Phillip M. Margolin is a criminal defence lawyer in Oregon, where he works as both an appellate and a trial attorney. He has represented over thirty people charged with murder, including a number of clients who have faced the death penalty.

His first novel, *Heartstone*, was published in 1978 and was nominated for an Edgar Award. This was followed by *The Last Innocent Man* and the bestselling *Gone, But Not Forgotten*, and he has also published short stories and contributed articles to law magazines, journals and books.

He lives in Portland with his wife (with whom he is also a partner in their law practice) and their two children.

D0716848

Also by Phillip M. Margolin

GONE, BUT NOT FORGOTTEN
HEARTSTONE
THE LAST INNOCENT MAN

AFTER DARK

PHILLIP M. MARGOLIN

WARNER BOOKS

A *Warner* Book

First published in the United States in 1995 by Doubleday
First published in Great Britain in 1995
by Little, Brown and Company

This edition published by Warner Books in 1996
Reprinted 1996 (four times)

A CIP catalogue record for this book
is available from the British Library.

ISBN 0 7515 1662 7

Typeset in Palatino by M Rules
Printed and bound in Great Britain by
Clays Ltd, St Ives plc

Warner Books
A Division of
Little, Brown and Company (UK)
Brettenham House
Lancaster Place
London WC2E 7EN

This book is dedicated to the much maligned, grossly underpaid and routinely overworked attorneys who represent the indigent accused.

Acknowledgments

Numerous people assisted me in the research for *After Dark*. Great thanks are due to Tony Ferreira, Earl Levin, Dr. Michael Kay, Michael Romanos, and Dr. William Brady, who shared their technical knowledge with me, to Judge Paul DeMuniz, who told me about *State ex rel. Beach v. Norblad*, to my good friend retired Chief Justice Edwin Peterson, and his law clerk Steven Briggs, who took me on a tour of the Oregon Supreme Court building and to the other justices of the court who let me wander around the court and their offices. I want to assure my readers that *all* of the Supreme Court justices portrayed in *After Dark* are fictional. The real justices work much too hard to have time for murder, sex and intrigue.

The comments of Susan Svetkey, Vince Kohler, Larry Matasar, Ben Merrill, Jerry, Joseph, Eleonore and Doreen

Margolin and Norman Stamm, who were kind enough to read drafts of *After Dark*, are much appreciated, as is the love and support of the three special people in my life, Doreen, Daniel and Amy.

It is impossible to give enough thanks to my agent, Jean Naggar, and everyone at her agency. They are terrific pros and really nice people, to boot. I am indebted to David Gernert, my tireless editor, whose excellent suggestions greatly improved *After Dark* and who would not let me stop writing until I got it right. Thanks also to Elisa Petrini, my editor at Bantam, and to Doubleday and Bantam for their incredible support.

Finally, on behalf of myself and the clients I have represented in death penalty cases, I want to thank Millard Farmer, who, in 1984, gave the chilling speech to the Oregon Criminal Defense Lawyer's Association that is the basis for some of the dialogue in Chapter Six. Mr. Farmer's words sobered and inspired me. I will never forget what he said that day and, in part, my clients owe their lives to him.

PART ONE
THE PRICE
IS RIGHT

Chapter One

1

The Multnomah County Courthouse occupied the entire block opposite Lownsdale Park. When it was completed in 1914, it had been the largest courthouse on the West Coast, as well as Portland, Oregon's largest building. There were no Art Deco frills or spectacular walls of glass decorating its exterior. Those who were summoned to face their fate here entered a solemn, brutish building of riveted structural steel and forbidding gray concrete.

Tracy Cavanaugh was too excited to be intimidated by the somber exterior of the courthouse. Her job interview at the public defender's office had ended at two-thirty, leaving her with a free afternoon. It would have been tempting to wander around Portland enjoying the balmy May weather, but Abigail Griffen was prosecuting a murder case and Tracy simply could not pass up an opportunity to watch one of the best trial lawyers in the state in action.

Potential employers had trouble taking Tracy seriously when they saw her for the first time. Today, for instance, she was wearing a lightweight navy-blue business suit that should have made her look like a young executive, but the suit highlighted a deep tan that conspired with Tracy's lean, athletic figure, bright blue eyes and straight blond hair to make her look much more like a college cheerleader than a law clerk to an Oregon Supreme Court justice.

Tracy did not worry about those first impressions. It never took the interviewers long to conclude that they were dealing with a *very smart* cheerleader. Degrees with honors from Yale and Stanford Law, and the clerkship, made Tracy a prime candidate for any legal position and, at the conclusion of today's interview, she had been offered a job. Now Tracy faced the pleasant predicament of deciding which of several excellent offers to accept.

When Tracy got out of the elevator on the fifth floor, the spectators were drifting back into the courtroom, where a young woman named Marie Harwood was being tried for murder. The courtroom was majestic with a high ceiling, marble Corinthian columns and ornate molding. Tracy found a seat seconds before the bailiff smacked down his gavel. A door opened at the side of the dais. Everyone in the courtroom stood. Judge Francine Dial, a slender woman with thick tortoiseshell glasses, took the bench. Most of the court watchers focused on her, but Tracy studied the deputy district attorney.

Abigail Griffen's long legs, full figure and classic Mediterranean features made her stand out in the most elegant surroundings. In Judge Dial's drab courtroom, her beauty was almost startling. The prosecutor was dressed in a black linen designer suit with a long, softly draped jacket and a straight skirt that stopped just below her knees. When Griffen turned toward the judge, her long black hair swept across olive-colored skin and her high cheekbones.

'Any more witnesses, Mr. Knapp?' Judge Dial asked Marie Harwood's lawyer.

Carl Knapp uncoiled dramatically from his chair and cast a disdainful look at Griffen. Then he said, 'We call the defendant, Miss Marie Harwood.'

The slender waif seated beside Knapp at the defense table was barely over five feet tall. Her pale, freckled face and loose blond hair made her look childlike, and the ill-fitting dress made her look pathetic. She struck Tracy as being the type of person a jury would have a hard time convicting of murder. Harwood trembled when she took the witness stand, and Tracy could barely hear her name when Harwood stated it for the record. The judge urged the witness to use the microphone.

'Miss Harwood,' Knapp asked, 'how old are you?'

'Nineteen.'

'How much do you weigh?'

'Ninety-eight pounds, Mr. Knapp.'

'Now, the deceased, Vince Phillips, how much did he weigh?'

'Vince was big. Real big. I think around two-seventy.'

5

'Did he wrestle professionally at one time?'

'Yes, sir.'

'And how old was he?'

'Thirty-six.'

'Was Mr. Phillips a cocaine dealer?'

'When I was living with him, he always had a lot around.'

Harwood paused and looked down at her lap.

'Would you like some water, Miss Harwood?' Knapp asked with fawning concern.

'No, sir. I'm okay now. It's just . . . Well, it's hard for me to talk about cocaine.'

'Were you addicted to cocaine when you met Mr. Phillips?'

'No, sir.'

'Did you become addicted while you lived with Mr. Phillips?'

'Yeah. He hooked me.'

'How bad?'

'Real bad. Cocaine was all I thought about.'

'Did you enjoy being an addict?'

Harwood looked up at Knapp wide-eyed. 'Oh no, sir. I hated it. What it made me become and . . . and the things I had to do for Vince to get it.'

'What things?' Harwood shivered.

'Sex things,' she said quietly.

'Did you ever try to resist Mr. Phillips's sexual demands?'

'Yes, sir, I did. I didn't want to do those things.'

'What happened when you protested?'

'He . . .' She stopped, looked down again, then dabbed at her eyes with a handkerchief. This time, Harwood accepted a glass of water.

'Go ahead, Miss Harwood,' Knapp said.

'He beat me up.'

Harwood's head hung down, her shoulders hunched and she folded her hands in her lap.

'How badly?'

'He broke my ribs once, and he closed . . . closed my eye. Sometimes he beat me so hard I passed out.'

Harwood's voice was barely above a whisper.

'Did you go to the hospital after one of these beatings?' Knapp asked.

'Yes, sir. That's where I escaped.'

'You ran away from the hospital?'

'They wouldn't let him take me home. So I knew it was my only chance, 'cause he kept me a prisoner when I was with him.'

'Where did you go from the hospital?'

'Back to John John's.'

'Who is John John?'

'John LeVeque.'

'Now, Mr. LeVeque is also a drug dealer, is he not?'

'Yes, sir.'

'Why did you run to him?'

'Protection. He was who I was stayin' with before I took up with Vince. He don't . . . didn't like Vince, and Vince was scared of John John.'

'Did John John take you in?'

'Yes, sir.'

'Let's move to the day that you killed Mr. Phillips. Can you tell the jury what happened around four-thirty in the afternoon?'

'Yes, sir. I'd been at John John's for about two weeks and I guess I was starting to feel safe, so I went out for a walk. The next thing I knew, Vince's car screeched up beside me and he jumped out and yanked me in it by my hair.'

'Did you resist?' Harwood shook her head slowly. She looked ashamed.

'It happened too quick. One second I was on the street, then I was on the floor of the car. Every time I tried to get up he'd pull my hair or hit me. Finally, I just stayed still.'

'What happened when you got to his house?'

'He drug me into the bedroom.'

'Please describe Mr. Phillips's bedroom.'

'It's real big with this king-size water bed in the middle and mirrors on the ceiling. There's a stereo and big-screen TV. And it's weird. Vince painted it black and there are these black curtains around the bed.'

'What happened in the bedroom?'

'He . . . He ripped off all my clothes. Just ripped them.' Harwood started to cry. 'I fought, but I couldn't do nothin'. He was too big. After a while I just gave up. Then . . . then, he . . .'

'It's okay Marie,' Knapp said. 'Just take your time.'

Harwood took two deep breaths. Then, in a trembling voice, she said, 'Vince made me get down on my knees.

Then he put cocaine on his . . . his thing. I begged him. I didn't want to do it, but Vince just laughed. He grabbed me by the hair and made me. I . . . I had to suck it . . .'

Harwood broke down again. Her testimony was getting to Tracy and she wondered how the jurors were handling it. While the defendant regained her composure, Tracy glanced toward the jury box. The jurors were pale and tight-lipped. Tracy looked over at Abbie Griffen and was surprised to see the deputy district attorney sitting quietly, and apparently unconcerned, while Harwood stole her jury.

'What happened next?' Knapp asked when Harwood stopped crying.

'Vince raped me,' she answered quietly. 'He done it a couple of times. In between, he'd beat me. And . . . and all the time he was screamin' at me on how he was gonna kill me and cut me up.'

'Did he tell you what he would use?'

'Yes, sir. He had a straight razor and he brung it out and held it to my face. I squeezed my eyes tight, 'cause I didn't want to see it, but he slapped me in the face till I opened them.'

'After he raped you the last time, what happened?'

'Vince fell asleep.'

'How did you finally escape?'

'It was the razor,' Harwood said, shuddering. 'He left it on the bed and forgot. And . . . and I took it, and I . . .'

Harwood's eyes lost focus. She ran a hand along her cheek.

'I didn't mean to kill him. I just didn't want him to hurt me anymore.' She turned pleading eyes toward the jury. 'It was almost an accident. I didn't even know the razor was there until I touched it. When I picked it up off of the bed Vince's eyes opened and I was so scared, I just did it. Right under his chin is all I remember.'

Harwood started to gulp air.

'Do you need a break, Miss Harwood?' Judge Dial asked, afraid Harwood might faint or hyperventilate.

The witness shook her head. Tears coursed down her cheeks.

'Marie,' Knapp asked gently, 'you've seen the autopsy photos. Mr. Phillips was cut many times on his body. Do you remember doing that?'

'No, sir. I just remember the first one, then it's a blank. But . . . but I probably done that. I just can't picture it.'

'And why did you kill Mr. Phillips?'

'To get away. Just to get away, so he wouldn't hurt me no more. And . . . and the cocaine. I didn't want to be a slave to the cocaine no more. That's all. But I didn't mean to kill him.'

Harwood buried her head in her hands and sobbed. Knapp looked at Griffen with contempt. In a tone that suggested a dare, he said, 'Your witness, Counselor.'

Just before Griffen rose to begin her cross-examination, the courtroom door opened. Tracy looked over her shoulder and saw Matthew Reynolds slip into a vacant seat in the rear of the court next to a prim gray-haired woman. As he sat down, the woman glanced toward him, then flushed and snapped her head back toward the front of the courtroom.

Tracy could understand the woman's reaction, but it angered her. She supposed that Reynolds was used to those shocked first impressions and had conditioned himself to ignore them. Tracy's own reaction to seeing Reynolds was not one of shock or disgust, but of awe. If she could pick any job in the country, it would be as Matthew Reynolds's associate, but Reynolds had responded to her employment inquiry with a tersely worded letter that informed her that his firm was not hiring.

Reynolds was America's most famous criminal defense attorney and his specialty was defending against death penalty prosecutions. He was a strange-looking man who had been battling the grim reaper in courtrooms across America for so long that he was starting to resemble his adversary. Six-five and gaunt to the point of caricature, Reynolds seemed always on the verge of collapsing from the weight he bore on his frail shoulders. Though he was only forty-five, his hair was ash gray and had receded well back from his high forehead. His paper-thin skin stretched taut across sunken cheeks and a narrow, aquiline nose. The skin was as pale as bleached bone, except for an area that was covered by a broad hemangioma, a wine-red birthmark that started at the hairline above Reynolds's left eye, extended downward over his cheek and faded out above his upper lip. You would have thought that jurors would be put off by Reynolds's odd looks, but by trial's end they usually forgot them. His sincerity had been known to move jurors to tears. No one he represented had ever been executed.

Griffen started her cross-examination and Tracy turned back to the front of the courtroom.

'Do you feel up to continuing, Miss Harwood?' Griffen asked solicitously.

'I'm . . . I'm okay,' Harwood answered softly.

'Then let me start with some simple questions while you regain your composure. And anytime you want me to stop, just say so. Or if you don't understand a question, just tell me, because I don't want to trick you. Okay?'

Harwood nodded.

'When you were living with Mr. Phillips, it wasn't all bad times, was it?'

'I guess not. I mean, sometimes he could be sweet to me.'

'When he was being sweet, what did you do together?'

'Drugs. We did a lot of drugs. We partied.'

'Did you go out together?'

'Not a lot.'

'When you did, what did you do?'

'Vince liked movies. We'd see lots of movies.'

'What kind did Vince like?'

'Uh, karate movies. Action movies.'

'Did you like them?'

'No, ma'am. I like comedy movies and romantic ones.'

'You mentioned a stereo and a big-screen TV in the bedroom. Did you guys listen to music or watch TV?'

'Well, sure.'

'You didn't go to the police after you killed Mr. Phillips, did you?' Griffen asked, quickly shifting the subject.

'No, I was too scared.'

'Where did you go?'

'I went back to John John.'

'And that's the gentleman you were staying with when we arrested you, a week and a half after you killed Mr. Phillips?'

'Yes.'

'You were John John's girlfriend before you took up with Mr. Phillips, weren't you?'

'Yes, ma'am.'

'And he was a rival of Mr. Phillips in the drug trade?'

'Yes.'

'When did you take the money, Miss Harwood?' Griffen asked without missing a beat.

'What?'

'The thirty thousand dollars.'

'What are you talking about?'

'Do you know Roy Saylor?'

'Sure. He was Vince's friend.'

'His crime associate.'

'Whatever.'

'Roy's going to testify that Vince was planning to buy two kilos of cocaine from his connection that evening for fifteen a kilo.'

'He never mentioned that. He was too busy beating

13

and raping me to mention business,' Harwood answered bitterly.

'Roy will also testify that Vince went to the bank at four to take the money out of a safety-deposit box.'

'That could be, too. I just never seen it.'

'That's fair. But if you took it, we'd understand. You're terrified. He's dead. You know you might have to run, so you take the money with you.'

'Man, I wasn't thinking about money. I just wanted out of there. If I wanted money, I'd've stayed. Vince was always generous with money. It just wasn't worth it to me.'

'He really scared you?'

'You bet he did.'

'In fact, as I recall your testimony, Mr. Phillips abducted you, dragged you inside his house, stripped you right away and forced you to perform oral sex.'

'Yes, ma'am.'

'Then he raped and beat you repeatedly and fell asleep?'

Harwood nodded.

'This was one right after the other? He was either beating you or raping you?'

Harwood's eyes were on the rail in front of her. Her nod was barely perceptible.

In her trial practice classes in law school, Tracy had been taught that you never gave an opposing witness a chance to repeat her testimony during cross-examination because it reinforced the story in the jurors' minds. Tracy could not understand why Griffen had just repeated

Harwood's pathetic tale three times. She glanced over at Reynolds to catch his reaction. The defense attorney was leaning forward and his eyes were riveted on Griffen.

'There wasn't a moment when you weren't scared silly from the time he abducted you until you escaped, was there?' Griffen asked, giving Harwood yet another chance to tell her story.

'That's true.'

'Either he was raping you or beating you or sleeping. How long do you figure this went on?'

'I don't know. I wasn't watching a clock.'

'Well, there was a clock on the VCR on the big TV.'

'Yeah, but I didn't look at it.'

'That's a cable hookup Vince had, wasn't it?'

'I guess.'

'HBO, Pay-per-View, Showtime?'

Harwood looked uncomfortable. Tracy caught Reynolds out of the corner of her eye. He was frowning.

'You've watched that big TV with Vince, haven't you?' Griffen asked.

'I told you he was beating me up.'

'I'm sorry. I meant on other occasions.'

'Yeah. He had all those movie channels.'

'What's your favorite movie, Miss Harwood?'

'Your Honor,' Knapp said, playing to the jury, 'I fail to see the relevance of this question.'

'Miss Harwood does,' Griffen answered.

Tracy studied the witness. Harwood looked upset. When Tracy looked over at Reynolds, he was smiling, as if he had just figured out an in joke that only he and Griffen understood.

'This is cross-examination, Mr. Knapp,' Judge Dial said. 'I'm going to give Ms. Griffen some latitude.'

'Can you please answer the question?' Griffen asked the witness. 'What is your favorite movie?'

'I . . . I don't know.'

The prosecutor took a letter-size sheet of paper out of a file.

'How about *Honeymoon Beach*? Have you seen that one?'

'Yeah,' Harwood answered cautiously.

'Tell the jury what it's about.'

'Your Honor, this has gone too far,' Knapp shouted as his client shifted nervously in the witness box. 'This is not the Siskel and Ebert show.'

'I promise I will show relevance,' Griffen told the judge, her eyes never leaving Marie Harwood.

'Overruled. You may continue, Ms. Griffen.'

'Is *Honeymoon Beach* a comedy?' Griffen asked.

'Yeah.'

'About two honeymoon couples who swap mates at a resort?'

'Yeah.'

'Where did you see it, Miss Harwood?'

'In the movies.'

Griffen walked over to Harwood. 'Then you saw it twice,' she said, handing the paper she was holding to the witness.

'What's this?' Harwood asked.

'It's a billing record of all the movies ordered on Pay-per-View from Vince Phillips's phone. *Honeymoon Beach* showed from five-thirty to seven on the day you killed him. Someone ordered it at four-fifty using Mr. Phillips's phone. Did you watch the movie before or after you slit his throat?'

'I didn't watch any movie,' Harwood insisted.

Reynolds stood up quietly and slipped out of the court-room just as Griffen said, 'Someone watched *Honeymoon Beach*, Ms. Harwood. According to your testimony, only you and Vince were in the house and the only Pay-per-View converter is in the bedroom. Did Vince order the movie while he was raping you or while he was beating you?'

'Never,' Harwood shouted. 'I told you we didn't watch that movie.

'Or was it you who watched it while John John was torturing Mr. Phillips to find out where he hid the money?'

Harwood glared at Griffen.

'Did you arrange to meet Vince after John John found out about the money? Did you get him in bed and slash his throat while he was watching *Honeymoon Beach*?'

'That's a lie!' Harwood shouted, her face scarlet with rage. 'I never watched no movie.'

'Someone did, Marie, and someone ordered it by phone. Who do you think that was?'

17

2

The day after Marie Harwood's conviction, Abbie Griffen was looking through a stack of police reports when Multnomah County district attorney Jack Stamm stepped into her office. The weather had unexpectedly turned from mild to torrid in twenty-four hours and the courthouse air conditioner was on the fritz. Stamm had taken off the jacket of his tan tropical-weight suit, pulled down his tie and rolled up his shirtsleeves, but he still looked damp and uncomfortable.

The district attorney was five feet eleven, rail thin and a bachelor, whose only passions were the law and distance running. Stamm's wavy brown hair was starting to thin on the top, but his kind blue eyes and ready smile made him look younger than thirty-eight.

'Congratulations on nailing Harwood,' Stamm said. 'That was good work.'

'Why, thank you,' Abbie answered with a big smile.

'I hear Knapp is making noises about reporting you to the Bar.'

'Oh?'

'He says you didn't tell him about the Pay-per-View bill before trial.'

Abbie grinned at her boss. 'I sent that arrogant creep a copy of the bill in discovery. He was just too stupid to understand its significance, assuming he even read it. I don't know what I enjoyed more, convicting Knapp's client or humiliating him in public.'

'Well, you did both and you deserve to enjoy your triumph. That's why I'm sorry to be the bearer of sad tidings.'

'What's up?'

'I just got this.'

Stamm handed Abbie the Oregon Supreme Court's slip-sheet opinion in *State of Oregon* v. *Charles Darren Deems*. Almost two years ago, Abbie had convicted Deems, an especially violent psychopath, for the pipe-bomb murder of a witness and his nine-year-old daughter. The Supreme Court had taken the case on automatic review because Deems had been sentenced to death. The slip sheet was the copy of the opinion that was sent to the attorneys in the case as soon as the Supreme Court issued its ruling. Later, the opinion would be published in the bound volumes of the official reporter that were sent to law libraries.

Abbie looked down the cover sheet past the caption of the case and the names of the attorneys until she found the line she was looking for.

'Oh no!'

'It's worse than that,' Stamm said. 'They threw out his statements to Rice.'

'That was my whole case,' Abbie said incredulously. 'I won't be able to retry him.'

'You got it,' Stamm agreed grimly.

'Which judge wrote this piece of shit?' Abbie asked, her rage barely contained as she scanned the cover sheet to find the name of the justice who had authored the opinion. Stamm could not meet her eye.

'That son of a bitch,' she said, so softly that Stamm barely heard her. Abbie crumpled the opinion in her fist. 'I can't believe he would stoop this low. He did this to make me look bad.'

'I don't know, Abbie,' Stamm said halfheartedly. 'He had to convince three other judges to go along with him.'

Abbie stared at Stamm. Her rage, disappointment and frustration were so intense, he looked away. She dropped the opinion on the floor and walked out of her office. Stamm bent down to retrieve the document. When he smoothed it out, the name of the opinion's author could be seen clearly. It was the Honorable Robert Hunter Griffen, justice of the Oregon Supreme Court and Abbie's estranged husband.

Chapter Two

Bob Packard, attorney-at-law, was a large man going to seed. His belt cut into his waist, because he stubbornly insisted on keeping it a notch too tight. There were fat rolls on his neck and a puffiness in his cheeks. At the moment, Packard was not feeling well. His trust and general account ledgers were open on his desk. He had checked them twice and the totals had not changed. Packard unconsciously ran a hand across his dry lips. He was certain there was more money in both accounts. His billings were up, clients were paying. Where had the money gone? His office overhead had not changed and his household expenses had not increased. Of course, there was the money he was spending for cocaine. That seemed to be increasing recently.

Packard took a deep breath and tried to calm down. He

rotated his neck and shrugged his shoulders to work out the tension. If the white lady was the problem, he would just have to stop. It was that simple. Cocaine was not a necessity. He could take it or leave it and he would just have to leave it. Once his current supply ran out, there would be no more.

Packard felt better now that his problem was solved. He put away the ledgers and picked up a case he needed to read in order to prepare a pretrial motion that was due in two days. It was imperative that he win the motion. If his client went to trial he was doomed. This motion had to be an A number one, slam-bang winner.

Packard started to read the case, but it was hard to concentrate. He was still thinking about his money problems and still worried about that other problem. His supplier. The one who had been arrested two days ago, just before Packard was going to pick up a little something to augment his dwindling supply.

Of course, he was going to stop, so there was no problem. But what if, just for the sake of argument, he needed some coke and couldn't get any. It made him jittery just thinking about it and he needed to keep calm and focused so he could write the motion.

Packard thought about the Ziploc bag in his bottom drawer. If he took a hit, he could whiz through the research on the motion and get it written. And there would be that much less cocaine to worry about. After all, he was quitting, and getting rid of his stash was an important first step.

Packard was working on his final rationalization for doing a line when his receptionist buzzed him on the intercom.

'Mr. Packard, a Mr. Deems is here to see you.'

Packard suddenly felt an urgent need to go to the men's room.

'Mr. Packard?' the receptionist repeated.

'Uh, yes, Shannon. I'll be right there.'

Bob Packard had never felt comfortable in Charlie Deems's presence, even when the two men were separated by the bullet-proof glass through which they had been forced to communicate while the former drug dealer was on death row. The facts underlying Deems's conviction were enough to unsettle anyone. A man named Harold Shoe was trying to cut into Deems's territory. Two boys found Shoe's mutilated body in a Dumpster. According to the medical examiner, Shoe had died slowly over a long period of time. Packard had looked at the autopsy photos when he was reviewing the trial evidence and had not been able to eat for the rest of the day.

Larry Hollins, twenty-eight, married, a union man who worked the swing shift, just happened to be driving by the Dumpster when Deems was depositing his bloody package. Hollins thought he'd seen a body, then convinced himself he was imagining things, until he read about the discovery of Shoe's corpse.

Hollins could not make a positive ID from Deems's mug shot, but he was pretty sure he could identify the man he saw if he was in a lineup. Someone leaked

Hollins's identity to the press and Deems disappeared for a few days. On one of those days, Hollins decided to drive his nine-year-old daughter to school so he could talk to her teacher. A pipe bomb attached to the underside of the car killed both of them.

Packard looked longingly toward the bottom drawer, but decided it was better to face Deems with all his wits about him. Besides, Charlie would be in a good mood. Packard had just won his appeal for him. He was probably in the office to show his appreciation.

When Packard walked into the reception area, Deems was reading a copy of *Newsweek*.

'Charlie!' Packard said heartily, extending a hand. 'It's great to see you.'

Charlie Deems looked up from the magazine. He was a man of average height, but thick through the chest and shoulders. A handsome man with dark, curly hair who reminded Packard a little of Warren Beatty. Deems's most engaging feature was his toothy grin, which was a bit goofy and put you at ease. Unless, that is, you had read the psychological profile in Deems's presentence report.

'You're looking good, Bob,' Deems said enthusiastically when they were seated in Packard's office.

'Thanks, Charlie. You're looking pretty good yourself.'

'I should. There's plenty of time to work out in the joint. You can't imagine how many sit-ups and push-ups you can do when you're locked down for twenty-three hours a day.'

Deems was wearing a short-sleeve maroon shirt. He flexed his left biceps and winked.

'Lookin' good,' Packard agreed. 'So, what's up?'

'Nothing much. I just wanted to drop by to thank you for winning my case.'

Packard shrugged modestly. 'That's what you paid me for.'

'Well, you did great. I bet that cunt Griffen is pissed,' Deems said with a laugh. 'You seen her since the decision came down?'

'Once, over at the courthouse, but I didn't bring up the case. No sense gloating.'

'Ah, Bob, you're too bighearted. Me, I'd love to have seen her face, because I know this case was personal for her. I mean, she wanted me dead. Now she ain't got nothin'.'

'Oh, I don't think it was personal, Charlie.'

'You don't?' Deems asked with a look of boyish curiosity.

'No. I just think she was doing her job. Fortunately, I did mine better.'

'Yeah, well, you might be right, but I don't think so. I mulled this thing over while I was on the row. I had lots of time to think about her there. I'm convinced that bitch had it in for me, Bob.'

Deems had an odd look on his face that worried Packard.

'You should let it rest, Charlie. The cops are going to be on your butt, night and day. You don't want to do anything even slightly suspicious.'

'Oh, right. I agree with that,' Deems said reasonably. 'Water under the bridge. No, Bob, I just want to get on with my life. Which brings me to the other reason for my visit.'

'What's that?' Packard asked uneasily.

'I wanted to ask you for a little favor.'

'What favor?'

'Well, it seems to me that you won my appeal pretty easily. I mean, they're not even gonna retry me, so the judge must have really fucked up, right?'

'Well, he did make a mistake,' Packard answered cautiously, 'but it wasn't that easy to win the case.'

Deems shook his head. 'That's not the way I see it. And that's not just my opinion. There's a lot of guys in the joint that know their law. I asked 'em about the appeal. They all knew you'd win. Said it was a cakewalk. So, seeing how easy it was, I was thinking that I'd like a little refund on my fee.'

'That's not how it works, Charlie,' Packard said, trying to convince himself that this would be like any business discussion between two civilized and rational men. 'The fee is nonrefundable and it's not dependent on results. Remember we discussed that?'

'I remember,' Deems answered with a shake of his head. 'But you know, Bob, I'm thinking PR here. Your reputation is what brings in the clients. Am I right? And happy clients talk you up. That's free advertising. I'd be real happy if you refunded half the fee.'

Packard blanched. 'That's fifteen thousand dollars, Charlie. I can't do that.'

'Sure you can. And if I remember right, that was only the cash half. The kilo of cocaine I gave you was probably worth a lot more than fifteen after you resold it. Am I right? But I don't want any blow back. And I don't care what your profit was. You did a great job for me. I'd just really appreciate the cash back.'

A thin line of sweat formed on Packard's upper lip. He forced a smile.

'I know you've been inside and can use some dough, so why don't I loan you a grand? Will that help?'

'Sure, but fifteen grand would help even more,' Deems said. This time there was no smile.

'Not possible, Charlie,' Packard said stubbornly. 'A deal's a deal. You were convicted of murder and now you're a free man. I'd say I earned my fee.'

'Oh, you did. No question. And I don't want you to do anything you don't want to do. If you give me back the money, I want it to be of your own free will. A good deed you can be proud of.'

Deems stopped talking and leaned back in his chair. Packard's heart was beating overtime and he strongly regretted not taking that hit of cocaine.

'Hey, you look upset, Bob,' Deems said suddenly. 'Look, let's forget about this. Okay? I'm sorry I even brought it up. Let's talk about something else. Say, do you like TV game shows?'

'Game shows?' Packard repeated, puzzled by the transition, but relieved that Deems had let him off the hook so easily.

27

'Yeah, like *Jeopardy!* or *Let's Make a Deal*. You know.'

'I work during the day, so I rarely get a chance to watch them.'

'I didn't watch them either until they put me on the row. We had a set outside the bars. One of our few luxuries. The guards let us watch the game shows. I really got hooked on them. At first I thought they were kind of stupid, but the more I watched, the more I realized that you can learn as much from game shows as you can at school. For instance, have you ever seen *The Price Is Right*?'

'Isn't that the one where the contestants have to guess the price of a refrigerator or a set of dishes?'

'Right!' Deems said, snapping upright in his chair and grinning broadly. Then, in an imitation of a game-show host, he said, 'Bob Packard of Portland, Oregon, come on down! You can play *The Price Is Right*!! Then you run up from the audience. Have you seen it?'

'A few times.'

'Well, that's a great show,' Deems said animatedly, 'because it teaches you about the value of things. For instance, if I put two rocks on your desk and asked you to guess at their value, you'd say they weren't worth much, am I right? I mean, we're talking about two rocks. But what if one was a chunk of common granite and the other was a diamond? You see? Two rocks, both the same size, but your judgment of their value would be really different.'

Packard nodded automatically to avoid insulting Deems and cast a quick glance at his watch.

'That's interesting, Charlie, and I'd like to talk about it

some more, but I have a motion I need to write. It's due in two days and it's rather complicated.'

'I'm sure it is,' Deems said, 'but I think it's more important for you, in the long run, to discuss values.'

The fear Packard felt initially had faded as he grew annoyed and he missed the menace in Deems's tone.

'What are you getting at, Charlie? Come to the point.'

'Sure. You're a busy man. I don't want to waste your time. But I do think this little talk will help you put things in perspective. For instance, what's worth more, a good night's sleep or the shoddy legal services of a coked-up junkie lawyer.'

Packard flushed. 'That's not fair, Charlie. If it wasn't for me, you'd be dead.'

'Maybe, maybe not. As I said, more than one person I talked to was of the opinion that this was a pretty easy win. That would make the value of your services a lot less than thirty thousand dollars. See what I mean? But putting a price on abstractions, like the value of legal services, is a lot tougher than dealing with diamonds and granite, Bob. So why don't you start by guessing the price of a common, everyday item.'

'Look,' Packard said angrily, 'I just told you. I don't have time for this nonsense.'

Deems ignored Packard and pulled a pair of soiled woman's underpants from his pocket, then laid them on Packard's desk. Packard leaned forward and stared. The cotton panties looked familiar, but he could not remember where he had seen them.

'What's the value of these panties, Bob?'

'Where did you get those?' Packard asked.

'Let's see if you can guess. I'll give you a hint.'

Deems leaned forward and grinned in anticipation of Packard's reaction to his clue. He pitched his voice high and, in a falsetto, said, '"Get off of me, now! If you can't get it up at least let me get some sleep."'

Packard turned white. His wife, Dana, had said that to him last night after a failed attempt at sex with the same tone of disgust Deems had so adequately imitated.

'You know, Bob,' Deems said with an air of feigned concern, 'your technique leaves a lot to be desired. You completely ignored Dana's nipples. They're yummy. Fiddle with them a while tonight. They're like the knobs on a radio. If you twirl them the right way, you can find a mighty nice station.'

Packard suddenly recognized the panties as the ones Dana had taken off just before they got in bed. Dana had dropped them next to the bed before they started to have sex. That meant that Deems had been in their room while they were sleeping.

'You were in my house?'

'That's right, Bob.'

Packard bolted to his feet and shouted, 'Listen, you prick . . .'

'Prick?' Deems interrupted in a bemused tone. 'That's a fighting word. Now, a fight between the two of us might be interesting. Speed and youth against size and power. But I want to give you a word of advice, Bob. If you start

30

a fight with me, you better be prepared to kill me. If you leave me alive, I'll come for you when you least expect it and you'll die like Harold Shoe.'

Packard remembered Shoe's autopsy photographs. It was the medical examiner's opinion that Shoe's hands and feet had been removed with a chain saw while he was still alive. All the fight went out of Packard and he collapsed in his chair. He tried to compose himself. Deems watched patiently while Packard took several deep breaths.

'What do you want from me, Charlie?'

'I want you to play the game,' he said grimly. 'You don't really have a choice. Now, what is the value of these panties?'

'Three-fifty? Four dollars?' Packard guessed, on the verge of tears. 'I don't know.'

'You're too literal, Bob. Think about how I got these undies and you'll know their true value. I'd put it at about the same price as a lifetime of good sleep. Wouldn't that be worth fifteen thousand dollars? I'd say a lifetime of sound sleep is cheap at that price.'

Packard's jaw trembled. 'Charlie, you have to be reasonable,' he begged. 'I don't have fifteen thousand extra dollars. You paid that retainer over a year ago. It's gone now. How about something less? What about three? Three thousand? I might be able to manage that.'

'Well, Bob, to me three thousand sounds like a kiss-off.'

Packard knew he could not afford to pay the money.

31

His rent was due, there were car payments. Then he thought about the price he would pay if he could be assured that Charlie Deems would never slip into his room at night and spirit him away to a twisted world of torture and pain.

Packard took his checkbook out of his drawer. His hand was shaking so badly that his signature was barely legible. Packard gave the check for fifteen thousand dollars to Deems. Deems inspected it, thanked Packard and opened the door. Then he turned, winked and said, 'Sleep tight and don't let the bedbugs bite.'

PART TWO
LAURA

Chapter Three

1

Salem, Oregon's capital, was a sleepy little city surrounded by farmland and located about fifty miles south of Portland on the I-5 freeway. The Oregon Supreme Court had been in its present location on State Street since 1914. The square four-story building was faced with terracotta and surrounded on three sides by a narrow lawn. In the rear was a parking lot that separated the court from the back of another building that housed the Department of Justice and the offices of the Court of Appeals.

There were vans with network logos parked in front of the court when Tracy Cavanaugh arrived for work at 8 A.M. She glanced at them curiously as she strolled down the side street that divided the court from the grounds of the State Capitol. A radiant July sun made the gold statue of the pioneer on top of the Capitol building shine and gave the grass in the small park that bordered the Capitol the brilliance of a highly polished emerald. In keeping with the spirit of the day, Tracy wore a bright yellow dress and wraparound shades.

Tracy was at the tail end of a year serving as Oregon Supreme Court Justice Alice Sherzer's law clerk. Judicial clerkships were plums that fell to top law school graduates. Each justice had a clerk who researched complex legal issues, drafted memos about other justices' positions and checked opinion drafts to catch errors before the opinion was published. A judicial clerkship was a demanding but exciting job that lasted one to two years. Most clerks moved on to good positions with top law firms, which coveted these bright young men and women for their skills as well as their intimate knowledge of the way the justices thought.

Laura Rizzatti was as pale as Tracy was tan and possessed the delicate features and soft, rounded figure of a Botticelli model. When Laura was deep in thought, she played with her long black hair. She had several strands wrapped tightly around her left index finger when Tracy poked her head into Laura's closet-sized office.

'Why are the TV reporters waiting outside?'

Laura dropped the transcript she was reading and rose halfway out of her chair.

'Don't do that!'

'Sorry.' Tracy laughed, tilting her head sideways to see what had occupied Laura's attention so completely. She saw the title of the case and 'Vol. XI' before Laura turned the transcript over so Tracy could no longer read the cover.

'The *Deems* case?' Tracy said. 'I thought we reversed that a month ago.'

'We did. What did you just ask me?'

Tracy looked up from the transcript and noticed the dark circles under Laura's eyes. Laura's clothes were disheveled and she looked like she'd been up all night.

'The TV people. What are they doing here?'

'Matthew Reynolds is arguing *Franklin* v. *Pogue* at nine.'

'Reynolds! Let me know when you go up to court.'

'I'm not going.'

'How come?'

'Justice Griffen took himself off the case, so there's no reason to sit in on the argument.'

'Why'd he recuse himself?'

'His wife is arguing for the state.'

'No shit.' Tracy laughed.

'No shit,' Laura answered bitterly.

'She is one smart cookie.'

'She's a bitch. She could have asked another DA to argue the state's position.'

'Then Justice Griffen would have sat on the case. Now he can't sit because the state is represented by a member of his family. So she gets rid of the most liberal justice on the court and ups her chance of winning. I call that smart lawyering.'

'I think it's unethical.'

'Don't take this so personally.'

37

'I'm not,' Laura said angrily. 'But the judge is such a nice guy. The divorce is eating him up. Pulling a stunt like this is just pouring salt in his wounds.'

'Yeah, well, if she's as big a bitch as you say, he's better off without her. And you should see Reynolds argue anyway. He's amazing. Do you know he's been defending death penalty cases all over the United States for twenty years and he's never had a client executed?'

'Reynolds is just another hired gun.'

'That's where you're wrong, Laura. These cases are like a mission for him. And he's a genius. Did you read his brief in *State* v. *Aurelio*? His Fifth Amendment argument was absolutely brilliant.'

'He's smart, and he might be dedicated, but it's to the wrong cause.'

'Don't be so uptight. Listen to the argument. Reynolds is really worth seeing. I'll check with you before I go up.'

2

The most conspicuous feature of the Oregon Supreme Court is a stained-glass skylight in the courtroom ceiling that displays the state seal. The stained glass is protected by a second, clear skylight above it. On this sunny day, the light filtering through the two sets of glass cast a soft yellow glow over six justices of the seven-member court as they assembled to hear argument in *State ex rel. Franklin* v. *Pogue*.

Tracy found a seat on a couch against the rear wall of

the courtroom just after the justices took their places. The judges sat on an elevated dais that stretched across the courtroom in a gentle curve. Directly in front of Chief Justice Stuart Forbes was the wooden podium on which Abbie Griffen calmly arranged her papers. When the Chief Justice told her to commence her argument, Abbie said, 'If it please the court, my name is Abigail Griffen and I represent the Multnomah County district attorney's office and the interests of Denise Franklin. We are asking this court to order trial judge David Pogue to withdraw an order commanding Mrs. Franklin to open her home to forensic experts employed by the defense.'

'Judge Pogue was acting on a motion for discovery filed by the defendant, Jeffrey Coulter, wasn't he, Ms. Griffen?' asked Justice Mary Kelly, an attractive woman in her mid-forties who was appointed to the bench after a stellar career in corporate law.

'Yes, Your Honor.'

'What was the basis for the discovery motion?'

'According to the affidavit of Mr. Reynolds, the defendant's attorney, Denise Franklin's son, Roger, promised to sell Jeffrey Coulter stolen jewelry. Coulter went to Franklin's house, but Franklin had no jewelry and tried to rob Coulter. Mr. Coulter claims he shot Roger Franklin in self-defense after Franklin shot at him.'

'And the defense wants to examine Mrs. Franklin's house for evidence that will corroborate the defendant's story?'

'Yes, Your Honor.'

'That seems pretty reasonable to me. What's wrong with Judge Pogue's order?'

'Mrs. Franklin is in mourning, Your Honor. She doesn't want agents of the man who killed her son traipsing through her home.'

'We're sympathetic to Mrs. Franklin, Counselor, but it's not unusual for witnesses to also be relatives of a murder victim. They're inconvenienced all the time by police interviews, the press. Your people went through the house, didn't they?'

'With Mrs. Franklin's consent and while the house was a crime scene. It's no longer a crime scene. The state has returned the house to its owner, Mrs. Franklin, who is not a party to the criminal case between the state and Mr. Coulter. A judge doesn't have the power to order a non-party to let the defense in her house.'

'Do you have legal authority for that contention, Counselor?'

Griffen smiled with the confidence of an attorney who has anticipated a question. While she told Justice Kelly about several Oregon cases that supported her position, Tracy looked across the courtroom at Griffen's opponent. The contrast between the two attorneys was stark. Abigail Griffen in her black tailored jacket, black pleated skirt, ivory silk blouse and pearls looked like a fashion model, while Matthew Reynolds in his plain, ill-fitting black suit, white shirt and narrow tie seemed more like a country preacher or an undertaker than America's premier criminal defense attorney.

A question by Justice Arnold Pope pulled Tracy's attention back to the legal argument.

'Mrs. Griffen, when Mr. Coulter was arrested did he claim he acted in self-defense?'

'No, Your Honor.'

'Did the police find the gun the defendant's counsel alleges was fired by the deceased?'

'No weapon was found at the scene.'

Pope, a barrel-chested ex-DA with a Marine crew cut, furrowed his brow, giving the impression that he was deep in thought. Justice Kelly rolled her eyes. Pope was a mental lightweight who tried to compensate for his lack of intelligence by being arrogant and opinionated. He was on the court because he had defeated a well-respected incumbent in one of the dirtiest judicial races in Oregon history.

'Could this self-defense business be hokum?' Pope asked.

'Yes, Your Honor. We believe Mr. Coulter manufactured the self-defense scenario.'

'Perhaps with the assistance of Mr. Reynolds?' Pope asked. Tracy was shocked by Pope's suggestion that Matthew Reynolds had sworn falsely in his affidavit. Reynolds was rigid, his face flushed.

'There is no evidence that Mr. Reynolds has been less than honorable in this case, Justice Pope,' Abbie answered firmly.

'Besides,' Justice Kelly interjected to shift the discussion from this unpleasant topic, 'that issue isn't before us, is it, Counselor?'

'No, Your Honor.'

'As I understand it,' Kelly continued, 'your position is that we must set aside the order of Judge Pogue, regardless of the truthfulness of the affidavit, because he had no power to order a nonparty to a criminal case to do anything.'

'Exactly.'

A tiny lightbulb at the front of the podium flashed red, indicating that Griffen's time was up.

'If the court has no further questions, I have nothing more to add.'

Chief Justice Forbes nodded to Griffen, then said, 'Mr. Reynolds?'

Matthew Reynolds uncoiled slowly, as if it took a great effort to stand, and walked to the podium. He was determined not to let his anger at Arnold Pope interfere with his duty to his client. Reynolds took his time arranging his papers and put the insult behind him. As soon as he looked up, Justice Frank Arriaga, a cherubic little man with an easy smile, asked, 'What about Mrs. Griffen's argument, Mr. Reynolds? I've read her cases and they seem to support the state's position.'

There was a hint of the Deep South when Reynolds spoke. His words rolled along softly and slowly, like small boats riding a gentle sea.

'Those cases should not control this court's decision, Justice Arriaga. The facts in the case at bar are substantially different. Mrs. Franklin is far more than a grieving mother. We believe she may be covering up her son's criminal involvement in an attempted robbery. Every moment we are barred from the Franklin home presents another chance for Mrs. Franklin to destroy evidence.

'And that leads me to my main legal point. The Due Process Clause of the United States Constitution imposes a duty on a prosecutor to preserve evidence in her possession that is favorable to an accused on either the issue of guilt or the issue of punishment. When we filed our motion with Judge Pogue, the Franklin home was still sealed as an official crime scene. Our affidavit put the state on notice that we believed the Franklin home contained evidence that would clear Mr. Coulter and it also put the state on notice that we believed that Mrs. Franklin might destroy that evidence. Soon after we filed our motion, the police unsealed the crime scene and returned the home to Mrs. Franklin. We consider that a violation of the state's duty to preserve evidence favorable to an accused.'

'Can we approve an order issued by a judge who lacks the authority to make it?' Justice Arriaga asked.

'No, but we believe the court should address this issue as if the house was still under seal and an official crime scene. Otherwise, the state can frustrate legitimate motions of this sort by simply unsealing the scene before the court has the opportunity to act.

'The Due Process Clause codifies the concept of fundamental fairness into our law. It's a wonderful thing to have a jurisprudence based on fairness rather than power. You can see the tension between these two ideas in this case. The state symbolizes power. It used that power to take over the home of a private citizen so it could investigate a crime. Once the state was satisfied that it had identified the criminal, it used its power to arrest my client and deprive him of his liberty.

'These were proper uses of power, Your Honors. Fair uses. But the state's final use of its power was unfair. As soon as my client stood up to the state and requested an opportunity to examine the crime scene for evidence that would clear his name, the state exercised its power unjustly.

'Legal motions should be decided by unbiased judges, not unilaterally by zealous advocates. When the police released the crime scene to thwart our motion, they acted in violation of the concept of fundamental fairness that is the foundation of the Due Process Clause. All Mr. Coulter is asking for, Your Honors, is a chance to examine the crime scene. The same thing the state was able to do through the exercise of its power. All he is asking for is a fair shake. Judge Pogue understood that and we ask you to be fair and permit his order to stand.'

Court recessed when the argument ended. Matthew Reynolds watched Abigail Griffen collect her papers and close her attaché case. In a moment, she would be fighting her way through the reporters who were waiting for them outside the courtroom on the third-floor landing. If he was going to talk to her, Reynolds knew it had to be now. Abbie started toward the door.

'Mrs. Griffen.'

Abbie turned to find Reynolds following her. With his suit jacket flapping behind him like the wings of an ungainly crow, Reynolds looked like Ichabod Crane in flight from the headless horseman.

'Thank you for telling the court that you didn't believe I would falsify my affidavit,' Reynolds said with a tremor Abbie had not heard when he was arguing. 'My reputation means so much to me.'

'No need to thank me, Mr. Reynolds. But I'm curious. That was such an odd accusation to make. Is there bad blood between you and Justice Pope?'

Reynolds nodded sadly. 'I tried a murder case against Arnold Pope when he was the district attorney for Walker County. It was poorly investigated and an innocent man was arrested. Justice Pope had a penchant for trying his cases in the press when he was a prosecutor and he promised a swift conviction.'

'I take it he didn't deliver.'

'No. After the trial, he threatened to indict me for jury tampering.'

'What happened?'

'The judge told Pope he lost because he should have, and promised to dismiss any jury-tampering indictment Pope obtained. That was the end of it as far as I was concerned, but I guess he still harbors a grudge.'

'I'm sorry to hear that.'

'That's gracious of you, considering that Pope's animosity guarantees you his vote.'

'On the other hand, some of the judges will side with

you simply to be on the other side of Pope's position.'

'I hope you're right, Mrs. Griffen,' Reynolds answered solemnly, the joke going right by him.

'Why don't you call me Abbie. We're going to see too much of each other during this case to stay on formal terms.'

'Abbie, then.'

'See you in court, Matt.'

Reynolds hugged his briefcase to his chest like a shield and watched Abigail Griffen glide through the courtroom doors.

The reporters converged on Matthew Reynolds as soon as he walked into the hall, and Abbie was able to escape down the marble stairway and leave the courthouse through the rear door. Her car was parked around the block from the court because she'd expected the press. Reynolds could go nowhere without them. When she rounded the corner, she saw Robert Griffen sitting in the passenger seat of her car.

Justice Griffen looked like a golf pro in tan slacks, a navy-blue Izod shirt and loafers. His long brown hair fell casually across his forehead. When she opened the rear door and tossed her attaché case in the back seat, he smiled. Abbie saw the sparkle in his clear blue eyes and almost forgot why she had walked out on him.

'How'd the argument go?' Griffen asked.

'What are you doing in my car?' Abbie answered sharply as she slid behind the wheel.

His smile wavered.

'I missed you. I thought we could talk.'

'You thought wrong, Robert. Maybe one of the women you were fucking behind my back has time for a chat.'

Griffen flinched. 'Can't you spare a minute?'

'I have a meeting in Portland and I don't want to be late,' Abbie said as she turned on the engine. 'Besides, Robert, I know what you want and the bank is closed. I suggest you either find a rich mistress or change your lifestyle.'

'You don't know what you're saying. I was never inter-ested in your money, and those other women . . . God, I don't know what got into me. But that's all behind me. I swear. It's you I love, Abbie.'

'Was reversing the *Deems* case a way of showing your love?'

Griffen paled. 'What are you talking about?'

'You reversed *Deems* to embarrass me.'

'That's nonsense. I decided that case on the law. So did the justices who joined the majority. Even Arnold Pope voted with me, for Christ's sake.'

'I'm not stupid, Robert. You adopted a rule that only three other states follow to reverse the conviction of a dangerous psychopath.'

'The rule made sense. We felt . . .' Griffen paused. 'This is ridiculous. I'm not going to sit here and justify my decision in *Deems.*'

'That's right, Robert. You're not going to sit here. You're going to get out of my car.'

'Abbie . . .'

Abigail Griffen turned in her seat and stared directly at her estranged husband. 'If you're not out of my car in ten seconds, I'm going to call the police.'

Griffen flushed with anger. He started to say something, then he just shook his head, opened the door and got out.

'I should have known I couldn't reason with you.'

'Please shut the door.'

Griffen slammed the car door and Abbie peeled out of the parking space. When Griffen walked back toward the court he was so angry that he did not notice Matthew Reynolds watching from the doorway of the Justice building.

3

In 1845, two Yankee settlers staked a claim to a spot on the Willamette River in the Oregon Territory and flipped a coin to decide if their proposed town would be called Portland or Boston. Portland was established in the most idyllic setting imaginable. Forest stood all around, backing up onto two high hills on the west side of the river. From the west bank you could look across the Willamette past the faraway foothills of the Cascade mountain range and see snow-covered Mount Hood, Mount Adams and Mount St. Helens pointing toward heaven.

The town had started on the water's edge at Front

Street and slowly moved away from the river as it became a city. Old buildings were torn down and replaced by steel and glass. But just below Washington Park, on the outskirts of downtown Portland, there were still beautiful Victorian mansions that now served as office space for architects, doctors and attorneys.

At 10 P.M. on the day he argued before the Oregon Supreme Court, the lights were off in the law offices and library on the first two floors of Matthew Reynolds's spacious Victorian home, but they still shone in the living quarters on the third floor. The argument had been hard on Reynolds. So much time had passed since the shooting that Reynolds's experts were no longer sure of the value of examining the Franklin home. No matter what the Supreme Court decided, Abigail Griffen's legal ploy might have cost his client the evidence that could win his case.

But that was not the only thing disturbing Reynolds. He was still shaken by his meeting with Abbie Griffen. Reynolds was captivated by Griffen's intellect. He considered her to be one of the few people who were his equal in the courtroom. But more than that, she was the most beautiful woman he had ever seen. Though he had spoken to her before in court as an adversary, it had taken all his nerve to approach Abbie in the Supreme Court chambers to thank her for standing up to Justice Pope, but her defense of his honor thrilled him and had given him the courage to speak.

Reynolds was dressed for bed, but he was not tired.

49

On his dresser were two photographs of his father and a framed newspaper article that showed his father outside a county courthouse in South Carolina. The article was old and the paper was starting to yellow. Matthew looked at the article briefly, then stared lovingly at the photographs.

Over the dresser was a mirror. Reynolds examined himself in it. There was no way of getting around the way he looked. *Time* had been charitable when the magazine described him as homely. As a boy, he had been the object of a million taunts. How many times had he returned home from school in tears? How many times had he hidden in his room because of the cruelty of the children in his neighborhood?

Matthew wondered what Abigail Griffen saw when she looked at him. Could she see past his looks? Did she have any idea how often he thought of her? Did she ever think of him? He shook his head at the temerity of this last idea. A man who looked like he did in the thoughts of someone like Abigail Griffen? The notion was ridiculous.

Matthew left his bedroom and walked across the hall. The law offices and his quarters were decorated with antiques. The rolltop desk in Matthew's study once belonged to a railroad lawyer who passed on in 1897. A nineteenth-century judge famous for handing down death sentences used to sit on Matthew's slat-back wooden chair. Reynolds took a perverse pleasure in crafting his arguments against death while ensconced in it.

Next to the rolltop was a chess table composed of green and white marble squares supported by a white marble base. Reynolds had no social life. Chess had been a refuge for Reynolds as a child and he continued to play it as an adult. He was involved in ten correspondence games with opponents in the United States and overseas. The pieces on the chessboard represented the position in his game with a Norwegian professor he had met when he spoke at an international symposium on the death penalty. The position was complicated and it was the only one of his games in which Reynolds did not have a superior position.

Reynolds bent over the board. His move could be crucial, but he was too on edge to concentrate. After a few minutes he turned off the ceiling light and seated himself at the rolltop desk. The only light in the study now came from a Tiffany lamp perched on a corner of the rolltop. Reynolds opened the bottom drawer of his desk and pulled out a large manila envelope. Not another soul knew it existed. Inside the envelope were several newspaper articles and many photographs. He took the articles and photographs out of the envelope and laid them on the desk.

The first article was a profile of Abigail Griffen that was featured in *The Oregonian* after her victory in *State* v. *Deems*. Reynolds had read the article so often, he knew it word for word. A black-and-white picture of Abbie took up a third of the first page of the profile. On the inside page, there was a picture of Abbie and Justice Griffen. The judge had his arm around her shoulder. Abbie, her silken hair held back by a headband, snuggled against her husband as if she did not have a care in the world.

51

The other articles were about other cases Abbie had won. They all contained pictures of the deputy district attorney. Reynolds pushed the articles aside and spread the photographs before him. He studied them. Then he reached forward and picked up one of his favorites, a black-and-white shot of Abbie in the park across from the courthouse, resting on a bench, her head back, face to the sun.

Chapter Four

1

When Alice Sherzer graduated from law school in 1958, she was one of three women in her class. Her job search in Portland consisted of interviews with one befuddled male after another, none of whom knew what to make of this lean, rawboned woman who insisted she wanted to be a trial lawyer. When one large firm offered her a position in its probate department, she politely declined. It was the courtroom or nothing. The partners explained that their clients would never accept a woman trial lawyer, not to mention the reactions they anticipated from judges and jurors.

Alice Sherzer would not bend. She wanted to try cases. If that meant going into practice for herself, so be it. Alice hung out her shingle. Four years later, a Greyhound bus totalled a decrepit Chevy driven by one of Alice's clients, a father of three who had lost his job in a sawmill. Now he was a quadriplegic. Alice sued Greyhound, which happened to be represented by the law firm that had offered her the position in probate.

Greyhound's lawyers would probably have advised the company to make a reasonable settlement offer if Alice's client was not represented by a woman, but the boys at the firm figured being represented by Alice was like not being represented at all. In court they ignored her, and when they spoke among themselves they made fun of her. The case was one big lark until the jury awarded four million dollars to the plaintiff, an award which stood up in the Supreme Court because the trial judge had ruled for his male buddies whenever he had the chance, leaving them nothing to appeal.

Money talks and four million dollars was a great deal of money in 1962. Alice was no longer a cute curiosity. Several firms, including the firm she had vanquished, made her offers. No, thank you, Alice answered politely. With her fee, which was a percentage of the verdict, and the new clients the verdict attracted, she did not need an associate's salary. She needed associates.

By 1975, Sherzer, Randolph and Picard was one of the top law firms in the state, Alice was married and the mother of two, and a seat opened on the Oregon Court of Appeals. In a private meeting, Alice told the governor that no woman had ever been appointed to an Oregon appellate court. When the governor explained the political problems inherent in making such an appointment, Alice reminded him of the large campaign contributions he had been willing to accept from a woman and the larger sums she had at her disposal for the campaign she would definitely run against any male he appointed. Seven years after her appointment to the Court of Appeals, Alice Sherzer became Oregon's first woman Supreme Court justice. She was now sixty-five. Every year brought new rumors of her retirement, but Alice Sherzer's mind was still in overdrive and she never gave a thought to leaving the bench.

Justice Sherzer had a corner office with a view of the Capitol and the red-brick buildings and rolling lawns of Willamette University. When Tracy knocked on her doorjamb on the day after Matthew Reynolds's argument at the court, the judge was sitting at a large desk that once belonged to Charles L. McNary, one of the first justices to sit in the Supreme Court building and the running mate of Wendell Willkie in the Republican's unsuccessful 1940 bid to unseat Franklin Delano Roosevelt. The antique desk contrasted sharply with the abstract sculpture and paintings Justice Sherzer used to decorate her chambers.

'Your clerkship is almost over, isn't it?' the judge asked when Tracy was seated in a chair across the desk from her.

'Yes.'

'Do you have a job lined up?'

'I have several offers, but I'm not certain which one I'm taking.'

'Justice Forbes asked me to find out if you're interested in something that's opened up.'

'What is it?'

'Matthew Reynolds is looking for an associate.'

'You're kidding!'

'One of his associates just went to the Parish firm and he needs someone right away.'

'I don't believe this. Working with Matthew Reynolds is my dream job.'

'It won't be easy, Tracy. Reynolds works his associates like dogs.'

'You know I don't mind hard work.'

'That's true, but with Reynolds we're talking slave labor. Most of his associates quit in less than two years.'

'Thanks for the warning, but nothing can stop me from giving it a try, if Reynolds takes me on.'

'I just want you to know what you're getting into. Reynolds lives at his law office. All he does is try cases and prepare for trial. He works fourteen-hour days, seven days a week. I know that sounds improbable, but I'm not exaggerating. Reynolds has no social life. He doesn't even understand the concept. He'll expect you to be at his beck and call and that can be at any hour of the night and weekends. I've been told Matt can exist on four hours' sleep and they say you can cruise by his office at almost any hour and see a light burning.'

'I'm still interested.'

'There's another thing. He's never had a woman associate. Quite frankly,' the judge said with a bemused grin, 'I'm not certain he knows what a woman is.'

'Pardon?'

'I don't know why, but he seems to shun women as if they were carrying the plague.'

'If he's never had a woman associate, why is he interested in me?'

The judge laughed. 'He's not. Reynolds has hired several clerks from our court because he went to school with Justice Forbes and trusts his recommendations. Reynolds called Stuart in a dither when he heard we wanted to send him a woman, but Stuart assured him you wouldn't bite. So he's willing to talk to you. This is his office number. His secretary will set up the interview.'

Tracy took the slip of paper. 'This is fantastic. I don't know how to thank you.'

'If it works out, you can thank me by doing such a good job that Reynolds will hire another woman.'

2

The library occupied most of the second floor of the Supreme Court building. The entrance was across from the marble staircase. A small glassed-in area with the checkout desk and an office for the librarians was directly in front of the doors. There were carrels on either side of the office. Behind the carrels, the stacks holding the law books stood two deep. A balcony overhung the stacks, casting shadows over the rows of bound volumes.

Laura Rizzatti was seated at a carrel surrounded by

law books and writing feverishly on a yellow pad. When Tracy touched her on the shoulder, Laura jumped.

'You up for a coffee break?' Tracy asked. 'I've got something fantastic to tell you.'

'I can't now,' Laura said, quickly turning over the pad so Tracy could not see what she was writing.

'Come on. A fifteen-minute break won't kill you.'

'I really can't. The judge needs this right away.'

'What are you working on?'

'Nothing exciting,' Laura answered, trying to appear casual, but sounding ill at ease. 'What did you want to tell me?'

'I've got an interview with Matthew Reynolds. He needs an associate and Justice Forbes recommended me.'

'That's great,' Laura said, but the enthusiasm seemed forced.

'I'd give my right arm to work with Reynolds. I just hope I make a good impression. Justice Sherzer says he's never had a woman associate and it sounds like he doesn't have much use for females.'

'He hasn't met you yet.' Laura smiled. 'I'm sure you'll knock him dead.'

'I hope so. If you change your mind about coffee, I'm going in about twenty minutes. I'll even buy.'

'I really can't. And congratulations.'

Tracy walked across the library and located the volume of the *New York University Law Review* she needed. She took it to her carrel and started making notes. Half an hour later, she walked over to Laura's carrel to try to convince her to go for coffee. She was really excited about the job interview and wanted to talk about it.

Laura wasn't at her desk. Tracy noticed the yellow pad on which Laura had been writing. There was a list of three criminal cases on it. Tracy studied the list, but could see nothing unusual about the cases. She wondered why Laura had turned over the pad to hide the list, then shrugged and went to look for her friend.

Tracy searched the long rows of books until she came to the section that held the Oregon Court of Appeals reporters. Laura was at the far end of the stacks near the wall and Tracy was surprised to see that she was talking with Justice Pope. She and Laura had discussed Pope on several occasions and Tracy knew that Laura despised him. Tracy's initial impulse was to walk up to her friend and the judge, but there was something about the attitude of their bodies that stopped her.

The space between the stacks was narrow and Laura and Pope were almost chest to chest. Laura looked upset. She moved her hands in an agitated manner when she spoke. Pope flushed and said something. Tracy could not hear what he said, because they were whispering, but the angry tone carried. Tracy saw Laura move away from the stocky judge until her back was against a bookshelf. Pope said something else. Laura shook her head. Then Pope reached up and touched Laura's shoulder. She tried to push his hand away, but the judge held her firmly. Tracy stepped into the aisle so Pope could see her.

'Ready for coffee?' Tracy asked loudly.

Pope looked startled and dropped his hand from Laura's shoulder.

'Laura and I have to discuss a case. I hope you don't mind, Judge,' Tracy said, in a tone that let Pope know she had seen everything. Pope flushed. His eyes darted to Laura, then back to Tracy.

'That's fine,' he said, stepping around Tracy.

'Are you okay?' Tracy asked, as soon as Pope was out of sight.

'What did you hear?' Laura asked anxiously.

'I didn't hear anything,' Tracy answered, confused by the question. 'It looked like Pope was coming on to you. Is he giving you a hard time?'

'No,' Laura said nervously. 'He was just trying to find out how Bob . . . Justice Griffen was going to vote on a case.'

'Are you being straight with me? Because you look pretty upset.'

'I'm okay, Tracy, really. Let's drop it.'

'Come on, Laura. I can help you, if you'll tell me what's bothering you.'

'How could you possibly help me?' Laura exploded. 'You have no idea what I'm going through.'

'Laura, I . . .'

'Please, I'm sorry, but you'd never understand,' Laura said. Then she edged away from Tracy and bolted out of the stacks. Tracy watched Laura go, stunned by her friend's reaction.

3

'Laura wants to see you, Judge,' Justice Griffen's secretary announced over the intercom.

'Send her in.'

The judge was preparing for the noon conference and hoped that Laura had finished her research in a tax case the justices would be discussing. The door opened as Griffen finished signing a letter. He looked up when the door closed and started to smile. But the smile disappeared when he saw his law clerk's face. She appeared to be on the verge of tears.

'We have to talk,' Laura said with a trembling voice.

Griffen stood up and walked around the desk. 'What's wrong?'

'Everything,' Laura answered. 'Everything.'

Then she started to cry.

The conference room of the Oregon Supreme Court was spacious, with few furnishings aside from a large conference table and some ancient glass-front bookshelves. Four former justices glowered down on their modern counterparts from portraits on the walls. Chief Justice Forbes sat at the head of the conference table with the sleeves of his white shirt rolled up and his tie loosened. Alice Sherzer put down her coffee cup and briefs at her place on Forbes's right. Vincent Lefcourt, snowy-haired and dignified, sat on Forbes's left.

Robert Griffen pushed through the door and almost ran

into Mary Kelly, who was working on her first cigarette of the conference.

'Sorry,' Griffen apologized.

Kelly was wearing a loose, sleeveless, forest-green dress. She brushed her honey-colored hair off her forehead and gave Griffen a casual smile.

'No damage done,' Kelly said. Then she noticed Griffen's face and her smile faded. Kelly touched Griffen lightly on his forearm. He stopped.

'What's wrong?' Kelly asked in a low voice.

Griffen shook his head. 'It's nothing.'

Kelly shifted so her back screened their conversation from the other justices.

'Tell me what happened,' she demanded.

Griffen looked away. Kelly's grip tightened. When Griffen looked at her, his face reflected his confusion. He was about to reply when Arnold Pope entered the room.

'Your wife looked terrific, Bob,' he said maliciously. 'Too bad you had to miss her argument.'

Griffen paled, and Kelly looked at Pope as if he was an insect she'd found in her salad. At that moment, Frank Arriaga rushed in. He held up a sack from the deli across the street.

'Sorry, guys. My clerk was late with my fuel. Did I miss anything?'

'Relax, Frank.' Forbes smiled. Arriaga sat next to Vincent Lefcourt, who looked on with amusement as Arriaga pulled a huge glazed jelly doughnut out of his brown paper bag.

'We're all here, so let's get started,' Justice Forbes said.

'We can talk later,' Mary Kelly assured Griffen.

Forbes squared the stack of briefs in front of him.

'I was going to begin with you, Frank, but you've got that monstrosity stuffed in your mouth, so how about it, Vincent? What's your take on the *State ex rel. Franklin*?'

4

Justice Sherzer needed a memo in the morning on a probate issue, but Tracy was so upset by what had happened in the library that she had trouble concentrating. At five o'clock, she decided to take a break and finish the memo after dinner.

Tracy's garden apartment was on the second floor of a two-story complex half a mile from the court. She had been a top student in college and law school, but she would have failed housekeeping. The front door opened into a living room that had not been cleaned in a week. Newspapers and mail were strewn across the sofa. Tracy rarely watched television, and her small black-and-white set was gathering dust in a corner. Tracy's rock-climbing equipment was well cared for, but it was piled high next to the television.

The apartment came furnished. The only marks Tracy had made on the personality of the place were several photographs detailing her athletic feats. One photo in the living room showed Tracy standing on a track in front of a grandstand with her hand gently touching the shoulder of a girl who was bent over from the waist. The two women were wearing Yale track uniforms. They had finished one-two in the 1,500 meters to clinch the Ivy League title and looked exhausted but triumphant.

Another photo showed Tracy climbing a snowcapped mountain. She was wearing a parka with the hood thrown back and was brandishing an ice ax over her head. A photo in the bedroom showed Tracy hanging upside down from a rockface on one of the more difficult ascents at Smith Rocks in eastern Oregon.

As soon as she arrived at her apartment, Tracy dumped her clothes on the bedroom floor and changed into her running gear. Then she set off along a seven-mile loop she had mapped out when she moved to Salem.

As Tracy ran, she thought about the incident in the library. She could not understand Laura's reaction. Laura disliked Justice Pope, so why would she protect him if he had made a pass at her? Maybe there was some other explanation for what she had seen, but Tracy could not think of one that made sense. Something was definitely going on in Laura's life. Tracy remembered how drawn and pale Laura looked when she surprised Laura reading the *Deems* transcript. Laura's angry outburst in the library was in keeping with the agitated state in which Tracy had observed her during the past few days, but what was causing Laura's anxiety?

After her run, Tracy showered, then ate a Caesar salad with baby shrimp and two slices of a thick-crusted sourdough bread. She threw the dirty dishes in the sink, then walked back to the courthouse across the Willamette University campus. In the daytime, the rolling lawns and old shade trees made Willamette a pleasant place to stroll. But at dusk, during summer break, the university was deserted. Streetlights illuminated the walking paths, and Tracy stayed on them when she could. The temperature had dropped and a cool breeze chilled her. Halfway across campus, Tracy thought she saw someone move in the shadow of a building. She froze and stared into the dying light. The wind rustled the leaves. Tracy waited a moment, then walked on, feeling silly for being so skittish.

The Supreme Court was deserted when Tracy let herself in at seven-thirty. It was eerie being alone in the empty building, but Tracy had worked at night before. The clerks' offices ran along the side of the Supreme Court building that faced the Capitol. An open area dominated by a conference table stood between their offices and the mail room. The top of the conference table was littered with staplers, plastic cups, paper plates and law books. No two chairs around the table were of the same type and none were in good repair. Behind the table was an alcove with a computer and the only printer. Scattered around the area were bookshelves, filing cabinets and a sagging couch. Tracy walked past the open area and down a short hall to her office. She found the notes she needed for the memo on the probate issue, turned off the lights in the clerks' area, and walked upstairs to the library.

A footnote in a law review article mentioned some

interesting cases. Tracy wandered around the stacks and found them. They led her to other cases and she became so absorbed in her work that she was surprised to discover it was almost ten o'clock when she was ready to write the memo. Tracy gathered up her notes and turned off the library lights. Her footsteps echoed on the marble staircase, creating the illusion that someone else was in the building. Tracy laughed at herself. She remembered how jittery she'd been earlier in the evening when she walked across the Willamette campus. What had gotten into her?

Tracy opened the door to the clerks' area and stopped. She was certain all the lights had been off when she went up to the library, but there was a light on in Laura Rizzatti's office. Someone must have come into the building while she was upstairs.

'Laura?' Tracy called out. There was no answer. Tracy strained to hear any sound that would tell her she was not alone. When she heard nothing, she looked in Laura's office. The drawers of Laura's filing cabinet were open and files were all over the floor. Transcripts were scattered around. Someone had ransacked the office while Tracy was upstairs in the library.

Tracy reached for the phone to call Laura. The door to the clerks' area closed. Tracy froze for a moment, then darted to the door and pulled it open. There was no one in the hallway. She ran to the back door and looked through the glass. No one was in the parking lot. Tracy tried to calm down. She thought about reporting what had happened to the police. But what *had* happened? Laura might have caused the mess in her office. That was not unreasonable, given the state Laura had been in recently. And she might have imagined hearing the door close. After all, she had not seen anyone in the building or the parking lot.

Tracy was too nervous to stay in the deserted courthouse. She decided to leave her notes and write the memo early in the morning. Tracy turned on the lights in the clerks' area and headed for her office. Out of the corner of her eye, she saw something under the conference table. Tracy stopped. A woman's leg stretched out into the light. The rest of the body was hidden in shadow. Tracy knelt down. The body was twisted as if the woman had tried to crawl away from her attacker. Blood ran through the curly black hair. The head was turned so that the dead eyes stared at Tracy. Tracy choked back a sob and lurched to her feet. She knew she should feel for a pulse, but she could not bring herself to touch Laura Rizzatti's slender wrist. She also knew instinctively that it would make no difference.

The first officers on the scene told Tracy to wait in her office. It was so narrow she could almost touch both walls if she stood sideways. Above her desk was a bulletin board with a chart of her cases. Next to the desk, on the window side, an old fan perched on top of a metal filing cabinet. Several briefs and some transcripts were stacked neatly on the desk next to a computer.

A slim woman in a powder-blue shirt, tan slacks and a light blue windbreaker walked into the office and held up a badge. She looked like she had been awakened from a deep sleep. Her blue eyes were bloodshot and her shaggy blond hair had an uncombed look.

'I'm Heidi Bricker, a detective with Salem PD.'

In Bricker's other hand was a container of hot coffee with a McDonald's logo. She offered it to Tracy.

'Can you use this?'

'Thanks,' Tracy answered wearily.

Bricker sat down beside Tracy. 'Was she a friend?'

Tracy nodded.

'It must have been some shock finding the body.'

Tracy sipped from the cardboard cup. The coffee was hot and burned the roof of her mouth, but she didn't care. The physical pain was a welcome distraction.

'What were you doing here so late?'

'I clerk for Justice Sherzer. She's working on a case with a complex probate issue and she needed a memo from me on a point of law, first thing in the morning.'

'What time did you start working?'

'Around seven-thirty.'

'Where were you working?'

'Upstairs in the library.'

'Did you hear or see anything out of the ordinary?'

'No. You can't hear anything that's said in the clerks' offices when you're upstairs in the library.'

Detective Bricker made some notes in a small spiral notebook, then asked, 'Was Laura a clerk?'

Tracy nodded. 'For Justice Griffen.'

'What did Laura do for Justice Griffen?'

'She researched legal issues being argued before the court, drafted opinions and read Petitions for Review filed by parties who've lost in the Court of Appeals.'

'Could she have been murdered because of something she was working on?'

'I can't imagine what. There isn't anything we know that isn't public record.'

'Why don't you explain that to me.'

'Okay. Let's say you were convicted of a crime or you lost a lawsuit and you didn't think you received a fair trial. Maybe you thought the judge let in evidence she shouldn't have or gave a jury instruction that didn't accurately explain the law. You can appeal. In an appeal, you ask the appellate court to decide if the trial judge screwed up. If the trial judge did make a mistake and it was serious enough to affect the verdict, the appellate court sends the case back for a new trial.

'A court reporter takes down everything that's said in the trial. If you appeal, the court reporter prepares a transcript of the trial that is a word-for-word record of everything that was said. An appeal must be from the record. If someone confesses to a crime after the trial, the confession can't be considered on appeal, because it's not in the record.'

'So there's nothing an appellate judge considers that's secret?' Bricker said.

'Well, sometimes there are sealed portions of the record, but that's rare. And no one is allowed to tell the public which justice is assigned to write the opinion in a case or what views the justices express in conference. But that wouldn't have anything to do with Laura.'

'Then why would someone ransack Laura's office?'

'I don't know. A burglar wouldn't be interested in legal briefs and transcripts. No one except the lawyers and judges involved in a particular case would be interested in them.'

'What about jewelry, cash?'

'Laura didn't have much money and I never saw her with any jewelry worth killing for.'

'Can you think of anyone who would want to hurt her? Did she have a boyfriend, an ex-husband with a grudge?'

'Laura was single. As far as I know, she didn't have a boyfriend. She kept to herself, so there might have been someone I didn't know about, but . . .'

Tracy paused.

'Yes?' Bricker asked.

'I feel odd about this.'

'About what?'

'Is what I tell you confidential?'

'Our reports have to be revealed to the defense in certain cases, if there's an arrest, but we try to keep confidences.'

'I don't know if I . . .'

'Tracy, your friend was murdered. If you know something that could help us catch the killer . . .'

Tracy told Detective Bricker how Laura had been acting and about the incident between Justice Pope and Laura in the library.

'It may have been nothing,' Tracy concluded. 'Laura never said Pope tried anything, but it was obvious to me he'd made a pass at her.'

'Okay. Thanks. If I talk to Justice Pope about this, I won't tell him my source. Can you think of anything else that might help?'

Tracy shook her head wearily.

'Okay. You've been a big help, but you look like you're at the end of your rope. I'm going to have someone drive you home. I may want to speak to you again,' Bricker said, handing Tracy her business card, 'and if anything else comes to you . . .'

'I'll definitely call, only I don't think I know anything I haven't told you. I can't imagine why anyone would want to kill Laura.'

5

Tracy waited on the landing while an officer checked her apartment. She was exhausted and had to lean against the railing to keep herself erect. It was hard to believe that Laura, to whom she'd spoken only hours before, was no longer alive.

'Everything's okay, miss,' the policeman said. Tracy hadn't heard him step out of the apartment and she jumped slightly. 'I checked the rooms, but you make certain you lock up tight. I'll cruise by every hour, just in case.'

Tracy thanked the policeman. She locked up, as he'd advised. Tracy wanted nothing more than to sleep, but she wondered if she could. The first thing she noticed when she entered her bedroom was the flashing light on her answering machine. Tracy collapsed on her bed and played back her only message. Laura's voice made her gasp.

'Tracy, I'm in trouble. I have to talk to you. It's nine-oh-five. Please call me as soon as you get in, no matter how late it is. I have to . . .'

Tracy heard a doorbell ringing in the background just before Laura stopped speaking. There was a pause, then Laura finished the message.

'Please call me. I don't know what to do. Please.'

Chapter Five

1

In the days following Laura's death, everyone at the court tiptoed around Tracy as if she had some rare disease, except for Justice Sherzer, who invited Tracy to move in with her. She declined, insisting on staying alone in her apartment and facing her fears.

Friday was oppressively humid. The portable fan barely stirred the air in Tracy's tiny office. The workmen's compensation case she was working on was as dry as dust and the heat made it hard to concentrate. Tracy was taking a sip from a diet Coke she had purchased more for the ice than the drink when Arnold Pope stormed in. His face was florid and he glowered at Tracy. With his bristly flattop and heavy jowls, he reminded her of a maddened bulldog.

'Did you talk to a woman named Bricker about me?' Pope demanded.

Tracy was frightened by the sudden verbal assault, but she refused to show it.

'I don't appreciate your yelling at me, Justice Pope,' she said firmly as she stood to confront the judge.

'And I don't appreciate a clerk talking about me behind my back, young lady.'

'What is this about?' Tracy asked, fighting to keep her tone even.

'I just had a visit from Detective Heidi Bricker of Salem PD. She said someone accused me of making a pass at Laura Rizzatti in the library. She wouldn't tell me who'd made the accusation, but only three of us were there. Did you think I wouldn't figure out who was slandering me?'

'I told Detective Bricker what I saw.'

'You never saw me make a pass at Laura Rizzatti, because that never happened. Now, I want you to call her and tell her you lied.'

'I'll do no such thing,' Tracy answered angrily.

'Listen, young lady, you're just starting your legal career. You don't want to make enemies. Either you call that detective or . . .'

'Is something wrong?' Justice Griffen asked from the doorway. He was wearing a short-sleeve white shirt. His top button was open and his red-and-yellow paisley-print tie was loosened. The heat had dampened his hair and it fell across his forehead. From a distance, he could have been mistaken for one of the clerks.

Pope whirled around. 'This is between Miss Cavanaugh and me,' he said.

'Oh? I thought I heard you threatening her.'

'I don't care what you think, Griffen. I'm not going to stand still while this girl makes false accusations about me behind my back.'

'Calm down, Arnold. Whatever happened between you and Ms. Cavanaugh, this is no way to deal with it. All the clerks can hear you yelling at her.'

Pope's shoulders hunched. He looked like he was going to say something to Griffen, then he changed his mind and turned back to Tracy.

'I expect you to make that call. Then I'll expect an apology.'

Pope pushed past Griffen and stormed down the hall and out of the clerks' area. As soon as the door slammed, Griffen asked, 'Are you okay?' Tracy nodded, afraid that the judge would see how frightened she was if she spoke.

'What was that about?'

Tracy hesitated.

'Please,' Griffen said. 'I want to help.'

'I told something to the police. Something about Justice Pope and Laura. That's why he was upset.'

'What happened between them?'

'I . . . I really shouldn't say. I don't have anything more than suspicions. Maybe I was wrong to tell the police in the first place.'

'Tracy, I feel terrible about what happened to Laura. If you know something, you have to tell me.'

Tracy hesitated, not certain if she should go on.

'What is it, Tracy?'

75

'I think Justice Pope was bothering Laura.'

'In what way?'

'Sexually. I . . . There was an incident in the library. I couldn't hear what Justice Pope said but it looked like he was making a pass at her. When I asked Laura what happened, she wouldn't come out and accuse him, but she was very upset. Laura was disturbed a lot recently. She looked like she wasn't sleeping and she was very jumpy.'

'And you think that was because Arnold was bothering her?'

'I don't know.'

Griffen considered what Tracy had told him. Then he closed the door to her office and sat down.

'I'm going to tell you something in confidence. You'll have to promise never to discuss this with anyone.'

'Of course.'

'We've had trouble with Arnold Pope since he came on the court. Justice Kamsky was highly respected. He was not only brilliant, he was very practical. I can't tell you how many times he was able to break a deadlock among the justices with his insights.

'When Pope beat Ted in the election we were crushed. Ted was not only the court's finest justice but a dear friend to us all. Still, we tried to treat Pope as a colleague. We bent over backward to be fair to him. But the man's been a disaster. And one of the worst problems we've had has been his relations with women.

'Stuart had a long talk with Pope about his conduct after we received complaints from a secretary and a woman clerk. We all hoped he learned his lesson, but it appears he hasn't.'

'What are you going to do?'

'I'll discuss what you've told me with Stuart, but I don't think there's anything we can do. You're our only witness and you can't say what really happened. But it helps us to know that there's still a problem.

'I hope you understand why you can't talk about this. The image of the court is very important. People have to believe that they are receiving justice when we decide matters. It's the public's acceptance of our decision-making authority that maintains the rule of the law. Any scandal weakens the public's image of what we do.'

'I've already told the police.'

'Of course. You had to. And I appreciate your candor with me.'

Now it was Griffen's turn to pause. He looked uncomfortable.

'You were Laura's friend, weren't you?'

'I'd like to think that, but Laura was tough to get to know.'

'Oh?' Griffen said, surprised. 'I had the impression you two were close.'

'Not really. We were the only woman clerks, so we gravitated toward each other, but Laura didn't make friends easily. She came over to my apartment a few times for dinner and I was at her place once, but she never let her hair down with me.'

Tracy paused, remembering Laura's last message.

'I think she wanted to that night. I think she was desperate for a friend. I wish . . .'

Tracy let the thought trail off. Griffen leaned forward.

'Alice told me about the call. Don't blame yourself. There's nothing you could have done.'

'I know that, but it doesn't make me feel any better.'

'Laura was a tough person to befriend. I try to get to know my clerks. We go fishing or hiking a few times during the year. You know, do something that has nothing to do with law. Laura always had some excuse. I tried to draw her out, but our relationship stayed strictly professional. Still, recently I also had the feeling that something was troubling her. She seemed on the verge of confiding in me a few times, then she would back off. When I heard she'd been killed . . . I don't know . . . I guess I felt I'd failed her in some way. I was hoping she'd told you what was troubling her.'

'You should take your own advice. If I'm not allowed to blame myself, how can you feel guilty?'

Griffen smiled. He looked tired. 'It's always easier to give advice than to take it. I liked Laura. She seemed to be very decent. I wish she trusted me more. Maybe she would have told me what was bothering her and I could have helped.'

'She trusted you a lot, Judge. She was your biggest fan. She looked up to you.'

'That's nice to know.'

Justice Griffen stood up. Before he left, he said, 'You should know that your reputation among the justices is excellent. You aren't only the best clerk we've had this term but one of the finest lawyers I've worked with since I started on the court. I'm sure you'll make an excellent attorney.'

Tracy blushed.

'Thanks for talking to me,' Griffen continued. 'I know this has been hard for you. If there's ever anything I can do for you, I'd be pleased if you would consider me a friend.'

2

Raoul Otero was wearing a custom-tailored gray suit with a fine blue weave, a white silk shirt and a yellow-and-blue Hermès tie. In the subdued lighting of Casa Maria, he could easily be mistaken for a successful executive, but a brighter light would have revealed the pockmarked face and wary eyes of a child of Mexico City's most dangerous slum.

'You're looking good for a dead man, amigo,' Otero said as he threw his arms around Charlie Deems. Otero was putting on weight, but Deems could still feel muscle as the big man smothered him.

'I'm feeling good,' Deems said when Otero let him go.

'You know Bobby Cruz?' Otero asked. A thin man with a sallow complexion and a pencil-thin mustache was sitting quietly in the center of the booth. He had not risen when Otero greeted Deems, but his pale eyes never left Charlie.

'Sure. I know Bobby,' Deems said. Neither seemed pleased to see the other. Cruz was wearing an open-necked white shirt and a sports jacket. Deems knew Cruz was armed, but he was not concerned about Otero's bodyguard.

'So,' Otero said, sliding back into the booth, 'how does it feel to be out?'

'Better than being in,' Deems cracked. Otero laughed.

'That's what I like about you, amigo. You got a sense of humor. Most guys, they'd come off the row all bitter. You, you're making jokes.'

Deems shrugged.

'We already ate,' Otero said, gesturing apologetically at the remains of his meal. 'You want a beer, some coffee?'

'That's okay, Raoul. I'd rather get down to business. I've got fifteen and I want a key.'

Otero looked uncomfortable. 'That may be a problem, Charlie.'

'Oh? That's not the price?'

'The price is right, but I can't deal with you right now.'

'I know one key ain't much, Raoul, but this is just the beginning. I'm going to be into some big money soon and I just need the key to help me reestablish myself.'

'I can't do it.'

Deems cocked his head to one side and studied Otero.

'My money was always good before. What's the problem?'

'You're hot. You start dealing and the cops gonna be all over you and everyone you're seen with. There's plenty people still pretty mad about you takin' out that kid. It caused trouble. We couldn't push shit for three months. The operation was almost shut down. I wish you'd talked to me before you done it, amigo.'

'Hey,' Deems asked, 'what was I supposed to do? Stand in a lineup and hope Mr. Citizen didn't pick me? The fuck should have minded his own business.'

Otero shook his head. 'If you'd come to me, I could have worked it out. Taking out that little girl was bad for business, Charlie.'

Deems leaned across the table. Cruz tensed. Deems ignored Cruz and looked directly into Otero's eyes.

'Was it bad for business when I took care of Harold Shoe?' Deems asked. 'Was it bad for business when I didn't tell the cops the name of the person who thought it would be neato if someone performed unnecessary surgery on Mr. Shoe while he was wide awake?'

Otero held up a hand. 'I never said you wasn't a stand-up guy, Charlie. This is business. I bet the cops been following you since you got out. Any business we do is gonna be on videotape. Things are back to normal and I want to keep it that way.'

Charlie smiled coldly and shook his head.

'This is bullshit, Raoul. You owe me.'

Otero flushed. 'I'm tryin' to say this politely, Charlie, 'cause I don't want to hurt your feelings, okay? I ain't gonna do business with you. It's too risky. Maybe, in the future, when things quiet down, but not now. I can't make it any clearer.'

'It might be worse for business to fuck with me.'

'What's that supposed to mean?'

'You're a smart guy. Figure it out.' Charlie stood up. 'I'm gonna be in a position to move a lot more than a key pretty soon. When I'm ready, I'll be back to see you. That will give you time to think about how intelligent it is to stiff a guy who went to the row instead of trading your fat ass for a life sentence. A person like that isn't afraid of death, Raoul. Are you?'

Cruz started to bring his right hand out from under the table, but Otero clamped a hand on Cruz's forearm.

'I'll think about what you said, amigo.'

'It's always better to think than to act rashly, Raoul. See you soon.'

Deems walked out of the restaurant.

'Charlie Deems has been too long on this earth, Raoul,' Cruz told Otero in Spanish, still watching the front of the restaurant.

'Charlie's just upset,' Raoul answered in a tone that made it clear he was not certain about what he was saying. 'He's just being the man. When he calms down, he'll do what he told me to do. Think. Then he'll see things my way.'

'I don' know. Charlie, he ain't like other guys. He don' think like other guys. He's fucked up in the head. Better I take him out, Raoul. That way we don' take no chances.'

Otero looked troubled. Killing people was bad for business, but Bobby Cruz was right when he said Charlie

Deems didn't think like other people. Charlie Deems was different from any man Raoul Otero had ever met and he had met some bad hombres in his time.

Charlie Deems sat in his car behind the restaurant. Anger was flowing through him like a red tide. The anger was directed at Raoul, whom he'd gone to death row to protect and who now turned his back on him. It was also directed at Abigail Griffen, the bitch who was responsible for all his troubles. If she hadn't made prosecuting him a personal crusade, he would not have lost almost two years of his life.

Charlie let his imagination run wild. In his fantasy, Deems saw himself gut-shooting Raoul, then sitting in a chair with a beer as he watched him die slowly and in excruciating pain. His fantasy about Abigail Griffen was quite different.

3

Caruso's did not have the best Italian food in Portland or great atmosphere, but it did have subdued lighting, stiff drinks and the privacy Abigail Griffen needed to brood about her bastard husband, who was in her thoughts because she had just come from a two-hour conference with the attorney who was handling her divorce.

At thirty-three, Abbie felt she had lived long enough to have some idea of what life was supposed to be about, but she was still in a state of tortured confusion when the subject was love. Abbie's parents were killed in a car accident when she was three and she grew up believing that she was missing a special kind of love that all the children with mothers and fathers received.

Abbie was afraid to form relationships with men, because she was afraid that the love she shared would disappear like the love that had been snatched away when her parents were taken from her. It wasn't until her sophomore year at the University of Wisconsin that she fell in love for the first time.

Abbie sipped from her wineglass and thought about Larry Ross, a sure sign that she was courting severe depression. When she married Robert, Abbie had been so happy that she stopped thinking about Larry, but she found herself clinging to his memory with increasing urgency as her marriage soured.

The alcohol Abbie had consumed since entering Caruso's was beginning to make her woozy. She tried to remember what Larry looked like, but his image was blurred and insubstantial. What if Larry's memory slipped away forever?

Larry Ross was a quiet, considerate pre-med student who was a friend for a year before he became Abbie's first lover. When Larry started medical school at Columbia University, Abbie sent out applications to every law school within commuting distance of New York. They both felt that they would be together forever. She was accepted at New York University exactly one week before

Larry was fatally stabbed during a mugging. Abbie fled home to the aunt who had raised her.

After Larry's death, Abbie ran away from every man who tried to form a relationship with her, because she was certain she could never survive love's loss a third time. Then she met Robert Griffen, who made her love him and then betrayed her.

Abbie had downed several Jack Daniel's in rapid succession soon after sliding into a deep leather booth well away from the front door of the restaurant. She was through most of a bottle of Chianti and a dinner of linguine con vongole when Tony Rose blocked what little light there was in the booth.

Tony was a cop who had testified in a few of Abbie's cases when she was in the drug unit. He was handsome, well built, and had the testosterone level of a teenager. After two cases, Abbie stopped prepping him for his testimony unless someone else was present. Putting together a good direct examination while trying to fend off a horny cop was too exhausting.

'Hi,' Rose said, flashing a wide smile. 'I thought that was you.'

Alcohol had dulled Abbie's reactions and Rose was sitting across from her before she could tell him to buzz off.

'How you doin'?' Rose asked cheerily.

'Not so good, Tony.'

'What's the problem?' Rose asked with phony concern.

'My son-of-a-bitch husband, the Honorable Robert

Hunter Griffen,' Abbie answered with a candor she would never have offered if she was sober.

'Hey, that's right. I forgot. You're married to a Supreme Court justice, aren't you?'

'Not for long.'

'Oh?'

'I walked out on the bastard,' Abbie said, slurring her words. Rose noticed the half-empty Chianti bottle and the melting ice cubes in Abbie's last glass of Jack Daniel's. He was an old hand at bedding inebriated women and he guessed that Abbie's inhibitions were way out of town by now.

'Hey! Isn't Griffen the judge who let out Charlie Deems?'

'He certainly is. The next time Deems kills somebody, they can thank good old Robert. And I'll tell you something else. I think he reversed the case just to embarrass me. Maybe next time Deems will do us all a favor and blow my asshole soon-to-be-ex to kingdom come.'

Abbie reached for her wineglass and knocked it over. A river of ruby-red Chianti flowed over the edge of the table. Abbie tried to slide away from it, but she was too slow.

'Ah, shit,' she said, dabbing at her lap with a napkin.

'Are you okay?'

'No, Tony. I'm fucked up,' Abbie answered distractedly.

'Look, I was on the way out. Can you use a lift home?'

'I've got a car.'

'You've got to be kidding.' Rose laughed. 'If I saw you driving tonight, I'd have to bust you.'

Abbie slumped down on a dry section of the booth and put her head back.

'What a terrific way to end a rotten day.'

'Leave your car and take a taxi in the morning. Come on. I'll get the check and you can pay me back.'

Abbie was too tired to fight Rose and too drunk to care. She let him take her arm.

'What?' Abbie mumbled.

'I said, watch your head.'

Abbie opened her eyes. She was staring at Tony Rose's chest and she had no idea where she was. Then Rose shifted and she could see her house through the car door.

'Come on,' Rose said, easing her out of the car. Abbie stood unsteadily. Rose wrapped an arm around her waist. Abbie tried to stand up. Her head swam and her vision blurred. She leaned back against Rose's shoulder. He smiled.

'Take it easy. We're almost there. Where's your key?'

Abbie realized she was holding her purse. She fumbled with the clasp and finally got it open, but missed the keyhole on the first try.

'Here,' Rose said, taking the key from her.

Rose helped Abbie into the house and switched on the light. Abbie shut her eyes against the glare and leaned against the wall. She heard the door close and felt Rose near her. Then she felt Rose's lips. His breath smelled minty. His kiss was gentle. So was his touch when he slipped his arm around Abbie's waist. 'What are you doing?' she asked.

'What you want me to do,' Rose answered confidently.

'Don't,' Abbie said, pushing against Rose. The cop's muscular arm tightened around her and she was crushed against his chest. Abbie strained against Rose's grip, but he was very strong. She felt his hands on her buttocks. Fear suddenly coursed through her, cutting through her haze. She pulled her head away and Rose pressed his lips against her neck while his right hand groped under her skirt. Abbie shifted until she could get her teeth around Rose's ear, then she bit down hard.

'Hey,' Rose yelped, jumping back and holding a hand to his

Abbie slapped Rose as hard as she could. The policeman looked stunned.

'What's wrong with you?' he asked in a shocked tone.

'Get out, you son of a bitch,' Abbie yelled.

'What's going on here? I was just trying to help you out.'

'Was that what you were doing just now?'

'Look, I thought . . .'

'You thought I'd fall into bed with you because I'm smashed.'

'No. It's not like that. You looked like you needed a friend.'

'And that's what you were doing? Being my friend?'

'Hey,' Rose said angrily, 'when I kissed you, you didn't exactly faint.'

'You bastard. I'm drunk.'

'Man, you are one cold bitch.'

'Cut the shit, Tony. You wanted to get me into bed. Well, it didn't work out.'

Rose looked hurt, like a little boy.

'It could,' he said. 'I mean, we got off on the wrong foot here, but that's not my fault. You're the one who was giving off signals.'

'Tony, haven't you been listening . . . ?' Abbie started. Then she stopped herself. Whatever had happened had happened. She just wanted Rose out of her house.

'Look, Tony, this was a major mistake. Let's just forget it. Okay?'

Rose took his hand away from his ear. It was covered with blood.

'Jesus,' he said. 'You really hurt me.'

'I'm sorry,' Abbie answered, too exhausted to be angry anymore. 'Can you please leave? I want to go to bed.'

'I guess you are as frigid as everyone says,' he snapped, getting in the last word. Abbie let him save face. It was worth it to get him out of her house. He slammed the door and she locked it immediately. The engine of Rose's car started and she heard him drive away.

Abbie turned away from the door. She saw herself in the hall mirror. Her lipstick was smeared and her hair looked like it had been permed in a washing machine.

'Jesus,' Abbie muttered. She imagined herself in court looking like this. She started to laugh. That would be something. She laughed harder and could not stop.

What a fool she was. How had she let herself get into this situation?

Abbie slumped down on the carpet. When she stopped laughing, depression flooded over her. She leaned against the wall and started to cry. It was Robert's fault she was falling apart. She had loved him without reservation and he had deceived her. She hated him more than she ever thought possible.

Abbie closed her eyes. She was so tired. She started to fade out, then jerked herself awake and struggled to her feet. She was going to sleep, but not on the floor in the entryway.

Abbie's bedroom was at the end of a short hall. She staggered inside. The shades in the bedroom were open and the backyard looked like a black-on-black still life. The only light came from the window of the house next door. Abbie reached for the light switch. In the moment before the bedroom light went on, a shape erased the glow from the next-door window. Abbie stiffened. Someone was in the yard. She switched off the light so she could see outside, but she had been blinded momentarily when the bedroom light flashed on.

Abbie pressed her face against the windowpane, trying to see as much of the backyard as possible. There was no one there. She must have imagined the figure. She sagged down on the bed and closed her eyes. A doorknob rattled in the kitchen. Abbie's eyes flew open. She strained to hear, but her heart was beating loudly in her ears.

Abbie had received a number of threats over the years

from people she had prosecuted. She had taken a few of them seriously enough to learn how to shoot a semiautomatic 9mm Beretta that she kept in her end table. Abbie took out the gun. Then she kicked off her shoes and walked on stocking feet down the dark hall to the kitchen. Abbie heard the doorknob rattle again. Someone was trying to break in. Was it Rose? Had he parked his car and returned on foot?

Abbie crouched down and peered into the darkened kitchen. There was a man on the deck outside the kitchen bent over the lock on the back door. Abbie could not see his face because he was wearing a ski mask. Without thinking, she ran to the door and aimed her gun, screaming 'Freeze!' as she pressed the muzzle to the glass. The man did freeze for a second. Then he straightened up very slowly and raised his arms until they were stretched out from his sides like the wings of a giant bird. The man was clothed in black from head to foot and wore black gloves, but Abbie had the strange feeling that she knew him. Their eyes met through the glass. No one moved for a moment. The man took one backward step, then another. Then he turned slowly, loped across the yard, vaulted the fence and disappeared.

It never occurred to Abbie to pursue him. She was just glad he was gone. The adrenaline began to wear off and Abbie started to shake. She dropped onto one of her kitchen chairs and put the Beretta on the kitchen table. Suddenly she noticed that the safety was on. She felt sick for a moment, then felt relieved that she was safe.

Abbie contemplated reporting the attempted break-in, but decided against it. She was so tired that she only wanted to sleep, and she could not describe the man anyway. If she called the police, she would be up all night. Worse, she would have to tell the officers about Tony Rose, even though she was certain he wasn't the intruder, and there was no way she was going to do that.

Abbie rested for a few moments more, then dragged herself back to the bedroom after checking to make sure that all the doors and windows were locked. She put the Beretta on the end table and stripped off her clothes. She was certain she would drop off to sleep immediately because she was so exhausted, but every sound primed the pump of her overwrought imagination and she did not slip into sleep until an hour before dawn.

PART THREE
THE
SORCERER'S
APPRENTICE

Chapter Six

The intense leather, glass and stainless-steel decor of the big law firms was nowhere to be found in Matthew Reynolds's reception area. The hand-knit antimacassar draped over the back of the country sofa, the Tiffany lamps and the deep old armchairs had a calming effect that was equally appreciated by clients facing prison or a nervous young woman waiting for a job interview.

Masterful black-and-white photographs of jagged mountain peaks, pristine lakes and shadowy timberland trails graced the walls. One picture in particular caught Tracy's eye. A doe and her fawn were standing in a clearing nibbling on a bush, apparently oblivious to the presence of the photographer. A wide ray of sunlight shone down through the trees and bathed the bush in light. The picture had a quiet, almost religious feel to it that touched something in Tracy. She was admiring the photograph when the receptionist beckoned her down a corridor on whose walls hung more of the exceptional wilderness photography.

'Mr. Reynolds took those,' the receptionist proudly told Tracy as she stepped aside to admit her to Matthew Reynolds's office.

'They're terrific,' Tracy answered, genuinely impressed by the use of light and the unique perspectives. 'Has Mr. Reynolds ever shown them in a gallery?'

'Not that I know of,' the receptionist answered with a smile. 'Why don't you have a seat. Mr. Reynolds will be with you shortly.'

The receptionist left Tracy alone in the large corner room. Law books and legal papers were arranged in neat piles on the oak desk that dominated it. Two high-backed, dark leather client chairs stood before the desk. Through the windows Tracy could see sections of a flower garden and the cheerful green of a well-manicured lawn.

Tracy wandered over to the near wall, which was covered with memorabilia from Reynolds's cases. There were framed newspaper clippings and the originals of courtroom sketches that had appeared in newspapers around the country. Tracy stopped in front of a frame in which was displayed the cover of a brief that had been filed in the United States Supreme Court. Above the cover, in a narrow recess, was a white quill pen.

'Those pens are specially crafted for the Court,' Matthew Reynolds said from the doorway. 'If you ever argue there you'll find them at counsel table. You're expected to take one as evidence that you have appeared before the highest court in the land. I've argued seven cases in the United States Supreme Court, but that pen means the most to me.'

Reynolds paused and Tracy was transfixed, the way she imagined his juries were, as his homely features were transformed by his quiet passion.

'I won that case on an insignificant technicality. A procedural point. Saved Lloyd Garth's life, though. Took him off death row as surely as any great legal point would have.'

A gentle smile played on Reynolds's lips.

'Two weeks before the retrial, another man confessed to the murder. Lloyd always swore he was innocent, but few people believed him. Sit down, Ms. Cavanaugh. Sit down.'

Tracy had been caught up in Reynolds's tale and it took her a moment to respond. While she took her seat, Reynolds studied her résumé. Tracy was rarely at a disadvantage, but she felt that Reynolds had already begun to dominate the interview. To regain the initiative, Tracy asked, 'Are all the wilderness photographs yours?'

'Why, yes,' Reynolds responded with a proud smile.

'They're incredible. Have you had formal training?'

Reynolds's smile vanished. A look of sadness passed over him.

'No formal training with a camera, but my father was a hunter – a great hunter – and he taught me all about the woods. He could stay with an animal for days in the forest.

The sheriff asked him to track men on occasion. Lost hunters, once an escaped convict. He found a little boy alive after everyone else had given up hope.

'He taught me to hunt. I was good at it, too. Eventually, I lost heart in the killing, but I still loved the woods. Photography is my way of getting out of myself when life gets too ponderous.'

'I know what you mean. I rock-climb. When you're on a cliff face, and the difference between life and death is the strength in your hands, you pull into yourself. You forget everything else except the rock.'

Tracy realized how pretentious she sounded as soon as she spoke. Reynolds seemed to close off a little. When he addressed her, there was less warmth.

'You're from California?'

Tracy nodded.

'What do your parents do?'

'My father works in motion pictures. He's a producer.'

'Successful?'

Tracy smiled. 'Very.'

'And your mother?'

'She doesn't work, but she's involved with charities. She devotes a lot of her time to volunteer work.'

Tracy hoped this would sound good, but she was afraid her background would be anathema to someone like Reynolds.

'Yale,' Reynolds went on, his voice giving away nothing of how he felt about her or her background, 'math major, *Stanford Law Review.*'

Tracy shrugged, wondering if she'd already blown the interview.

'And you placed fifth in the NCAA cross-country championships. You appear to have been successful at everything you've tried.'

Tracy considered a modest answer, then decided against it. If she got this job, it would not be by being a phony.

'I've been lucky. I'm very smart and I'm a natural athlete,' Tracy said. 'But I also work my butt off.'

Reynolds nodded. Then he asked, 'Why did you choose the law as a profession?'

Tracy thought about the question, as she had many times before.

'When I was young, I couldn't understand the world. It made no sense that the earth and sun didn't collide. Why didn't we fly off into space? How could a chair be made of tiny, unconnected atoms, yet be solid enough to prevent me from putting my hand through it? Mathematics imposes order on the sciences. Its rules helped me to make sense out of insanity.

'Human beings like to think of themselves as rational and civilized, but I think we are constantly on the brink of chaos. Look at the madness in Africa or the carnage in Eastern Europe. I was attracted to the law for the same reason I was fascinated by mathematics. Law imposes order on society and keeps the barbarians in check. When the rule of law breaks down, civilization falls apart.

'America is a nation of laws. I've always marveled that

a country with so much power shows such restraint in the way it treats its citizens. Not that I think the country is perfect. Not by a long shot. We've condoned countless injustices. Slavery is the most obvious example. But that's because human beings are so fallible. Then I think of what the President could do if he wanted to. Especially with today's technology. Why don't we live in a dictatorship? Why did Nixon resign, instead of trying a coup d'état? I think it's because we are a nation of laws in the truest sense and lawyers are the guardians of the law. I really believe that.'

Tracy felt she was running on. She stopped talking and studied Matthew Reynolds, but his face revealed nothing and she could not tell if her speech had impressed him or made him think she was a fool.

'I understand that the young woman who was murdered at the court was a friend of yours.'

Reynolds's statement shook her and all Tracy could do was nod. An image of Laura, strands of curly black hair wrapped around her fingers as she worked through a legal problem, flashed into her mind. Then another image of Laura, dead, her curly black hair matted with blood, superimposed itself on the first image.

'What punishment should your friend's killer receive if he's caught?'

Tracy knew Reynolds would ask about her views on the death penalty, but she never expected him to come at her in this way. She had spent several hours reading articles about the death penalty, including some by

Reynolds, to prepare herself for the interview, but dealing with punishment in the abstract and asking her to decide the fate of Laura's murderer were two different things.

'That's not a fair question,' Tracy said.

'Why not?'

'She was my friend. I found the body.'

Reynolds nodded sympathetically.

'There's always a body. There's always a victim. There's always someone left alive to mourn. Don't you want revenge for your friend?'

It was a good question that forced Tracy to decide what she really thought about the death penalty. She looked across the desk at Matthew Reynolds. He was watching her closely.

'If I found the man who murdered Laura, I would want to kill him with my bare hands, but I would hope that the sober people around me would stop me. A civilized society should aspire to higher ideals. It should be above legalized killing for revenge.'

'Would you be in favor of the death penalty if it deterred crime?'

'Maybe, but it doesn't. I don't have to tell you that there's no statistical evidence that the penalty deters killing. Oregon had a record murder rate a few years after the penalty was reinstated.

'And then there's the mistake factor. I read recently that four hundred and sixteen innocent Americans were convicted of capital crimes between 1900 and 1991 and twenty-three were actually executed. Every other sentence can be corrected if the authorities realize they've made a mistake, except for a sentence of death.'

'Why do you want to work for me, Ms. Cavanaugh?'

'I want to work for you because you're the best and because everything in my life has been easy. I don't regret that, but I'd like to give something back to people who haven't been as fortunate.'

'That's very noble, but our clients are not the "less fortunate." They are sociopaths, misfits, psychotics. They are men who torture women and murder children. Not the type of people you associated with in Beverly Hills or at Yale.'

'I'm aware of that.'

'Are you also aware that we work very long hours? Evenings and weekends are the norm. How do you feel about that?'

'Justice Sherer warned me about your version of a workweek and I still called for this interview.'

'Tell me, Ms. Cavanaugh,' Reynolds asked in a neutral tone, 'have you ever been to Stark, Florida, to the prison, after dark?'

'No, sir,' Tracy answered, completely stumped by the question.

'And I suppose you have never been to Columbia, South Carolina, to visit after dark?'

Tracy shook her head. Reynolds watched her carefully, then continued.

'Several attorneys of my acquaintance have visited their clients in prison after dark. These attorneys have a number of things in common. They are brilliant, extremely skilled legal practitioners. They are what you would call the top of the bar in morality, ethics and commitment. They are people we can admire very much for what their lives are about and what their commitment to the criminal justice system is.

'These people have something else in common. They all visited these prisons after dark and left before sunrise with their clients dead.'

A chill ran up Tracy's spine.

'There is something else they have in common, Ms. Cavanaugh. They all left before dawn with their clients dead because of some act of another lawyer in not preserving an issue, in failing to investigate competently, in not seeing that that client was represented in the way that a co-defendant was. And the fact is that these co-defendants are on the street today, alive, just because of the quality of the words written or spoken in some court or some act by some lawyer.'

Reynolds paused. He leaned back in his chair and formed a steeple with his slender fingers.

'Ms. Cavanaugh, I've been a lawyer for more than twenty years and neither I nor any associate of mine has ever visited a prison in this country after dark. Not once. I take no pride in that fact, because pride has no place in the work we do. It is backbreaking, mind-numbing work. If you work for me, you won't sleep right, you won't eat right, and you certainly won't have time to climb or run. This work tears the soul out of you. It requires dedication to men and women who are pariahs in our society. It is work that will earn you no praise but will often earn you the hatred and ill will of decent citizens.'

Tracy's throat felt tight. There was a band around her heart. She knew she had never wanted anything more in life than to work for this man.

'Mr. Reynolds, if you give me this chance I won't let you down.'

Reynolds watched Tracy over his steepled fingers. Then he sat up in his chair.

'You know I've never worked with a woman?'

'Justice Sherzer told me.'

'What special gifts do you think you'll bring to this job as a woman?'

'None, Mr. Reynolds. But I'll bring several as a lawyer. I'll bring an exceptional ability to analyze legal issues and total dedication to my work. Justice Forbes knows my work. He wouldn't have told you to talk to me if he didn't think I could cut it. If you hire me, you won't have to worry about the quality of the words I write or speak.'

'We'll see,' Reynolds said. He sat up. 'When can you start?'

Chapter Seven

1

Tracy Cavanaugh was sitting on the floor in jeans and a faded Yale Athletic Department tee shirt taking law books out of a carton and putting them on bookshelves when she heard someone behind her. Standing in the doorway of her new office was a lean man with a dark complexion, curly black hair and a wide grin. To her surprise, Tracy felt an immediate attraction to him, and she hoped her deep tan was hiding the blush that warmed her cheeks.

'You must be the new associate. I'm Barry Frame, Matt's investigator.'

Frame was a little over six feet with wide shoulders and a tapered waist. He was wearing a blue work shirt and khaki slacks. The sleeves of his shirt were rolled back to the elbow, revealing hairy forearms that were corded with muscle. Tracy stood up and wiped her hand on her jeans before offering it to Frame. His grip was gentle.

'Getting settled in okay?' Frame asked, looking at the cardboard cartons.

'Oh, sure.'

'Can I help?'

'Thanks, but I don't have that much stuff.'

'Have you found a place to stay?'

'Yeah. I've got a nice apartment down by the river. I found it just before I moved up.'

'You were living in Salem, right?'

Tracy nodded. 'I was clerking for the Supreme Court.'

'Which justice?'

'Alice Sherzer.'

'I clerked for Justice Lefcourt five years ago.'

Tracy was confused. She was certain Frame had said he was an investigator. Frame laughed.

'You're wondering why I'm not practicing, right?'

'Well, I . . .' Tracy started, embarrassed that she was so transparent.

'It's okay. I'm used to getting that look from lawyers. And no, I didn't flunk the bar exam. After the clerkship with Justice Lefcourt, Matt hired me as an attorney, but I liked being a detective more than I liked practicing law. When his investigator quit, I asked for the job. I don't get paid as much, but I'm not stuck behind a desk and I don't have to wear a tie.'

'Does Mr. Reynolds have you do any legal work?'

'Not if I can help it, although I did fill in while we were

waiting for you to come on board. The last associate left precipitously.'

'Why did he go?'

'Burnout. Matt expects a lot from people and some of his requests are above and beyond the call of duty.'

'For instance . . . ?' Tracy asked, hoping Frame would give her examples of the horror stories others had hinted at when talking about the demands Reynolds put on his associates, so she could prepare herself for the worst.

'Well, Matt handles cases all over the country. Sometimes he'll expect an associate to become an expert on another state's law.'

'That doesn't sound unreasonable.'

'I've seen him give that type of assignment to some poor slob a week before trial.'

'You're kidding?'

'Absolutely not.'

'Boy, that would be tough,' Tracy answered, a bit worried. The work at the Supreme Court was demanding, but Justice Sherzer always emphasized that good scholarship was more important than speed. Tracy hoped she wasn't in over her head.

'Do you think you could do it?' Frame asked.

'I'm a quick study, but that's asking a lot. I guess I could in a pinch, if the area was narrow enough.'

'Good,' Frame said, grinning broadly, 'because you leave for Atlanta next Monday.'

'What!'

'Did I mention that Matt also uses me to bear grim

tidings? No? Well, I'm frequently the messenger that everyone wants to kill.'

'What am I supposed to do in Atlanta?' Tracy asked incredulously. 'I'm not even unpacked.'

'You'll be second-chairing the Livingstone case. The file is in the library. You'll want to get to it as soon as you get your stuff put away. It's pretty thick.'

'What kind of case is it?'

'A death penalty case. Matt rarely handles any other kind. The legal issues are tricky, but you can get up to speed if you work all week. There's a good place for Chinese takeout a few blocks from here. They stay open late.'

'Mr. Reynolds wants me to become an expert on Georgia law and learn everything I can about this case in five days?' Tracy asked with an expression that said she was certain this was some bizarre practical joke.

Frame threw his head back and laughed. 'There's nothing I enjoy more than that look. But cheer up. I hear Atlanta is lovely in August. A hundred twenty in the shade with one hundred percent humidity.'

Frame cracked up again. Tracy could hear him laughing long after he was out of sight. She sat back down on the floor and stared at the boxes that still had to be unpacked. She had planned on running after squaring away her office, but that was not possible now. It looked like the only exercise she would get in the near future would be from lifting law books.

2

'Thank you for seeing me on such short notice,' Matthew Reynolds said as Abigail Griffen ushered him into her office, three weeks after their argument at the Supreme Court.

'I don't have much choice,' Abbie answered, flicking her hand toward the slip-sheet opinion in the *State ex rel. Franklin* case. 'The court bought your due process argument. When can your people go into Mrs. Franklin's house?'

'I phoned California. The criminologist I'm working with can be here Tuesday. My Portland people are on call.'

'I'll tell Mrs. Franklin you'll be there sometime Tuesday. She doesn't want to see you. There'll be a policeman at the house with a key to let you in.'

'I'll be in Atlanta for a few weeks trying a case. Barry Frame, my investigator, will work with the forensic experts.'

'I'll be out of the office myself.'

'Oh?'

'Nothing as exotic as Atlanta. I'm taking a week of R. and R. at my cabin on the coast. Dennis Haggard can handle any problems while I'm away. I'll brief him.'

'Can we have a set of the crime-scene photographs and the diagrams your forensic people drew?'

'Of course.'

Abbie buzzed her trial assistant on the intercom and

asked her to bring what Reynolds had requested. While she talked, Reynolds took in the line of Abbie's chin and her smooth skin. She was wearing a black pantsuit and a yellow shirt that highlighted her tan. A narrow gold necklace circled her slender neck. A diamond in the center of the necklace matched her diamond earrings.

Abbie turned and caught Reynolds staring. He blushed and looked away.

'It's going to be a few minutes,' Abbie said, as if she had not noticed. 'Do you want some coffee?'

'Thank you.'

Abbie left, giving Matthew a chance to compose himself. He stood up and looked around her office. He had expected to see pictures of Abbie and her husband and was surprised to find the office devoid of personal items. Abbie's desk was covered with police reports and case files. One wall was decorated by her diplomas and several civic awards. Framed newspaper clippings of some of her cases hung on another. They were a testimonial to Abbie's trial skills and her tenacity. Death sentences in almost every case where she had asked for one. Lengthy sentences for Oregon's most wanted criminals. Abigail Griffen never gave the opposition an inch or a break.

Matthew noticed a blank spot on the wall. The framed article that had been hanging there lay facedown on top of a filing cabinet. Matthew turned it over. The headline read: BOMBER CONVICTED. There was a picture of Charlie Deems in handcuffs being led out of the courthouse by three burly guards.

'I forgot to ask if you take cream or sugar,' Abbie said as she reentered the office with two mugs of coffee.

Reynolds had not heard her come in. 'Black is fine,' he answered nervously, sounding like a small boy caught with his hand in the cookie jar. Abbie held out his coffee, then noticed what Reynolds was looking at.

'I'm sorry about Deems,' Reynolds told her.

'I never thought I'd hear Matthew Reynolds bemoaning the reversal of a death sentence.'

'I see nothing inconsistent in opposing the death penalty and being sorry that a man like Deems is not in prison.'

'You know him?'

'He tried to hire me, but I declined the case.'

'Why?'

'There was something about Deems I didn't like. Will you retry him?'

'I can't. The court suppressed statements Deems made to a police informant. Without the confession we don't have a case. He's already out of prison.'

'Are you concerned for your safety?'

'Why do you ask?'

'Deems struck me as someone who would hold a grudge.'

Abbie hesitated. She had forgotten about the man who tried to invade her home, assuming he was simply a burglar. Reynolds's question raised another possibility.

'Deems is probably so happy to be off death row that he's forgotten all about me,' Abbie answered, forcing a smile.

The trial assistant entered with a manila envelope. Abbie checked the contents then handed it to Matthew.

'I'd like to set a trial date,' she said. 'After your forensic people are through, you should have an idea of what you want to do. Get in touch with me.'

'Thank you for your cooperation,' Reynolds said, as if he was ending a business letter. 'I'll have the photos returned when my people are done.'

What a peculiar man, Griffen thought, after Reynolds was gone. So serious, so stiff. Not someone you'd go out with for a beer. And he was so awkward around her, blushing all the time, like one of those stiff-necked South Seas missionaries who didn't know how to deal with the naked Tahitian women. If she didn't know better, she'd guess he had a crush on her.

Abbie thought about that for a moment. It wouldn't hurt if Reynolds was a little bit in love with her. It might make him sloppy in trial. She could use any edge she could get. Reynolds might be an odd duck, but he was the best damn lawyer she'd ever gone up against.

Chapter Eight

1

Joel Livingstone was a handsome, broad-shouldered eighteen-year-old with soft blue eyes and wavy blond hair. On the most important day of his life, Joel wore a white shirt, a navy-blue blazer, gray slacks with a knife-sharp crease and his Wheatley Academy tie. This outfit was similar to the one he was wearing when he raped Mary Harding in the woods behind the elite private school before beating her to death with a jagged log.

Outside the office of Matthew Reynolds's Atlanta co-counsel, a torrid sun was shining down on Peachtree Street, but inside the office the mood was dark. Joel sprawled in a chair and regarded Reynolds with a smirk. An observer might have concluded that Joel was contemptuous of anything Matthew had to say, but the rapid tapping of Joel's right foot betrayed his fear. Reynolds imagined the tapping foot was asking the same question the boy had asked him over and over during the year they had spent as lawyer and client: 'Will I die? Will I die? Will I die?' It was a question Reynolds was uniquely qualified to answer.

'Are we going to the courthouse?'

'Not yet, Joel. There's been a development.'

'What kind of development?' the boy asked nervously.

'Last night, when I returned to my hotel, there was a message from the prosecutor, Mr. Folger.'

'What did he want?'

'He wanted to resolve your case without going to trial. We conferred in my hotel room until midnight.'

Matthew looked directly at his client. Joel fidgeted.

'Mary Harding was very popular, Joel. Her murder has outraged many people in Atlanta. On the other hand, your parents are prominent people in this community. They are well liked and respected. Many people are sympathetic to them. Some of these people are in positions of power. They don't want your mother and father to suffer the loss of their only son.'

Joel looked at Reynolds expectantly.

'Mr. Folger has made a plea offer. It must be accepted before the judge makes his ruling on our motions.'

'What's the offer?'

'A guilty plea to murder in exchange for his promise to not ask for a death sentence.'

'What . . . what would happen then?'

'You would be sentenced to life in prison with a ten-year minimum sentence.'

'Oh no. I'm not doing that. I'm not going to jail for life.'

'It's the best I can do for you.'

'My father paid you a quarter of a million dollars. You're supposed to get me off.'

Matthew shook his head wearily. 'I was hired to save your life, Joel. No one can get you off. You killed Mary and you confessed to the police. The evidence is over-whelming. It was never a question of getting you off. We talked about that a lot, remember?'

'But if we went to trial . . .'

'You would be convicted and you might very well die.'

Matthew held up a photograph of Mary Harding at her junior prom next to a full-face autopsy photograph of the girl.

'That's what the jury will see every minute of their deliberations. What do you think your sentence will be?'

Joel's lip quivered. His teenage bravado had disap-peared. 'I'm only eighteen,' he pleaded. A tear trickled down his cheek. 'I don't want to spend my life in prison.' Joel slumped in his chair and buried his face in his hands.

Matthew leaned forward and placed a hand on Joel's shoulder. 'What, Joel?'

'I'm scared,' the boy sobbed.

'I know, Joel. Everyone I've ever represented has been scared when it was time to decide. Even the tough guys.'

Joel raised his tear-stained face toward Matthew. He was just a baby now and it was impossible to imagine what he must have looked like when he straddled Mary

Harding's naked body and slammed the log down over and over until he had smashed the life out of her.

'What will I do, Mr. Reynolds?'

'You'll do what you have to to make a life for yourself. You won't stay in prison forever. You'll be paroled. Your parents love you. They'll be there for you when you get out. And while you're in, you can take college courses, get a degree.'

Matthew went on, trying to sound upbeat, wanting Joel to have hope and knowing it was all a lie. Prison would be hell for Joel Livingstone. A hell he would survive, but one from which he would emerge a far different person from the boy he was today.

2

Matthew Reynolds and Tracy Cavanaugh had been in court for three solid days of pretrial motions when Joel Livingstone's late-afternoon guilty plea abruptly ended the case. As the judge took the plea, Tracy had glanced at Joel's parents, who were elegantly dressed, barely under control and totally at sea in the Fulton County Circuit Court.

Bradford Livingstone, a prominent investment banker, sat stiffly, hands folded in his lap, uncomfortable in the company of cops, court watchers and other types with whom he did not normally associate. On occasion, Tracy caught Bradford staring at his son in disbelief. Elaine

Livingstone pulled into herself, becoming more distant, pale and fragile every day. When the judge pronounced sentence, the couple seemed to age before Tracy's eyes.

After court, there was a tearful meeting between Joel and his parents, then an exhausting meeting between the parents and Matthew, which Matthew handled with great compassion.

It was almost seven when Tracy joined Reynolds in the hotel dining room for their final dinner in Atlanta. Tracy noticed that Reynolds was indifferent to food and every night had ordered steak, a green salad, a baked potato and iced tea. This evening, Tracy was as disinterested in food as her boss. She was toying with her pasta primavera and replaying the events of the day when Reynolds asked, 'What's bothering you?'

Tracy looked across the table. She knew Reynolds had said something, but she had no idea what it was.

'You've been distracted. I was wondering if something was wrong,' he said.

Tracy hesitated, then asked, 'Why did you convince Joel to take the deal?'

There was a piece of steak on Reynolds's fork. He put the fork on his plate and leaned back in his chair.

'You don't think I should have?'

Reynolds's tone gave no clue to what he was thinking. Tracy had a rush of insecurity. Reynolds had been trying cases for twenty years. She had never tried a case and she had worked for the man she was questioning for all of one week. Then again, Reynolds struck her as a man who welcomed ideas and would not take offense if she had a sound basis for her views.

'I think Folger made the offer because he was afraid he might lose our motion to suppress the confession.'

'I'm sure you're right.'

'We could have won it.'

'And we could have lost.'

'The judge was leaning our way. Without the confession, we might have had a shot at manslaughter. There's no minimum sentence for manslaughter. Joel would have been eligible for parole anytime.'

'There's no minimum sentence with death either.'

Tracy started to say something, then stopped. Reynolds waited a moment, then asked, 'What was our objective in this case?'

'To win,' Tracy answered automatically.

Reynolds shook his head. 'Our objective was to save Joel Livingstone's life. That is the objective in every death case. Winning is one way of accomplishing that objective, but it must never be your main objective.

'When I started practicing, I thought my objective was always an acquittal.' Reynolds's lips creased into a tired smile. 'Unfortunately, I won my first three murder cases. It's difficult to avoid arrogance if you're young and undefeated. My next death case was in a small eastern Oregon county. Eddie Brace, the DA, was only a few years older than I and he had never tried a murder case. The rumor was that he'd run for DA because he wasn't making it in private practice. The first time we were in court, Brace stumbled around and spent half his time apologizing to the Judge.

'The night before we were to start motions, Mr. Brace came to my hotel, just like Folger did. We jawed for a while, then he told me flat out that he felt uncomfortable about asking a jury to take a man's life. He wanted to know if my client would take a straight murder if he'd give up the death penalty. Well, I had a winnable case and I'd gotten not-guilty verdicts in every murder case I'd tried, so I figured what you figured with Folger, that Brace was afraid to lose. I knew I was so good I'd run right over him.'

Reynolds looked down at his plate for a moment, then directly at his associate.

'The worst words a lawyer can hear is a verdict of death for his client. You don't ever want to hear those words, Tracy. I heard them for the first time in the case I tried against Eddie Brace.'

'What went wrong?'

'Only one thing. Brace stumbled along, I tried a brilliant case, but the jury was for hanging. They really wanted to see my client die. With hindsight I could see that it really didn't matter who tried the case, my man was going to die if a jury was deciding the matter. Brace knew that. He knew his people. That's why he tried so hard to convince me to take the deal. Not because he was afraid he would lose, but because he knew he couldn't lose.'

'But Joel's case . . . It's different. The judge might have . . .'

'No, Tracy. Not while there was any kind of argument on Folger's side. I know you don't believe that now, but you will after a while. What's important is that I know the judge would have found a way to keep the confession in and the jury would have no sympathy for a spoiled rich kid who took the life of that lovely girl.'

Reynolds looked at his watch.

'I'm going to take a walk then turn in. There'll be a limousine waiting to take us to the airport at seven. Get a good night's sleep. And don't let this case keep you up. We did a good job. We did what we had to do. We kept our client alive.'

3

Matthew Reynolds closed the door to his hotel room and stood in the dark. The sterile room was immaculately clean, the covers on his bed neatly tucked in at the corners, a chocolate mint centered on the freshly laundered pillowcase. It looked this way every night.

Reynolds stripped off his jacket and laid it over the back of a chair. The conditioned air dried the sweat that made his shirt stick to his narrow chest. Outside the hermetically sealed window, Atlanta sweltered in the sultry August heat. The lights of the city flickered all around. This was the last time Reynolds would see them. Tomorrow he would be home in Portland and away from the reporters, his client and this case.

Reynolds turned away from the window and saw the red message light blinking on the phone next to his bed. He retrieved the message and punched in Barry Frame's number, anxious to hear what he had uncovered in the Coulter case.

'Bingo!' Frame said.

'Tell me,' Reynolds asked anxiously.

'Mrs. Franklin hung a picture over the bullet hole. This horrific black velvet Elvis. The cops never thought to move it because they have no aesthetic taste. Fortunately for Jeffrey Coulter, I do.'

Frame paused dramatically.

'Stop patting yourself on the back and get to it.'

'You can relax, Matt. We don't have to worry about this case anymore. I guarantee Griffen will dismiss once she reads the criminologist's report. See, the picture was too high. No one would hang it like that. Not even someone with Mrs. Franklin's awful taste. It bothered me in the crime-scene photos and it was worse when I walked into the hall.

'In Jeffrey's version of the shooting, he fell back when Franklin pulled out the gun. When he tripped, Franklin's shot missed him. Jeffrey is tall. If Franklin shot for the head, he'd be aiming high. We found a snapshot in the family album showing the hallway three months before the shooting with the Elvis on another wall. I moved the picture and there was a freshly puttied hole. We've got everything on videotape, as well as stills. We dug out the putty. The expert's pretty certain it's a bullet hole. The bullet's gone. Ma Franklin must have deep-sixed it.'

'When will we have the criminologist's report?'

'By the end of the week.'

'Let's step up the background investigation of Franklin. Put another man on it if necessary.'

'What for? The fact that Mrs. Franklin puttied over the bullet hole, then moved the picture to conceal it, proves she was covering up for her son. Griffen will have to drop the charges.'

'Never bank on the prosecution acting reasonably, Barry. Abigail Griffen is not the type to roll over. She may not draw the same conclusions from the evidence that we did. We go full-bore until the moment the indictment is dismissed.'

'You got it,' Barry said wearily. 'I'll put Ted French on the backgrounder. How are things in Atlanta?'

'Joel took the deal.'

'That's what you hoped, isn't it?'

'Yes.'

'How are his parents doing?'

'Not well.' Matthew paused for a moment and rubbed his eyes. 'I'm flying back tomorrow, Barry, but don't tell anyone. I want to take a few days off.'

'Are you okay? You don't sound so good.'

'I'm tired. I need some time to myself.'

'I've been telling you that for years. When do you land? I'll pick you up at the airport.'

'I'll be in at three-ten. And, Barry, that was good work at the Franklin house. *Very* good work.'

Matthew hung up. His eyes were glazed with fatigue and he was bone weary. He lay back on the bed in the dark and thought about Joel Livingstone and Jeffrey Coulter back in Portland and Alonso Nogueiras in Huntsville, Texas, and all the other people for whom he was the sole difference between life and death. It was too much for one man to do and he was beginning to think he just couldn't do it anymore.

Matthew thought about Tracy Cavanaugh's drive and desire. There had been a time when he moved from one cause to another with the energy of a zealot. Now the cases just seemed to grind him down, and it was taking all his strength to stand up after he was done with them. He needed time away from the clients and the ever present specter of death. He needed something . . . someone.

Matthew turned on his side and hugged a pillow to his cheek. The linen felt cool and comforting. He closed his eyes and remembered the way Abigail Griffen looked in one of the photographs he kept in the manila envelope in the lower right drawer of his desk. The photo was his favorite. In it, she stood relaxed and happy outside the French windows of her home, her arms at her side, her right knee slightly bent, looking toward the woods, as if she was listening to some faint sound that carried to her on the wind.

Chapter Nine

1

The morning had been cool and overcast, but the fog burned off by noon and the sun was shining. Abbie circled the cabin taking pictures from different angles with her Pentax camera. She tried to capture the cabin from every angle, because she needed a photographic record of the place that in all the world had come to be her favorite.

When she was finished photographing the cabin, Abbie followed a narrow dirt path through the woods to a bluff overlooking the Pacific. She took some shots from the bluff, then walked down a flight of wooden steps to the beach.

Abbie was wearing a navy-blue tee shirt, a bulky, hooded gray sweatshirt and jeans. She hung the camera around her neck and took off her sneakers and socks. There had been a storm the previous day and the Pacific was still in turmoil. Abbie pushed her toes through the sand until she reached the waterline. Gulls swooped overhead. She set up a shot, stepping sideways toward the bluff whenever the freezing water came too close. A wave rose skyward, spraying foam, then fell in a fury.

Abbie finished the roll of film and continued down the beach. She loved the ocean and she loved the cabin. The cabin was the place she came to escape. She would awake with the sun, but stay in bed reading. When she was hungry, Abbie would whip up marionberry, ginger or some other type of exotic pancakes and a *caffé latte*. She would nurse the *latte* while reading the escapist fiction she had no time for when she was in trial and which helped her to forget the grim work of prosecuting rapists and murderers. Then, for the rest of the day, she would continue to do absolutely nothing of importance and revel in her idleness.

Abbie hunched her shoulders against a sudden gust of wind. The sea air was bracing. The thought of losing the cabin was unbearable, but she was going to lose it. The cabin belonged to Robert and he had made it clear that she would never use it once the divorce was final, taunting her with the loss because he knew how dear the place was to her. It gave Abbie one more reason to hate him.

The sun began to set. Abbie reached a place where the beach narrowed at the base of a high bluff. She turned for home, leaning forward to fight the tug of the sand. By the time she arrived at the stairs that led back up to the cabin, she was feeling melancholy. She sat on the lowest step and tied her sneakers. She would be able to buy another cabin, but she doubted she would find one that suited her so perfectly.

Abbie rested her forearms on her thighs and lost herself in the rhythm of the waves. What would she do after the divorce? She would not mind being alone. She had lived alone before. She was living alone now. Living alone was better than living with someone who used you and lied to you. What she would miss was the special feeling of being in love she had experienced with Larry Ross and during the early days of her marriage to Robert. Abbie wondered if she would take the risk of falling in love again, knowing how easily love could be snatched away.

When the chill reminded her of the advent of night, Abbie hoisted herself to her feet and climbed the stairs. She walked slowly along the short path through the woods. Something moved deep in the forest and Abbie froze, hoping it was a deer. She had been on edge since the attempted break-in at her house. When Matthew Reynolds commented that Charlie Deems was the type of person who would seek revenge, Abbie remembered that the burglar's physique vaguely resembled Deems's. The thought that a man like Deems might be stalking her was profoundly unsettling.

Abbie waited nervously in the shadows cast by the pines, but the source of the sound remained a mystery. She returned to the cabin, showered, then ate dinner on the front porch. She sipped a chilled Chardonnay that went well with the trout amandine and saffron rice pilaf. Overhead, the stars were a river of diamonds so sharp they hurt her eyes. They never looked like this in the city.

Abbie loved to cook and usually felt upbeat after consuming one of her creations. Tonight, she was thinking about losing the cabin and she felt logy and maudlin. After dinner, she sipped a mug of coffee, but soon felt her eyelids drag. She emptied the coffee onto the packed earth below the porch rail and went inside.

Abbie sat up in bed, certain she had heard a noise but unable to tell what it was. Her heart was beating so loudly, she had to take deep breaths to calm herself. The moon was only a sliver and the room was pitch black. According to the clock on her nightstand, she had only been asleep for an hour and a half.

Abbie tried to identify the sound that had awakened her, but heard only the waves breaking on the beach. Just as she convinced herself that she was only having a bad dream, a stair creaked and her heart raced again. Abbie had taken to carrying her handgun since the attempted break-in, but as she reached for it, she remembered that her purse was downstairs.

She had been too exhausted to change her clothes when she went to bed, so Abbie was wearing her tee shirt and panties and had tossed her sneakers, socks and jeans onto the floor next to the bed. She rolled onto the floor and slipped on her jeans and sneakers.

There was a deck outside the bedroom window. Abbie grabbed the doorknob and tried to open the door quietly, but the salt air had warped the wood and the door stuck.

Abbie pulled a little harder, afraid that the intruder would hear her if she jerked open the door. It would not move.

Another step creaked and she panicked. The second she wrenched the door open footsteps pounded up the stairs toward her room. Abbie ran onto the deck. She slammed the deck door closed to slow the intruder, then she rolled over the low deck rail just as the door to her bedroom slammed open. For a brief moment, Abbie could see the silhouette of a man in her doorway. Then she was falling through the air and slamming against hard-packed earth.

The deck door crashed against the outside wall and Abbie was up and running. A dirt trail ran between the woods and the edge of the bluff for a mile until it reached the neighbors' property. There was no fence and the trail was narrow, but Abbie streaked along it, praying she would not be followed.

A hundred yards in was a footpath that led into the woods. Abbie's brain was racing as she weighed her choices and decided her chances of survival were better in the woods, where there were more places to hide. She veered to the left and shot down the trail, then moved off it and into the woods as silently as she could.

Abbie crouched behind a tree and strained to hear the man who was chasing her. A second later, footsteps pounded by on the path. Abbie gulped air and tried to calm herself. She decided to move deeper into the woods. She would hide until daylight and hope the man would give up before then. She had almost regained her composure when she heard a sound on her right.

Adrenaline coursed through her and she bolted into the underbrush, making no effort to be quiet. Her feet churned. She surged into the woods and away from the cliff, oblivious to the pain from branches that whipped across her face and ripped her shirt. Then she was airborne. She tried to cushion her fall but her face took the brunt of it. Blinding lights flashed behind her eyes. The air was momentarily crushed from her lungs. She hugged the earth, praying she would be invisible in the dark. Almost immediately, she heard the loud crack of branches breaking and the snap of bushes as they swung back after being pushed apart.

The sound was nearby and there was no way she could run. On her right was a massive, rotting tree trunk. Abbie burrowed under it, pressing herself into the earth, hoping that the mass of the log would shield her.

Something wet fell on Abbie's face. It started to move. Tiny legs scrambled across her lips and cheek. An insect! Then another and another. Abbie desperately wanted to scream, but she was afraid the insects would crawl into her mouth. She clamped her jaws shut and took in air through her nose. Every part of her wanted to bolt, but she was sure she would die if she did.

The woods were silent. The man had stopped to reconnoiter. Abbie brought a hand to her face and brushed off the bugs. She expelled air slowly. Her heart was beating wildly in her ears and she calmed herself so she could hear.

There was cool earth against her cheek and the silhouettes of tall evergreens against the night sky. Suddenly the space between two large trees was filled by the outline of a man. His back was to her, but she was certain he would see her if he turned and looked down. Abbie pressed herself closer to the log, praying that the man would not turn. He did. Slowly. A few inches more and he would see her. Abbie felt for a rock or a thick tree limb she could use as a weapon, but her hand closed on nothing of substance. Now the man was facing the log. He started to look directly at Abbie. Then the sky lit up.

2

The ringing of the phone wrenched Jack Stamm out of a deep sleep. He groped for the receiver. When he knocked it off the cradle, the ringing mercifully ceased.

'District Attorney Stamm?'

Stamm squinted at the bright red numerals on his digital alarm clock. It was 4:47 A.M.

'Who's this?'

'Seth Dillard. I'm the sheriff in Seneca County. We met at a law-enforcement conference in Boise two years ago.'

'Right,' Stamm said, trying to picture the sheriff and coming up blank. 'What couldn't wait until morning?'

'We have one of your people here. Abigail Griffen.'

'Is she all right?' Stamm asked, suddenly wide awake.

'Yes, sir, but she's mighty shaken up.'

'Why? What happened?'

'She says someone tried to kill her.'

*

Seneca County was two hours west of Portland and it was almost seven-thirty when Jack Stamm stopped beside one of the two county police cars that were parked in front of an A-frame that belonged to Evelyn Wallace, Abbie's neighbor. When Stamm stepped out of his car, he could see the sun through breaks in the trees and heard the dull *shoosh* of the surf through the woods behind the house.

A Seneca County sheriff's deputy opened the front door and Stamm showed his ID. The A-frame was small. A kitchen and the living room took up the ground floor. Abbie was huddled on the living-room couch wrapped in a blanket and sipping a cup of coffee. Evelyn Wallace, a slender woman in her mid-sixties, sat beside her.

Stamm was shocked by the way Abbie looked. Her hair was uncombed, there were streaks of dirt on her cheeks and her eyes were bloodshot. Stamm also noticed a number of cuts and bruises on her face.

'My God, Abbie. Are you all right?' Stamm asked.

Abbie looked up at the sound of Stamm's voice. At first she did not seem to recognize her boss. Then she mustered the energy for a tired smile.

'I'm exhausted but I'm okay. Thanks for coming.'

'Don't be ridiculous. Do you think I'd let you drive yourself to Portland after what the sheriff said?'

Before Abbie could answer, the door opened and a tall man with leathery skin and a salt-and-pepper mustache entered. He wore a Stetson and the uniform of the Seneca County sheriff's office.

'Mr. Stamm?' asked the uniformed man.

'Sheriff Dillard?'

'Yes, sir. Thanks for comin'.'

The sheriff turned his attention to Abbie.

'Do you think you're up to going back to the cabin? My men are almost through and I'd appreciate it if you could walk me through what happened.'

Abbie stood up. The blanket slipped down. She was wearing a tee shirt without a bra, jeans and sneakers without socks, and she was covered with caked brown-gray mud from head to toe.

'You're sure you're up to it, dear?' Mrs. Wallace asked.

'I'm fine. Thank you so much, Mrs. Wallace. You've been wonderful.'

When Abbie was ready, she got in the sheriff's car. Stamm followed along a short driveway until they reached the highway. The sheriff turned left and drove for a little over a mile, then turned down the narrow dirt road that led to the Griffen cabin. Abbie and the sheriff were going inside by the time Stamm parked and climbed the steps to the front porch.

The front door of the Griffen cabin opened into a large living room with a stone fireplace. There were two bedrooms and a kitchen on the first floor and two more bedrooms, plus the deck, upstairs.

'Forensic people through?' Sheriff Dillard asked a lanky deputy who was waiting in the living room holding a Styrofoam cup filled with lukewarm coffee.

'Left a few minutes ago.'

'Before you tell us what happened,' the sheriff asked

Abbie, 'can you check to see if anything was stolen?'

Abbie went through the downstairs as quickly as possible, then led everyone upstairs to the bedroom. Her terrifying ordeal had drained her physically and emotionally, and she climbed the stairs slowly. When she reached the bedroom doorway, she paused, as if expecting to find the intruder inside. Then she took a deep breath and entered.

The shades on the big picture window were open and pale morning light filled the room. Only a lamp that lay with its shade askew on the floor next to an oak chest of drawers suggested an intruder, but Abbie could feel a presence in the bedroom that made her skin crawl. She hugged herself and shivered slightly. She had been scared after the burglary attempt, but the fear passed quickly because she convinced herself that the attempted burglary was a random incident. Now she knew it wasn't.

'Are you all right, Mrs. Griffen?' Sheriff Dillard asked.

'I'm fine, just tired and a little scared.'

'It wouldn't be normal if you weren't.'

Abbie checked the chest of drawers and her end table. She went through her wallet carefully. Then she looked in the closets.

'As far as I can see, nothing's missing.'

'Why don't you come on out to the deck so you can sit down and get some fresh air,' the sheriff said solicitously.

Abbie walked out of the room into the bracing salt air and sat on one of the deck chairs. She looked out past the rail and saw the wide blue plain that was the sea.

'Do you think you're up to telling us what happened?' the sheriff asked.

Abbie nodded. She started with the sound she had heard in the woods before dinner and walked Stamm and Sheriff Dillard through the events of the night, stopping occasionally to give them specific details she hoped would prove helpful to the investigation. Remembering what happened was almost more terrifying than experiencing it, because now she had time to think about what would have happened if she hadn't escaped. To her surprise, Abbie found she had to pause on occasion to fight back tears.

When Abbie told the sheriff about seeing the intruder in the doorway, Sheriff Dillard asked her if she could describe the man.

'No,' Abbie replied. 'I only saw him for a second before I dropped off the deck. I just had an impression of someone dressed in black. I'm certain he wore a ski mask or a stocking over his face, but I saw him for such a short time and it was just before I jumped. I was mostly concentrating on the ground.'

'Go on.'

'When I hit I rolled and took off. There's a dirt trail along the bluff. I heard the deck door slam. He must have pushed it hard. Then I was running in the dark. I could hear the ocean and see the whitecaps, but that was it. I was scared I'd go off the trail and fall from the bluff.

'About a hundred yards along the cliff, the trail branches into the woods. I saw a gap in the woods and took the offshoot, hoping the man would go straight. I tried to be quiet. He passed on the trail. I could hear his footsteps and his breathing. I was starting to feel like I'd gotten away when I heard something off to my right.'

'What kind of thing?'

'I don't know. Just . . .' Abbie shook her head. 'Just something. It spooked me.'

'Could there have been a second person?'

'That's what I thought. When I heard the sound, I jumped off the trail and dodged through the undergrowth. I was really scared and not making any effort to be quiet. Just plunging away from the bluff and the place where I'd heard the sound.'

Abbie told Stamm and the sheriff about her hiding place under the log. She remembered the insects and shivered involuntarily.

'For a while it was quiet,' she continued. 'I hoped the man had gone off. Then a shadow moved between two large trees a short distance from me. I think it was the man I'd seen in the doorway.'

'Couldn't you be sure?' the sheriff asked.

'No. He seemed to be the same size and shape, but it was so dark and I only saw the man in my room for a second.'

'Go on.'

'I knew if he turned and looked down he'd see me. I was certain he could hear me breathing. Suddenly, he did turn and I was sure I'd been discovered. Then the woods lit up.'

'Lit up?' Sheriff Dillard repeated.

'There was a brief, but intense flash. It came from the other side of the log.'

'Do you know what caused the flash?' the sheriff asked.

'No. I was under the log. I could just see a change in the light.'

'Did you recognize the man?' the sheriff asked.

Abbie hesitated. 'Two weeks ago, a man tried to break into my house in Portland. I scared him away, but I got a good look at him while he was on my back porch. He was dressed like the man who broke into the cabin tonight. I'm certain it was the same person. I could never identify him in a lineup. He was wearing something over his face both times, but something about him reminded me of Charlie Deems.'

Stamm looked startled.

'Who is Charlie Deems?' the sheriff asked.

'A man I convicted on a murder charge more than a year ago. He was sentenced to death, but the Supreme Court reversed his sentence recently and he's out of prison.'

'Right. I knew the name sounded familiar. But why do you think it was Deems?'

'The size, his build. I could never swear it was Deems. It was just a feeling.'

'Did you report the attempted break-in in Portland?' the sheriff asked.

'No. I didn't see any purpose in reporting it. I couldn't identify the man and nothing was taken. He wore gloves, so there wouldn't be any prints. And at the time I thought he reminded me of someone, but I didn't make the connection with Deems then.'

The sheriff nodded and said, 'Okay. Why don't you finish telling us what happened tonight, so you can go home.'

'After the flash, the man froze for a second, then took off in the direction of the light. I heard him crashing through the underbrush away from me. After a while, I couldn't hear him anymore. I decided to stay still for a long time. I wanted to be sure he wasn't waiting for me to move. I didn't have a watch, so I don't know how long I stayed put, but it seemed forever. When I thought I was safe I made my way to the Wallace cabin and Mrs. Wallace called you.'

'When the man ran off, did you hear anything else?'

'No, but there had to be someone else out there. The flash, those sounds.'

'Okay. I guess you'd like to shower and change. Why don't I take Mr. Stamm downstairs. We'll be in the living room when you're ready to go.'

'Tell me some more about Charlie Deems,' Sheriff Dillard said when they were downstairs.

'If Deems is after Abbie, she's in serious trouble,' Stamm said. 'He's a stone killer. As cold as they come. He tortured a rival drug dealer to death, then he killed a little girl and her father to keep the father from testifying. I sat in on Deems's interrogation. He never blinked. Smiled the whole time. Super polite. He treated the whole thing as if it was a joke. I watched his face when the jury came in with the death sentence. I'll bet his heart rate didn't go up a beat.'

'Would he try to kill Mrs. Griffen?'

'If he wanted to, he would. Charlie Deems is basically a man without restraints. I just don't know why he'd go to the trouble, now that he's out. Then again, rational thought is not one of Deems's biggest assets.'

Sheriff Dillard looked distracted and troubled.

'I'll tell you what concerns me, Mr. Stamm. Nothing was stolen. That could mean that the intruder was a thief who panicked. But I don't think so. If he was a thief, why follow Mrs. Griffen into the woods? Why hunt for her? No, I think the intruder was here to do your deputy harm.'

Chapter Ten

1

The Griffens' yellow three-story colonial stood at the end of a winding gravel drive on five acres of wooded land. A sawhorse blocked entry to the driveway. Despite the late hour, curious neighbors milled around in front of the barrier straining for a glimpse of the house and debating the cause of the explosion that had shattered the silence of their exclusive Portland residential neighborhood.

Nick Paladino drove through the crowd slowly, pausing in front of the sawhorse. A uniformed officer ducked his head down and looked through the driver's window. Paladino had the face of a gym-scarred boxer. The officer studied him suspiciously until the homicide detective flashed his badge, then he quickly moved the barrier aside.

Jack Stamm stared morosely out of the passenger window as the unmarked police car rolled slowly up the drive. The news of the explosion had stunned Stamm, who spent the ride to the crime scene blaming himself for not doing 'something' in the week following the attack on Abigail Griffen.

Paladino parked near a Fire Rescue Unit. The men from Fire Rescue were watching the bomb squad work. There was nothing else for them to do. There was no fire, just the shattered remains of a new Mercedes-Benz. There was definitely no one to rescue. The driver of the Mercedes was unquestionably dead.

Paul Torino, the Team Leader of the Explosive Disposal Unit, intercepted the district attorney and the detective before they crossed the barriers the squad had erected around the blast site. Torino was balding, five-eleven, thick through the neck and shoulders and bowlegged. He was wearing the unit's black combat fatigues under a Tyvex paper throwaway chemical suit, which protected against blood-borne pathogens.

'Put these on and I'll give you the grand tour,' Torino said, handing Stamm and Paladino Tyvex suits. Stamm slipped into his easily, but Paladino struggled to pull the paper suit over his beer gut.

'When did the bomb explode?' Stamm asked.

'The 911 came in at 10:35 P.M.,' Torino answered as he led them through the police barrier. Portable lighting had been set up to illuminate the front yard and someone had turned on all the lights in the house. The bomb squad members were searching the crime scene for parts of the bomb so they could discover how it had been made. One officer had been designated evidence custodian. Another sketched the area to show where each piece of evidence was found.

Stamm noticed a man photographing a jagged hole in the garage door. The ruined Mercedes was just outside the garage, facing the door. Stamm guessed that the car had been parked in the driveway and was backing out when the bomb exploded. He circled the Mercedes before looking inside. An acrid smell that had not been dispersed by the evening breeze hung in the air. The safety glass in the windshield was shattered but intact, but the side and rear windows had been blown out by the blast. There were shards of glass and chunks of bent and twisted metal scattered across the driveway and the front lawn. The roof on the driver's side was puffed out from the inside as if a giant fist had struck upward with tremendous force. Torino pointed out two one-inch holes in the roof and explained that they'd been made by pipe fragments. Then he motioned the two men toward the driver's window.

'When we get the chance to examine the underside,' Torino said, 'we're gonna find a large hole in the floorboard under the driver's seat. That's where the bomb was attached. Notice the seat belt.' It had been sheared in two. 'The victim was blown up into the roof, breaking the restraint. Then the body settled back in the bucket seat.'

Stamm took a deep breath and looked inside. Viewing a murder victim was never easy. It was infinitely harder if the victim was someone you knew. What helped here was the impression that the victim, slumped to the right, eyes closed, seemed merely asleep. The upper torso and head were intact, as was the body from the knees down, but there were massive injuries to the body between the knees and the torso. The pieces of flesh Stamm discerned were confined to the roof and the inside of the windshield on the driver's side and there was not as much blood as Stamm expected because death was the result of internal injuries. Stamm gathered himself and focused on the face once more, remembering it in life. He felt light-headed and turned away.

'Paul,' someone shouted from the garage. 'Look at this.'

The garage door was up now. Inside, a member of the bomb squad squatted in front of a white refrigerator that stood against the back wall. Torino bent over him and Paladino and Stamm looked in from the side. Embedded in the refrigerator door was a rounded piece of metal.

'Did it come through the hole in the garage door?' Torino asked the man who had summoned them into the garage.

'Yeah. We measured the trajectory. I'm glad I wasn't looking in here for a beer. I'd have me two assholes.'

'Have Peterson photograph this,' Torino said. 'Don't pry it out until he gets here.'

Stamm bent closer and noticed two short pieces of copper wire and something he could not identify embedded in the piece of metal.

'That's one of the end caps from the bomb,' Torino explained, 'and that's the remains of a lightbulb that was used as the bomb's initiator. When the bomb exploded, the end caps flew off like bullets in the direction they were pointing. This one penetrated the garage door and wedged itself in the refrigerator door.'

The squad member returned with the sketch artist and the evidence custodian.

'It's getting crowded in here,' Torino said. He led Stamm and Paladino outside.

'Paul,' Stamm asked the captain, 'you worked the Hollins bombing, didn't you?'

'The *Deems* case?'

Stamm nodded.

'I'm not surprised you asked,' Torino said, 'because I started getting a dose of déjà vu as soon as I saw that end cap. I just didn't want to say anything until the investigation was complete. I'll know for sure when we get all the pieces of the bomb, but I'd bet a year's salary that this bomb is identical to the bomb that killed Hollins and his little girl.'

2

Shortly before midnight, Jack Stamm followed Harvest Lane through Meadowbrook, a development consisting of twenty small but attractive homes scattered over three winding streets on the outskirts of Portland, a twenty-minute drive from the site of the explosion. Stamm parked in the driveway of a modern, one-story gray house with an attached garage. By the time a marked police car was parked at the curb, Stamm was ringing the bell and pounding on the front door. The small house was only a few years old. The development was so new that the trees provided no shade. The house was loaded with glass to catch the sun in the daytime. Stamm peered into the dark interior of the living room through the front window, then he turned to the uniformed officers whom he had ordered to follow him.

'Check the rear. See if there's any sign that someone's broken in.'

The officers separated and circled the house. Stamm was worried. Why was the house deserted? Just then headlights appeared at the end of the street. A car started to turn into the driveway, then braked. The driver's door opened and Abbie got out. She was dressed in jeans, a dark long-sleeved cotton shirt and a navy-blue windbreaker. Her hair was tied back in a ponytail.

Abbie looked at the marked patrol car just as the police officers came around the side of the house. Abbie looked from the officers to Stamm.

'What's wrong, Jack?' Abbie asked anxiously.

'Where were you?' Stamm said, avoiding her question.

'On a wild-goose chase. What's going on?'

Stamm hesitated. Abbie gripped his arm.

'Tell me,' she said.

Stamm put his hands firmly on Abbie's shoulders. 'I've got bad news,' Stamm said. An array of emotions flashed across Abbie's face. 'It's Robert. He's dead.'

'How?' was all she managed.

'He was murdered.'

'Oh my God.'

'It was a car bomb, Abbie. Just like the one Charlie Deems used to kill Larry Hollins and his little girl.'

Abbie's legs gave way and Stamm helped her to the front stoop, where he eased her down.

'I want you to listen carefully,' Stamm told Abbie. 'There's no evidence Deems did this, but the bombs are very similar. So I'm not taking chances. These officers are going to stay with you tonight and I'm going to arrange twenty-four-hour police protection.'

'But why Robert?' Abbie asked in apparent disbelief. 'He's responsible for taking Deems off of death row.'

'Deems is a sadist. Maybe he wants to kill you, but only after he's made you suffer by killing someone close to you.'

Abbie looked dazed. 'First the attempted break-in, then the attack on the coast. Now Robert is dead. I don't believe this is happening.'

'You're going to be all right, Abbie. We'll protect you and we'll find the person who killed Robert. But you have to be careful. You have to take this very seriously.'

Abbie nodded slowly. 'You're right. I can't believe I went off by myself tonight.'

'What were you doing out so late?'

'I got a call about a case. This man wanted me to meet him, but he didn't show up.'

'What time was this?'

'Around nine.'

Abbie paused, suddenly realizing why Stamm was asking about the call.

'You don't think the call and the bombing are connected, do you?' Abbie asked, but Stamm was not listening. He turned to one of the officers.

'Move your car away from the house, fast. Then get on the radio to Paul Torino. He's still at Justice Griffen's house. Tell him I need the bomb squad over here, right away.'

Stamm pulled Abbie to her feet and started dragging her toward his car.

'What are you doing?' Abbie asked, still too dazed to realize what was frightening the district attorney.

'I'm getting you away from the house until the bomb squad's checked it thoroughly. If you've been out since nine, the person who set the bomb in your husband's car would have had plenty of time to rig something here.'

Chapter Eleven

1

The small windowless room in the basement garage of the Portland Police Bureau looked more like a storeroom than the office of the bomb squad. Its walls were unpainted concrete and the floor was littered with cardboard cartons filled with scraps of metal, copper wire and pieces of pipe. A gray gunmetal desk next to the door was the only hint that the room was used for something other than storing junk, but the desk was covered with an unorganized collection of miscellaneous clutter and could have been mistaken for abandoned furniture.

Paul Torino opened the door and let Nick Paladino into his workroom. Paladino had taken the elevator from the Homicide Bureau to the basement after Torino called.

'What's up, Paul?'

'I want to show you something.'

Torino sat at the desk and gestured Paladino into a chair beside him. Then Torino cleared the top of the desk by shoving everything into a big pile on one of the edges. There was a torn cardboard carton next to one of the desk legs. Torino pulled several items out of it and placed them on the desk in a line. Then he drew a side view of a piece of pipe on a yellow writing tablet.

'This is a rough drawing of the pipe bomb that killed Justice Griffen. The bomber has to attach the bomb to the underside of the car and there is a simple way to do that.'

Torino bent over the yellow sheet again and drew a rectangle. Then he drew a horseshoe on the left end of the rectangle and another on the right end and placed a black dot in the center of the curve of each horseshoe.

'This is a strip of metal,' Torino said pointing to the rectangle. 'These are magnets,' he continued, pointing to the horseshoes. 'You drill holes in the strip and affix the magnets to the plate with nuts and bolts, then you tape the magnetic strip to the pipe bomb. When you're ready to use the bomb, you just have to stick it to the underside of the car.'

'Okay.'

Torino picked up a charred and twisted strip of flat metal approximately six inches in length, one and a half inches wide and one quarter of an inch thick.

'What do you think this is?' Torino asked Nick Paladino.

Paladino studied the object and the drawing. 'The metal strip that the magnets are attached to?' he guessed.

'Right. I took this from the evidence room this morning. It was part of the pipe bomb that killed Larry and Jessica Hollins. Do you notice anything unusual about it?'

Paladino took the metal strip from Torino and examined it closely. It was heavy. One end of the rectangle was flat and looked like it had been shaped by a machine. The other end was uneven and there was a notch in the metal that formed a jagged vee.

'The ends are different,' Paladino said.

'Right. This steel strip came from a longer strip. Someone put it in a vise and used a hacksaw to cut it so it would fit the top of the pipe.'

Torino pointed to the uneven end. 'Notice how this notch overlaps. That's because the person who cut it cut from two directions.'

Torino picked up a clear-plastic bag with another twisted and charred metal strip.

'When the bomb exploded yesterday, Justice Griffen was seated directly over it. This strip was blown through the bottom of the car into the judge. It's what killed him. The medical examiner found it during the autopsy. Take a look at the right edge.'

The similarities between the notch on the metal strip that had killed Robert Griffen and the notch on the end of the strip from the Hollins bomb were obvious.

'So you think the same person cut both strips?' Paladino asked.

'There's no way I could say that for sure, but I *can* say that I've only seen a bomb constructed like this once before. This is the bomber's signature. It's unique like a fingerprint.'

'So Deems is probably our man?'

Torino did not answer. Instead, he picked up the last item on the desk. It was also in a clear-plastic bag along with some metal shavings. Paladino examined it. It was a clean steel rectangle with one machine-cut end and one end that had been cut by hand.

'What's this?' Paladino asked, certain he knew the answer.

2

'Detective Bricker,' Tracy Cavanaugh said when the receptionist connected her to the Salem Police Department's Homicide Bureau, 'I don't know if you remember me . . .'

'Sure I do. You're Justice Sherzer's clerk.'

'Well, I used to be. I'm working in Portland now. I've got a new job.'

'I hope you didn't leave because of what happened to your friend.'

'No, no. The clerkship was only for a year.'

'How are you doing? Emotionally, I mean.'

'I think about Laura a lot, but I'm okay. The new job helps. I'm pretty busy.'

'That's good. What's up?'

'I wanted to know how you're doing with the investigation. Are there any suspects?'

'No. We believe Ms. Rizzatti was the intended victim rather than someone a burglar chanced upon, because someone ransacked Ms. Rizzatti's cottage. It may have been the person who rang the doorbell while she was leaving the message on your answering machine. But we have no idea who killed her, yet.'

'Oh.'

There was dead air for a moment. Then Detective Bricker asked, 'Did you have another reason for calling?'

'Yes, actually. It's . . . Did you hear about Justice Griffen?'

'Yes,' Bricker answered. Tracy thought she heard a little caution in the detective's tone.

'When I heard he was murdered, I couldn't help thinking . . . Have you considered the possibility that the two murders might be connected? Doesn't it seem like too big a coincidence? First Justice Griffen's clerk, and now the judge.'

'I contacted Portland PB as soon as I heard Justice Griffen was killed. Both agencies are looking into the possibility that there's a connection between the two murders, but right now we don't have any evidence to support that theory. Do you know anything that suggests the cases are related?'

'No. I just . . . I didn't know if you'd thought about it. I wanted to help.'

'I appreciate your interest.'

'Okay. That's all, I guess. Thanks for talking to me.'

'Anytime.'

3

When Nick Paladino finished explaining what he had learned from Paul Torino, Jack Stamm stood up and walked over to his window. Summer in Oregon was a dream. Snowcapped mountains loomed over miles of bright green forest. Pleasure boats cruised the Willamette, their sails a riot of color. Crime and despair should not exist in such a place, but the real world kept intruding on paradise.

'What about Deems? Do you know where he is?'

'He's vanished.'

'That's the same thing he did before he killed Hollins. And what about the similarity between the two bombs?'

'Torino described how to make that bomb at Deems's trial.'

Stamm turned away from the view. Paladino waited patiently for the district attorney.

'Is Paul certain about the metal strips?'

'I know you don't want to hear this, Jack. You don't need Torino's opinion. You can see the fit.'

'That's not what I asked, damn it.'

The detective looked down, embarrassed. 'Paul will swear they fit.'

Stamm picked up a paper clip from his desk and began to unbend it absentmindedly as he paced around the room. Paladino watched him. He knew exactly what Stamm was thinking, since he had been going through the same mental anguish since his meeting with Torino.

'Jesus,' Stamm said finally.

'I know how you feel, Jack. It's ridiculous. I don't believe it for a minute. But we have to deal with the possibility. Abbie has a motive, she has no alibi for the time the bomb was attached to Griffen's car, she knows how to make the bomb. Paul says he walked her through it step by step when they prepared his direct examination at Deems's trial.'

'This is total bullshit,' Stamm said angrily. He threw the mangled paper clip into his wastepaper basket. 'Nick, you know Abbie. Can you see her killing anyone?'

'No. And that's the biggest reason why I'm not gonna continue on this investigation. I know Abbie too well to be objective. You have to get out, too.'

Stamm walked back to his desk and slumped in his chair.

'You're right. I might even be a witness. I'll have to get a special prosecutor from the Attorney General's office. Shit. This is impossible.'

'I think you should call the AG right now and set up a meeting.'

Stamm was furious. He knew Abbie did not murder her husband. If anyone did, it was Charlie Deems. But even the possibility that one of his deputies was guilty made it imperative that his office turn over the investigation and prosecution to another agency.

The intercom buzzed. 'Mr. Stamm,' Jack's secretary said, 'I know you don't want to be disturbed, but Charlie Deems is here. He says he wants to see you.'

'Charlie Deems?'

'At the front counter. He said it was important.'

'Okay. Tell him I'll be right out.'

Stamm looked across the desk at Nick Paladino. The detective seemed as surprised as the district attorney.

'What the fuck is going on, Nick?'

'I don't have a clue, Jack.'

'You don't think he's turning himself in?'

'Charlie Deems? Not a chance.'

Stamm put on his jacket and straightened his tie. His office was only a few steps from the reception area. When he stepped into the narrow hall that led to it, he saw Deems sitting in one of the molded plastic chairs reading *Sports Illustrated*.

'Mr. Deems, I'm Jack Stamm.'

Deems looked up from the magazine, grinned and walked over to the low gate that separated the reception area from the rest of the office.

'I hear you've been looking for me,' Deems said.

'Yes, sir. We have.'

' Here I am.'

'Would you like to step into my office?'

'Okay,' Deems answered agreeably.

Stamm led Deems past his secretary and into his office.

'You know Nick Paladino.'

'Sure. He arrested me, but I don't have any hard feelings. Especially since we'll be working together.'

'Oh?' Stamm said.

'Yeah. I'm turning over a new leaf. I want to work for the forces of justice.'

'What brought about this miraculous conversion, Charlie?' Paladino asked sarcastically.

'While you're sitting on death row you have plenty of time to think about life. You know, life, what does it all mean. I don't want to waste mine anymore. I'm a new man.'

'That's very nice, Charlie. Is that why you came here? To tell us about your change of heart?' Paladino asked.

'Hey, I know how busy you guys are. If all I wanted to do was to tell you I turned over a new leaf, I'd have dropped you a letter. No, I'm here to help you catch criminals.'

'Anyone in particular?' Stamm asked.

'Oh, yeah. Some people I'm gonna enjoy sending to prison for a long, long time.'

'And who might they be?'

'How about Raoul Otero? I know everything about his operation: how he brings the stuff into the country, where they cut it and who's working for him. Interested?'

'I might be.'

'"Might be,"' he repeated. Then Deems chuckled. 'Mr. Stamm, right now you're creaming in your pants, but it's okay to play it cool. I respect you for that. Hell, if you acted real excited it would just encourage me to boost the price I'm gonna ask for the information.'

'And what is your price?' Paladino asked.

Deems turned slowly toward the detective. 'I'm glad you asked. First, I'm gonna need protection. Raoul isn't the forgive-and-forget type.'

155

'Get to the good part, Charlie,' Paladino said.

'Naturally, I'd appreciate some remuneration.'

'Why doesn't that surprise me?'

'Hey, if I'm working for you I can't be working for me. Let's not quibble over money. I'm risking my life here.'

'I'll check to see about the money. But you're going to have to prove you can deliver.'

'That's fair. Oh, and there's something else to sweeten the pot.'

'What's that?' Jack Stamm asked. 'Not what, who.'

'Who, then?'

Deems grinned broadly. He paused to savor the moment. Then he asked Stamm and Paladino, 'How would you like to know who iced Supreme Court Justice Robert Griffen?'

4

'All work and no play makes Tracy a dull girl,' Barry Frame said from the doorway of the office law library.

'Don't I know it,' Tracy said, looking up from the case she was reading. Barry sat down next to Tracy at the long polished oak conference table that took up the center of the room. Around them were floor-to-ceiling bookshelves filled with Oregon and federal statutes and cases.

'It's after eight, you know.'

Tracy looked at her watch.

'And I bet you haven't eaten dinner.'

'You win.'

'How about some Thai food?'

'I don't know . . .' Tracy stared at the stack of law books in front of her.

Frame smiled and shook his head. 'He's really got you going, doesn't he?'

'No, it's just . . .'

'I bet he gave you his "If you work for me, you won't sleep right, you won't eat right" speech.'

Tracy's mouth opened in astonishment, then she grinned sheepishly.

'He gives that speech to all the new associates and everybody falls for it. He even had me going for a while, but I wised up. Just because Matt practices what he preaches, that doesn't mean you have to become a machine. Whatever you're working on can wait until tomorrow. You won't be able to write your memo if you die of malnutrition.'

'I guess I am a little hungry.'

'So?'

'So take me to this Thai place. But we go Dutch.'

'I wouldn't have it any other way.'

Outside, the night air was warm, but not oppressive. Tracy stretched and looked up at the sky. There was a quarter moon and a sprinkling of stars. In the hills that towered over downtown Portland, the house lights looked like giant fireflies.

'Is the restaurant close enough to walk? I need the exercise.'

'It's about seven blocks. No sweat for someone who placed in the NCAA cross-country championships.'

'How did you know that?'

'Matt has me read the résumés he receives.'

'Oh. Did you read the one I sent about six months ago?'

'Yup.'

'Why didn't I get an interview?'

'You're a broad,' Frame joked. 'For what it's worth, I told him he was a jerk for ignoring you, but the Sorcerer's got no use for women. I couldn't believe it when he hired you. Justice Forbes must have made some pitch.'

'Why did you call Mr. Reynolds the Sorcerer?'

'Three years ago, Matt won that acquittal at Marcus Herrera's retrial. *Time* did a cover story and called him the Sorcerer because everyone was saying that only a magician could save Herrera. He hated it.'

'I think it's romantic.'

'It's also accurate. There are a lot of people who owe their lives to Matt's magic.'

'Why do you think he's so successful?'

'It's simple. Matthew Reynolds is smarter than anyone he's ever faced.'

Tracy thought about that for a moment. Matthew Reynolds was smart, but there were a lot of smart lawyers. If someone had asked her the question she had just posed to Barry, Tracy would have emphasized the hours Reynolds devoted to his cases. She had never met anyone who worked harder at any job.

'What drives him, Barry? What makes him push himself the way he does?'

'Do you know about his father?' Barry asked.

'Mr. Reynolds mentioned him during my interview. It sounds like he loves him very much.'

'Loved. Oscar Reynolds was executed at the state penitentiary in Columbia, South Carolina, when Matt was eight years old. He was sentenced to death after being convicted of rape and murder.'

'My God!'

'Two years later, another man confessed to the crime.

'Matt doesn't talk about it, for obvious reasons. His mother had a nervous breakdown when Matt's dad was sentenced to prison. She committed suicide a week after the execution. Matt stayed in a series of foster homes until a distant relative took him in. He never talks about what happened there, but I think it was pretty bad.'

Tracy felt she should say something, but she could not think of anything even remotely appropriate. What Barry had just told her was too enormous. And it certainly explained all of the questions she had about Reynolds's fanatic devotion to his cause.

Tracy tried to imagine what life must have been like for eight-year-old Matthew Reynolds, growing up with a mother who committed suicide, a father who was executed for a sex crime and murder and a disfiguring birthmark that would be an easy target for the cruelty of children.

'He must have been so alone,' Tracy said.

'He's still alone. I'm probably the closest thing he has to a friend.'

Barry paused. They walked together in silence, because Barry was obviously struggling with what he wanted to say and Tracy sensed it was important enough to wait to hear.

'There's another reason Matt's so successful,' Barry said finally. 'Other lawyers have a life outside the law. Matt's life is the law. And I'm not exaggerating. He literally has no interests outside of his job, except maybe his correspondence chess. I think the real world has been so unbearably cruel to him that he uses the law as a place to hide, a place where he can feel safe.

'Think about it. It's like his chess. There are rules of law, and he knows every damn one of them. In the courtroom, the rules protect him from harm. He can bury himself in his cases and pretend that nothing but his cases exist.

'And as a lawyer, he's needed. Hell, he's the only friend some of his clients have ever had.'

Barry looked down and they walked in silence again. Tracy waited for him to talk about his boss some more, so she could better understand him. Instead, Barry suddenly asked, 'Do you still run?'

'What?'

'I asked if you still run.'

'I've been getting in a workout on the weekends,' Tracy answered distractedly, finding it hard to switch to this innocuous topic after what she had just learned. 'I'm lucky if I get out at all during the week.'

'How far do you go?'

'Seven, eight miles. Just enough to keep the old heart and lungs going.'

'What's your pace?'

'I'm doing six-and-a-half-minute miles.'

'Mind if I join you sometime?'

Tracy hesitated. She wasn't sure if Frame wanted a workout partner or a date. Then she decided it didn't matter. It was more fun running with someone than running alone. Frame was a good-looking guy and she wasn't seeing anyone. She would go with the flow.

'I used to run after work on weekdays back in the good old days. But now I run before work, which means before dawn, when I can, and on the weekends.'

'Tell you what,' Frame said. 'Why don't we run about nine on Sunday, then eat brunch at Papa Haydn's.'

'You're on,' Tracy said, smiling, as she started to detect the direction the river was running.

Chapter Twelve

Assistant Attorney General Chuck Geddes reluctantly agreed to wait until the day after the funeral to interview Abigail Griffen, but only after Jack Stamm suggested that confronting a widow on the day her husband was buried might be seen as insensitive and in bad taste. It was the 'bad taste' part that swayed Geddes, who prided himself on his impeccable judgment in all things.

Geddes had the rugged good looks of the men who modeled in cigarette commercials, and he walked like a man with a steel rod for a spine. He had developed this marching style while in the Judge Advocate's office during his military service. His views were as unbending as his posture. When he lost a trial, it was always due to the judge's intellectual deficits, the underhanded tactics of an unscrupulous opponent or the stupidity of the jurors.

To give him his due, Geddes did win his share of tough cases. He had been appointed attorney-in-charge of the District Attorney Assistance Program at the Department of Justice because he was the most successful trial attorney in the section. Geddes was relentless, possessed of animal cunning and quite able to charm a jury.

The policeman guarding Abbie's house relaxed when he recognized Jack Stamm. As soon as Stamm parked, Geddes got out of the front passenger seat and straightened the jacket of his tan lightweight Brioni suit. Neil Christenson, his investigator, got out of the back seat while Geddes was adjusting his French cuffs. Christenson was third-generation law enforcement and a former state trooper who had been with the Department of Justice for nine years. He had the type of heavy build you would expect from an ex-Oregon State lineman who was too busy to keep in top shape but still managed to jog a little and pump iron on occasion. Christenson wore his hair in a crew cut, but his friendly blue eyes and easy smile made him less intimidating than normal for a man his size. While Geddes dressed to kill, Christenson wore a worn tweed sports jacket that was too heavy for summer, lightweight tan slacks, a blue oxford dress shirt with a frayed collar and no tie.

Abbie looked exhausted when she opened the door. She wasn't wearing makeup, her hair had only received a perfunctory brushing and there were dark circles under her eyes. She had made only the briefest attempt to clean up after the mourners who had followed her home from the cemetery. Overflowing ashtrays, dirty plates and partially filled cups of coffee littered the living room.

'How are you feeling?' Stamm asked.

'I'm doing okay.'

Abbie looked past Stamm to the two men who were standing behind him.

'This is Chuck Geddes. He's with the District Attorney Assistance Program at the Department of Justice, and this is his investigator, Neil Christenson.'

'My condolences. Justice Griffen's death was a terrible tragedy,' Geddes said, stepping around Stamm and offering his hand.

Abbie looked confused and a little wary. 'What's going on, Jack?'

'Can we come in?' Stamm asked. Abbie stepped aside. She looked at the mess in the living room and led everyone into the kitchen, where there had been some damage control.

'I've got coffee if anyone's interested.'

'Is it decaf?' Geddes asked.

'Not this morning,' Abbie answered.

Stamm and Christenson asked for theirs black, but Geddes demurred.

The kitchen window looked out at a small deck and beyond to a fenced backyard. A flower garden separated the fence from the lawn. Scarlet fuchsias, yellow gladioli and pink tea roses created a bouquet of bright colors that contrasted with the gloom in the kitchen.

'What brings you here?' Abbie asked when everyone

was seated around the kitchen table. Stamm looked at Abbie briefly, then looked down at his cup.

'I'm in a very unpleasant position. One that makes it impossible for me to continue the investigation of Justice Griffen's murder. The Portland police are also stepping aside. Chuck has been appointed as a special deputy district attorney for Multnomah County. It's his case now.'

Abbie looked perplexed. 'Why do you have to bow out? What happened?'

'There's no easy way to put this, Abbie. You've become a suspect in Robert's murder.'

Abbie stared at Stamm. 'Are you serious?' she asked with a confused smile.

'I'm very serious,' Stamm answered quietly.

Abbie looked back and forth between the three men. Then her features clouded. 'This is utter nonsense.'

Geddes had been sitting back, legs crossed, observing Abbie's reaction. 'We have a witness who claims you solicited him to kill Justice Griffen and evidence to support his story.'

'That's ridiculous. What witness? What evidence?' Abbie challenged.

'I'm not at liberty to say at the moment, but you can assist us in clearing up this matter by answering a few questions. Of course, I do have to warn you that you have a right to remain silent and that anything you say can be used to convict you in a court of law. You also have a right to consult with an attorney and, if you cannot afford an attorney, the court will appoint one to assist you, free of charge. Do you understand these rights?'

Abbie stared at Chuck Geddes in disbelief. 'Are you being intentionally insulting?'

'I'm being a professional,' Geddes answered with unruffled calm.

Abbie turned to Stamm. 'Is this for real, Jack? Am I a suspect?'

'I'm afraid so. And you should think seriously about talking to Chuck without counsel.'

Geddes glared angrily at Stamm for a second, then regained his composure.

'I don't need a lawyer, Jack. I didn't kill Robert. Ask me anything you want to.'

'Abbie . . .' Stamm started.

'She says she's willing to talk to us, Jack,' Geddes interjected forcefully. 'Maybe she can clear up the confusion. If we're on a wild-goose chase, let's straighten this out, so I can go back to Salem.'

Stamm did not regret warning Abbie, but he backed off. This was Geddes's case now.

'Mrs. Griffen, why don't you tell us where you were from nine to midnight on the evening Justice Griffen was killed?'

'I already explained that to Jack.'

'I know, but Neil and I would like to hear what you have to say firsthand.'

'I'm prosecuting a murder case involving a defendant named Jeffrey Coulter, who is represented by Matthew Reynolds.' At the mention of Reynolds's name Geddes leaned forward slightly. 'Reynolds's forensic experts conducted experiments in the Franklin home recently. The results were favorable to Coulter. The night my husband was killed, a man called around nine o'clock and told me that Reynolds's experts manufactured evidence at the Franklin home. He wanted to meet me immediately at the rose garden at Lewis and Clark College.'

'The rose garden is in an isolated area of the campus, isn't it?' Geddes asked.

'That's right. It's on the edge of the campus behind the outdoor pool.'

'Jack told me about your close call at the coast. Weren't you afraid of meeting someone in such a deserted spot so soon after being attacked?'

'I couldn't pass up the chance to nail Coulter. And I went armed. I was almost hoping it was the bastard who broke into my cabin.'

'Did you think about bringing backup with you?'

'The caller told me to come alone or he wouldn't talk to me. I didn't want to scare him off. It didn't matter anyway, because no one showed.'

'Can someone substantiate your story?'

'No. The parking lot was deserted by the time I got there and I didn't meet anyone.'

'Mrs. Griffen, was your divorce acrimonious?'

'I don't want to discuss my private life.'

'That's going to be a difficult subject to avoid.'

'I'm sorry. Robert is dead. What went on between us is over.'

'I can appreciate your reluctance, but this is a murder investigation. How many times have you asked that question of a suspect or a witness?'

'Many times, but I won't talk about my personal relations with Robert.'

'Okay. I can accept that, for now. What about your financial relationship?'

'What do you mean?'

'Is it fair to say that a divorce would have hurt you financially.'

'Yes, but I knew that when I filed.'

'Can you tell us about your relative financial positions?'

Abbie looked from Geddes to Christenson. Their faces showed no emotion. Then she turned to Jack Stamm. Stamm was hunched forward slightly and he looked like he wanted to be anywhere but where he was.

'I don't like the tone of this conversation, Mr. Geddes, or where it's going, so I'm going to end it. Jack is right. I should consult an attorney.'

'As you wish.'

'What is my status, Jack?' Abbie asked.

'Status?'

'Can I work? Am I suspended, fired?'

Stamm could not look Abbie in the eye.

'I think it's best if you take some time off with pay. You would have anyway, because of the funeral. I'll assign your cases to the other assistants.'

'And if I don't want to take time off?'

Stamm looked up. He was in obvious distress. 'You can't be at the office. You're under investigation.'

'I see,' Abbie said slowly.

'This isn't what I want personally, Abbie. For what it's worth, I'm sure you're innocent. That's part of the reason I stepped aside and turned over the investigation to the Attorney General. It's what I have to do as an officer of the law.'

Abbie stood up. 'I'm sorry if I was rude, Mr. Geddes. I'm very tired. I'll contact you after I've spoken to my attorney.'

'I understand,' Geddes said with a condescending smile. 'This is very unpleasant for me as well, Mrs. Griffen, but there is one more thing.'

'Yes?'

Geddes held out his hand. Christenson was carrying an attaché case. He opened it and handed a legal document to Geddes. Geddes gave it to Abbie.

'This is a warrant to search your home.'

'What!'

'I obtained it from Judge Morosco this morning.'

Abbie turned on Jack Stamm. 'You bastard. I thought you were my friend. I can't believe you'd do this.'

Stamm's face flushed in anger. 'I didn't know anything about the warrant, Abbie.'

'That's true, Mrs. Griffen. I didn't inform Jack. Neil, please signal the troopers.'

Christenson walked out the front door and waved a hand toward the far end of the block. Several car engines came to life and, moments later, three Oregon State Police cars pulled up in front of the house.

'I'd like you to confine yourself to one place in the house, Mrs. Griffen,' Geddes said. 'Or if you prefer, you can visit someone. We're going to search your car, so I can offer you a ride.'

Everything was happening so fast that Abbie had to fight to keep from being overwhelmed, but her anger gave her strength. She looked directly at Geddes.

'I'm staying right here,' she said, 'and I'm going to watch every move you make.'

PART FOUR

THE
PRISONER

Chapter Thirteen

1

'Mrs. Griffen,' Matthew Reynolds said as he walked across his reception area, 'there was no need to meet with me so soon after your husband's funeral. Mr. Coulter's case could have waited a few more days.'

'I'm not here about the Coulter case. Can we go to your office?'

A look of curiosity and concern crossed Reynolds's face as he guided Abbie down the hall. As soon as they were seated, Abbie asked, 'What can you tell me about Chuck Geddes?'

Reynolds didn't ask why Abbie wanted this information. Instead, he studied her while he gathered his thoughts. She was beautiful in black with a single strand of pearls, but she looked exhausted and sat stiffly, her hands folded, her face tight, as if she was afraid that she might break apart if she moved.

'Chuck Geddes is intelligent and single-minded, but he is rigid. As long as a trial goes as he's foreseen, he does a good, workmanlike job, but let the slightest thing go wrong and he can't bend with it.

'About four years ago, the La Grande district attorney called in the Attorney General's office to help in the prosecution of a complex murder case I was defending. Mr. Geddes was condescending to me at first. Then, as his case began to get away from him, he became strident, demanding and rude. I had the feeling he thought my legal motions were part of some conspiracy aimed at him.

'Two years later, we tried a case in John Day. He was offensive from the start. Paranoid about every detail. I prevailed on a motion to suppress the state's key evidence, so the case never came to trial. Later, I learned that he violated the discovery rules by failing to notify me about a witness whose testimony would have been damning. I have the impression that when he's under pressure he'll do anything to win.'

'Is Geddes ambitious?'

'Very. And now, if I may,' Reynolds asked, sighting Abbie over his tented fingers, 'why this sudden interest in Mr. Geddes?'

An array of emotions crossed Abbie's face. She looked down and gathered herself. When she raised her head, her features showed the strain of maintaining her composure.

'I need a lawyer to represent me.'

'In what type of case?'

'Yesterday, Geddes came to my home to question me about Robert's death. I'm a suspect.' Reynolds sat up. 'He had a warrant to search my house. They have a witness who says I'm involved and evidence that supposedly supports the accusation.'

'Who is the witness?'

'They won't tell me. Geddes treated me like a criminal.' Abbie's heart was beating furiously and she had to breathe deeply before she could say the next sentence. 'I have the feeling that it's only a matter of time before I'm . . . before they arrest me.'

'This is preposterous. Have you talked with Jack Stamm?'

'Jack is off the case. Geddes has been appointed a special deputy district attorney. He'll run the investigation and he'll prosecute.'

'I can give you the names of several excellent defense attorneys.'

'No. I want you to represent me.'

Reynolds looked at Abbie and she sensed that he was torn by conflicting emotions.

'I'm flattered, Mrs. Griffen, but I don't see how I can do that when you're prosecuting Jeffrey Coulter.'

'I'm not. I'm suspended. Dennis Haggard has the Coulter case.'

'Jack Stamm suspended you?'

'I was angry at first. I'm still angry. I'm furious. But Jack had no choice. I'm a suspect in a murder case his office is investigating. In any event, there is no conflict.'

'Why me?' Matthew asked.

Abbie's expression was grim. 'You're the best, Matthew. If I'm charged I'll need the best. They wouldn't have gone this far if they didn't think they had a case. Searching the home of a deputy district attorney . . .' Abbie shook her head. 'There's no way Geddes would have done that unless there was strong evidence of guilt.'

'Are you guilty?'

Abbie looked directly at Matthew. 'I did not kill my husband,' she said firmly.

Matthew studied her, then said, 'You have yourself a lawyer.'

The uncertainty that clouded Abbie's features vanished like mist evaporating in sunlight. Her shoulders relaxed and she slumped down, visibly relieved. 'I was afraid you wouldn't help me.'

'Why?'

'Because . . . I don't know. Coulter. The fact that I'm a prosecutor.'

'You're a human being in trouble and I'm going to do everything I can to protect you.'

'Thank you, Matthew. You don't know what that means to me.'

'It means our relationship has changed. First, we're no longer adversaries. We work together from now on. Second, I'm still an attorney, but in this relationship you're not. You're my client. That's going to feel strange to you. Especially since you're used to being in charge. From now on, I'm in charge. Can you accept that?'

'Of course. But I can help. I want to participate in my defense.'

'Of course you'll participate, but not as an attorney. It wouldn't work. You've seen what happens when a defendant represents himself. You're too emotionally involved to be objective.'

'I know, but . . .'

'If we're going to work together you've got to trust my judgment. Can you do that?'

'I . . . I don't know. I'm not used to being helpless.'

'I'm not asking you to be helpless. I'm asking you to trust me. As of this moment, your case is the single most important matter in this office. Do you believe that?'

Matthew's bright blue eyes blazed with a passionate intensity that transformed his plain features. Abbie had seen Reynolds like this before, in the Supreme Court, when he challenged the justices to be fair to Jeffrey Coulter. A calm feeling flooded over her.

'Yes, I believe you.'

'Good. Then we can begin. And the first thing I want to do is explain the attorney-client relationship to you.'

'I'm aware of . . .' Abbie started, but Matthew held up his hand.

'Do you believe that I respect your intelligence and your abilities as an attorney?'

'I . . . Yes.'

'I am not trying to insult you. I am trying to help you.

177

This is not a position you've been in before. You're a client and a suspect in a murder. I'm going to give you every piece of advice I give to every other client. I'm going to assume nothing, because I don't want to make the mistake of skipping a step because of the respect I have for your abilities.'

'Okay.'

'Abbie, everything you tell me is confidential. I will guard your disclosures completely. I am the only person on earth in whom you can confide with the certainty that what you say will not be repeated to the people investigating you.

'I don't want you to be upset by what I say next. I am a criminal defense attorney. Many of the people I represent are criminals and many of these people lie to me at some point during my representation. I am never upset when they lie. I know that people under pressure do things that they would never do under normal circumstances. So if you intend to lie to me, I won't be upset, but you could cause me to go off and do something that would put you in a worse position than you would be in if you told me the truth.'

Abbie sat up straight in her seat and looked into Matthew's eyes. 'I will never lie to you, Matthew,' she said with great intensity. 'I promise you that.'

'Good. Then tell me why Chuck Geddes thinks you murdered your husband. Let's start with motive.'

'We were separated, if that's what you mean,' Abbie said, coloring slightly.

'Was the separation amicable?'

'No.'

'Whose idea was it to separate?'

'Mine,' Abbie said firmly.

'Justice Griffen wanted to stay married?'

'Robert liked to live well,' Abbie answered, unable to hide her bitterness, 'but he couldn't do a lot of that on a judge's salary.'

'Surely he had his own money? I thought Justice Griffen had a successful law practice before he went on the bench.'

'Robert was intelligent, and he was certainly charming, but he was not a good attorney. He was lazy and he didn't care about his clients. He used to talk about what idiots they were. How much he was overcharging them. After a while, the clients caught on and complained to the other partners. Robert was losing clients. He was making good money at one time, but he spent what he earned and more. As I said, Robert really enjoyed the good life. He put his name in for the bench because his partners were carrying him and he knew his time at the firm was limited.'

'Why did the governor appoint Justice Griffen if his reputation was so bad?'

'It wasn't. Most people saw Robert's corner office with a view of the Willamette, read his name on the door of one of Portland's most prestigious firms and met him in social settings, where he shined.

'Then there were the markers. The firm contributed a great deal of money to the governor's campaign and they wanted Robert out. In all honesty, he wasn't a bad judge. He was always smart. And for a while he tried hard to do a good job. Robert wasn't evil so much as he was self-absorbed.'

Matthew made some notes, then asked, 'Who stood to gain if the divorce became final?'

'Robert. My attorney said he wanted a two-million-dollar settlement.'

Reynolds was surprised by the amount. He had never thought of Abbie as a wealthy woman, always assuming that Robert Griffen was the one with the money because he had been a partner in a prestigious law firm while Abbie worked in the district attorney's office.

'Could you afford that?' Reynolds asked.

'Yes. It would have been worth it to get him out of my life.'

'Two million dollars is a very good motive for murder.'

'He would have settled for less and I could have survived nicely, even if it cost me that much to get rid of him.'

'Most jurors would find it hard to believe that you could give away two million dollars and not care.'

'It's the truth.'

'I didn't say it wasn't. We're talking about human nature, Abbie. What the average person will think about a sum that large.'

Abbie thought about that for a moment.

'Where did your money come from?' Reynolds asked.

'My parents were both killed in an auto accident when

I was very young. There was a big insurance policy. My Aunt Sarah took me in. She made certain the money was invested wisely.'

'Tell me about your aunt.'

'Aunt Sarah never married and I was her only family. A few years before I came to live with her, she started Chapman Accessories in her house to supplement her income. It kept growing. She sold out to a national chain when she was fifty for several million dollars. I was seventeen and I'd just graduated from high school. We went around the world together for a year. It was the best year of my life. Aunt Sarah died five years ago. Between the money she invested for me and the money she left me, I'm quite wealthy.'

'I take it that you were very close to your aunt.'

'I loved her very much. As much as if she was my real mother. She made me strong and self-sufficient. She convinced me that I didn't have to be afraid of being alone.'

Abbie paused, momentarily overcome by emotion. Then she said, 'I wish she was here for me now.'

Reynolds looked down at his desk, embarrassed by Abbie's sudden display of emotion. When Reynolds looked up, he looked grim.

'You must never think you're alone, Mrs. Griffen. I am here for you, and so are the people who work for me. We are very good at what we do. You must believe that. And we will do everything in our power to see that you are cleared of this terrible accusation.'

2

Jack Stamm had assigned Chuck Geddes a room in the Multnomah County district attorney's office that overlooked the Fifth Avenue transit mall. With the window open, Geddes could hear the low hum of the city. The white noise was lulling him into a state of somnolence when he was suddenly struck by an idea.

Geddes sat up and grabbed his legal pad. If Neil Christenson could find evidence to support his new theory, that evidence would not just put a nail in Abigail Griffen's coffin, it would seal it hermetically.

When Geddes was through with his notes he made a call to the Supreme Court in Salem. Then he buzzed Neil Christenson and told him to come to his office immediately. While he waited, Geddes marveled at his ability to make this type of intuitive leap. There were lots of good prosecutors, Geddes thought with a smile of smug satisfaction, but the truly great lawyers were few and far between.

Geddes was so lost in thoughts of self-congratulation that the ringing phone startled him.

'Geddes,' he barked into the receiver, angered by the inopportune interruption.

'Mr. Geddes, this is Matthew Reynolds.'

Geddes stiffened. He genuinely hated Reynolds because of the way the defense attorney had humiliated him in court both times they had faced each other, but he would never give Matthew the satisfaction of knowing how he felt.

'What can I do for you, Matt,' Geddes asked in a tone of false camaraderie.

'Nothing right now. I'm calling because I understand you are in charge of the investigation into Justice Griffen's murder.'

'That's right.'

'I have just been retained to represent Abigail Griffen and I would appreciate it if neither you nor any other government agent contacts her in connection with this case. If you need to speak to her, please call me and I'll try to assist you, if I can. I already mailed you a letter that sets out this request. Please put it in your file.'

Listening to Reynolds give him orders as if he was some secretary set Geddes's teeth on edge, but you could never tell that from the way he calmly responded to Abbie's attorney.

'I'll do that, Matt, and I appreciate the call, but I don't know why Mrs. Griffen is so bent out of shape. You both know that the wife is always a natural suspect. I was sorry to have to upset her so soon after her husband's funeral, but we're not looking at her any more than anyone else.'

'Then you have other suspects?'

'Now, you know better than that. I can't discuss an ongoing investigation.'

'I understand,' Reynolds said abruptly, to let Geddes know that he was in no mood to play games. 'I won't keep you any longer.'

'Nice talking to you,' Geddes said, just as Neil Christenson walked in.

'Well, well,' Geddes mused, breaking into a grin. 'If we needed any more proof that Abigail Griffen is guilty, we just got it.'

'What proof is that?'

'She's hired Matthew Reynolds as her attorney.'

Christenson wasn't smiling.

'What's bothering you?' Geddes asked, annoyed that Christenson did not react to his joke.

'I think we should move slowly with this investigation. Something just doesn't feel right to me.'

Geddes frowned. 'For instance?'

'There's Deems for one thing. He's the worst possible person we could have for a key witness, especially now with Reynolds defending. Can you imagine what a lawyer like Reynolds will do to Deems on cross? He has a terrific motive to lie. Griffen put him on death row, for God's sake. And don't forget, Deems was the prime suspect before he waltzed into Stamm's office with his story.'

'Good points, Neil. But think about this. You'll admit Deems is intelligent?'

'Oh, that's for sure. Most psychopaths are.'

'Then why would he kill Justice Griffen with a bomb that is identical to the bomb he used to kill Hollins? Does that make sense? Or does it make more sense that someone who knew how Deems made the Hollins bomb, and who knew that the bomb squad would immediately connect the Griffen bomb to Deems, would use the bomb to frame Deems?'

'The point's well taken, Chuck, but I don't trust him.

Why is he here? Why would someone like Deems want to help the police?'

'That's simple. He hates Griffen for putting him on death row. Revenge is one of man's oldest motives.

'And don't forget the metal strip and her alibi, or lack of one. You don't buy that fairy story about the meeting in the rose garden, do you? Talk about leading someone down the garden path.'

Geddes laughed at his own joke, but Christenson looked grim. 'There's still the attack on the coast. Griffen said the man could have been Deems.'

'If there was an attack. Remember what Sheriff Dillard told you when you talked to him yesterday. But let's assume the attack did take place. Does it make sense that Griffen would go off in the middle of the night alone, and meet someone in an isolated place, a week after someone tried to rape or murder her? No, Neil, this little lady is weaving a web of bullshit and a jury won't buy it any more than I do.'

Christenson frowned. 'What you say makes sense, but I still . . .'

Geddes looked annoyed. 'Neil, I have no doubts about Griffen. She's guilty and I'm going to get her. I need an investigator on this case who's going to nail Griffen to the wall. If you feel uncomfortable working on this, say so. I can get someone else.'

'It's not that . . .'

'Good, because I respect your work.'

Geddes turned his chair sideways. He looked out the

window. 'You know, Neil, I'm not staying in this job forever.' Geddes paused. 'Gary Graham is not going to run
for Attorney General after his term is up.'

'I didn't know that.'

'It's not public knowledge, so let's keep it between us,
okay?' Geddes swiveled back toward Christenson. He put
his forearms on the desk and leaned forward. 'If I put a
top prosecutor away for the murder of a Supreme Court
justice, with Matthew Reynolds defending, I can write my
own ticket, Neil.'

Geddes let that hang in the air for a moment, then he
said, 'When I make my move, I'm going to need good
men with me. Men I can count on. Do you catch my drift?'

'Yeah, Chuck. I hear you.'

'It's not enough to hear me, Neil. I need your undi-
vided loyalty. Do I have it? Are you going to give me one
hundred percent on this?'

'I always give one hundred percent, Chuck.'

Geddes smiled. 'That's good, because I've just figured
out how to bust this case wide open. Have a chair and
hear me out.'

Christenson sat down. Geddes leaned back and folded
his hands behind his neck.

'I've always believed that you solve a crime by figuring
out the motive behind it,' Geddes pontificated. 'Now, what
was Abbie Griffen's motive? We know the divorce would
have cost her money, but she has a lot of money. So I asked
myself, what other motive could she have had? Then I
thought about *the way* Justice Griffen was killed.' Geddes

shook his head. 'That type of carnage tells me that this was a crime of passion. The person who killed Justice Griffen hated him so much that she wanted to destroy him totally.

'Now, what breeds that kind of hate? Sex, Neil. Lust, jealousy. So I thought about the Griffens' divorce. Why were they splitting up? It had to be sex. Either she was cheating on him or he was cheating on her. That's when I got my idea.'

Geddes paused dramatically. Christenson was used to his boss's theatrics and he endured them stoically.

'Laura Rizzatti, Neil. Laura Rizzatti. It was under our noses all the time.'

Now Geddes had his investigator's attention.

'Did you ever see her, Neil? I have. The Supreme Court clerks use the cafeteria in the basement of the Justice building all the time. I once had lunch with her and Justice Griffen. That's what gave me the idea. Seeing them together.

'She was attractive. *Very* attractive. One of those full-bodied Italian girls with pale skin and beautiful eyes. I think the judge noticed just how good-looking she was.' Geddes paused. 'I think the good judge was fucking her.'

'Now, wait a minute . . .' Neil started.

Geddes held up a hand. 'Hear me out. It's just a theory, but it makes sense. Abbie Griffen's a good-looking woman, but she might be as cold in bed as she is in the courtroom. Suppose the judge got frustrated and started hitting on his clerk. The next thing you know, they're in the sack together.'

'We don't know that.'

'Don't we?' Geddes answered smugly. 'I've already done a little investigating on my own. Before I buzzed you, I talked to Ruth McKenzie at the Supreme Court. She was Justice Griffen's secretary. I asked her if she was aware of any unusual occurrences involving Rizzatti and the judge around the time Laura was killed. Do you know what she told me? On the very day she was murdered, Laura came to the judge's office in a highly emotional state. Mrs. McKenzie couldn't hear what they talked about, but Laura looked like she had been crying and the judge was very upset.

Christenson thought about Geddes's theory and had to admit that there might be something to it.

'First Griffen's clerk is murdered, then Griffen,' Geddes said. 'It's too big a coincidence, Neil. I think Abbie Griffen found out that her husband and Laura Rizzatti were having an affair and killed them both.'

3

As soon as Matthew Reynolds hung up on Chuck Geddes he told his secretary to hold his calls, then he went upstairs to his living quarters. Dreams come true, he thought as he climbed the stairs to the third floor. Sometimes we do have our greatest wish fulfilled.

Matthew entered his study without even glancing at his chessboard and locked the door. The bright midday light illuminated the room. Motes of dust floated on the sun-beams. He took the manila envelope from the bottom drawer and spread the photographs of Abigail Griffen across his desk. The photos did not capture her essence. How much more beautiful she was in person. How perfect. And she was his now.

Chapter Fourteen

'You're awfully quiet,' Barry Frame said as Tracy Cavanaugh turned off Macadam Boulevard onto the side street that led to the house where Robert Griffen died. It was a beautiful day and the top was down on Tracy's convertible, but Tracy was off in a world of her own.

'I knew him, Barry, and I liked him. He went out of his way to be nice to me after Laura was killed.'

'And it bothers you to work for a woman who might have murdered him.'

Tracy didn't answer.

'What if Mrs. Griffen is innocent? Matthew believes in her. If she's innocent and she goes to prison that's worse than dying. When you're dead, you don't feel anything. If you're alive and living in a cage for a crime you didn't commit, you suffer every second of every interminable day.'

'What are we supposed to be doing?' Tracy asked, intentionally changing the subject. Barry was tempted to push her, but decided against it.

'Now that the police have released the crime scene, Matt wants us to go through the house to see if we can find anything that might help Mrs. Griffen.'

'Didn't the police search the house after the explosion?'

'Sure, but they might have missed something.'

'It sounds like a waste of time.'

Barry turned toward Tracy.

'Matt doesn't consider any time spent on a case a waste of time. If we don't turn up anything, we can move on to something else. But Matt always asks, "What if we didn't search and there was something?" I've seen some good results in situations where I didn't think a job was worth the effort and Matt made me do it anyway.'

Tracy turned into the driveway. Matthew's car was parked in front of the house. He was sitting on the ground, his back against an old shade tree, his knees bent and almost touching his chin, looking impossibly out of place on the wide green lawn in his black suit, thin tie and white shirt.

Abigail Griffen drove up as Tracy was parking. Tracy studied their new client as Griffen got out of her car. She was dressed in a blue sleeveless blouse and a tan skirt, looking regal and self-assured in spite of the strain Tracy knew she had to be under. A woman who could take care of herself in any situation, a woman who was always in control. Tracy wondered how far this woman would go if she was threatened. Would Abigail Griffen kill if that was the only way to end the threat?

Griffen ignored Tracy and Barry Frame and walked over to Reynolds.

'Have you been waiting long, Matt?'

'I've been enjoying the solitude,' Reynolds said as he stood up awkwardly while brushing dirt and blades of grass from his pants. 'I'd like you to meet Tracy Cavanaugh, my associate. She'll be working with us. And this is Barry Frame, my investigator.'

Abbie acknowledged them with a nod, but didn't offer to shake hands.

'Let's go in,' she said.

The Griffen house had the musty smell of a summer home on the first day of the season. The doors and windows had been closed since the murder, trapping the stifling summer heat. Tracy felt queasy, as if there was insufficient air.

All the curtains were drawn and only a hint of sunlight filtered through them, giving the living room a pale yellow cast. Abbie went from window to window pulling back the curtains to let in the light. Tracy stood to one side near the entrance and watched Abbie move around her domain. The living room was spacious with a high ceiling. A white couch and several highbacked armchairs faced a stone fireplace. To one side of the grate, a set of wrought-iron fireplace tools hung on a long, twisted black metal hook. As Abbie opened the last curtain, a ray of sunlight illuminated the rich greens and browns of a forest scene portrayed in an oil painting that hung above an oak side-board. Then Abbie threw open a set of French windows. A fresh breeze rushed into the room. Just outside the doors were a patio and a circular metal table shaded by an umbrella. Beyond the patio was a rambling lawn with several large trees and a pool. The lawn ended where woods began.

'That's better,' Abbie said. She turned slowly, taking in the room.

'Where would Justice Griffen have kept his personal papers?' Matthew asked.

'In here.'

Abbie entered the den through a door at the far end of the living room and the others followed her. The room was windowless with dark wood paneling and floor-to-ceiling bookshelves filled with a combination of classics, popular fiction, history books, law books and legal periodicals. There was a Persian rug on the hardwood floor and a desk against one wall. A computer took up one side of the desk.

Abbie opened the desk drawers, but they were empty.

'It looks like the police were already here,' Abbie said.

'I assumed they had been,' Matthew answered as he looked around. 'Do you have a safe? Something the police wouldn't have been able to get into, where Justice Griffen might have put something he didn't want anyone to see?'

Abbie walked over to a small portrait that hung in a space between two bookshelves and lifted it off, revealing a wall safe. Abbie spun the dial and it opened. Matthew and Barry Frame crowded around Abbie as she reached in to bring out the contents. Tracy walked around the edge of the desk to try to see what Abbie had pulled out.

'Stock certificates, tax records,' Abbie said. 'I don't see anything unusual, Matt.'

The front door opened. Abbie turned her head. Barry left the den and stepped into the living room.

'District attorney's office,' someone said. 'Please identify yourself.'

'I'm Barry Frame, an investigator for Matthew Reynolds. We represent Abigail Griffen. This is her house and she let us in. We're in the den.'

A moment later, Barry reentered the room followed by Chuck Geddes, Neil Christenson and two uniformed officers.

'Hello, Matt,' Geddes said.

'Good afternoon, Mr. Geddes.'

'Mind telling me what you're doing here?'

'I'm Mrs. Griffen's attorney. This is Mrs. Griffen's home. We're here at Mrs. Griffen's invitation.'

'How did you get in and what are you doing in my house?' Abbie demanded. Matthew put a restraining hand on his client's arm and stepped between Abbie and Geddes.

'I was about to ask the same questions,' Reynolds said.

Geddes flashed a condescending smile at Reynolds. 'I'll be glad to answer them. I opened your front door with a key that the medical examiner found in your husband's pocket, Mrs. Griffen, and I'm here to place you under arrest for Justice Griffen's murder.'

Reynolds turned to Abbie. 'Not another word,' he said sternly. Then he turned back to Geddes. 'May I see your warrant?'

'Sure,' Geddes answered with a smirk. Christenson handed the warrant to Matthew, who read it carefully. Tracy was impressed with Reynolds's calm demeanor.

'I assume you'll agree to release Mrs. Griffen pending arraignment, after she's been booked and printed,' Matthew said when he was done.

'No, sir,' Geddes answered. 'Your client is charged with the murder of a Supreme Court justice. She's wealthy enough to be a serious flight risk. We're holding Mrs. Griffen in jail pending arraignment. You can ask for a bail hearing.'

'You're not serious. Mrs. Griffen is a deputy district attorney with an excellent reputation.'

'Save the passionate oratory for the judge. You got lucky the last time we were in front of one. Maybe you'll get lucky again.'

'This isn't about us, Mr. Geddes. Mrs. Griffen is a human being. There's no need to strip her of her dignity by making her spend several days in jail.'

'Mrs. Griffen is accused of premeditated murder,' Geddes shot back. 'She's the worst kind of criminal – a prosecutor who's broken the law. She's going to be convicted for the murder of her husband and I'm going to see that she gets a death sentence.'

Abbie paled. Tracy felt a shock go through her and she was suddenly very frightened for their client.

Reynolds stared at Geddes with contempt. 'You are a little man,' he said quietly. 'A tiny little man. I'm going to enjoy destroying you in front of everyone.'

Geddes flushed with anger. He turned to one of the policemen. 'Cuff her and take her downtown.'

Abbie turned to Reynolds. She looked scared.

'Go with them,' Matthew said. 'You know you have to. And don't say anything to anyone about the case. Not the police, not a cellmate, not a soul.'

'Matt I can't go to jail.'

Reynolds placed his hands on Abbie's shoulders.

'You have to be strong. Don't let them demean you. And trust me. I'll have you out as soon as possible.'

The policeman with the handcuffs looked embarrassed. He waited until Reynolds stepped aside, then politely asked Abbie to put her hands behind her back. When he'd secured the cuffs, he asked if they were hurting her. Abbie shook her head.

'Let's go,' Geddes said, executing a military turn and striding out of the den. Tracy followed Matthew outside and watched the officer help Abbie into the back seat of a police car.

'Do you think it was smart to insult Geddes that way?' Barry asked Matthew as soon as the police were gone.

'Mr. Geddes is no concern of mine,' Matthew said.

'Geddes has a thin skin. He's going to make everything extra hard now.'

Reynolds turned to Frame. Tracy saw an almost frightening determination on his face and in the way he held himself. She imagined his body as pure energy, and for the first time realized what a formidable adversary he would be.

'Leave Chuck Geddes to me, Barry. I have other work for you. If Geddes has an indictment, he'll have to make discovery available to us immediately. We'll soon know the identity of this mystery witness and their evidence. You're going to be very busy.'

Chapter Fifteen

1

The fourth floor of the Justice Center jail was reserved for security risks, prisoners with psychiatric problems and prisoners who had to be isolated. The jail commander had known Abbie for years and liked her. When she appeared at the jail on the preceding day, he booked her in personally, then made sure she was held in her own cell on the fourth floor, because he knew what would happen if he put a deputy district attorney in with the other inmates.

The jail elevator opened onto a narrow hall of concrete blocks painted in yellow and brown pastels. The fourth-floor contact visiting room was across from the elevator. It was small with a circular wooden table and two plastic chairs. Matthew stood when the guard brought Abbie into the room through a heavy metal door that opened into the jail.

Abbie's hair was combed, but she wore no makeup. There were dark circles under her eyes. The guard took off Abbie's handcuffs. She sat down and rubbed her wrists. Her face stayed expressionless while the guard was in the room. As soon as he left, she spread her arms to show Reynolds the blue cotton pants and short-sleeved blue pullover shirt that all the women prisoners wore. Then she flashed him a tired smile.

'Not exactly high fashion, huh?'

'I'm glad to see you haven't lost your sense of humor.'

'I know exactly what Geddes is trying to do. Do you think I'd let that asshole spook me?' Abbie paused. Her smile disappeared and she was suddenly subdued. 'It ain't been easy, though. I barely slept. It's so noisy. The woman next to me cried all night.

'There was one time, last night, when I was so tired I let my defenses down and started thinking about what it would be like to spend the rest of my life in a place like this. That's when I understood why the woman in the next cell was crying.'

Abbie caught herself. 'Sorry. I'm getting maudlin and I promised myself I wouldn't do that.'

'It's okay. That's what I'm here for. To listen. To help relieve some of the pressure.'

Abbie smiled again. 'I appreciate that. When's the arraignment?'

'Late this afternoon. They couldn't hold the hearing

sooner because they had to bring in a judge from another county. All the Multnomah County judges have a conflict, because they know you.'

'Who's the judge?'

'Jack Baldwin. He's from Hood River. Don't worry. I've appeared in front of him and he's all right.'

'Can you get me out of here?' Abbie asked, trying not to sound desperate.

'I don't know. Geddes won't give an inch. He'll want you held without bail and, as you well know, there's no automatic bail in murder cases.'

'What are you going to do?'

'I'm going to try an end run. Meanwhile, I've sent Tracy to your house to pick out an outfit for court.'

'Thank God. I don't know if I'm more afraid of the death penalty or having to appear in public in these awful rags.'

Matthew couldn't help smiling. 'You'll have to run a media gauntlet and I don't want you looking like Squeaky Fromme.'

Abbie smiled. Then her eyes lost focus and she looked tired and dispirited.

'What's wrong?' Matthew asked.

Abbie took a deep breath. 'I'm afraid I'll lose everything, Matt. My reputation, my career.'

'You haven't lost a thing and you're not going to. Geddes can't rob you of your pride unless you let him. You know you're innocent. It doesn't matter what the papers say or what the public thinks, if you can look at yourself in the mirror and know you're right.'

Abbie laughed. 'They don't let me have a mirror. Broken glass. It's a suicide precaution.'

Matthew smiled back. It was a perfect moment. The shared fears the shared intimacy, the trust she showed in him. He didn't want the visit to end.

'I have to go,' Matthew said reluctantly. 'I have an appointment with Jack Stamm in a few minutes.'

'Your end run?'

'If we're lucky.'

2

'It's been a while, Matt,' Jack Stamm said after they shook hands and Reynolds was seated across from him in the district attorney's office.

'Thank you for seeing me.'

'I'm not sure I should be,' Stamm said, unconsciously picking up a paper clip that lay on top of a stack of legal documents.

'You know what Geddes has done, don't you?'

Stamm nodded noncommittally.

'Do you think it's right?'

Stamm looked uncomfortable. He unbent one end of the paper clip.

'Abbie is a friend of mine,' he said evenly. 'I have a conflict. That's why I called in the Attorney General. I can't get involved in this case.'

'You're the district attorney of this county. As long as

Geddes is a special deputy district attorney, he's your employee.'

'That's true in theory, but you know very well that I can't interfere with Geddes.'

'Geddes is using this case to settle a score with me and for self-aggrandizement. You saw his press conference after the arrest.'

'We shouldn't even be having this conversation. I have to let him try his case.'

'I'm not asking you to interfere with the way he tries this case. I'm asking you to talk to him about his position on bail. You can't believe it's right for Abbie to stay in jail for months while we get ready for trial. I just came from visiting her. She looks terrible. She's trying to hold herself together, but you can see the toll the effort is taking.'

'Abbie is wealthy. She can afford to go to a country that doesn't have an extradition treaty with the United States. Geddes is afraid she'll rabbit.'

'Only if she's guilty. You know her far better than I, Jack. Do you think Abbie killed Robert Griffen?'

Stamm straightened the paper clip, then bent it in two. After a moment, he said, 'No. I don't think she's guilty.'

'Then how can you let Geddes keep her in a cage?'

'Look, Matt, you've tried cases against Geddes. You know how he gets. I've spoken to him, and he knows I think he's wrong. But he won't budge. What more can I do?'

'You can call the Attorney General. Tell Gary Graham what Geddes is doing. Tell him it's not right.'

'I don't know . . .'

'When you talk to Graham, tell him I assured you that Abbie will surrender her passport and she'll submit to ESP, the electronic surveillance program. I've already checked with the people who run the program and they'll supervise Abbie. She won't be able to leave her house without Geddes knowing immediately and she won't have to endure the jail.'

Stamm worried the paper clip while he thought over Reynolds's proposal. Then he said, 'I don't know if Geddes will agree but I think I can convince Gary to order him to go along.'

'Then please call Graham.'

Stamm hesitated. 'If I call Gary, there's something you'll have to do.'

'Name it.'

'Geddes is going to be furious because I went behind his back. And he'll be right. If I do this for Abbie, you've got to let Geddes save face. I want you to let him make the house arrest suggestion in open court and praise him for his thoughtfulness.'

Reynolds's lips quivered for a moment as he held back a smile. Then, without any emotion, he said, 'I have nothing personal against Mr. Geddes. I only want what's best for my client.'

'I'm glad to hear that. Now I want you to listen carefully.' Stamm put down the paper clip and leaned toward Reynolds. 'I'm going way out on a limb with this. I'm probably violating the Canon of Ethics to help a friend. Once it's done, I won't do anything more. Do you understand?'

'Yes.'

Stamm stood. He held out his hand. 'Do everything you can for Abbie. Good luck.'

3

The sun was fading by the time the technician from the electronic surveillance program finished hooking up an oblong foot-long box to Abbie's phone. Abbie was now wearing a bracelet with a tapered piece of metal attached to it. A computer at a monitoring center was programmed to call her at her home phone at random intervals. When the calls came, she had to answer the phone and state her name and the time, then insert the metal piece into a slot in the box. People at the monitoring center would be trained to identify Abbie's voice and the insertion of the metal strip confirmed her presence in the house. A unit in the bracelet also broadcast a radio frequency. If Abbie went more than one hundred and fifty feet from the box, a signal would go off in the monitoring center and trigger a pager that would alert the staff.

Matthew accompanied the technician to the door, then returned to the living room. The French windows were open and Abbie was standing on the patio, her arms wrapped around herself, looking at the sunset. Matthew paused to watch her. Abbie closed her eyes and tilted her head back, savoring the warm and comforting breeze.

The scene was something Matthew had dreamed about. He and Abbie alone at dusk at the end of a perfect summer day. Already there were long shadows creeping across the wide expanse of lawn, changing green into black where the silhouettes of the oaks and evergreens fell. On the horizon, the scarlet sun shimmered above the trees, its dying rays reflecting in the cobalt blue of the pool.

Abbie sensed Matthew's presence. She opened her eyes and turned slightly. He started, afraid she could read his mind, and frightened of what she would think of him if she knew his deepest thoughts. But Abbie just smiled and Matthew walked toward her.

'The police are gone,' he said.

'It's so nice just being alone.'

'I can go, if you'd like.'

'No, stay. I didn't mean you.'

Matthew stopped beside Abbie. It was part of the fantasy. Abbie at his side.

'I bought this house because I fell in love with it,' Abbie said wistfully, 'but I just couldn't stay with Robert after I found out he'd betrayed me. When I was living in Meadowbrook, I missed not being here. Still, I don't think I ever really appreciated how beautiful it is until tonight. Maybe everyone should spend a few days in jail.'

Matthew didn't answer right away, wanting the

205

moment to last as long as possible. Finally he said, 'It is beautiful.'

They stood quietly for a moment more. Then Abbie looked up at Matthew. 'Are you hungry?' she asked.

'A little.'

'The jail chow lived up to its reputation and I'm famished for real food. Will you join me?'

'I had Barry stock the refrigerator.'

'I know. You've thought of everything.'

Matthew blushed. Abbie laughed.

'When are you going to stop doing that? We're going to be spending a lot of time together and I can't always walk on eggshells so as not to embarrass you.'

'I'm sorry.'

'Don't be. So will you stay for dinner?'

'If you'd like.'

'Good, but you'll have to wait until I shower. I've got to get this jail smell off of me. Then I'll fix us bacon and eggs. Lots of eggs. Soft scrambled. And stacks of toast. Will that be okay? For some reason, bacon and eggs sounds so good to me.'

'That's fine.'

'There's coffee in the cupboard over the refrigerator. Why don't you make a pot while I'm upstairs.'

Matthew wandered into the kitchen, taking his time, savoring each moment. He lingered in the hall and ran his hand over the molding and along the wall. Somewhere on the second floor the shower started. Matthew strained to hear, imagining Abbie with the water cascading down her body. He was suddenly terrified by the possibility, no matter how fanciful, no matter how remote, of intimacy with a woman like Abigail Griffen.

After starting the coffee, Matthew sat at the kitchen table waiting for Abbie to come downstairs. She had asked him to stay with her. Would she have asked *anyone* to stay with her, just to have someone with her after her ordeal in the county jail? Was he special to Abbie in any way or was he simply an object she was using to ward off loneliness, like a television kept on through the night for the comfort of the sound?

The shower stopped. The silence was like an alarm. Matthew was as nervous as a schoolboy. He stood up and rummaged through the kitchen drawers and cupboards for silverware, cups and plates. When he was almost done setting the table, he heard Abbie in the doorway of the kitchen. Matthew turned. Her hair was still damp, falling straight to her shoulders. Her face was fresh-scrubbed. She wore no makeup, but she looked like a different person from the woman he had visited in the jail. There was no sign of despair or exhaustion. She glowed with hope.

The phone rang. They froze. Abbie looked at the bracelet on her wrist and the glow vanished. The phone rang a second time and she crossed to it slowly, her arm hanging down as if the bracelet was a great weight.

Abbie raised the receiver on the third ring. She listened for a moment, then in a lifeless voice said, 'This is Abigail Griffen. The time is eight forty-five.'

She put down the receiver and inserted the tapered metal strip that was attached to the bracelet into the slot in the box. The effort to answer the phone and complete this simple task exhausted her. When she turned around, the face Matthew saw was the face he had seen in the visiting room. He felt helpless in the presence of such grief.

Chapter Sixteen

1

'You are not going to believe who the mystery witness is,' Barry Frame said as he dropped the police reports in Abbie's case on Matthew Reynolds's desk.

'Tell me,' Matthew said, looking at Frame expectantly.

'I should make you guess, but you'd never get it.' Frame flopped into a chair. 'So I'll give you three choices: Darth Vader, Son of Sam or Charlie Deems.'

Matthew's mouth gaped open. Frame couldn't hold back a grin.

'Is this good news or what?' he asked Reynolds. 'Geddes is basing his case on the word of a drug-dealing psychopath who murders nine-year-old girls.'

Matthew did not look happy.

'What's the matter, boss?'

'Have you read all the discovery?' Reynolds asked,

pointing toward the thick stack of police reports.

'I barely had time to pick it up from the DA's office and make your copy. But I did read the report of Jack Stamm's interview with Deems. That was also a piece of luck. If Geddes had been the first one at him, he'd never have written a report.'

'Something is wrong, Barry. Geddes would never base a case on the testimony of Charlie Deems unless he could corroborate it. I want you and Tracy to go over the reports. I'll do the same.'

'Tonight?' Barry asked, knowing that his plans for the evening had just set with the sun. Reynolds ignored him.

'I want a list of our problem areas and areas where the prosecution is soft. I want your ideas on what we should do. It scares me to death that Geddes is confident enough to base his case on the testimony of Charlie Deems.'

2

Abbie was wearing tan shorts and a navy-blue tee shirt when she answered the door. Her hair was pulled back into a ponytail. Her legs and arms were tanned and she looked rested. When she saw Matthew her face lit up and he could not help smiling back.

Matthew was wearing his undertaker's uniform and Tracy looked businesslike in a gray linen dress, but Barry Frame was casually dressed in a denim work shirt and a pair of chinos.

Abbie ignored Barry and Tracy and took Matthew's arm.

'Let's sit outside,' she said, leading Reynolds onto the patio. A tall pitcher of iced tea and a bowl of fruit were standing on a low glass table next to Abbie's copies of the police reports. Matthew waited until Tracy and Abbie were seated, then he took a chair and placed his copies of the discovery on his lap. Barry took out a pad and pen. Tracy leaned back and listened.

'You've read everything?' Matthew asked.

Abbie nodded.

'What do you think?'

'The whole case is preposterous. The things Deems says, they're simply not true.'

'Okay, let's start with Deems's story. What's not true?'

'All of it. He says I asked him to come to the beach house the day of the attack and offered to pay him to kill Robert. That never happened. I haven't seen Deems since his trial and I've never spoken to him, except in court.'

'What about the dynamite?'

Abbie looked concerned. 'Robert did buy dynamite to clear some stumps on the property.'

'How would Deems know about the dynamite if you didn't tell him?' Barry asked.

'Robert kept the dynamite in a toolshed. Maybe Deems cased the cabin when he was planning the attack and saw the dynamite in the shed.'

'Was there dynamite in the shed on the day of the attack?' Matthew asked. 'Is it possible that Justice Griffen used all of it when he blew up the stumps?'

'I don't know. Robert told me he cleared the stumps, but he didn't say if he used all the dynamite.'

'Do you remember looking in the shed, the day of the attack?' Matthew asked.

'No. The shed's in back of the cabin. I wasn't in the back that much. Mostly I was on the beach or the front porch or in the house.'

'Have you gone to the coast since the attack?' Barry asked.

'No. I don't think Robert was there either. The court heard arguments in Salem that week.'

'Barry, make a note to go out to the cabin. We can check the shed,' Matthew said. Then he asked Abbie, 'Can you think of a way we can show Deems is lying?'

'No. It's just his word against mine, but his word shouldn't carry much weight. My God, he's the worst scum. I can't imagine why even someone like Geddes would give credit to anything he said.'

'But he did,' Matthew said. 'And Jack Stamm thought there was enough to it to call in the AG's office. Why, Abbie? What evidence do they have that corroborates Deems's story?'

Abbie shook her head. 'I've been over and over the reports. I don't get it.'

Tracy felt nervous about interrupting, but an idea occurred to her.

'Excuse me, Mr. Reynolds,' she said, 'but I know where we might be able to get evidence to show that Charlie Deems is a liar. Deems received a death sentence when

Mrs. Griffen prosecuted him. To get a death sentence from the jury, she had to prove he would be dangerous in the future . . .'

'Of course,' Abbie said to Reynolds. 'How stupid of me.'

Matthew beamed. 'Good thinking, Tracy.'

Abbie studied Tracy, as if noticing her for the first time.

'Who handled Deems's appeal?' Reynolds asked Abbie.

'Bob Packard.'

'Tracy,' Reynolds said, 'call Packard. He may have the transcripts of Deems's trial. It could be a gold mine of information about Deems's background.'

It was warm on the patio. While Tracy made a note to contact Packard, Matthew took a sip of iced tea. When Tracy looked up, she noticed the interplay between her boss and his client. From the moment he entered the house, Matthew rarely took his eyes off Griffen, and Abbie's attention was totally focused on him. Even when Tracy or Barry was asking a question, Abbie directed her answers to Matthew.

'How did you meet Justice Griffen?' Reynolds asked.

'I was prosecuting a sex-abuse case involving a minor victim. The defendant was from a wealthy family and they talked the victim's family into settling the case out of court for a lot of money. Robert represented the victim in the civil matter. We consulted about the case. He asked me out. The relationship became serious about the time the governor appointed Robert to the Supreme Court.'

'That's about five years ago?'

'Yes.'

213

'Was it a bad marriage from the start?'

'No,' she answered quietly, shifting uneasily in her chair and casting a brief look at Tracy. Tracy could see that the question made Abbie uncomfortable and she wondered if their client would have felt less self-conscious if there were no other woman present.

'At first the marriage was good,' Abbie continued. 'At least I thought it was. With hindsight, I can't really be sure.'

'What went wrong?'

'I guess you could say that our relationship was like the relationship Robert had with his clients,' Abbie said bitterly. 'He romanced me. Robert knew the right things to say, he could choose wines and discuss Monet and Mozart. He was also a wonderful lover.' Matthew colored. 'By the time I realized it was all bullshit, it was too late. I'm certain he talked about me to his other women, the way he talked about his clients to me.'

'Justice Griffen was cheating on you?' Barry asked.

Abbie laughed harshly. 'You could say that. I don't know their names, but I'm pretty sure there were more than one.'

'How do you know he was cheating?'

'He slipped up. One time I overheard the end of a conversation on an extension and confronted him. He denied everything, of course, but I knew he was lying. Another time, a friend said she'd seen Robert with a woman at a hotel in Portland on a day he was supposed to be in Salem. That time, he admitted he'd been with someone, but he wouldn't tell me who. He promised he would stop.

I told him I would leave him if it ever happened again.'

'And it did?'

'Yes. On May third. A woman called me at work and told me Robert was meeting someone at the Overlook Motel. It's a dive about twenty-three miles south on I-5, roughly halfway between Salem and Portland. The caller didn't identify herself and I never learned who she was. I drove down immediately hoping to catch Robert in the act, but the woman was gone by the time I got there. Robert was getting dressed. It wasn't a pleasant scene. I moved out the next day.'

'Check out the Overlook,' Matthew told Barry. 'Get their register and see if you can find out the identity of the woman.'

Frame made a note on his pad.

'Abbie,' Matthew asked, 'who do you think killed Justice Griffen?'

'Charlie Deems. It has to be. This is his revenge on me for sending him to prison. I'm more certain than ever that he's the man who tried to kill me at the cabin. And he may have tried to break into my house in Portland.'

'Tell us about that,' Barry said.

Abbie told them about the man she had frightened away on the evening Tony Rose accosted her.

'Did you report the burglary attempt?' Frame asked.

'No. I thought it would be a waste of time. He didn't take anything and I couldn't identify the man.'

'Barry,' Reynolds said, 'we have to find Deems.'

'There's no address for him in the discovery, Matt.'

Reynolds's brow furrowed. 'The discovery statutes require the state to give us the address of all witnesses they're going to call.'

'I know, but it's not there.'

Reynolds thought for a moment. Then he said, 'Don't ask Geddes for it. Get it from Neil Christenson. He's working out of the Multnomah County DA's office.'

'Gotcha,' Barry said, writing himself another note.

Matthew turned his attention back to Abbie.

'If Deems *didn't* kill Justice Griffen, who did? Do you have any other ideas?'

'No. Unless it was a woman. Someone he seduced then threw over. But I'm just guessing. If it's not Deems, I don't know who it could be.'

Matthew reviewed his notes, then said, 'There doesn't seem much more to discuss about the discovery material. Do you have any more questions, Barry? Tracy?'

They shook their heads.

'Why don't you take Tracy back to the office,' Matthew told Barry. 'Set up an appointment to view the physical evidence and get Deems's address. I have a few more things I want to discuss with Mrs. Griffen.'

'Okay,' Barry said. 'We'll find our way out.'

'Thanks for the iced tea,' Tracy said. Abbie flashed her a perfunctory smile.

'What did you want to ask me?' Abbie said when Barry and Tracy were out of earshot.

'Nothing about the case. Are the security guards working out?'

'I guess so. One reporter made it through the woods, but they got him before he could get to me.'

'Good. How are you holding up?'

'I'm doing okay, but I get depressed if I drop my guard. When I get blue, I remind myself how much nicer this place is than my cell at the Justice Center.' Abbie held up her wrist, so Matthew could see the bracelet. 'I'm even getting used to this.'

'Do you have friends who can visit?'

'I'm not the kind of woman who makes friends, Matt. I've always been a loner. I guess the closest I've come to a friendship is with some of the other prosecutors, like Jack or Dennis Haggard, but they can't visit me now that I'm under indictment.'

'But you must have friends outside of work?'

'I met a lot of people when I was married but they were Robert's friends.'

Abbie made a halfhearted attempt to smile and shrugged.

'My work was my life until I met Robert. Now I'm pretty much on my own.'

'Abbie, I understand how it is to be alone. All of my clients know they can call me at any time. I'm here for them and I'm here for you.

'I know, Matt,' Abbie said softly, 'and I appreciate that.'

'Please, don't give up hope. Promise me you'll call anytime you feel all this getting the best of you. Anytime you need someone to talk to.'

'I will. I promise.'

*

Barry turned his Jeep Cherokee onto Macadam Boulevard and headed toward downtown Portland. The road ran along the river and they had occasional glimpses of pleasure boats cruising the Willamette. Barry envied the weekday sailors and watched them longingly, but Tracy seemed oblivious to the scenery.

'What's bothering you?' Barry asked.

'What?'

'What's bothering you? You haven't said a word since we left the house.'

Tracy shook her head.

'Come on, we're a team. What's on your mind?'

'It's our client,' Tracy said.

'What about her?'

'I don't trust her.'

'Matt sure does.'

'You've noticed, have you?'

'I didn't have to be much of a detective to pick up on that,' Barry said.

'I mean, it's like a mutual admiration society,' Tracy went on. 'I don't think she gave either of us more than a glance the whole time we were at the house.'

'So?'

'Barry, Matthew Reynolds is a brilliant attorney and a nice man, but he is not the type of guy a woman like Abigail Griffen makes goo-goo eyes at.'

'Hey, don't put down the boss.'

'I'm not. I really like him. I just don't want to see Abigail Griffen take advantage of him.'

'How would she do that?'

'By using her obvious attractions to convince a vulnerable man she's innocent when she's not.'

'You think she did it?'

'I think it's possible.'

'Based on the statement of a scumbag like Deems?'

'Based on what I know about Justice Griffen. This business about his affairs . . . I don't buy it. If he was seeing other women, I'll bet she drove him to it.'

'Why does Mrs. Griffen have to be the bad guy?'

'Laura respected the judge.'

'Laura is . . . ?'

'I'm sorry. Laura Rizzatti. She was his clerk. She was murdered just before I left the court.'

'That's right. You found the body. Sorry, I didn't recognize the name.'

'That's okay. I don't talk about it.'

'Do the police know who killed her?'

'No. I call the detective in charge of the case occasionally, but she says they don't have any leads.'

'Let's get back to our client. Talk it out. If you've got something, we need to know. You were saying that Laura respected Justice Griffen.'

'She did. I don't think she'd feel that way if she knew he was a womanizer.'

'Maybe she didn't know. She only saw him at work. He might have been very different around his law clerk.'

Tracy stared out the window without speaking for a while. They rounded a curve and the Portland skyline

219

appeared, tall buildings of glass and steel dwarfed by the green hills that loomed behind them.

'You're right, I guess I really didn't know Justice Griffen. I only saw him at work, too. It's just . . . Barry, he was a really nice guy. He was so concerned about Laura. I just don't see how he could be the way Mrs. Griffen portrays him.'

'What I'm getting from this is that you don't know the truth about Justice Griffen, but you don't like Abigail Griffen, so you don't want to believe what our client is saying. That ain't the way it works, Tracy. Nothing you've told me disproves anything Mrs. Griffen told us. We represent Abigail Griffen and our job is to save her butt. So until we learn otherwise, we've got to assume the worst about the deceased and the best about our client. If evidence turns up that convinces us otherwise, we'll deal with it. But for now let's operate on the theory that Justice Griffen was a cheat and a slimeball and see where that leads us.'

Chapter Seventeen

1

'I've got good news and bad news,' Barry Frame told his boss as soon as Reynolds walked through the front door. 'Which do you want first?'

'The good news,' Reynolds said as he headed for his office with Barry in tow.

'Christenson set up a time for us to view the physical evidence. He's bringing it to a conference room at the DA's office on Friday at ten.'

'Good. What's the bad news?'

'Geddes talked Judge Baldwin into issuing a protective order for Deems. They don't have to give us his address.'

Reynolds looked furious. 'That's preposterous.'

'Yeah, but Geddes convinced the judge to do it. The affidavit in support of the order is sealed, so I've got no idea what story Geddes cooked up to convince Baldwin to issue the order. The bottom line is I'm going to have to find another way to get the address.'

'Do it, then. Whatever it takes. We have to talk to Deems. He's the key to their case. I'm certain Deems is framing Abbie.'

'Why would he do that?'

'For revenge, of course. She put him in prison.'

'I know that's Mrs. Griffen's theory, but it doesn't make sense. Now that he's off death row, why risk going back to prison for perjury or worse, if he killed Justice Griffen?'

Matthew thought about that. 'Could someone have paid Deems to kill Griffen and frame Abbie?' he asked Barry.

'Sure, but why?'

Matthew shook his head. 'I don't know. We have to look deeper into Justice Griffen's background.'

Reynolds paused. Barry waited patiently.

'Barry, see if Deems has a bank account. If someone paid him to kill Griffen, it would have been a substantial amount. He may have put the money in an account.'

Barry laughed. 'You're kidding. A guy like Deems doesn't deal with banks, unless he's robbing them.'

Reynolds flashed Barry a patient smile. 'Humor me.'

'Sure thing. Oh, before I forget. Neil Christenson and I engaged in a little small talk. He let it slip that Geddes is really pissed at you.'

'Oh?'

'You did insult him when he arrested Mrs. Griffen.

Then there's the business with Mrs. Griffen's release. Geddes blames you for getting the Attorney General involved. We won't be getting any breaks from him. He's determined to get a death sentence in the case and he's going to fight us every step of the way.'

'Is that so?' The tiniest of smiles creased Reynolds's lips, as if he was enjoying a private joke. 'Well, back to work.'

Reynolds turned abruptly and walked away. Frame was about to go to his office when a thought occurred to him. When Deems was arrested for the Hollins murders, he tried to hire Reynolds to represent him. Barry was certain Matthew had talked to Deems two or three times before declining the defense, and he wondered if there was a file on the case with phone numbers and addresses for Deems and his acquaintances. Barry walked toward the back of the house where a rickety flight of stairs led down to the damp concrete basement where the old files were stored.

Tracy's office was near the basement door. She was at her desk, working at her word processor.

'Hi,' Barry said.

Tracy didn't move. Her thoughts were focused on the words that were scrolled across her monitor.

'Earth to Tracy.'

This time she turned.

'The Griffen case?' Barry asked, pointing at the computer screen.

'No. It's the Texas case. One of the issues in the brief.

The Supreme Court just handed down an opinion that had some useful language and Matt wanted me to expand our assignment of error to include a new argument.'

'Are you going to be working all weekend?'

'I'll be here Saturday, but I don't have any plans for the Sabbath.'

'I'm going to take some pictures at Griffen's cabin on Sunday. Want to come out to the coast with me?'

'I don't know. I should stay in town in case Matt needs me.'

'Matt will survive without you for one day. Come on. There's a beautiful spot I want to show you a few miles from the cabin.'

Barry held his hands out in front of him like a film director framing a shot.

'Picture this. We hike a mile or so through verdant woods and a field covered with wildflowers that create a riot of colors worthy of an artist's palette. Finally, weary, but at peace, we arrive at a rugged cliff overlooking a boiling ocean.'

Tracy laughed. 'And then what?'

'We have a picnic lunch. I've got a terrific Merlot I've been saving for a special occasion. Whaddaya say?'

Tracy looked at the pile of work on her desk. Then she made some quick mental calculations.

'Okay, but I want to clear it with the boss.'

'Tell him you're helping me investigate,' Barry said. Then he was gone. Tracy watched Barry walk away and smiled. He sure had a cute butt. They'd run together a few times and it had been fun. So far Barry had been a perfect gentleman, which was fine, but Tracy had decided she liked him enough to take matters a little further herself, if he didn't make a move. A romantic picnic in a beautiful setting seemed an ideal time to get started.

Tracy knew she was going to enjoy the coast, no matter what happened between her and Barry. She tried to remember what fresh air and sunshine were like. She had not seen much of either since she started as Reynolds's associate. Not that she was complaining. Working for Matthew Reynolds was everything she thought it would be. Still, the coast would be a great change of scenery after being cooped up with law books all week.

2

There were two addresses listed in the file Reynolds had opened for Charlie Deems. The first was for the apartment where Deems lived when he was arrested for the Hollins murders. Deems never returned to it. He had been in the county jail or on death row until his conviction was reversed. The apartment was rented to someone else now and the landlord had no idea how to reach Deems.

The second address was in a run-down section of north Portland. Barry Frame peered out the passenger window into the fading daylight and tried to read the numbers on a bungalow that stood back from the street. A chain-link fence surrounded the bungalow. Its gray paint was peeling. The yard had not been mown in weeks. One of the metal numbers on the front door was missing, but the other three numbers were right.

Barry opened the gate and walked up a slate path. Loud music blasted through the front door. Barry recognized grating guitars, rowdy drums and a sound that was closer to screaming than singing and quickly identified the group as another Pearl Jam knockoff. He rang the doorbell twice, then tried heavy pounding. Someone turned down the volume and Barry knocked again.

'Stop that racket. I'm coming,' a woman shouted.

The living-room curtains moved. Barry stepped away from the door and tried his best to look nonthreatening. A moment later, the front door was opened by a slender, barefoot blonde who was dressed in cutoffs and a bikini top. The shadows cast by the setting sun smoothed the lines hardship had etched into her features and for a moment Barry was fooled into thinking she was a teenager.

'Who are you?' the woman asked belligerently.

Barry held out his identification. 'My name's Barry Frame. I'm an investigator working with Matthew Reynolds. He's an attorney.'

'So?'

'Are you Angela Quinn?'

'What's this about?' she asked, cocking her hip and leaning against the doorjamb. The pose was intended to distract him and it worked. Barry could not help noticing her long, smooth legs and the impression her nipples made on the fabric of the bikini top.

'We're trying to get in touch with Charlie Deems. Mr. Deems consulted with Mr. Reynolds a few years ago and he gave him this address and phone number for messages. Are you Angela?'

Barry saw fear flicker in Angela Quinn's blue eyes.

'I don't know where Charlie is,' Angela said as she started to close the door.

'Wait. You were his girlfriend, right?'

'Look, mister, I'll make this simple. I dance at Jiggle's. Charlie used to hang out there and we were friends for a while. Then he killed that kid.'

Angela shook her head, as if she still couldn't believe it.

'Charlie wrote me from death row. I'm a sucker. I wrote him back, once or twice, because the guy doesn't have anyone else and I never figured I'd see him again. My mistake. The first place he goes after they let him out is my house. I let him stay. But he's gone now, and I don't know where he is.'

'If you dislike Deems so much, how come you let him stay?'

Angela laughed, but there was no humor in it.

'Mister, you must not know Charlie very well. You just don't say no to him.' Angela shuddered. 'The bastard stayed more than a month and that was a month too long. I hope I never see him again.'

'Can you remember when Charlie left?'

'It was about two weeks ago.'

'Do you remember hearing about a Supreme Court justice who was killed by a car bomb?'

Barry saw the fear again. 'Why do you want to know?' Angela asked, suddenly suspicious.

'Mr. Reynolds, my boss, is representing the woman who's charged with killing the judge. Charlie is going to be a witness in the case and we want to talk to him about his testimony.'

'I told you I don't know where he is.'

'Did Charlie ever say anything about the judge's murder to you?'

Angela looked like she was debating whether to talk to Barry.

'This is just between us,' he said, giving her his most reassuring smile.

'Why should I believe that?'

Barry stopped smiling. 'Look, Angela, I know how dangerous Deems is and I'm not going to put you in danger. I just want this as background. Did Charlie discuss Justice Griffen's murder with you?'

'No, he didn't say nothin' to me, but he was watching a story about it on the news when I was getting ready for work one night, and he seemed real interested. He even asked me if I had the paper, because he wanted to read about the killing. Now that I think about it, Charlie left right after that.'

'And there hasn't been any contact since he left? He's never called? You didn't have to send him any clothes? Stuff he left behind?'

'Nope. I have no idea where he is.'

'Well, thanks. You've been a real help. Here's my card.

If he does contact you, I'd appreciate it if you'd let me know where I can find him.'

'Yeah, sure,' Angela said. The door closed and Barry wondered how long it would take for his business card to find its way into the trash.

3

Charlie Deems sat on the back porch of a farmhouse in Clackamas County smoking a cigarette and watching the grass sway back and forth. It was the most exciting thing that happened at the farm, but that was okay with Charlie. Two years of living in a cell the size of a broom closet, locked down twenty-three out of every twenty-four hours, had taught him how to deal with idle time.

Out past the high grass was a stand of cottonwoods. Past the cottonwoods were low rolling hills behind which the sun was starting to set. Charlie felt content. His plans were moving forward slowly, but steadily. He was living rent-free and, except for a steady diet of pizza and Big Macs, he didn't have much to complain about.

As soon as Charlie was released from the Oregon State Penitentiary, but before he contacted Raoul, he reestablished contact with people who worked for Otero. Raoul had changed some of his ways of doing business, but for the most part the cocaine flowed along the same river it was travelling when Deems was working the waterways. For instance, there was a certain rest stop on the interstate where trucks from Mexico stopped on their way to Seattle. While the drivers relieved themselves, shadowy figures relieved the drivers of a part of their cargo that never showed on the manifest, then faded into the night. This evening, one of his babysitters had told him that several arrests had been made at that rest stop and a large amount of cocaine had been confiscated. Charlie's steak dinner reflected the DA's appreciation.

Charlie took another drag on his cigarette. He smiled as he pictured the confusion Raoul would experience as each piece of his organization crumbled. Soon the cops would catch the fish who was more afraid of prison than Raoul. Someone would wear a wire and Raoul's own words would weave themselves into the rope that would hang him. Then the grand jury would start to meet. It would take a while, but Charlie could wait.

What he could not wait for was the day he would testify against Abigail Griffen. He wanted to look her in the eye as his testimony brought her down. For two years, the bitch had been at the center of every one of his sexual fantasies. If he had a dollar for every time he had raped or tortured her in his dreams, he would be living in a villa on the French Riviera. And while he would certainly enjoy a chance to visit with Ms. Griffen personally, he felt greater satisfaction at the thought of Abbie pacing back and forth in the same concrete cell where he had spent interminable hours that crept by so slowly that sometimes he felt he could actually see the progress of each second.

Maybe Charlie would write to Abbie. He would send

her postcards from faraway places to let her know that he was thinking of her always. He imagined Abbie's beauty fading, her dark skin turning pale from lack of sunlight, her body withering. But even more satisfying would be the destruction of the bitch's spirit. She, who was so proud, would weep interminably or stare with dead eyes at the never-changing scene outside her cell. The thought brought a smile to Charlie's lips.

He glanced at his watch and stood up. It was almost 7 P.M., time for *Jeopardy!*, his favorite game show. He ground out his butt on the porch railing and flicked it into the grass. Free pizza, peace and quiet and all the game shows he could watch. Life was good.

Chapter Eighteen

1

Tracy parked her car in front of the Griffen cabin shortly after ten on Sunday morning. She got out while Barry reached into the back seat to retrieve his camera. It was cool for early September and Tracy was glad she'd brought a sweatshirt.

'I'm going to have a look around,' Barry said. 'I've gone over the crime-scene photos the Seneca County deputies shot and I've read the police reports. I thought I'd retrace Mrs. Griffen's steps. I doubt I'll find anything this long after the incident, but you never know.'

'Go ahead. I'm going down to the beach.'

Tracy saw the shed as soon as she rounded the corner of the cabin. It was tall and square and constructed from graying timber. The door was partly open. From where Tracy was standing, she could see a rake and a volleyball

232

resting on a volleyball net, but no dynamite. She walked over and opened the door the whole way. There was an empty space that would have been big enough for a box of dynamite, but there was no box. She saw some rusted gardening tools and a barbecue grill. Tracy repositioned the door as it had been. She put her hands in her pockets, hunched her shoulders against the bracing sea air and walked down the path.

A flight of wooden steps led from the top of the bluff to the beach. Tracy sat down on the top step and let the wind play havoc with her long blond hair. High waves curled onto the beach, crashing against the sand with a sound that shut out the world. Tracy scanned the beach slowly, focusing on the low dunes and the gulls cruising the blue-green water, and thought about Barry Frame.

It had been a while since she'd had anything that could be classified as a relationship, but it wasn't anything she regretted. Tracy had decided long ago that being alone was preferable to being with someone she did not really care about. She missed sex sometimes, but having sex just to have sex never appealed to her. Tracy wanted love, or at least affection, from a partner. What she really missed was intimacy. Of course, sex with the right guy could be pretty good, too.

Tracy liked Barry's openness, his casual independence and his easy humor. And she thought he enjoyed her company as much as she enjoyed his. She also thought he was damn good-looking. Tracy had imagined what he would look like naked on more than one occasion. She also wondered what he would be like in bed and had a feeling she would enjoy finding out.

'Look what I've got.'

Tracy turned around. Barry was smiling and lipping the volleyball Tracy had seen in the shed from hand to hand.

'Are you finished?' she asked.

'All done.'

'Find anything?'

'Except for a vial of exotic poison, a Chinese dagger and a series of hieroglyphics written in blood, I struck out. Let's go down to the beach.'

Tracy stood up and they walked down the steps. When they reached the bottom, she ran ahead and Barry heaved the ball as if it was a football. Tracy caught it easily and returned it with a fancy overhand spin serve.

'Whoa!' Barry said. 'Very impressive. All you need are those weird shades and you're ready for ESPN.'

'You can't grow up in California and not play beach volleyball.'

'I love it here,' Barry said, tossing the ball back to Tracy underhand. 'When I retire, I'm gonna get a house at the beach.'

'If I had a beach house,' Tracy said as she served the ball back to Barry, 'I'd want it to be just like this place, so I could see the ocean. I'd have a huge picture window.'

Barry tried an overhand serve but the ball sailed over Tracy's head and bounced toward the water. They both raced toward it.

'You know the best thing?' Barry asked as they met over the ball at the water's edge. Tracy shook her head.

'Storms.' Barry bent down and picked up the volley-ball. 'Have you ever watched a storm when the waves are monstrous and the rain comes down in sheets? It's incredible. When it's dark, you build yourself a fire and drink some wine and watch the whitecaps through the rain.'

'I had no idea you were such a romantic,' Tracy kidded.

Barry stopped smiling. 'I can be under the right circumstances,' he said softly.

Tracy looked at him, shielding her eyes because the sun was perched on his shoulder. Barry dropped the ball. Tracy was surprised, but pleased, when Barry took her in his arms and kissed her. His lips tasted salty and it felt good being held. She rested her head on his shoulder and he stroked her hair.

'Not a bad kiss for a lawyer,' he murmured. 'Of course, it could be beginner's luck.'

'What makes you think I'm a beginner?' Tracy asked with a smile. Then she grabbed a handful of his hair, pulled Barry's head back, planted a wet kiss on his forehead and dumped him in the sand.

'That was just like a lawyer.' Barry laughed as he pulled himself to his feet.

'Don't forget the volleyball.'

Barry held it in one hand and draped his arm around Tracy's shoulder.

'You ready to visit one of the most beautiful spots on the planet?' he asked.

'Yup.'

'Then let's go have our picnic. We'll hit the Overlook on the way back to Portland.'

They climbed the stairs. Tracy liked the feel of his hip bumping against hers and the pressure of his arm across her shoulder. Barry tossed the volleyball into the shed. Tracy saw it roll to a stop in the empty space as they headed for the car.

2

Barry's special place was everything he had promised and they had lazed around enjoying Barry's Merlot and each other's company until the setting sun reminded them that they still had work to do. Tracy drove fast along the winding mountain roads that traversed the Coast Range and they hit I-5 a little before six o'clock and started looking for the Overlook Motel.

'There it is,' Barry said finally, pointing past the freeway exit. Tracy took the off-ramp and drove down an access road for two hundred feet, then turned into the parking lot of the Overlook Motel. Sunset would save the Overlook's dignity by cloaking its shabby exterior in shadow, but by daylight it was a tired, fading, horseshoe-shaped failure with an empty pool and a courtyard of chipped concrete and peeling paint.

Tracy pulled up in front of the office. She took a close look at three bikers who were parking their Harleys in front of one of the rooms and locked her car. A heavyset woman in a flower-print muumuu was sitting behind the registration desk eating potato chips and watching a soap opera. She put down the chips and struggled to her feet when the office door opened.

'Hi,' Tracy said as she took her business card out of her wallet and handed it across the counter. 'I'm Tracy Cavanaugh. I'm an attorney. This is Barry Frame, my investigator.'

The woman read the card carefully, then studied Tracy through her thick-lensed glasses, as if she didn't believe Tracy could possibly be a lawyer. Tracy didn't blame her. She was wearing shades, her hair was pulled back in a ponytail and she was still dressed in the cutoffs and navy-blue tank top she had worn all day.

'We're working on a murder case and we'd like your help.'

'What murder case?' the woman asked suspiciously.

'You may have seen it on TV, Mrs . . . ?' Barry said.

'Hardesty. Annie Hardesty.'

'. . . Mrs. Hardesty. It's the case where the judge was blown up in his car. We represent Abigail Griffen, his wife.'

The woman's mouth opened. 'You're kidding.'

'No, ma'am.'

'I've been following that case and I don't think she did it. A bomb isn't a woman's weapon.'

'I wish you were on our jury,' Tracy said with a smile.

'I was on jury duty once. The lawyers wouldn't let me sit on any of the cases, though.'

Barry nodded sympathetically. 'Isn't that the way it always goes. Mrs. Hardesty, can you spare a few minutes to talk to us?'

'Sure.'

'You're not too busy?' Tracy asked.

'No, it's slow on Sundays. What can I do for you, honey?'

'We'd like to see your guest register for May third of this year.'

'I don't know if Mr. Boyle would like that.'

'Well, we could subpoena it, but then Mr. Boyle would be the witness.'

'You mean I might have to testify in court?' Mrs. Hardesty asked excitedly.

'If you're the one who shows us the register.'

Mrs. Hardesty thought for a moment, then bent down behind the desk and came up with the register. Tracy opened the ledger to May and scanned the entries for May 3, the day Abigail Griffen said she had confronted Justice Griffen at the motel. Seven people had checked into the motel that day. She took out a pen and copied the names. Craig McGowan, Roberto Sanchez, Arthur Knowland, Henrietta Rainey, Louis Glass, Chester Walton and Mary Jane Simmons.

'If Justice Griffen checked into the Overlook, he didn't do it under his own name,' she said.

'I wasn't expecting him to,' Barry said, laying a brochure about the Supreme Court on the counter. There were pictures of all the justices in it.

'Does anyone look familiar to you, Mrs. Hardesty?' Barry asked. The woman studied the pictures intently. Then she put her finger on Justice Griffen's picture. 'I've seen him a few times, but I can't say when. Is that the judge who was killed?'

'Yes, ma'am,' Barry said as he started to pick up the brochure. Mrs. Hardesty stopped him. Then she put her finger on the picture of Mary Kelly.

'Is that the wife?'

'No. Why?'

'She was with him one of the times he came here.'

3

'Tracy,' Mary Kelly said with surprise when she opened the door to her condominium. Even wearing reading glasses and without makeup, the judge was an impressive-looking woman, and Tracy could see why Justice Griffen would have been interested in her.

'I'm sorry to bother you so late, Justice Kelly. This is Barry Frame. He's Matthew Reynolds's investigator.'

The judge studied Barry for a moment, then invited the couple in. The condominium had a high ceiling and a view of the Willamette. Her taste was modern and there was a lot of glass and designer furniture in the living room. A cigarette was smoking in an ashtray that balanced on the arm of a deep alabaster armchair. A biography of Louis Brandeis was open on the seat where

Justice Kelly had left it when she answered the door.

'How's your new job?' Kelly asked. Tracy had the impression that the judge was asking the question to forestall her own.

'It's a lot of work, but it's exciting, most of the time. Sometimes, though, it's not so much fun.'

Tracy paused. During her year at the court, she had come to respect Justice Kelly and she felt very uncomfortable about questioning her, especially about her private life.

'I've been following Abigail Griffen's case in the papers,' Kelly said. 'How is it going?'

'We've just come from the Overlook Motel,' Tracy answered, her voice catching slightly.

'I see,' Kelly said, growing suddenly thoughtful.

'The desk clerk identified your picture and Justice Griffen's.'

Justice Kelly took a moment to think about that. Then she said, 'You two look too healthy to smoke. Do you want a drink?'

'No, thanks,' they answered.

'Sit down.' She placed the book on the floor, sat in the armchair and took a drag on her cigarette. 'I was hoping to avoid talking about Robert and me, but it looks like the cat's out of the bag. What do you want to know, Tracy?'

'Were you having an affair with Justice Griffen?'

Kelly laughed self-consciously. 'An affair sounds a little too formal for what we were doing.'

Kelly suddenly sobered. She looked very tired.

'Poor Robert.' She shook her head. 'I just can't imagine him dying like that.'

Kelly took a long drag on her cigarette and stared out the window. Tracy waited respectfully for the judge to continue. After a moment, Kelly looked up. Then she stubbed out her cigarette.

'Look, I'll make this simple,' she told Tracy quietly. 'My husband and I are separated. The whole thing is very amicable. I'm going to file for divorce as soon as I'm certain I have no opposition in next year's election. If my relationship with Robert makes the papers, the bad publicity could give someone the courage to run against me. If possible, I would appreciate it if you didn't go public about us. I doubt it has anything to do with Robert's murder anyway.'

'We have no interest in hurting you,' Tracy said, 'but I'll have to tell Mr. Reynolds. It's his decision.'

'I guess I'll have to live with that.'

'How did you two get together?' Barry asked.

'My problems at home were fairly obvious to an astute observer of human nature, like Robert. He was having his own problems with the ice princess. Since we had a problem in common, it was natural for us to talk. One thing led to another. Both of us were consenting adults. Neither one of us took the sex that seriously.'

'How long did it go on?'

'Two years, off and on. It wasn't a regular thing.'

'Why the Overlook?' Barry asked.

Kelly chuckled. 'Good question.' She lit another cigarette. 'It certainly wasn't the ambience.'

Justice Kelly laughed nervously again, then took a drag.

'Robert and I are public figures. We needed an out-of-the-way place where we wouldn't be seen by anyone we knew. None of our friends would be caught dead at the Overlook.'

'Did you meet Justice Griffen there on May third?'

'Yes.'

'Someone called Mrs. Griffen anonymously and told her Justice Griffen would be at the Overlook that day.'

'Robert told me about that. I gather Little Miss Perfect was pissed. She must have missed me by a minute or so. Robert, always the gentleman, assured me he didn't tell the little woman who I was.'

'You don't seem to like Mrs. Griffen,' Barry said.

Kelly drew in some smoke. She looked thoughtful.

'I guess I'm not being fair, since I only met Abbie a few times. I'm really echoing what Robert told me. Though Abbie did live up to her advance billing on the occasions we met.'

'How so?'

'Have you ever tried talking to her? To say she was a bit chilly would be generous.' Kelly laughed again. 'I guess I shouldn't throw stones. I've heard that I had a nasty reputation when I was practicing with my firm. It was just tough to get the time of day from her.'

'Maybe she suspected you were sleeping with her husband,' Tracy said, shifting uncomfortably when she realized that the statement, which she had not intended to be a reproach, could be interpreted as one.

Kelly stared at her for a second.

'That would explain it,' she answered bluntly.

'What did Justice Griffen say about his relationship with Mrs. Griffen?' Barry asked.

'He told me his wife was all work and no play, and barely tolerated sex. That would be tough for someone like Robert.'

'Who do you think tipped off Mrs. Griffen to your meeting at the Overlook on May third?' Barry asked.

'Probably someone he was sleeping with who was jealous.'

'Was there someone else?'

'I always assumed so. Robert was a rabbit where women are concerned.'

The statement shocked Tracy, but she concealed her surprise. She found it hard to reconcile her image of Justice Griffen with the blatant womanizer Justice Kelly and Abbie Griffen believed him to be.

'Do you have any idea who the other woman is?' Barry asked.

'No.'

'Do you have any idea who killed him?' Tracy asked.

Kelly crushed out her cigarette. Tracy thought she was debating whether to give her opinion. Then Kelly shrugged her shoulders and said, 'Abbie, of course. She's the first person I thought of when I heard Robert had been murdered.'

Chapter Nineteen

1

Bob Packard did not look well. He seemed jittery. His complexion was pasty and his skin was slack, as if he'd lost weight rapidly. Tracy wondered if Charlie Deems's lawyer had been ill recently.

'Thanks for seeing me,' she said as she took a seat in his office.

'No problem. What can I do for you?'

'I'm an associate of Matthew Reynolds. Mr. Reynolds is representing Abigail Griffen, who has been accused of killing Oregon Supreme Court Justice Robert Griffen.'

'Of course. I read about that in the paper. Boy, that was awful. You know, I won a case in the Supreme Court a few months ago and he wrote the opinion.'

'That's why I wanted to see you. Mr. Reynolds would like to borrow the transcript in the *Deems* case.'

Packard looked uncomfortable. He shifted nervously in his chair.

'If you don't mind my asking, why do you need the transcript?'

'Charlie Deems is the key witness against Abigail Griffen.'

Packard's jaw dropped and he looked at Tracy as if he was waiting for a punch line. When none came, Packard said, 'This is a joke, right?'

'Mr. Deems claims Mrs. Griffen hired him to murder her husband.'

Packard remembered worrying that Deems might try to harm Abigail Griffen. He'd been thinking about violence, but framing Griffen for murder was diabolical.

'The DA is buying Charlie's story?' Packard asked incredulously.

'He seems to be.'

'Well, if it was me, I'd be looking at Charlie long before I'd peg Abbie Griffen as a suspect.'

'Do you have any specific reason for suspecting Deems?'

'Are you kidding? Blowing people up is Charlie's thing, and he has plenty of reason to frame Griffen. She made putting Charlie on death row a personal crusade.'

'Mr. Reynolds thinks Deems is framing Mrs. Griffen, too. We're going after Deems and he thought there might be something useful in the transcript. Especially the penalty-phase testimony.'

'I'd be careful about going after Charlie if I were you.'

'Why's that?'

Packard remembered playing *The Price Is Right* and his stomach turned. He had been off cocaine, cold turkey, since Deems's visit, but he wished he had some snow right now.

Packard was quiet for so long, Tracy wondered if he had heard the question. Finally he said, 'If I tell you something, will you swear not to say where you heard it?'

'That depends. Our first loyalty is to our client.'

'Yeah, well, I have to think of myself. I don't want it getting back to Charlie that I talked to anyone about this. I've got him out of my life now, and I don't want him back in.'

Packard was fidgeting in his chair and Tracy noticed beads of sweat on his upper lip. She was surprised at how nervous he was.

'It isn't anything concrete anyway,' Packard went on. 'Not like a confession. It's just something you should know about Deems. I don't want to see anyone get hurt.'

'Okay. Go ahead,' Tracy said, curious to find out what Deems had done to scare Packard so much.

'Charlie Deems is crazy. I mean really crazy. He thinks he can do anything and nothing will happen to him. And the funny thing is, he's right. I mean, look at what happened with the case I handled. He tortures this guy Shoe, then he kills Hollins and his kid. The jury says death, but he walks away.'

'Most criminals don't think they'll get caught.'

'You don't understand. How do I say this?'

Tracy waited patiently while Packard searched for the words to explain why Charlie Deems terrified him.

'Charlie not only believes he can break the law with impunity, he believes he's impervious to any kind of harm.'

'I'm not following you.'

'He doesn't think he can be killed. He thinks he's immortal.'

Tracy's mouth opened. Then she laughed out loud.

'It's not funny,' Packard said.

'I'm sorry, but I'm not sure I understand you. Are you saying that Deems thinks nothing would happen if I shot him?'

'That's exactly what I mean.'

'Oh, come on.'

'I visited Charlie at the penitentiary when I was handling his appeal. At some point, we got to talking about what steps he should take if he lost in the Oregon Supreme Court. I noticed he wasn't paying attention, so I tried to shock him into listening by talking about his death sentence. Charlie just smiled. He told me he wasn't worried about dying because he has an angel who protects him.'

'An angel?' Tracy asked, thinking she had not heard Packard correctly.

'That's right. An angel. At first I thought he was kidding. I told him that with the stuff he'd done, the last thing he had was an angel. But he was dead serious. He said his angel is a dark angel. Then he told me this story.

'When Deems was in his late teens there was this woman he was screwing. An older woman. Maybe thirty-five. She was the wife of Ray Weiss, who was doing time for murder. Weiss was paroled. When he got home he beat up his wife because he heard she was cheating on him. She named Charlie as the guy.

'The wife had kept Weiss's handgun and ammunition in the house all those years. As soon as Weiss got the name, he loaded the gun and went looking for Charlie. He found him sitting on his front stoop. Weiss pulled the gun and accused Charlie of fucking his wife. Charlie denied everything. Weiss called Charlie a liar. Then he shot him. Charlie told me he was sure he was a dead man. The bullet hit him right in the chest. But the thing is, it bounced off.'

'It what?'

'The bullet bounced off Charlie's chest, just like in the Superman comics.'

'But how . . . ?'

'I asked a ballistics expert about the story. He said it was possible. The bullets had been sitting around all that time. Ten years. The powder could have gotten damp or oil might have seeped into it. Whatever the reason, Weiss was in shock. He fired again and the same thing happened. Charlie said Weiss's eyes bugged out of his head. Then he threw the gun at Charlie and took off running.

'Now, here's the scary part. Charlie told me that when the first bullet hit him, he saw the dark angel. She was dressed in a black gown that went from her neck to her feet. She was wearing sandals. He remembered that. And she had wings. Beautiful wings, like the wings of a dove, only huge and black. The angel loomed over Charlie with her wings spread out. When the bullet struck him, he saw a flash of light and the angel said, "I'll protect you, Charlie."

'From that minute on, Charlie Deems has believed that he can do anything he wants and nothing can hurt him. That means he can't be scared off and he can't be stopped, once he sets his mind to something.'

The story was so bizarre that Tracy didn't know what to say. How did you deal with someone who thought he was immortal?

'Tell Reynolds to tread very carefully where Charlie Deems is concerned,' Packard warned her.

'I will.'

'Good. Now, I'll get you those transcripts.'

'Thanks.'

'Don't thank me. I'm all too glad to get rid of anything that reminds me of Charlie Deems.'

2

Matthew Reynolds watched the light blinking on his personal phone line. All calls to the office were handled by an answering service after the receptionist left, but the personal line bypassed the service. Few people knew his private number, but he had given it to Abbie.

Matthew picked up the receiver, hoping it was Abbie. He had not seen her for two days, but she had never left his thoughts.

'Matt?'

'Yes.'

Matthew's heart raced.

'I remembered something. I don't know if it will help.'

'Tell me.'

'I shot a roll of film the day I was attacked at the coast. I forgot all about it in the excitement. When Jack drove me back to Portland, he packed up the car. He must have put my camera in the trunk. Then he brought my things in when we got to the rental house in Meadowbrook. Your investigator must have brought the camera when he moved my belongings here. I just found it. The film is in the camera. I think I took some shots behind the cabin. There might be a shot of the shed where the dynamite was stored.'

'Barry was at the cabin on Sunday. He looked in the shed and there was no dynamite. If we had an earlier picture of the shed . . .'

Matthew thought for a moment. 'What make is the camera?'

'It's a Pentax 105-R.'

'That could be a break. The Pentax date-stamps the negatives. That will prove the date the pictures were taken. If there is something useful on the film, Geddes won't be able to argue that the pictures were taken at a later date.'

'What should I do?'

'Don't do anything. Leave the film in the camera. I'm going to send Tracy Cavanaugh to pick it up. I'll want the camera, too.'

'Couldn't you come?' Abbie asked.

'I can't tonight.'

'Oh.'

Matthew could hear the disappointment in her voice and could not help smiling.

'I'm sorry. I'm handling an appeal in Texas. The man is on death row. The brief is due in two days.'

'You don't have to explain, Matt. I know you have other people who depend on you. It's just that . . .'

'Yes.'

'Oh, I was feeling sorry for myself. You cheer me up, that's all.'

'Good. That's the part of my job I like the best.'

Abbie laughed. 'Will I see you soon? I'm getting a little stir crazy.'

'I promise. As soon as this brief is done.'

Tracy brought the transcripts and a takeout order of kung pao chicken to the office as soon as she left Bob Packard. Deems's trial had lasted several weeks, so the transcript was twenty-nine volumes long. She was reading Volume III when Matthew Reynolds said, 'I'm glad you're still here.'

Tracy looked up from the transcript and saw Reynolds and the time simultaneously. It was 8:15. How had that happened? She was certain she had started reading at 5:30. Where had the hours gone?

'Mrs. Griffen just phoned me. We could be in luck. She shot a roll of film at the coast the day she was attacked. In the excitement, she forgot about it. I want you to drive to her home and get the camera and the film. Bring the film to a commercial developer first thing in the morning. I want a receipt showing the date the film was delivered for processing. Then bring me the camera.'

'I'll go right now.'

Reynolds turned to leave.

'Mr. Reynolds.'

Matthew paused.

'These are the transcripts from Deems's trial.'

'Ah. Good. I want a synopsis of everything you think will be of use. Make certain you give me cites to the pages in the transcript, so I can find the information quickly.'

'I'm working on it now,' Tracy said, holding up a yellow pad to show Reynolds her notes. 'Oh, and there's something Bob Packard thought you should know.'

Tracy told Reynolds about Charlie Deems's dark angel. As she talked, she watched Reynolds's face show surprise, disbelief and, finally, a look of amused satisfaction. She expected him to ask her questions about Packard or Deems when she was done, but all he said was 'That's very interesting, Tracy. Excellent work.'

When Reynolds was gone, Tracy shook her head. She could never tell what her boss was thinking and he rarely expressed his thoughts. He acted like an all-wise and all-knowing Buddha who silently weighed the worth of what he heard but never let on what he was thinking until it was absolutely necessary.

During the pretrial motion to suppress evidence in the Livingstone case in Atlanta, Tracy was unaware of the direction his cross-examination was taking until the moment before Reynolds sprang his trap. Tracy had been very impressed by Reynolds's technique, but she had also been a little upset that he had not confided to her what he was planning.

When Tracy clerked for Justice Sherzer there were never any secrets between them and she felt as if she was part of a team. Reynolds worked alone and at times made her feel like a piece of office equipment. Still, the opportunity to work with a genius like Reynolds was adequate compensation for her bruised feelings.

As she drove along the dark highway toward the Griffen place, Tracy realized that her feelings about Abigail and Robert Griffen had changed since her talk with Justice Kelly. The judge had cheated on his wife and to Tracy that was indefensible. She was also upset with herself for being so quick to conclude that Abigail was lying about her husband simply because she liked the judge.

On the other hand, Tracy had been around Mrs. Griffen enough to concur in Mary Kelly's opinion that Griffen was a cold, calculating woman who could easily have been frigid enough to drive Justice Griffen into the arms of other women. And the fact that the judge had been cheating gave Abigail Griffen a powerful motive for murder.

The Griffens' driveway had been resurfaced as soon as the police removed the crime-scene tapes, but here and there, on the edges, Tracy's headlight beams picked out burn marks and scarred asphalt. When she parked, Tracy saw Abigail Griffen standing in the doorway. Abbie was smiling, but the smile looked forced. Tracy wondered how long Mrs. Griffen had been waiting for her near the front door.

'It's Tracy, right?'

Tracy nodded. 'Mr. Reynolds sent me for the film and the camera.'

Tracy expected Abbie to be holding them, but her hands were empty. She did not see the camera on the hall table.

'Come in,' Abbie said. 'They're upstairs. Would you like a cup of coffee?'

'No, thanks. It's a little late.'

The smile left Abbie's lips for a moment. 'Oh, come on. I was going to pour myself a cup when you drove up.'

Tracy was going to decline again, but Mrs. Griffen sounded a little desperate.

'Okay. Sure.'

There were two settings on the kitchen table. Tracy realized that Abbie had been counting on her to stay. Tracy sat down. She felt uncomfortable. Abbie carried over the coffeepot.

'Do you take milk or sugar?'

'Black is fine.'

Abbie filled Tracy's cup. 'How long have you worked for Matt?' she asked nervously, like a blind date fishing for a way to start a conversation. Tracy got the feeling that making small talk was not one of Abbie's strengths.

'Not long,' Tracy answered tersely, unwilling to have their relationship be anything more than a professional one while she still harbored doubts about Abbie.

'You clerked for Alice Sherzer, didn't you?'

'Yes. How did you know?'

Abbie smiled. 'You looked familiar. I visited Robert at the court occasionally. He may have pointed you out. Did you enjoy your clerkship?'

'Yes. Justice Sherzer is a remarkable woman.'

Abbie sipped at her coffee. Tracy sipped at hers. The silence grew. Tracy shifted in her seat.

'Are you working with Matt on my case?'

'I'm reviewing the evidence to see if we've got any good legal motions.'

'And what have you concluded?'

Tracy hesitated. She wasn't sure that Reynolds would want her to answer the question, but Abigail Griffen was no ordinary client. She was also a brilliant attorney. And Tracy was relieved to be freed from making small talk.

'I haven't reached a final decision, but I don't think we're going to win this case on a legal technicality. Do you have any ideas for a pretrial motion?'

Abbie shook her head. 'I've thought about it, but I don't see anything either. What's it like working for Matt?'

'I like it,' Tracy answered guardedly, not willing to discuss her boss with Griffen.

'He seems like such a strange man,' Abbie said. When Tracy didn't respond, she asked, 'Is he as passionate about all his cases as he is about mine?'

'He's very dedicated to his clients,' Tracy answered in a neutral tone.

Abbie's eyes lost focus for a moment. Tracy waited uncomfortably for the conversation to resume. 'He used to watch my trials. Did you know that?'

There was no rhythm to their discussion and the statement fell into the conversation like a heavy object. Tracy remembered seeing Reynolds at the Marie Harwood trial, but she wasn't certain where Mrs. Griffen was going, so she didn't respond. Abbie went on as if she had not expected a response.

'I saw him more than once in the back of the courtroom, watching me. He would sit for a while, then leave. I don't think he realized that I'd seen him.'

Abbie looked directly at Tracy when she said this. Tracy felt compelled to say something.

'What do you think he was doing there?'

Abbie warmed her hands on her cup. Instead of answering Tracy's question, she changed the subject.

'Does Matt like me?'

'What?'

The question made Tracy very uncomfortable.

'Has he said anything . . . ?' She paused and looked across the table at Tracy. 'Do you think he likes me?'

All of a sudden, Abigail Griffen seemed terribly vulnerable to Tracy.

'I think he believes you,' she replied, warming to Abbie a little.

'Yes. He does,' Abbie said, more to herself than to Tracy.

Tracy was surprised to find herself feeling sorry for Abbie. She had thought a lot about her as a defendant, but she suddenly saw her as a person and she wondered what it must be like to be confined, even if the prison was as luxurious as the Griffen house. Mary Kelly had portrayed Abbie as an ice princess, but she did not seem very tough now.

Tracy suddenly realized how sad it was that Mrs. Griffen had looked forward to her visit and she reevaluated her earlier opinion that Abbie was coming on to Reynolds to blind him to her possible guilt. Abbie was totally alone and Matthew was one of her few links to the outside world. Tracy had read about hostages in the Middle East and kidnap victims, like Patty Hearst, who became dependent on their kidnappers and developed a bond with them. The condition even had a name, the Stockholm syndrome. Maybe Abbie's enforced isolation was making her dependent on Reynolds and that was why she appeared to be playing up to him.

'Are you getting along okay?' Tracy asked.

'I'm lonely. I'm also bored to death. I tried to convince myself that this would be like a vacation, but it's not. I read a lot, but you can't read all day. I even tried daytime

television.' Abbie laughed. 'I'll know I'm completely desperate when I start following the soaps.'

'The trial will start soon. Mr. Reynolds will win and
your life will go back to normal.'

'I'd like to think that, but I doubt my life will ever be
normal again, even if Matt wins.' Abbie stood up. 'I'll get
you the camera.

When Abbie went upstairs, Tracy waited in the entryway. Abbie returned with a camera case. She handed it to
Tracy.

'Thank you for having the cup of coffee. I know you
didn't want to.'

'No, I . . .'

'It's okay. I was hungry for company. Thanks for
putting up with me.'

They shook hands and Tracy took the camera. As she
pulled out of the driveway, she glanced back at the house.
Mrs. Griffen was watching her from the front door.

3

2313 Lee Terrace was a single-story brown ranch-style
house with a well-tended yard in a pleasant middle-class
neighborhood. A nondescript light blue Chevy and an
equally nondescript maroon Ford were parked in the
driveway. As the officers assigned to raid the house drew
closer to it, they could hear the muted sounds of music.

Inside the living room of the house, three young

women sat in front of a low coffee table talking and laughing while they worked. In the center of the table was a large plate piled high with cocaine. The woman on the end of the couch closest to the front door picked up a small plastic bag from a pile and filled the bag with cocaine. The next woman folded over the Baggie, then used a Bic lighter to seal it. The third put the sealed Baggie in a cooking pot that was close to overflowing with packaged dreams.

Two men in sleeveless tee shirts lounged in chairs, smoking and watching MTV. One man cradled an Uzi. A MAC-10 submachine gun was lying next to the second man's chair within easy reach. Two other men with automatic weapons were in the kitchen playing cards and guarding the back of the house.

Bobby Cruz watched the women work. He was doing his job, which was to protect Raoul Otero's product. From his position he would see if one of the women tried to slip a Baggie down her blouse or up her skirt. Cruz knew that the women were too frightened of him to steal, but he hoped they would anyway, because Raoul permitted him to personally punish the offender.

'Julio,' Cruz said. One of the men watching TV turned around. 'I'm going to pee.'

Julio picked up the MAC-10 and took Cruz's post against the wall. Cruz knew that Julio would not be tempted to look the other way by a glimpse of breast or thigh and a promise of future delights. Once upon a time, Cruz had forced Julio to assist him while he interrogated

259

a street dealer Raoul suspected of being a police informant. Ever since, Julio had been as frightened of Cruz as the
women were.

As Cruz walked down the hall toward the bathroom,
the front and back doors exploded.

'Police! Freeze!' echoed through the house. Cruz heard
the women scream. One of them burst down the hall
behind him as he ducked into the bedroom. There were
more screams in the front room and shots from the
kitchen. Someone was shrieking in Spanish. An Anglo
was bellowing that he'd been hit. Cruz calmly ran through
his possible courses of action.

'Put 'em down,' someone yelled in the living room.
Cruz opened the clothes closet and moved behind the
clothes hangers. The closet was crowded with dresses
because two of the women who were packaging the
cocaine lived here. Cruz pressed himself into a corner of
the closet and waited. The odds were that someone would
search the closet. If it was his fate to be arrested, he would
go peacefully and let Raoul fix things later. But he would
try to cheat fate if that was at all possible.

There were heavy footfalls in the bedroom. He heard
the voices of two men. The closet door opened. Cruz could
see a man in a baseball cap and a blue jacket through a
break in the dresses. He knew these jackets. They were
worn on raids, and POLICE was stenciled on the back in
bold yellow letters.

'Sanchez, get in here,' someone called from the hall.
'This asshole claims he doesn't *habla inglés*.'

The man at the closet door turned his head to watch Sanchez leave. When he turned back, Bobby Cruz stepped through the curtain of dresses and calmly stuck his knife through the officer's voice box. The policeman's eyes widened in shock. His hands flew to his throat. He tried to speak, but he could only gurgle as blood and spittle dripped out of his mouth. Cruz pulled the policeman through the dresses and laid his body on the floor. He was still twitching when Cruz worked off his jacket, but he was dead by the time Cruz adjusted the baseball cap and slipped out of the bedroom into the hall.

A policeman rushed by Cruz without seeing him. Cruz followed the man into the kitchen. Two men lay on the floor, their hands cuffed behind them. They were surrounded by police. A wounded officer was moaning near the sink and several men huddled around him. A medic rushed through the back door into the kitchen. Cruz stepped aside to let him in, then drifted into the backyard and faded into the night.

Two houses down, Cruz cut through the backyard, dropping the police jacket and cap. Then he headed toward a bar that he knew had a phone. In the three years Raoul had been using 2313 Lee Terrace they had never had any problems. The people at the house were all family or trusted employees and they were all extremely well paid. They might cop some cocaine, but they would never go to the police. But someone had, and whoever it was knew a lot about Raoul's operation if he knew about Lee Terrace.

PART FIVE
THE MAGIC SHOW

Chapter Twenty

1

Matthew Reynolds chose five o'clock on the Friday before the trial to review the questions he would ask during jury selection. Tracy knew better than to complain. With the trial so close, all hours were working hours.

Reynolds was explaining his system for questioning jurors about their views on the death penalty when his secretary buzzed to tell him that Dennis Haggard was in the reception area.

'Do you want me to leave?' Tracy asked.

'No. I definitely want you to stay. This could be very interesting.'

Dennis Haggard was balding, overweight and unintimidating. He was also Jack Stamm's chief criminal deputy and an excellent trial attorney. Reynolds walked over to Haggard as soon as the secretary showed him in.

'Don't you ever quit?' Haggard asked as he looked at the files, charts and police reports strewn around Matthew's office.

Matthew smiled and pointed to his associate. 'Do you know Tracy Cavanaugh?'

'I don't think we've met.'

'She just started with me. Before that, she clerked for Justice Sherzer.'

As Haggard and Tracy shook hands, Haggard said, 'The Department of Labor takes complaints. If he works you more than seventy-six hours straight, there's a grievance procedure.'

Tracy laughed. 'I'm afraid we're way past seventy-six hours, Mr. Haggard.'

Reynolds seated himself behind his desk. Tracy took a stack of files off the other client chair so Haggard could sit on it.

'What brings you here, Dennis?' Reynolds asked.

'I've come because Chuck Geddes wouldn't.'

'Oh?'

'He's still mad about the bail decision and this put him through the roof.'

'And "this" is?'

'A plea offer, Matt. Geddes wouldn't consider it, but the AG insisted. Then Geddes said he'd quit rather than make the offer, so everyone agreed I would carry it over.'

'I see. And what is the offer?'

'We drop the aggravated-murder charge. There's no death penalty and no thirty-year minimum. Abbie pleads to regular murder with a ten-year minimum sentence. It's the best we can do, Matt. No one wants to see Abbie on death row or in prison for life. Christ, I can't even believe we're having this conversation. But we wanted to give her the chance. If she's guilty, it's a very good offer.'

Reynolds leaned back and clasped his hands under his chin. 'Yes, it is. If Mrs. Griffen is guilty. But she's not, Dennis.'

'Can I take it that you're rejecting the offer?'

'You know I can't do that without talking to Mrs. Griffen.'

Haggard handed Matthew a business card. 'My home number is on the back. Call me as soon as you talk to Abbie. The offer is only good for forty-eight hours. If we don't hear by Sunday, Geddes takes the case to trial.'

Haggard let himself out. Reynolds turned back to his notes on jury selection. When he looked up, Tracy was staring at him.

'What's wrong?'

Tracy shook her head.

'If you're concerned about something, I want to know.'

'You're going to advise Mrs. Griffen to reject the offer, aren't you?'

'Of course.'

Tracy frowned.

'Say what's on your mind, Tracy.'

'I'm just . . . That was a good offer.'

Reynolds cocked his head to one side and studied his associate like a professor conducting an oral examination.

'You think I should advise Mrs. Griffen to accept it?'

'I don't think you should reject it out of hand. I can't help remembering what you told me in Atlanta.'

'And what was that?'

'When I asked you why you accepted the plea bargain for Joel Livingstone, you said that the objective in every death penalty case was to save our client's life, not to get a not-guilty verdict.'

Reynolds smiled. 'I'm pleased to see you've learned that lesson.'

'Then why won't you advise Mrs. Griffen to take this offer?'

'That's simple. Joel Livingstone murdered Mary Harding. There was no question of his guilt. Abigail Griffen is innocent of the murder of Robert Griffen. I have never advised an innocent person to plead guilty.'

'How can you know she's innocent?'

'She's told me she's innocent and until she tells me otherwise, I will continue to believe in her innocence.'

Tracy took a deep breath. She was afraid to ask the next question and afraid not to.

'Mr. Reynolds, please don't take offense at what I'm going to say. I respect your opinion and I respect you very much, but I'm concerned that we're making a mistake in not recommending this plea.'

Tracy paused. Reynolds watched her with icy detachment.

'Go ahead,' Reynolds said, and Tracy noticed all the warmth was gone from his voice.

'I can't think of another way to put this. Do you think it's possible that you're being influenced by your personal feelings toward Mrs. Griffen?'

Reynolds colored angrily. Tracy wondered if she had overstepped her bounds. Then Reynolds regained his composure and looked down at the jury selection questions.

'No, Tracy,' he said, his calm restored. 'I am not being influenced by personal feelings. And while I appreciate your concern, I think we've spent too much time on this matter. Let's get back to work.'

2

The days and nights were endless. Minutes seemed like hours. Abbie never expected it to be this way. She prided herself on being able to live alone. When she lost her parents, she built a shell around herself to keep out the horror of loneliness. Then she survived the death of her lover, Larry Ross. When her aunt passed on, she pulled inside the shell once more and she had been able to walk out on Robert Griffen without a backward glance, because she needed no one but herself. But now, trapped in the house, virtually helpless and almost totally deprived of human contact, her shell was cracking.

Even the weather was conspiring against her. The sunny days of summer had given way to the chill of fall and it was often too cool to sit outdoors. She would have given anything to take a walk, but the bracelet on her wrist was a constant reminder that even such simple pleasures were forbidden to her.

On Friday night, the weather was balmy. A last-gasp attempt by nature to fight off the cruel and depressing rains that were sure to come. Abbie sat on the patio, close to her invisible electronic wall, and watched the sunset. A large glass of scotch rested on the table at her elbow. She was drinking more than she wanted to, but liquor helped her sleep without dreams.

A flock of birds broke free from the trees at the edge of her property and soared into the dying light in a black and noisy cloud. Abbie envied them. Her spirit was weighted down by the gravity of her situation and confined to a narrow, airless place in her breast. Even Matthew's boundless confidence could not give it wings.

The sound of tires on gravel made Abbie's heart race, as it did whenever there was any break in the monotony of her routine. She left the glass of scotch on the table and hurried to the front door. She smiled when she saw that it was Matthew. He had been so good to her, visiting almost every day on the pretext that he was working on her case, when she knew that most of what they discussed could have been covered in a short phone call.

'How are you?' Matthew asked, as he always did.

'I was on the patio, enjoying the weather.'

'May I join you?'

'Of course. A drink?'

'No, thanks.'

They walked through the living room in silence, then

stood side by side on the patio for a moment without speaking.

'Are you ready for trial?' Matthew asked.

'I should be asking you that.'

Matthew smiled. Abbie was pleased to see that he was not as stiff around her as he had been when they first met.

'Actually,' she said, 'I can't wait. I would endure anything to get out of here.'

'I can't imagine how hard it's been for you.'

Abbie turned toward Matthew. She felt she could say anything to him.

'It hasn't been hard, Matt, it's been hell. Do you know what the worst part is? The absence of phone calls. Except for you and the electronic surveillance monitors, my phone never rings. Before the indictment, I had my work to occupy me. I guess it kept me from realizing how alone I've been. I think you may be the last person left who cares about me.'

'The people who have deserted you aren't worthy of your friendship,' Matthew said. 'Don't waste your time worrying about them.'

Abbie took his hand. 'You've been more than my attorney, Matt. You've been my friend and I'll never forget that.'

Matthew needed all of his courtroom skills to keep from showing how happy her simple words had made him.

'I'm glad you think of me that way,' he said as calmly as he could.

Abbie squeezed his hand, then let it go. 'Why did you come out?'

'Business. Dennis Haggard visited me. He made a plea offer . . .'

'No,' Abbie said firmly.

'I have an ethical obligation to communicate the offer. They'll take a plea to murder. Life with a ten-year minimum sentence. There would be no possibility of a death sentence.'

'I'm innocent. I will not plead guilty to a crime I did not commit.'

Matthew smiled. 'Good. That's what I hoped you'd say.'

'You're that certain you'll win?'

'I'm positive.'

'I'm scared, Matt. I keep thinking about what will happen if we lose. I used to think I could take anything, but I can't. If I have to go to jail . . .'

Abbie looked as frightened and vulnerable as a child. Matthew hesitated for a second, then put his arms around her. Abbie collapsed into him, letting go completely. Matthew wished he could make time stop, so he would never have to let her go.

Chapter Twenty-one

1

Matthew Reynolds was right. While working on *State of Oregon* v. *Abigail Griffen*, Tracy did not have time to run or rock-climb or eat right, and she sure wasn't sleeping right. But she didn't care. Trying a death penalty case was more exhilarating than anything she had ever done.

All her life Tracy had been fiercely competitive. That was why she had turned down jobs at several corporate law firms, which offered more money, to work for Matthew Reynolds. Criminal law provided the biggest challenge. There were no higher stakes than life or death. She played for those stakes occasionally when she climbed, but the life that was at risk was her own. It surprised her how much more difficult it was when the life in the balance was someone else's and that person was totally helpless and dependent on her skills.

When Reynolds spoke about the lawyers who visited

their clients after dark during her interview, Tracy felt an electric current passing through her. Reynolds had never faced the ultimate failure of watching a client die, and she vowed that it would never happen to her.

Matthew had put her in charge of the legal research so he could concentrate on the facts of the case. This was tremendously flattering because Reynolds was known nationally for his innovative legal thinking. But it also meant working in the library from morning to night, learning everything there was to know about the specialized area of death penalty law, as well as the legal issues that were specific to Abbie's case. Tracy's head was so crammed with information that she was waking up at odd hours with ideas that had to be jotted down. When the alarm startled her out of bed each morning, she was groggy, but an adrenaline high kicked in and carried her through days that passed in a flash.

Once the trial started, Tracy set her alarm even earlier so she could meet Reynolds at the office at six-thirty for the day's pretrial briefing. At eight-thirty, Barry Frame would arrive with Abigail Griffen and they would drive to the Multnomah County Courthouse, where they would fight their way through the crowd of reporters and spectators who mobbed the fifth-floor corridor outside the courtroom.

Their judge, the Honorable Jack Baldwin, was a gaunt, diminutive man with curly gray hair and a pencil-thin mustache. His complexion was unnaturally pale. When they were introduced, Tracy noticed liver spots on the back of the judge's hand and felt a slight tremor when they shook. Lines on his face showed Baldwin's seventy-four years. The Oregon constitution made it mandatory that judges retire at seventy-five.

Although Baldwin was dwarfed by Geddes and Reynolds, he carried himself with an easy authority that commanded respect and made him seem equal in stature to the attorneys. Baldwin had a reputation for being fair and his intelligence was unquestioned. The judge let the parties know that his last major trial was going to be a model for death penalty litigation.

The first week and a half in court was taken up with jury selection and opening statements. On Thursday of the second week, Geddes called his first witness, the attorney who represented Justice Griffen in his divorce. When he was through testifying on direct examination, the jury was fully aware that Abigail Griffen stood to lose a lot of money if the divorce became final. Tracy was worried about the damage the testimony had caused, but Matthew's cross-examination left everyone in the courtroom convinced that two million dollars was chump change for a woman like Abbie Griffen.

Next Geddes called Jack Stamm, who reluctantly told the jury about Abbie's angry reaction when she learned that Justice Griffen had authored the opinion that reversed the conviction of Charlie Deems. Stamm's testimony was no surprise to the defense. He believed in Abbie's innocence and had spoken freely with Matthew and Barry Frame before the trial.

'Mr. Stamm,' Matthew asked the district attorney when

275

it was his turn to cross-examine, 'are your deputies usually overjoyed when the case of a convicted criminal is overturned on appeal?'

'No, sir.'

'Have you heard deputy district attorneys other than Mrs. Griffen curse a particular judge because that judge wrote an opinion reversing a conviction?'

'Yes.'

'So Mrs. Griffen's reaction was not unusual?'

'No, Mr. Reynolds. She reacted the way a lot of my deputies react when a case is reversed.'

Reynolds smiled at Stamm. 'I suspect even you have taken the name of a few appellate judges in vain?'

'Can I take the Fifth on that?' Stamm answered with a grin. Everyone in the courtroom laughed, except Chuck Geddes.

'I'm going to let him exercise his rights here, Mr. Reynolds,' Judge Baldwin said with a smile.

'Very well, Your Honor. I'll withdraw the question. But I do have another for you, Mr. Stamm. How seriously does Mrs. Griffen take her cases?'

Stamm turned to the jury.

'Abigail Griffen is one of the most dedicated prosecutors I have ever met. She is brilliant, thorough and scrupulously fair.'

'Thank you, sir. No further questions.'

'Mr. Geddes?' Judge Baldwin asked. Geddes thought about going after Stamm, but he knew Stamm would try to help Griffen if given the chance.

'No further questions, Your Honor. The state calls Anthony Rose.'

Tony Rose entered the courtroom looking impressive in his police uniform. He would not look at Abbie. When he took the witness stand, he sat with his shoulders hunched and shifted uncomfortably in his seat. Geddes established that Rose was a police officer who had testified in several cases which Abigail Griffen had prosecuted. Then he stood up and walked over to the end of the jury box farthest from the witness.

'Officer Rose, when did you learn that the Supreme Court had reversed the conviction of Charlie Deems?'

'The day it happened. It was all over the station house.'

'At some point after you learned of the reversal, did you have an opportunity to talk about it with the defendant?'

'Yes, sir.'

'Tell the jury about that conversation.'

'There's an Italian place, Caruso's. It's downtown on Second and Pine. I eat there every once in a while. One night I saw Mrs. Griffen, the defendant, as I was leaving. She was by herself, so I went over to say hello. While we were talking, I told her I was sorry the case was reversed.'

'What was her reaction?'

'She was furious.'

'Did she mention her husband, Justice Griffen?'

'Yeah, and, uh, she wasn't too complimentary.'

'What did she say about him?'

'She called him a son of a bitch and she said he reversed the case to get her. I guess she was going through a divorce and figured he was trying to make her look bad.'

Geddes paused long enough to get the jurors' attention. Then he asked, 'Officer Rose, did Mrs. Griffen tell you about something she wished Charlie Deems would do to Justice Griffen?'

'Yes, sir. She did.'

'Tell the jury what she said.'

'Right after she said she thought the judge had reversed the case to make her look bad, she said she hoped Deems would blow Justice Griffen to kingdom come.'

Geddes nodded. 'Blow him to kingdom come. Those were her words?'

'Yes, sir. They were.'

Geddes turned toward Matthew Reynolds. 'Your witness, Counselor.'

Rose turned toward the defense counsel table, but he still refused to look Abigail Griffen in the eye. Matthew Reynolds stood and walked slowly toward the witness stand.

'You don't like Mrs. Griffen, do you?' Matthew asked, after taking a position that would not block the jurors' view of the witness.

Rose shrugged nervously. 'I've got nothing against her.'

'Do you respect her, Officer Rose?'

'What do you mean?'

'Is she a woman you treat with respect?'

'Well . . . Yeah. Sure. I respect her.'

'Did you treat her with respect on the evening you have spoken about?'

Rose shifted nervously in his seat.

'Your Honor, will you instruct Officer Rose to answer.'

'You must answer the question,' Judge Baldwin said.

'Look, that was a misunderstanding.'

'I don't believe we were discussing a misunderstanding, Officer. We were discussing the concept of respect in the context of the respect a gentleman should have for a lady. Did you treat Mrs. Griffen with respect that evening?'

'I thought she was sending signals. I was wrong.'

'Signals that indicated she wished to be raped?'

'Objection,' Geddes shouted.

'This goes to bias, Your Honor.'

'Overruled,' Judge Baldwin said. 'Answer the question, Officer.'

'I didn't try to rape the defendant.'

'Then why did she have to slap you to make you leave her house?'

'She . . . Like I said, there was a misunderstanding.'

'That reached the point where she had to use physical force to make you leave her home?'

'That wasn't necessary. If she'd asked I would have left.'

'At the time Mrs. Griffen slapped you, was she pinned to the wall?'

'I . . . I'm not certain.'

'Was your hand up her dress?'

'Look, everything happened very fast. I already said it was a mistake.'

'This was not the first time Mrs. Griffen had rebuffed you, was it?'

'What do you mean?'

'On two occasions, when she was trying to prepare your testimony for trial, did you make sexual advances to her?'

'It wasn't like that.'

'How was it, Officer Rose?'

'She's a good-looking woman.'

'So you suggested a date?'

'I'm only human.'

'And she was married. You knew that when you propositioned her, did you not?'

Rose looked toward Chuck Geddes for help, but the prosecutor was stone-faced.

'Did you know she was married when you propositioned her the first time?'

'Yes.'

'And the second time? You were still aware that she was a married woman?'

'Yes.'

'Nothing further, Officer Rose.'

2

'You were fantastic,' Abbie said as soon as her front door closed. 'You crucified Rose.'

'Yes, but the jury heard that you wished Deems would blow up Justice Griffen.'

'It doesn't matter. Rose's credibility was destroyed. You weren't watching the jurors. You should have seen the way they were looking at him. They were disgusted. If that statement's all they've got . . .'

'But we know it isn't. There has to be something more.'

'Well, I don't want to think about it now. I want to relax. Can I get you a drink?'

'I have to work tonight. Geddes is calling several important witnesses tomorrow.'

'Oh,' Abbie said, disappointed.

'You know I want to stay.'

'No, you're right. It's just . . . I don't know. I'm so happy. Things went well for once. I want to celebrate.'

'We'll celebrate when you're acquitted.'

'You believe I will be, don't you?'

'I know you'll never go to prison.'

Abbie was standing inches from Matthew. She reached out and took his hand. The touch paralyzed him. Abbie moved into his arms and pressed her head against his chest. She could hear his heart beating like a trip-hammer. Then she looked up and kissed him. Matthew had imagined this moment a thousand times, but never believed it would really happen. He felt Abbie's breasts press against his chest. He let his body fit into hers. Abbie's head sank against his chest.

'When this is over, we'll get away from here,' Abbie said. 'We'll go to a quiet place where no one knows us.'

'Abbie . . .'

She placed her fingertips against Matthew's lips.

'No. This is enough for now. Knowing you care for me.'

'I do care,' Matthew said, very quietly. 'You know I care.'

'Yes,' Abbie said. 'And I know you'll win I know you'll make me free.'

Chapter Twenty-two

1

'The state calls Seth Dillard,' Chuck Geddes said. Tracy checked off Dillard's name on the defense witness list. Dillard followed Mrs. Wallace, who told the jury about Abbie's hysterical appearance at her door on the evening of the attack at the coast.

'What is your profession?' Geddes asked.

'I'm the sheriff of Seneca County, Oregon.'

'Sheriff, if I wanted to buy some dynamite to clear stumps on property in Seneca County, what would I have to do?'

'You'd have to come to my office and fill out an application for a permit to purchase explosives. There's a fifteen-dollar fee. We'd take a mug shot and print you to make certain you weren't a felon. If everything checked out, you'd go to the fire marshal, who'd issue you a permit.

Once you had the permit, you'd take it to someone who sells explosives.'

'Did Justice Griffen secure a permit from your office for dynamite to clear stumps on his property?'

'Yes.'

'When did he do that?'

'Middle of the summer. July third.'

'Now, Sheriff, a week or so before Justice Griffen was killed did you investigate a complaint by the defendant that she had been attacked by an intruder in her cabin?'

'I did.'

'Can you tell the jury what the defendant told you about the alleged attack?'

'Early Saturday morning, August thirteenth, I interviewed Mrs. Griffen at a neighbor's house. She claimed that a man broke into her cabin close to midnight on the twelfth and she escaped by jumping from her second-story deck. According to Mrs. Griffen, the man chased her and she hid in the woods until she thought he was gone. About three-thirty A.M., she woke up the neighbor, Mrs. Wallace, by pounding on the door.'

'Did the defendant see the face of this alleged intruder?'

'Mrs. Griffen said the man wore something over his face.'

'I see. Now, Sheriff, did the defendant tell you about another alleged attack that occurred two weeks before this alleged attack at the coast?'

'Yes, sir. She said she thought the same person tried to break into her house in Portland.'

'Did she report this alleged break-in to the police?'

'Mrs. Griffen said she didn't.'

'Did she see who attempted this alleged break-in in Portland?'

'She told me that the man also wore a mask in Portland, so she didn't see his face.'

'Now, Sheriff, despite the fact that Mrs. Griffen never saw this person's face, did she suggest a person for investigation?'

'Yes. She said she thought her attacker might be a man she put on death row a year or so ago, who just got out of prison.'

'Charlie Deems?'

'Right, but it wasn't much of an ID. More like a guess.'

'She was the one who brought up the name?'

'Yes.'

'Sheriff Dillard, did you find anything at the crime scene linking Charlie Deems to the alleged attack?'

'No.'

'What did your investigation turn up?'

Dillard weighed his answer carefully. Then he told the jurors, 'Truthfully, we haven't found much of anything.'

'I don't follow you.'

'We don't have any evidence that anyone besides Mrs. Griffen was there. We did not find Mr. Deems's prints in the cabin. There was no sign of forced entry and nothing was taken. Mrs. Griffen says that she and the intruder jumped from the deck. Well, someone did jump from the deck, but the ground was so churned up we can't say if it was one person or two. When it got light I walked the trail along the bluff where she said she was chased by this fella and I searched the woods. I didn't find anything to support her story. Neither did my men.'

'Thank you, Sheriff. No further questions.'

Matthew Reynolds reviewed his notes. The jurors shifted in their seats. A spectator coughed. Reynolds looked up at the sheriff.

'How did Mrs. Griffen seem to you when you questioned her?' Matthew asked.

'She was shaken up.'

'Would you say her behavior was similar to other assault victims you've interviewed?'

'Oh, yeah. She definitely acted like someone who'd been through an ordeal. Of course, I wasn't looking for deception. After all, she's a district attorney. I naturally assumed she'd be telling the truth and she didn't do anything that raised my antennas.'

'You've testified that you haven't found any evidence to corroborate Mrs. Griffen's story. If the intruder wore gloves, you wouldn't find fingerprints, would you?'

'That's right. And I don't want to be misunderstood here. I'm not saying Mrs. Griffen wasn't attacked. I'm just saying we haven't found any evidence that there was an intruder. There could have been. She sure seemed like someone who'd been attacked. I just can't prove it.'

'One thing further, Sheriff. About a week or so after Justice Griffen was killed, did you receive a call from Mr. Geddes's investigator, Neil Christenson?'

'Yes, sir.'

'Did he ask you to go to the Griffen cabin and check in a shed behind it to see if there was a box of dynamite in the shed?'

'Yes, sir.'

'Did you find any dynamite?'

'Well, there was a cleared space on the floor of the shed big enough for the kind of box that holds it, but there wasn't any dynamite there.'

'Nothing further.'

'I have a few questions on redirect, Your Honor.'

'Go ahead, Mr. Geddes,' Judge Baldwin said.

'Did you or your men look in the shed on the day Mrs. Griffen reported the attack?'

'No, sir. There wasn't any reason to.'

'Did you post a guard at the Griffen cabin?'

'No reason to do that either.'

'So there was plenty of time and plenty of opportunity between the day of the alleged attack and the day you searched the shed for someone to remove the dynamite, if there was some in the shed on the day of the attack?'

'Yes, sir.'

Barry Frame was waiting in the courtroom when Matthew Reynolds returned from lunch. As soon as Reynolds walked through the door, Frame broke into a grin.

'Bingo,' he said, handing Reynolds a thick manila envelope.

'What's this?'

'Charlie Deems's bank records.'

'You found an account?' Reynolds asked excitedly.

'Washington Mutual. The branch across from Pioneer Square.'

'Have you reviewed the records?'

'You bet.'

'And?'

'See for yourself.'

Geddes's next witness was the neighbor who called 911 to report the explosion that killed Justice Griffen. He was followed by the first officers at the crime scene. Then Geddes called Paul Torino to the stand.

'Officer Torino, how long have you been a Portland police officer?'

'Twenty years.'

'Do you have a special job on the force?'

'Yes, sir. I'm assigned to the bomb squad.'

'What is your official title?'

'Explosive Disposal Unit Team Leader.'

'Officer Torino, will you tell the jury about your background and training in police work with an emphasis on your training in dealing with explosive devices?'

'Yes,' Torino said, turning toward the jury. 'I enlisted in the Army immediately after high school and was assigned to an Explosive Ordnance Disposal Unit. I received training in dealing with explosive devices at the United States Navy Explosive Ordnance Disposal training center at Indian Head, Maryland. Then,' Torino said with a grin, 'I served four years in Vietnam and received more practical experience in dealing with explosive devices than I really wanted.'

Two male jurors chuckled. Tracy noted that they were both veterans.

'What did you do after the Army?'

'I went to college and received an AA from Portland Community College in police science. Then I joined the force. After three years, which is the minimum experience you need, I qualified for the month-long course run by the FBI at the Hazardous Device Division of Redstone Arsenal in Huntsville, Alabama.'

'Did you graduate from that course?'

'Yes, sir.'

'Do you have any more formal training in dealing with explosive devices?'

'I'm a graduate of a two-week post-blast investigative school run by the Bureau of Alcohol, Tobacco and Firearms. I'd estimate that I have a total of more than fourteen hundred hours of formal education in bomb disposal through the military and the government.'

'How long have you been doing post-blast investigation for the Portland police?'

'Around twelve years.'

'Did you go to the home of Oregon Supreme Court Justice Robert Griffen in your capacity as Team Leader of the Explosive Disposal Unit?'

'Yes.'

'Were you the first unit to arrive at the scene?'

'No, sir. A Fire Rescue Unit and uniformed officers were the first to respond. As soon as it was determined that an explosive device had been detonated, they secured the scene, notified us, the medical examiner and the homicide detectives, then backed off until we checked the scene to make certain there were no more unexploded bombs.

'We made a determination that it was safe to proceed with the investigation. Before the victim was removed from the car, my people photographed the area to make a record of the scene.'

'What did you do then?'

'A bomb breaks up when it explodes and parts of the bomb are propelled to different areas of the crime scene. My people have a routine we follow. We roped off the area around the car and divided it into search areas. I had two men working at the seat of the blast, the place where the bomb was located. They examined the radius around the car to pick up pieces of the car and the bomb that were thrown off by the blast. I had other men working in other sections of the roped-off area. Whenever a piece of the bomb, or other relevant evidence, was found, an officer recorded where on the grid it was located and another officer took possession of the item and logged it in.'

'Officer Torino, can you tell the jury a little about how this bomb was constructed?'

'Certainly. All bombs have four things in common: explosives, an initiator, a power source and a switch or delay. When you look for a bomb, you see if you can find these components. This bomb consisted of a piece of pipe two inches in diameter and ten inches long that was filled with smokeless powder. A nine-volt battery was the power source. End caps sealed in the powder. These end caps flew off like they'd been shot from a rifle when the bomb exploded. The back end cap was found in the trunk, lodged in the frame of the car. The front end cap went through the garage door and was found embedded in the door of a refrigerator that was in the garage.

'The metal tube that made up the body of the bomb shattered into three pieces. One large part was found in the interior of the car lodged in the rear seat. Two other parts went through the roof of the car and were found on the lawn.'

'What set the bomb off?'

'A flashlight bulb was placed inside the body of the bomb in contact with the powder. The glass of the bulb was shattered. Wires from the bulb were threaded through one of the end caps and attached to a nine-volt battery. The wires were peeled back and the copper ends were wrapped around the teeth of a clothespin. Then a strip of plastic from a Clorox bottle was placed between the teeth of the clothespin, preventing the teeth from closing. The bomber attached a lead sinker to the strip of plastic. When Justice Griffen moved the car, the sinker held down the plastic strip and the strip was pulled out from between the teeth of the clothespin. That permitted the copper wires to touch, completing the circuit. A spark from the exposed wires in the lightbulb ignited the powder and caused the explosion.'

'How do you know all this about the bomb?'

'We located two short pieces of copper wire and the remains of the lightbulb embedded in the end cap we removed from the refrigerator door in the garage. A wooden clothespin was found in the front yard on the south side of the car. The plastic strip, monofilament fishing line and a lead sinker were found on the ground near the right front wheel. We also found a shattered battery, mostly intact.'

'Officer Torino, how was the bomb attached to the car?'

'We found chunks of magnets and nuts and bolts that had been bent and twisted from the blast. These did not match anything in the car, but I was familiar with them already, so I knew they were part of the bomb.'

'We'll get to that in a moment. Would you explain to the jury how the magnets were used?'

'Yes. A strip of metal eight inches long and two inches wide and a quarter inch thick was used. Holes were drilled in it and four magnets were affixed to the strip with nuts and bolts. Black electrical tape was then used to tape the strip to the bomb. When the bomb was ready to be used, it was pressed against the undercarriage of the car and the magnets held it in place.'

'Officer Torino, you mentioned that you were familiar with this bomb. Explain that statement to the jury.'

'A bomb of almost identical construction was the murder weapon in a case tried approximately two years ago.'

'Who was the defendant in that case?'

'Charles Deems.'

Geddes paused for effect, then faced the jury.

'Who was the prosecutor?'

'Abigail Griffen.'

'The defendant in this case?'

'Yes, sir.'

'Did the defendant know how to construct the bomb that killed her husband?'

'Yes.'

'How do you know that?'

'I showed her how to make one. We went into great detail so she could examine me about the construction of the bomb on direct examination. Then I told the jury the same information in court. It's in the record of the case.'

Geddes walked back to his table and picked up several plastic evidence bags. He returned to the witness stand and handed one of the plastic bags to Torino.

'This has been marked as State's Exhibit 35. Can you tell the jury what it is?'

Torino opened the plastic bag and took out a charred and twisted strip of metal approximately six inches long, one and a half inches wide and a quarter inch thick.

'Yes, sir. I personally took this from the Portland Police Bureau evidence room. This is the strip to which the magnets were attached by the bomber in the case Mrs. Griffen prosecuted against Mr. Deems.'

'Is there anything unusual about it?'

Torino held out one end of the strip to the jury. 'You can see that this end is flat and looks like it was shaped by a machine.' Torino turned the other end toward the jury.

'But this end is uneven and there is a notch that forms a jagged vee in the middle. That's because this strip came from a longer strip. Someone sawed it off of the large strip to shorten it so it would fit onto the top of the pipe bomb.'

'Is it unusual to find a notch like this in the strip that secures the magnets?'

'Yes, sir. With one exception, I've never seen a notch like this on another pipe bomb.'

'Was the defendant aware of the unique nature of the notch?'

'Oh yes. I told her that several times. She knew it was like a fingerprint.'

'So,' Geddes asked with heavy emphasis after turning toward the jury, 'the defendant was also aware that a Portland police explosives expert who found a strip of metal like this one with such a notch at the site of a bombing would immediately think that Mr. Deems was responsible for making the bomb?'

'Yes, sir.'

'Thank you. I now hand you State's Exhibit 36. What is it?'

Torino held up another strip of charred and twisted metal that was eight inches long, two inches wide and a quarter inch thick and very similar in appearance to State's Exhibit 35.

'This is the strip of metal to which the magnets were attached in the bomb that killed Justice Griffen. When the bomb exploded, it was blown through the bottom of the car into the judge. The medical examiner found it during the autopsy.'

'Is it similar to the strip used by the killer in the case which the defendant prosecuted against Mr. Deems?'

'Yes. One end is flat and the other has an almost identical notch.'

'How was that notch formed?'

'By putting the strip in a vise and using a hacksaw to cut it from the larger strip. The person who used the hacksaw cut from two directions and that's why the notch overlaps here,' Torino said, pointing to the center of the vee.

'And you say you've only seen one other magnet strip with a similar notch?'

'Yes, sir. The only other time I've seen one like it was in the case Mrs. Griffen prosecuted against Mr. Deems.'

'As an expert in the area of explosive devices, what conclusion do you draw from the similarity in appearance of these two strips?'

'Either the same person cut them or someone intentionally tried to make the second strip look like the first.'

'Why would someone intentionally do that?'

'One reason would be to frame Mr. Deems.'

'Objection,' Reynolds said, standing. 'That is pure speculation.'

'Sustained,' Judge Baldwin said, turning toward the jury. 'You jurors will disregard that last remark.'

'Officer Torino, you did say that the defendant knew about the unusual notch in the end of Exhibit 35?'

PHILLIP M. MARGOLIN

'Yes, sir. I pointed it out to her during the investigation of the Hollins murders.'

'Thank you. Now, Officer Torino, on the evening that Justice Griffen was killed, were you called to another location to search for explosive devices?'

'I was.'

'Where did you go?'

'To a home the defendant was renting. District Attorney Stamm was concerned that the same person who killed the judge might have rigged a bomb at Mrs. Griffen's house.'

'In the course of your search did you look in Mrs. Griffen's garage?'

'Yes, sir.'

'Describe it.'

'It was a typical two-car garage with a work area in one corner. The work area consisted of a workbench and table with a vise. Tools were hanging from hooks on the wall.'

Geddes handed Torino a photograph. 'Can you identify State's Exhibit 52 for the jury?'

'That's a shot of the garage.' Torino held up the photograph so the jury could see it and pointed to the left side of the picture. 'You can see the workbench over here.'

Geddes took the photograph and handed Torino the last plastic bag. It contained a clean strip of metal. It was not charred or twisted. One end was flat and obviously shaped by a machine. The other end came to a point. The point was jagged and appeared to have been cut by hand.

'This is State's Exhibit 37. Can you tell the jury what it is?'

Torino took Exhibit 36 in one hand and Exhibit 37 in the other and fit the jagged point from Exhibit 37 into the notch at the end of Exhibit 36.

'Exhibit 37 appears to be the other part of the longer strip from which Exhibit 36 was cut. They don't fit exactly because Exhibit 36 was mangled in the explosion.'

Geddes paused and turned toward Abigail Griffen.

'Did you find Exhibit 37, Officer Torino?'

'Yes, sir.'

'Where did you find it?'

'Under the workbench in Abigail Griffen's garage. You can see the strip in the bottom right corner of Exhibit 52. We also have a close-up in another photo.'

Tracy suddenly felt sick. Torino's testimony was devastating. She glanced quickly at the jurors. Every one of them was leaning forward and several were writing furiously on their notepads. Then she looked at Matthew. If he was feeling any stress as a result of Torino's testimony, Tracy could not see it.

'Officer Torino, there are what appear to be metal shavings in the plastic bag that we've been using to hold Exhibit 37. Where did they come from?'

'They were found on the floor under the vise.'

Geddes went back to counsel table and pulled a plastic Clorox bottle from a shopping bag.

'Can you tell the jury where State's Exhibit 42 was found?'

'It was also found in Mrs. Griffen's garage.'

Tracy glanced at Reynolds. He still appeared to be unconcerned.

'Your Honor, at this time I move to introduce State's Exhibits 35, 36, 37, 42 and 52,' Geddes said.

'Any objection, Mr. Reynolds?'

'May I see 42, please,' Reynolds said calmly as he climbed to his feet. Tracy could not believe how well he concealed the shock he had to be experiencing. Geddes handed Reynolds the Clorox bottle.

'May I ask a question in aid of objection, Your Honor?'

'Go ahead.'

'Officer Torino, this Clorox bottle is in one piece, is it not?'

'Yes.'

'Then it could not be the bottle from which was cut the plastic strip used in the detonating device?'

'That's true.'

Matthew turned toward the bench. 'I object to the admission of State's Exhibit 42. It has no relevance.'

'Mr. Geddes?' the judge said.

'It is relevant,' Geddes answered. 'This is obviously not the bottle from which the strip was cut, but it proves that the defendant uses the brand.'

'I'll let it in. It has limited relevance, but as long as it has some, it meets the evidentiary threshold for admissibility.'

'I have no further questions of this witness, Your Honor. Mr. Reynolds may examine.'

'Mr. Reynolds?' Judge Baldwin asked.

'May I have a moment, Your Honor?'

Baldwin nodded. Matthew turned to Abbie. His features were composed, but Tracy could tell that he was very upset.

'What was that metal strip doing in your garage?' he asked in a tone low enough to keep the jurors or Geddes from hearing what was said.

'I swear, I don't know,' Abbie answered in a whisper. 'My God, Matthew, if I made that bomb in the garage, don't you think I'd have the brains to get rid of anything that could connect me to it?'

'Yes, I do. But we're stuck with the fact that the strip was found in the garage of the house you were renting together with metal shavings that would be created when it was sawed off the rest of the strip. When was the last time you remember being around the worktable?'

'I put the car in the garage every evening. The people I'm renting from own the workshop furniture and the tools. I've never used them. Deems planted the strip and the shavings. Don't you see that? I'm being framed.'

'This is very bad,' Matthew said. 'Now I understand why Stamm felt he had to get off the case.'

Reynolds turned to Tracy. 'Do you remember seeing the three strips when we examined the physical evidence?'

'Of course, but I didn't think anything about them. They weren't together, I'm sure of that. If I recall, they were scattered among the other pieces of metal from the bomb and there were a lot of metal chunks on the table.'

'Geddes did that on purpose,' Matthew muttered. 'He set us up.'

'What are we going to do?'

Reynolds thought for a moment, then addressed the judge.

'Before I cross-examine, I have a matter I would like to take up with the court.'

Judge Baldwin looked up at the clock. Then he turned to the jurors. 'Ladies and gentlemen, this is a good time to take our morning recess. Let's reconvene at ten forty-five.'

As the jurors filed out, Barry came through the bar of the court and stood next to Tracy.

'As soon as we break for the day,' Reynolds told them, 'I want you two to look at all of the physical evidence again, to make certain there aren't any more surprises.'

The door to the jury room closed and Judge Baldwin said, 'Mr. Reynolds?'

'Your Honor, I would like to reserve my cross-examination of Officer Torino. His testimony, and this exhibit, are a complete surprise to the defense.'

'Will you explain that to me? Didn't Mr. Geddes let you know that he was introducing it?'

'There are no written reports about the metal strips that were used in the bombs and the strip found in Mrs. Griffen's garage . . .'

Chuck Geddes leaped to his feet. He was fighting hard to suppress a smile of satisfaction.

'Exhibits 35, 36 and 37 were listed on evidence reports supplied to the defense, Your Honor. We also made all

300

of the physical evidence available to the defense for viewing.'

'Is that so, Mr. Reynolds?'

Matthew cast a withering glance at Geddes, whose lips twisted into a smirk.

'Mr. Geddes may have listed the exhibits, Your Honor, but no report furnished to the defense explained the significance of the items. If I remember correctly, the strips were noted on the evidence list simply as pieces of metal and the three metal strips were scattered among the remnants of the bomb that killed Justice Griffen, giving the impression that all three strips were unconnected and found at the crime scene.'

'What do you have to say about that, Mr. Geddes?'

'The discovery rules require me to list all the witnesses and exhibits I intend to introduce at trial. They do not require me to explain what I intend to do with the exhibits or what my witnesses have to say about them. I did what was required by law. If Mr. Reynolds was unable to understand the significance of the exhibits, that's his problem.'

'Your Honor, there is no way any reasonable person could have understood the significance of this evidence,' Matthew answered angrily. 'Mr. Geddes made certain of that by scattering them among the other exhibits. Ask him why he did that and ask him why he didn't have Officer Torino write a report about them.'

'If you're implying that I did anything unethical . . .' Geddes started.

'Gentlemen,' Judge Baldwin interrupted, 'let's keep this civilized. Mr. Reynolds, if Mr. Geddes gave you notice that Officer Torino was testifying and he listed the strips as exhibits, he complied with the law. However, I want you to have a fair opportunity to cross-examine on this matter, which is of obvious importance. What do you suggest we do?'

'Your Honor, I would like to have custody of the three strips so I can have them examined by a defense expert. I have someone in mind.'

'How long will you need the evidence, Mr. Reynolds?'

'I won't know until I talk to my expert. He may be able to accomplish what I want this weekend.'

'I object, Your Honor,' Geddes said. 'We're in the middle of trial. Mr. Reynolds had ample opportunity to examine and test the evidence.'

'And I'm sure he would have if you'd given him some notice of the use to which you were putting it,' Judge Baldwin said sternly. 'Quite frankly, Mr. Geddes, while you're within the letter of the law on this, I don't think you're within its spirit.'

'Your Honor . . .' Geddes began, but Judge Baldwin held up his hand.

'Mr. Geddes this could have been avoided if you had informed Mr. Reynolds about Officer Torino's testimony in advance of trial. I'm going to let Mr. Reynolds have the metal strips, if he can find an expert to examine them.'

2

The rest of the afternoon was taken up with the testimony of several bomb squad members, who identified evidence taken from the crime scene and explained where each item was found. Outside, a gentle rain was falling, but the heat was on in the courthouse and the drone of the witnesses was putting Tracy to sleep. She sighed with relief when the judge called the weekend recess.

As soon as court was out, Matthew took custody of the three metal strips and left with Abigail Griffen. Tracy and Barry Frame looked over all of the evidence that was in the courtroom. When they were through, Neil Christenson escorted them to a conference room in the district attorney's office that was being used to store the physical evidence that had not been introduced. Some of the evidence was spread over the top of a long conference table. Other evidence was in cardboard boxes on the floor of the conference room. Christenson parked himself in a chair at the far end of the room.

'How about some privacy?' Barry asked.

'Sorry,' Christenson replied. 'If it was up to me, I'd be home with a cold beer, but Chuck told me to keep an eye on you.'

'Suit yourself.'

Tracy started with the items on the table, conferring with Barry in whispers if she saw anything that might be significant and making notes on a legal pad. When they were done with the items on top of the table, Barry cleared a space at one end and emptied the contents of the first cardboard carton, which contained items taken from Abbie's rented house.

Tracy's stomach was starting to growl by the time they finished with the evidence from the rented house and Barry emptied the first box of items from Justice Griffen's den. The box contained personal papers, household receipts, bills and other documents of this type. Tracy emptied a second box that contained papers found in the bottom right drawer of Justice Griffen's desk. At first glance, the papers looked like they would be similar to the papers in the other box. Then Tracy spotted something that was out of place. At the bottom of the pile was a volume from a trial transcript. A sheet from a yellow legal pad was jutting out from between two of the transcript pages. Tracy thought that Barry must have gone through this box when they looked through the evidence the first time, because she did not remember seeing the transcript before.

When Tracy saw the cover page of the transcript, she concealed her surprise. She was looking at Volume XI of *State of Oregon, Plaintiff-Respondent* v. *Charles Darren Deems, Defendant-Appellant*, the transcript Laura Rizzatti had been reading the day Matthew Reynolds and Abigail Griffen argued at the Supreme Court. Tracy remembered how nervous Laura had seemed when she found her reading it.

Tracy glanced over at Christenson. He was reading the sports section of *The Oregonian* and looked bored stiff.

Tracy shifted her body to block Christenson's view, then opened the transcript enough to see what was written on the sheet from the legal pad. The sheet was wedged between pages 1289 and 1290 of the transcript. It was a sheet from the legal pad on which Laura was writing in the library on the day Justice Pope accosted her. The names of three criminal cases were written on the page. Tracy remembered how quickly Laura had turned over the yellow pad to prevent Tracy from seeing what was on it. Tracy wrote down the names of the cases and the volume numbers of the Oregon reports in which they were published.

What was so special about the transcript and these cases, and what were this transcript and Laura's notes doing in Justice Griffen's den? The transcript was part of the official record of the *Deems* case and should be with the rest of the transcripts in the case in the file room of the Supreme Court.

Twenty minutes later, Barry stretched and announced, 'That's the lot.'

Christenson showed them out, then returned to the conference room. Barry pressed the down button on the elevator. As they waited for it to arrive, he asked, 'Any brilliant insights?'

Tracy was tempted to tell him about the transcript, but there was nothing to tell. She had no idea what was in Volume XI. Whatever was there wouldn't have anything to do with Abbie's case anyway.

'I didn't see anything I didn't spot the first time we

went through this stuff. If there are any more surprises, Geddes slipped them past me.'

'I agree. Are you up for dinner?'

Tracy wanted to get to the office so she could read Volume XI in the set of transcripts she'd taken from Bob Packard.

'I'll pass. I'm going to grab some takeout and head for the office. There are a few things I have to go over tonight.'

'Hey, it's the weekend. *Casablanca* is on. I thought we'd whip up some gourmet popcorn, crack open a bottle of wine and watch Bogie. You don't want to pass that up, do you?'

Barry sounded disappointed. The elevator doors opened. They stepped into the empty car. Tracy touched him on the arm.

'I'll tell you what. I'm big on Bogie myself. When's the movie start?'

'Nine.'

'Save me a seat. I should be able to finish by then.'

Barry grinned. 'I'll be waiting. Do you like red or white wine with your popcorn?'

'Beer, actually.'

'A woman after my own heart. I'll even spring for imported.'

Neil Christenson showed Barry Frame and Tracy Cavanaugh out of the district attorney's office, then he returned to the conference room and emptied the box with the evidence that had been found in the bottom right drawer of Justice Griffen's desk onto the conference table. Christenson had only been pretending to read the paper while Barry and Tracy went through the evidence and he noticed that Tracy was intentionally blocking his view when she went through this box. Christenson was determined to discover the piece of evidence that had created so much interest.

The transcript and yellow paper attracted his attention immediately because they were out of place. Christenson frowned when he saw that the transcript was from the *Deems* case. Then he remembered that Justice Griffen had written the opinion that reversed Deems's conviction. How ironic, he thought, that the person Justice Griffen had freed from prison was going to help convict the judge's killer.

Christenson flipped through the transcript, but found nothing that looked important. He put it down on the table and started on the other documents. There were miscellaneous papers, a file filled with correspondence between Justice Griffen and his stockbroker, another file with paperwork about his beach property and an envelope stuffed with credit card receipts. Christenson went through the receipts. Several were from a restaurant in Salem that was close to the court, a few were from stores in Salem and Portland, three were from a motel called the Overlook and a number of receipts were from gas stations. Nothing relevant to the case.

Christenson went through the contents of the box once

more, then gave up. It was late and he was tired. If Tracy Cavanaugh had spotted something important, it had gone right by him. Christenson yawned, closed the door to the conference room and headed home.

3

As soon as she was alone in the office, Tracy found Volume XI. To her great disappointment, it was incredibly dull. It contained the testimony of the police officers who searched Charlie Deems's apartment after his arrest. They told about items they had discovered during the search. Tracy could not imagine why Laura Rizzatti would have been interested in anything she read.

The sheet from Laura's yellow legal pad had been stuck between pages 1289 and 1290. Tracy wondered if that meant those pages contained something important or if the yellow sheet with the list of cases had ended up there by chance. When she reached pages 1289 and 1290, she found nothing that helped clear up the mystery.

Portland police detective Mark Simon's testimony started on page 1267 and continued past the two pages. He was the detective in charge of the search of Deems's apartment. In the early part of his testimony, he outlined the assignments of the officers who searched the apartment. Then he talked about various items found during the search and their significance to the homicide investigation. Deems had been arrested at a nightclub. Several people had phoned him while he was out. The direct examination by Abigail Griffen on pages 1289 and 1290 concerned messages found on Deems's answering machine.

'GRIFFEN: So these were messages that were waiting for the defendant, which he was unable to return because he was arrested?'

'SIMON: Yes, ma'am.

'Q: The jury has heard the message tape. I'd like to go through the messages with you and ask you to comment on their significance, if you can.'

'A: All right.

'Q: The first message is from "Jack." He leaves a number. What significance do you attach to that call?'

'A: I don't have enough information to comment on that call. The number was for a pay phone. We did send someone to the phone, but there was no one there when the officers arrived.'

'Q: Okay. Message number two was from Raoul. He leaves a pager number and asks the defendant to call him when he gets in. What is the significance of that call?'

'A: Okay. Well, with this one, I can comment. Subsequent investigation revealed that the pager was rented from Continental Communications by Ramón Pérez, a known associate of Raoul Otero. Mr. Otero is reputed to be one of the major players in an organization that distributes cocaine in Oregon, Washington, Texas and Louisiana. I believe this call indicates a connection between the defendant and this organization.'

'Q: Thank you. Now, the next call was from Arthur Knowland. He did not leave a phone number. He did say that he needed some "shirts" and wanted the defendant to call him as soon as possible.'

'A: Okay. I believe this call is from someone who wants to buy drugs from the defendant. We see this all the time when we have electronic surveillance on individuals who are talking about drug deals. They rarely use the names of narcotics in their discussions. They will call heroin or cocaine "tires" or "shirts" or whatever they have agreed on in the belief that this will somehow protect them if the person they are dealing with is an undercover officer or a recording is being made of their conversation.'

'Q: The last message is from Alice. She leaves a message and a phone number.'

'A: We contacted the person who subscribes to the phone number. Her name was Alice Trapp. She admitted that her call was an attempt to purchase cocaine.'

The examination continued on the next page, but it changed to a discussion of the contents of a notebook that had been found in Deems's bedroom. Tracy reread the two pages, but had no idea why they might be significant. Then she glanced at her watch. It was eight-thirty. Tracy put Volume XI back with the other transcripts and turned out the lights.

The idea of watching *Casablanca* with Barry Frame seemed like heaven compared to reading another page of boring transcript. In fact, spending the evening with Barry was preferable to anything else she could imagine.

The trial was leaving Tracy so exhausted that sex had been completely banished from her thoughts. Until now. She and Barry had not made love yet, but the way they felt about each other meant it was only a matter of time and the right setting.

Chapter Twenty-three

1

'You know the drill. Keep your head up, keep moving and let me do the talking,' Matthew told Abbie when Barry Frame stopped his car in front of the Multnomah County Courthouse on Monday morning. A torrential rain cascaded off the car as Matthew opened the back door on the driver's side. Huge drops bounced off of the hood and windshield. Matthew held up a large black umbrella to shield Abbie from the downpour. Tracy grabbed the huge leather sample case with the trial files, smiled quickly and shyly at Barry, then ran around the car to help screen Abbie from the crowd that blocked the courthouse entrance. She was soaking wet by the time they fought their way through the reporters and into the elevator.

The court guards recognized the defense team and

waved them around the metal detector that stood between the courtroom door and the long line of spectators. Matthew led the way through the low gate that separated the spectators from the court. He set his briefcase next to the counsel table and shook the water off the umbrella. When he turned around, Abbie was staring at Charlie Deems, who was lounging on a bench behind Chuck Geddes inside the bar of the court. Deems looked surprisingly handsome in a blue pinstripe suit, freshly pressed white shirt and wine-red tie that Geddes had purchased for his court appearance. His shoes were polished and his hair had been cut.

'Howdy, Mrs. Prosecutor,' Deems said, flashing his toothy grin. 'You learnin' what it feels like to be in the frying pan?'

Before Abbie could respond, Matthew stepped in front of her. He stared down at Deems. Deems stopped grinning. Reynolds held him with his eyes a moment more. Then he spoke in a voice so low that only Charlie Deems heard him.

'You are a hollow man, Mr. Deems. There is no goodness in you. If you tell lies about Mrs. Griffen in this courtroom, not even a dark angel will protect you.'

Charlie Deems turned pale. Reynolds turned his back to Deems. Deems leaped to his feet.

'Hey,' Deems shouted, 'look at me, you freak.'

Reynolds sat down and opened his briefcase. Deems took a step toward Matthew, his face tight with rage.

'What did you just say?' Geddes demanded of Reynolds

as he and Christenson restrained Deems. Matthew ignored Geddes and calmly arranged his notes while the prosecutor tried to calm his star witness.

'Mr. Deems,' Chuck Geddes asked, 'are you acquainted with the defendant?'

'In a manner of speaking.'

'Please explain how you two first met.'

'She prosecuted me for murder.'

'Had you ever met the defendant before she prosecuted you?'

'No, sir.'

'What was the result of your case?'

'I was convicted and sentenced to death.'

'Where did you spend the next two years?'

'On death row at the Oregon State Penitentiary.'

'Why aren't you still on death row?'

'The Oregon Supreme Court threw out my case.'

'It reversed your conviction?'

'Right.'

'And the Multnomah County district attorney's office elected not to retry you?'

'Yes.'

'Shortly after your release from prison, did the defendant contact you?' Geddes asked.

'Yes, sir. She sure did.'

'Did that surprise you?'

Deems laughed and shook his head in wonder. 'I would have been less surprised if it was the President.'

The jury laughed.

'Why were you surprised?' Geddes asked.

'When a woman spends a year of her life trying to get you executed, you start to think she might not like you.'

Deems smiled at the jury and a few jurors smiled back.

'Tell the jury about the conversation.'

'Okay. As I recollect, she asked me how it felt to be off death row. I said it felt just fine. Then she asked how I was fixed for money. I asked her why she wanted to know. That's when she said she had a business proposition for me.'

'What did you think she had in mind?'

'I knew she didn't want me to mow her lawn.'

The jurors and spectators laughed again. Tracy could see them warming to Charlie Deems and it worried her. She glanced at Reynolds, but he seemed completely unperturbed by Deems's testimony. Tracy marveled at the way he kept his cool.

'Did you ask the defendant what she wanted?' Geddes continued.

'I did, but she said she didn't want to discuss it over the phone.'

'Did you agree to meet the defendant?'

'Yes, sir.'

'Why?'

'Curiosity. And, of course, money. I was dead broke when I got off the row and she implied there was a lot of money to be made.'

'Where did you meet?'

'She wanted me to come to a cabin on the coast. She gave me directions.'

'Do you remember the date?'

'I believe it was Friday, August twelfth.'

Abbie leaned toward Reynolds. She was upset and Tracy heard her whisper, 'These are all lies. I never called him and we never met at the cabin.'

'Don't worry,' Tracy heard Reynolds say. 'Let him hang himself.'

'What happened when you arrived at the cabin?' Geddes asked.

'Mrs. Griffen was waiting for me. There were some chairs on the porch, but she wanted to sit inside, so no one would see us.

'At first she just made small talk. How was I getting by, did I have any jobs lined up? She seemed real nervous, so I just went along with her, even though it didn't make any sense.'

'What do you mean?'

'I knew damn well she wasn't concerned about my welfare. Hell, the woman tried to get me lethally injected. But I figured she'd get to it soon enough.'

'And did she?'

'Yes, sir. After we'd been talking a while, Mrs. Griffen told me she was real unhappy with her husband and wanted a divorce. But there was a problem. She was very rich. Justice Griffen's divorce lawyer was asking for a lot of money and she was afraid the court would give it to him. I asked her what that had to do with me. That's when she led me out back of the cabin and showed me the dynamite.'

'Where was this dynamite?'

'In a toolshed behind the house.'

'Describe the shed and its contents.'

'It's been a while and I only looked in a minute, but it seems like the shed was made out of weathered gray timber. The dynamite was in a box on the floor. I know there were some gardening tools in the shed, but I can't remember what kind.'

'What did Mrs. Griffen say to you when she showed you the dynamite?'

'She said she knew I was good with explosives and wanted to know if I could use the dynamite to kill her husband. She told me she had a workshop in her garage and I could make the bomb there. She also said no one would suspect us of working together since she was the one who prosecuted me.'

'What did you tell her?'

'I told her she'd made a big mistake. I said I didn't know anything about making bombs and that I hadn't killed any of the people she thought I'd killed. But even if I had, I wasn't going to kill the guy who was responsible for taking me off death row. Especially when that guy was a justice of the Oregon Supreme Court. You'd have to be an idiot. I mean, every cop in the state would be hunting you down if you killed someone important like that and they'd never give up.'

'What did the defendant say to that?'

'She offered me fifty thousand dollars. She told me I was smart and could figure out how to do it without being caught.'

'How did you respond?'

'I said I wasn't going to do it.'

'What did the defendant say then?'

'She got real quiet. I'd seen her in court like that. It made me a little nervous. Then she said she was sorry she'd troubled me. I didn't want to hang around any more than I had to, so I took off.'

'Did you go to the police after you left?'

'Are you kidding? She warned me about that. She said no one would believe me if I accused her, because the cops still thought I killed that kid and her father. She also said she'd have dope planted on me and send me away forever if she even heard I was in spitting distance of a police station or the DA's office.'

'Was that the last time you had any contact with Mrs. Griffen?'

'Yes, sir.'

'Despite her warning, you did come to the district attorney and explain what happened.'

'Yes, sir.'

'Why did you come forward?'

'Self-preservation. As soon as the judge was blown up, I knew she was trying to frame me. Hell, she did it once with that phony confession, and the newspapers said the bomb was similar to the one that killed Hollins and his kid. Then I heard the cops were looking for me. I figured my only chance was to go to the DA and hope he'd believe me.'

Geddes reviewed his notes, then said, 'No further questions.'

Deems had stared at Reynolds frequently during his testimony, growing frustrated when Matthew refused to pay any attention to him. The slight had been intentional. Matthew wanted Deems angry and combative.

'Did you know a man named Harold Shoe, Mr. Deems?' Matthew asked.

'Yeah, I knew Shoe.'

'Was he a drug dealer?'

'So they said.'

'Did "they" also say he was a rival of yours in the drug trade?'

'I don't know everything people said about Shoe.'

'Did you know that Mr. Shoe was tortured to death?'

'I heard that.'

'Did you also hear that Larry Hollins was prepared to identify you as the man he saw putting Mr. Shoe's body in a Dumpster?'

'My lawyer told me that after Hollins was killed. That's the first I knew of it.'

'While you were awaiting trial for the murder of Larry Hollins and Jessica Hollins, his nine-year-old daughter, did you have a cellmate named Benjamin Rice?'

'Yeah. The cops planted him in my cell.'

'Did you tell Benjamin Rice that Shoe was "a worthless piece of shit who couldn't even die like a man"?'

'I never said that. Rice made that up.'

'Did you tell Mr. Rice that it was "tough that the kid had to die, but that's the risk a snitch takes"?'

'I never said that either.'

Tracy cast a quick look at the jurors. They no longer looked amused by Charlie Deems.

'What time of day did you meet with Mrs. Griffen at the coast?'

'Late afternoon.'

'Can you be more specific?'

'She said to come out around four.'

'The sun was still shining?'

'Right.'

'And this meeting was arranged during the phone call you received from Mrs. Griffen?'

'Right.'

'Where were you when you received the call?'

'A friend's.'

'What friend?'

'Her name is Angela Quinn.'

'Did you go to Ms. Quinn's as soon as you were released from prison?'

'Yeah.'

'And you were in prison for two years?'

'Two years, two months and eight days.'

'And before that, you were in jail, awaiting trial?'

'Yes.'

'And before that, you lived in an apartment?'

'Right.'

'Not with Ms. Quinn?'

'No.'

'How did Mrs. Griffen know where to call you?'

'What?'

'You testified that you were living in an apartment when you were arrested, then jail, then prison. You've also testified that the first conversation you ever had with Mrs. Griffen was the phone call you received at Angela Quinn's residence. How would Mrs. Griffen know where to contact you? How would she know Angela Quinn's phone number?'

Deems looked confused and glanced at Chuck Geddes for help.

'While you're trying to think up an answer to that question, why don't you tell the jury what Mrs. Griffen was wearing when you met at the cabin.'

'Uh, let's see. Jeans, I think, and a tee shirt.'

'What color tee shirt?'

'Uh, blue, I think.'

'How long were you with Mrs. Griffen?'

'Forty-five minutes. An hour.'

'Face to face?'

'Yeah.'

'And you can't recall what she was wearing?'

'I wasn't paying attention,' Deems snapped angrily. 'I'm not a fashion expert.'

Deems sounded flustered and Geddes leaned over to confer with Neil Christenson.

'You talked inside the cabin, did you not?'

'Right.'

'Maybe you'll have better luck describing the furnishings of the cabin to the jury.'

'What do you mean?'

'Tell the jury what the inside of the cabin looked like. You should have no trouble if you were inside it for forty-five minutes to an hour.'

Several of the jurors leaned forward.

'Uh, there's a kitchen and a living room.'

'When you spoke with Mrs. Griffen, where did you sit?'

'In the living room.'

'Where in the living room?'

'Uh, on the couch.'

'What color is the couch?'

Deems paused for a moment. Then he shook his head. 'I don't really remember. Look, I told you, the woman wanted me to murder her husband. I wasn't paying attention to the furniture.'

'How about the living-room rug, Mr. Deems?' Reynolds asked, ignoring Deems's discomfort.

'I don't remember. Brown. Maybe, it was brown.'

'Can you tell the jury the color of anything in the Griffen cabin?'

Deems was upset. He shifted in his seat.

'Do you want to know why you can't recall the colors, Mr. Deems?' Deems just stared at Reynolds. 'It's because you were in the Griffen cabin but not when you claim you were there. You entered the cabin at night, after sunset, when you tried to kill Mrs. Griffen. In the absence of light, the human eye cannot distinguish colors.'

Deems flushed. He shook his head and glared at Reynolds.

'That's not it. I wasn't paying attention to colors. I was nervous. I mean, this woman prosecuted me for a murder I didn't commit. Then she turns around and asks me to kill her husband. Colors were the last thing on my mind.'

Reynolds picked up a stack of photographs and crossed the courtroom to the witness box. Then he smiled at Deems, but there was no warmth in it.

'By the way,' Matthew said, handing Deems one of the pictures, 'there is no rug in the living room. It's hardwood.'

'What are those photographs?' Geddes asked as he leaped to his feet.

'They are pictures of the cabin taken on August twelfth, the day Mr. Deems claims he visited Mrs. Griffen. The pictures were mentioned in discovery.'

'Objection,' Geddes said desperately. 'There's no foundation for them.'

'All of these photographs were taken by Mrs. Griffen. The camera she used date-stamped the negatives. I'll lay the foundation later,' Reynolds said.

'With that assurance, I'll permit you to use them,' Judge Baldwin ruled.

Deems examined the picture quickly. While the attorneys argued, he looked over at Abigail Griffen. She was smiling a hard, cold smile at him. Deems flushed with rage. He wanted Abbie to suffer, but she looked triumphant.

'Well?' Matthew asked. 'Is there a rug?'

'No,' Deems answered grudgingly. 'At least not in these pictures.'

'Do you have other photographs showing a rug in the Griffen cabin, Mr. Deems?' Reynolds snapped.

Suddenly, it appeared to Tracy that Charlie Deems had thrown a switch and cut off all of his emotions. The anger disappeared to be replaced by a deadly calm. The witness relaxed visibly and leaned back in his chair. Then he grinned at Matthew and answered, 'No, sir. These are the only photos I know about.'

Tracy was suddenly frightened for Matthew and glad that he was not alone with Charlie Deems.

'Thank you, Mr. Deems. Now, you've explained that Mrs. Griffen wanted you to use dynamite that was in a shed behind the house?'

'Right,' Deems replied evenly.

'You remember the dynamite because she showed it to you?'

'Definitely.'

Matthew Reynolds handed another picture to Deems. 'I remind you that the negative of this picture of the shed is date-stamped. Where is the dynamite?'

In the photograph, the shed door was ajar enough to show the interior. Deems saw gardening tools, a volleyball net and an empty space with a volleyball resting dead center. What he did not see was a box of dynamite.

'I don't know,' Deems said with a marked lack of interest. 'Maybe she moved it.'

Reynolds left the pictures and returned to the defense table. He picked up a manila envelope and walked back to Deems.

'I believe you said that you were tempted by Mrs. Griffen's offer of fifty thousand dollars because you could use the money?'

'Yes.'

'I assume you were broke when you left prison?'

'You assume right.'

'Have you gotten a job yet?'

'No.'

'Any savings?'

'No.'

'Did someone hire you to blow up Justice Griffen and frame Mrs. Griffen for the murder?'

Deems laughed. 'That's nonsense.'

'Then how do you explain this?' Reynolds said as he withdrew a sheaf of papers from the envelope and handed them to Charlie Deems. Deems completely lost his cool and his mouth gaped open. He looked at the bank records, then at Reynolds.

'What the hell is this?'

'A bank account at Washington Mutual in your name with a hundred thousand dollars in it.'

'I don't know anything about this,' Deems shouted.

'I see. Then I have no further questions.'

'Any redirect, Mr. Geddes?' Judge Baldwin asked.

'May I have a moment, Your Honor?'

Baldwin nodded and Geddes continued the intense

conversation he had been having with Neil Christenson since Matthew Reynolds announced the contents of the manila envelope. After a moment, Geddes stood. He had learned how to look composed in the worst situations from years of courtroom combat and he appeared to be unconcerned about the destruction of his key witness.

'Nothing further,' Geddes said. 'And the state rests.'

'I imagine you have some motions, Mr. Reynolds?' Judge Baldwin said.

'Yes, sir.'

'How many witnesses do you have?' the judge asked Matthew.

'Twenty-seven.'

'Can you put any of them on this afternoon?'

'I'd prefer to start tomorrow.'

'Why don't we take our morning recess now. I'll send the jury home. We can take up your motions after the recess, then take witnesses in the morning.'

The jurors filed out. As soon as the judge left the bench, Charlie Deems left the witness box. Chuck Geddes and Neil Christenson hustled Deems out of the courtroom and up the stairs to the sixth floor.

'Where did you get that money?' Geddes demanded as soon as they were in his office.

'That's not my account,' Deems said.

'It's in your name.'

'But I don't know anything about it. That fucker Reynolds set me up.'

'And I suppose he took the pictures of the shed, too?'

'I don't know anything about those pictures. There was dynamite in the shed when I was at the cabin.'

Geddes swiveled his chair toward the window. The picture of the shed and the bank account were devastating. There had to be an explanation. He hoped it did not have something to do with being duped by Charlie Deems.

'Wait outside,' Geddes told Deems. Deems seemed only too happy to leave the room.

'What the fuck is happening, Neil?' the prosecutor demanded when they were alone.

'Either Deems was paid off to pin Justice Griffen's murder on Abbie Griffen or someone set him up.'

'Damn it. Reynolds is making me look like a fool.'

'What do you want to do with Deems?'

'Keep him at the farm until we figure out what's going on. If that son of a bitch lied to me, I'll have his balls.'

2

Raoul Otero was staring at the gray roiling clouds and sheets of rain that obscured the view from his penthouse apartment in downtown Portland when Bobby Cruz sat down across from him. Raoul's mood was as black as the weather and the fifth of scotch he'd been working on all afternoon had only stoked his rage.

'You want some?' Otero asked, holding up the bottle.

'*No, gracias,*' Cruz answered politely. Otero was not

surprised. Except for violence, Bobby Cruz had no vices.

'Well?'

'It don' look good, Raoul. Deems testified for the DA.'

Otero stared at the Willamette River. No ships were moving on its turbulent waters. It was so dark the cars crossing the Hawthorne Bridge were using their headlights even though it was only four o'clock.

'Why is Charlie doing this? He beat his case. The cops don't have no leverage on him.'

'What I think is, he's doin' it to get even with the Griffen woman for putting him on the row.'

Raoul nodded in agreement. 'That piece of shit was always big on revenge. Remember how happy he was when I let him do Shoe?'

'Sí, Raoul. He could barely contain his joy. Our problem is that Griffen isn't the only one Charlie's mad at.'

'How can he be stupid enough to talk to the cops about me?' Raoul asked incredulously.

'Charlie isn't stupid, but he's mean. He's also loco. Charlie does what Charlie wants to do. That's why I told you not to have no dealings with him in the first place. Remember I said you can't control Charlie, because Charlie is always out of control?'

'And you were right. José called from Tijuana while you were at the courthouse. The feds busted the two border guards we had on the payroll. Charlie knew about them, just like he knew about Lee Terrace and the rest area on I-5.'

'There's only one thing to do,' Cruz said calmly.

Otero knocked down what was left of the scotch in his glass. He did not like being in this position, but that fuck Deems had put him in it. Killing someone always hurt business, because the cops had to work hard on a murder case. Still, normally the risk was small with someone like Charlie, because the cops wouldn't spend too much time looking into the murder of a dealer who'd offed a kid. But 'normally' might not apply anymore. Charlie was on the side of the angels. The cops were going to work overtime if someone took out the key witness in the murder of a Supreme Court justice. But that shit-for-brains, loco son of a bitch gave him no choice.

'Do you know where the cops have Charlie?'

'They're hiding him at a farmhouse. I followed them from the courthouse.'

'Can you do it?'

'It won't be easy. He has two cops guarding him.'

'You need help?'

Cruz smiled. '*No, gracias.* I think I will handle this myself.'

Raoul nodded. A red mist clouded his eyes. He wanted to smash something. He wanted to smash Charlie Deems. If the situation wasn't desperate, if they had not lost three shipments already, he would wait and personally carve up Charlie Deems like a fucking turkey. But there would be no more shipments until Charlie was dead, so he would have to let Bobby Cruz have the honor.

3

Neil Christenson arrived home at ten o'clock Monday night, after spending all evening listening to Chuck Geddes scream at Charlie Deems. Christenson changed into jeans and an OSU sweatshirt, then he settled into his favorite armchair and tried to get into a sitcom his wife, Robin, was watching.

At a commercial, Christenson went into the kitchen to fix himself a snack and Robin put on some water for tea. It was quiet in the house because the kids were asleep.

'Are you okay?' Robin asked.

'I'm just tired, but I'm thankful for a chance to forget about the *Griffen* case for a few hours.'

Robin gave him a sympathetic smile. 'Is it that bad?'

'Worse. Geddes has been driving me crazy ever since Reynolds took apart Deems this morning.'

Robin put her arms around her husband and gave him a compassionate kiss.

'The trial will be over soon,' she said. 'Maybe we can get away for a few days.'

Christenson held his wife and kissed the top of her head.

'What did you have in mind?'

'I don't know,' she answered coyly. 'Maybe we could shack up in a motel on the coast for a weekend. Mom can watch the kids.'

Christenson froze. 'That's it,' he muttered to himself.

Robin pulled back and looked at her husband. He was staring into space. Christenson gave her a tremendous hug and kissed her on the cheek.

'I've got to go,' he said.

'What? You just got home.'

'It was the receipts, Robin. You're a lifesaver.'

'What did I do?'

'You may have won the *Griffen* case.'

Christenson walked back into the living room and put on his shoes.

'You're not going out?'

'I'm sorry. I have to check something to see if I'm right. If I don't do it now, I won't be able to sleep.'

Robin sighed. She had been married to Neil for twelve years and she was used to his odd hours.

As he laced up his shoes, Christenson thought about the afternoon he had watched Tracy Cavanaugh and Barry Frame sift through the state's evidence. He had never figured out what piece of evidence had intrigued Tracy so much that she had felt it necessary to hide it from his view. Now he thought he knew what she had been looking at. Some of the credit card receipts in the box of evidence from the bottom right drawer in Justice Griffen's den had been from the Overlook Motel. Christenson knew that motel. Three years ago, there had been a murder there and he had visited it during the investigation. The Overlook was a dive. What was a Supreme Court justice doing there on three occasions? Robin had given him the answer. He was shacking up. But with who? Geddes's guess was Laura Rizzatti, and Christenson was going to see if Geddes was right.

4

Charlie Deems paced back and forth across his small bedroom on the second floor of the farmhouse. The rain had trapped him inside and he was going stir crazy. Not even the game shows made this dump bearable anymore. To make matters worse, that asshole Geddes and his flunky Christenson had grilled him all evening.

'Why wasn't there dynamite in the photo of the shed? Where did the money in the bank account come from? Did he kill Justice Griffen and frame Abigail Griffen?' And on and on, over and over again.

Deems was certain he knew what had happened, but he wasn't going to tell Geddes. What he was going to do was take care of this himself. He'd been set up by that bitch Griffen. How else could Reynolds have made a fool out of him? According to Geddes, the whole case was in the toilet and that smirking whore was going to walk. Well, she might walk away from this case, but she was never going to walk away from Charlie Deems. When he was through with her, Abigail Griffen was going to wish she had been convicted and sentenced to death, because what he had planned for her would make dying seem like a fucking picnic.

Chapter Twenty-four

1

'As our first witness,' Matthew said on Tuesday morning, 'the defense calls Tracy Cavanaugh.'

Tracy could not remember being this nervous since the finals of the NCAA cross-country championships. She knew that she was only a chain-of-custody witness, but being under oath was nerve-racking.

'Ms. Cavanaugh, what is your profession?'

'I'm an attorney, Mr. Reynolds.'

'What is your current position?'

'I'm an attorney in your office.'

'Have you assisted me in defending Mrs. Griffen since she retained my firm?'

'Yes, sir.'

'On September thirteenth, did I ask you to do something?'

'Yes.'

'Please tell the jury what I asked you to do.'

'You asked me to go to Mrs. Griffen's home and pick up a Pentax camera and film from her.'

'Where was the film?'

'In the camera.'

'What did you do with the film?'

'It was late evening when I picked up the camera, so I waited until morning and took it to FotoFast, a commercial developer. The clerk took the film out of the camera and signed a receipt stating that he had done so. Then I brought you the camera.'

Matthew handed Tracy a slip of paper. 'Is this the receipt you received from the clerk?'

'Yes, sir.'

'Later, did you go to FotoFast to pick up the developed film?'

'Yes. And I had the clerk sign a second statement.'

Reynolds picked up the envelope with the photographs and Abbie's camera and walked over to Tracy.

'I am handing you what has been marked as Defense Exhibit 222. Is this the camera you picked up from Mrs. Griffen?'

'Yes,' Tracy said after examining the small black Pentax.

'I hand you Defense Exhibit 223. Is this the envelope you picked up from FotoFast?'

'Yes.'

'Did you give this envelope to me?'

'Yes.'

'Did you review the photographs?'

'No, sir.'

'Thank you.'

Tracy handed the envelope back to Reynolds. As she did, she noticed that the photographs Matthew had shown to Deems were still on the ledge in the witness box where witnesses place exhibits they are viewing. She picked them up and gave them to Reynolds to put with the other photographs.

Just before Reynolds took the photo of the shed from her, Tracy frowned. She was certain there was something odd about the picture, but she could not figure out what it was in the brief moment she had to view the photograph.

'Nothing further,' Reynolds said as he placed the photographs in the envelope and walked to his seat.

'Mr. Geddes?'

Tracy looked at the prosecutor. He was sitting alone this morning and Tracy wondered why Neil Christenson was missing.

'No questions,' Geddes said, and Tracy was relieved to return to her seat at counsel table.

'The defense calls Dr. Alexander Shirov,' Matthew said.

Tracy wanted to look at the photograph of the shed, but Reynolds had placed the envelope with the pictures under a stack of exhibits by the time she was back at the counsel table.

When Dr. Shirov entered the courtroom, Tracy turned to look at him. She had questioned Reynolds about the identity of his expert and the results of the tests on the metal strips, because she was dying to know what he could possibly do about this seemingly incontrovertible evidence, but Reynolds just smiled and declined to name his witness or discuss the results.

Dr. Shirov walked with a slight limp and carried his notes in both hands. He was tall and heavy, a man in his mid-fifties with a slight paunch, salt-and-pepper hair and a full beard. He looked relaxed when he took the oath and he smiled warmly at the jury when he took his seat in the witness box.

'What is your profession?' Matthew Reynolds asked.

'I'm a professor of chemistry at Reed College in Portland.'

'Do you hold any other positions at Reed?'

'Yes. I'm also the director of the nuclear reactor facility.'

'What does that job entail?'

'I'm responsible for the maintenance, opération and use of the research reactor and its licensing.'

'What is your educational background?'

'I obtained a BS in chemistry from the University of California at Berkeley in 1965. In 1970, I received a doctor of science degree from the Massachusetts Institute of Technology with a specialty in the area of nuclear chemistry.'

'Do you have any special expertise in the use of neutron activation analysis?'

'I do.'

'Would you please explain neutron activation analysis to the jury?'

'Certainly,' Dr. Shirov said, turning toward the jury box. His smile was light and easy and his thick glasses magnified the St. Nick's twinkle in his blue eyes. Some of the jurors smiled back.

'If we take a sample of any material and place it in a source of neutrons – atomic particles – the material will absorb the neutrons and become radioactive. There are ninety-two basic elements and fourteen man-made elements. More than fifty of the basic elements emit gamma rays when they become radioactive. We have instruments that measure how many gamma rays are given off by the material and their specific energy.

'A nuclear reactor is a source of neutrons. If I have material I want to analyze, I place it in the reactor. Once the substance is radioactive it is removed from the reactor and taken to a gamma ray analyzer, a machine that detects gamma rays and measures their energy. The information obtained from the analyzer is printed on a magnetic disk and stored so we can analyze the data and determine what elements are present and how much of each element is present.'

'Dr. Shirov,' Matthew said, 'if you were asked to compare two items which appeared to come from the same source, what could you tell about their similarities and differences by using neutron activation analysis?'

'I could tell a great deal. You see, materials in nature contain traces of other materials. Sometimes there are large amounts of one material in the other, but other times there may only be a small amount. Neutron activation analysis is a very sensitive technique for determining the amount of minor elements that exist in a particular object.

'For example, if you filled a thimble with arsenic and thoroughly mixed it with four railroad tank cars of water, neutron activation analysis would be able to determine the amount of arsenic in a one-ounce sample of the water.

'Now, getting back to the comparison of our two samples, if the trace elements in the two are greatly different, it is possible to reach a conclusion with a high degree of certainty that they came from different sources.

'On the other hand, if we see no differences between the two samples, we can say that there is no scientific evidence to support an assertion that they are from different sources.'

'Dr. Shirov, I'm handing you what has previously been marked as State's Exhibits 36 and 37. Do you recognize them?'

Dr. Shirov took from Reynolds Exhibit 36, the charred and twisted metal strip with the notch that had been part of the bomb that killed Justice Griffen, and Exhibit 37, the clean metal strip with the point that had been found in Abbie's garage.

'You brought these two items to the college this weekend.'

'What did I tell you I needed to know?'

'You told me that you wanted to know if the two pieces of steel plate were attached at one time.'

'What did you do to find out?'

'There was no need to irradiate both exhibits in their

entirety, so I took samples of each. This presented a small problem. How to cut a sample without contaminating it. Most of the usual ways of cutting steel involve the possibility of contamination. For example, the steel of a hacksaw blade might transfer elements to the samples that would give off gamma rays when irradiated. I chose a silicon carbide saw because these elements do not give off gamma rays.

'You explained the importance of the two pieces of steel plate, so I took my samples from the middle of one side so as not to affect the end with the tool markings. I placed each exhibit in a vise and made a vee-notch cut that allowed me to obtain two one-hundred-milligram-size samples.'

'How big is that, Dr. Shirov?'

'Oh, say the size of a sunflower seed.'

'And that was enough for an accurate test?'

'Yes.'

'What did you do after you obtained the samples?'

'I put each sample in a pre-cleaned vial and washed it in distilled water to remove adhering material. Then I dried the samples overnight.

'The next day, I placed each sample in a pre-cleaned polyethylene vial and heat-sealed the vials. The sealed vials were then placed inside a polyethylene irradiation container, called a "rabbit," for irradiation in the nuclear reactor's pneumatic tube facility. This is similar to the pneumatic tube system used in drive-in banks, but ours ends up in the core of the reactor.'

Reynolds returned to the counsel table and picked up two lead containers, approximately two inches in diameter and four inches tall and handed them to Dr. Shirov.

'Dr. Shirov, I am handing you what have been marked as Defense Exhibits 201 and 202. Can you identify these exhibits?'

'Certainly. These are what we call lead pigs and they are used for housing radioactive samples.'

'Are the samples dangerous?'

'No. Not at this time.'

'What is in these lead pigs?'

'The samples I took from Exhibits 36 and 37.'

'If the state wished, could its own scientists retest these samples?'

'Yes, but they would probably want to use fresh samples from the steel plates.'

'Thank you. Go on with your explanation, Doctor.'

'I performed a five-minute irradiation on each sample. Then I retrieved the samples. Next I punctured the vials with a hypodermic needle and flushed out the radioactive argon gas produced when argon, which occurs naturally in air, is irradiated in a reactor. The vials were then placed in a clear plastic bag and put in front of a high-resolution gamma ray analyzer.'

'Explain what you did next.'

'When a substance is exposed to neutrons some of the atoms may absorb a neutron and become radioactive. These atoms decay differently depending on the identity of the original atom. No two radioactive nuclides decay with the same half-life and energy. Therefore, by measuring the energy of the gamma rays emitted during decay at known times after these samples were removed from the reactor, I was able to identify many of the elements in the samples by analyzing the data from the gamma ray detector. I counted the gamma rays emitted at one, five, ten and thirty minutes after the end of the irradiation. I counted the sample again at two and twenty-four hours after the end of the irradiation. The data for each gamma ray count was stored on a disk for later analysis. After the data was on the disk, I used a computer program to identify the energies of the gamma rays.'

'Dr. Shirov, what conclusions did you draw from the test data?'

'Mr. Reynolds, I have concluded, after reviewing the information obtained from the analysis, that there is no evidence to support a conclusion that the sample from Exhibit 36 and the sample from Exhibit 37 could have come from the same piece of steel plate. Furthermore, they could not have a common source of origin.'

Tracy was stunned and she could tell by the look on Chuck Geddes's face that she was not alone. The two metal pieces so obviously fit that she had assumed they were joined once. Now it looked like she was wrong and the state's case was in shambles.

'Are you saying that Exhibit 36 and Exhibit 37 were never connected?' Reynolds asked Dr. Shirov.

'I am.'

'What is the basis for your conclusion?'

'The fragments from Exhibit 37, the clean piece of steel plate, contained observable arsenic, antimony, manganese and vanadium. Exhibit 36, the sample that is charred and twisted, contains manganese, vanadium and aluminum, but no arsenic or antimony. It would not be possible for one piece of steel from a common plate to contain arsenic and antimony and another piece of steel from the same plate to be missing these elements.'

'Exhibit 36 was in an explosion. Could that account for the missing elements?'

'Mr. Reynolds, it is not possible that the explosion changed the composition of the steel by removing two elements. It would be more likely that an explosion would add material.'

'Dr. Shirov, did you conduct any more tests on the samples?'

'No. Since the observations were conclusive at this point, there was no purpose in further analysis.'

'Thank you, Doctor. I have no further questions.'

Chuck Geddes stood up. He was obviously fighting to control his emotions in front of the jury.

'May we approach the bench, Your Honor?'

Judge Baldwin motioned Geddes and Reynolds forward.

'Mr. Reynolds gave me Dr. Shirov's test results this morning . . . ,' Geddes whispered angrily.

'No need to go any further, Mr. Geddes,' Judge Baldwin said. 'I assumed you'd want to reserve cross. Any objection, Mr. Reynolds?'

'No, Your Honor,' Reynolds said graciously.

'Then let's take our morning recess.'

As soon as the jurors filed out, Tracy grabbed Reynolds's arm.

'How did you know the two pieces of steel were different?' she asked, unable to keep the awestruck tone out of her voice.

Reynolds smiled. 'I had no idea they were different, Tracy. When I'm dealing with the state's evidence, I follow a simple rule. I never assume any of it is what it appears to be. I thought I was wasting my time when I hired Dr. Shirov this weekend, but I couldn't think of anything else to do. Fortunately, whoever is trying to frame Abbie didn't know there was a foolproof method of telling if the two metal strips were once joined.'

Reynolds turned his attention to Dr. Shirov, who had walked over to the defense table as soon as Judge Baldwin left the bench. Tracy shook her head. Reynolds was astonishing. Now she understood why so many people, especially other lawyers, spoke of him with such reverence. And why so many clients literally owed him their lives.

Tracy saw Chuck Geddes rushing out of the courtroom and away from the humiliating events of the morning. Just as he reached the door, Neil Christenson came in with a big smile on his face. The investigator said something that made Geddes stop. The two men conferred. Geddes's back was to Tracy, so she could not see his face, but she could see Christenson gesturing animatedly and Geddes nodding vigorously. Then Christenson stopped talking and Geddes turned and stared at Reynolds and Abbie Griffen. There was a cruel smile on his face, an expression that was hard to reconcile with the stunning blow that had been dealt to his case moments ago.

2

Barry Frame lived in the Pearl District, an area of northwest Portland once filled with decaying warehouses that had been rejuvenated by an infusion of art galleries and an influx of young professionals and artists who lived in the renovated lofts. Some of the bare brick walls in Barry's loft were decorated with Matthew Reynolds's nature photography. A poster from the Mount Hood Jazz Festival showing a piano floating on a pristine lake with Mount Hood in the background hung above a low white sofa. Across from the sofa, a metal bookcase stood next to a twenty-seven-inch TV set and a state-of-the-art stereo system. Barry was listening to a CD of Stan Getz blowing a mellow sax when Tracy knocked on his door. She had called from the courthouse as soon as court ended. Barry had been in the field interviewing witnesses during the day and was anxious to be brought up to date on what had happened in the courtroom.

As soon as the door opened, Tracy threw her arms around Barry's neck and kissed him. Then she broke free and grabbed Barry by the shoulders.

'Matthew Reynolds is unreal. I mean, I'd heard he was

a grade A genius, but I didn't really believe it until I saw him this afternoon.'

'Slow down,' Barry said with a laugh.

'I can't. I'm on a fantastic high. You should have seen Geddes. He's such a pompous ass. God, the look on his face as soon as the jurors were out of the room. He went ballistic. It was priceless.'

'What happened?'

Tracy grinned wickedly. 'What are you willing to do to find out?'

Tracy was loaded with energy and wanted to expend it the same way they had when they missed the last half of *Casablanca* on Friday night.

'Jesus, I'm involved with a sex maniac. Is this the only way I can get information out of you?'

'Yup.'

'I feel like I'm being used.'

'Yup.'

'And here I thought it was my mind that attracted you.'

'Nope,' Tracy said as she started taking off her dress.

'Tell me what happened in the goddamn courtroom while I still have the strength to listen,' Barry said.

They were lying naked on Barry's king-size bed. Tracy rolled over on her side.

'I guess you've earned the information,' she said, smiling impishly. Then she told Barry about Dr. Shirov's testimony.

'Man, I wish I'd been there,' Barry said when she was finished.

'Didn't you know about Shirov?'

'No. This was Matt's baby. He's pulled stuff like this before. He gets in this zone only he can get to and comes up with these ideas. If there's a better lawyer in the country, I haven't heard of him.'

'Or her,' Tracy said, nestling against Barry's chest.

'Excuse me for being politically incorrect,' Barry answered as he kissed Tracy's forehead.

'It's all over but the shouting,' she said. 'Matt destroyed Deems and Dr. Shirov has wiped out Geddes's key evidence. The jury has to have at least a reasonable doubt.'

'I never like to get overconfident,' Barry said, 'but I have to agree with you. It looks like Matt has this one in the bag.'

PART SIX
THE MAGIC
TRICK

Chapter Twenty-five

1

On Wednesday morning, Tracy noticed that no one was sitting at the prosecution counsel table when the defense team entered the courtroom. The judge's bailiff hurried over to Reynolds as soon as he spotted him.

'The judge wants you in chambers with your client. Mr. Geddes and Mr. Christenson are already there.'

'Any idea what's going on, George?' Reynolds asked.

'Not a clue.'

Brock Folmer, the judge whose chambers Judge Baldwin was using, was a Civil War buff. A bookcase with volumes about the great conflict stood next to the door to the courtroom and a table covered with miniature blue and gray soldiers reenacting the Battle of Bull Run sat against the wall under the window. Judge Baldwin seemed lost behind a huge oak desk that stood in the center of the room. In back of him was a complete set of the Oregon Court of Appeals and Supreme Court reports and the Oregon Revised Statutes. The court reporter was sitting at Judge Baldwin's elbow.

There were three high-backed, brown leather, upholstered chairs in front of the judge's desk. One was empty and Reynolds took it. The other two were occupied by Chuck Geddes and Neil Christenson. Christenson looked nervous, but Geddes looked like he had just won the lottery.

'Good morning, Matt,' Judge Baldwin said. 'Miss Cavanaugh and Mrs. Griffen, why don't you have a seat on that couch over by the wall, and we'll get started.'

'What's going on, Judge?' Reynolds asked.

'Let's go on the record and Mr. Geddes can tell us. He asked for this meeting this morning.'

Geddes lounged in his chair. There was a smug smile on his face. 'I want to reopen the state's case,' he said.

Judge Baldwin looked a little put out. 'That's highly unusual, Mr. Geddes. We're well into the defense case.'

'I'm aware that my request is unusual, Your Honor, but Mr. Christenson has discovered new evidence that changes the complexion of our case.'

'And what evidence is that?' the judge asked.

'Evidence that Abigail Griffen also murdered her husband's lover, Laura Rizzatti.'

Tracy was stunned and Abbie bolted out of her seat.

'You sick bastard,' she started, but Reynolds was up, blocking the judge's view and holding out a hand to his client.

'Please, Mrs. Griffen,' he said forcefully.

Abbie caught herself and sank down onto the couch. She was clearly shaken by the accusation. And so, to Tracy's surprise, was Matthew Reynolds.

'Let's everyone calm down so we can sort this out,' Judge Baldwin commanded. Geddes had not moved during Abbie's outburst. Reynolds made certain that Abbie was under control, then he turned back to the judge.

'I object to Mr. Geddes's motion to reopen,' Reynolds said forcefully. 'The state has rested. Mr. Geddes had months to uncover evidence of this sort, if it exists. The introduction now of evidence of another murder would be untimely. I also believe it would require a mistrial or a lengthy continuance so the defense could prepare to meet this evidence. Both actions would be highly prejudicial to the defense case, which, as the court knows, is in an excellent posture at this point.'

Reynolds paused and cast a cutting look at Geddes.

'Frankly, Your Honor, I'm a bit skeptical of the timing of this motion, coming, as it does, right after Mr. Geddes's key witness and key evidence have been discredited.'

'Mr. Reynolds's points are well taken, Mr. Geddes,' Judge Baldwin said, 'but I suppose I have to hear the evidence you want to introduce before I can make a ruling. Why don't you enlighten us?'

'Certainly, Your Honor. That's why Mr. Christenson is here. Neil, please tell the judge what you discovered.'

Christenson shifted uncomfortably in his chair and faced the judge. 'Laura Rizzatti was Justice Griffen's clerk at the Supreme Court, Your Honor. She was murdered a little less than a month before Justice Griffen was killed. Mr. Geddes thought it was suspicious that the two murders had been committed so close to one another, but we had no evidence that they were connected, so we assumed that we were probably just dealing with a coincidence.

'Then, Monday night, I remembered that I had seen several credit card receipts to the Overlook Motel in evidence we had taken during a search of Justice Griffen's home office.'

Tracy's stomach tightened at the mention of the Overlook. She saw exactly where Christenson was going and she could not believe it. Until now, the defense was convinced that the prosecutors knew nothing about Justice Griffen's extramarital affairs. But it was clear that not only did they know about Griffen's trysts at the Overlook, they had drawn an unexpected inference.

'Initially, the receipts meant nothing to me,' Christenson continued. 'Then I recalled that the Overlook was a very seedy motel. Not a place where someone like Justice Griffen would normally go. On a hunch, I brought a photograph of Laura Rizzatti to the Overlook and showed it to Annie Hardesty, who is a clerk at the motel. Mrs. Hardesty confirmed that Justice Griffen used rooms at the motel on several occasions to meet women. She also told me that she had seen Laura Rizzatti with the judge more than once.'

Christenson paused to let the implications sink in.

'Then she told me two other facts that I considered

important. First, she told me that Miss Cavanaugh and Barry Frame, Mr. Reynolds's investigator, came to the motel well before the trial and learned that the judge was using the motel as a love nest.'

'Which will make it difficult for Mr. Reynolds to claim surprise, Your Honor,' Geddes interjected.

'Let's hold off on your argument until I've heard all of Mr. Christenson's statement,' the judge said sternly. 'Mr. Christenson, you said there was something else Mrs. Hardesty related.'

'Yes, sir. She said she started watching the news about the case after Miss Cavanaugh's visit because she thought she might be a witness, and she recognized the defendant, Mrs. Griffen, as someone she'd seen at the Overlook. She remembered the incident quite clearly because Mrs. Griffen and her husband were arguing so loudly that one of the other guests complained.

'Mrs. Hardesty told me that she went over to the room the judge was renting to get them to quiet down when the door burst open and Mrs. Griffen came flying out. Before the door opened, though, she heard part of the argument and she is willing to testify that Mrs. Griffen threatened to kill her husband if she caught him cheating again.'

'When did you discover this information, Mr. Christenson?' Judge Baldwin asked.

'Yesterday and the day before, Your Honor.'

Geddes leaned forward. 'I believe this evidence lays a strong foundation for our theory that Mrs. Griffen learned that Laura Rizzatti and the judge were lovers and that she

killed them both when the judge did not heed her warning
to stop his affair with Miss Rizzatti.'

'What do you have to say, Mr. Reynolds?' the judge
asked.

Reynolds had carried a paperback copy of the Oregon
Rules of Evidence into chambers. As he was flipping
through the pages, looking for the section he wanted, the
book slipped from his hand and fell to the floor. The pages
crumpled and the cardboard cover bent. Reynolds leaned
over to retrieve the book and Tracy saw his hand tremble
as he smoothed out the pages. When he spoke, there was
an uncharacteristic quiver in his voice.

'Rule 404 (3) states that evidence of other crimes is not
admissible to prove that a defendant is likely to have
committed the crime for which she is on trial simply
because she committed another, similar crime before.'

'Yes, Mr. Reynolds,' the judge interrupted. 'But the
rule also states that proof of prior crimes is admissible
for other purposes, such as proof of motive or to show a
plan involving both crimes. If there is proof that Mrs.
Griffen had a plan to kill both victims or that she killed
her husband because he and Miss Rizzatti were lovers,
wouldn't the evidence of Miss Rizzatti's murder be
admissible?'

'It's possible, Your Honor, but you've forgotten a step
the Supreme Court set out in *State* v. *Johns*, the case that
set up the procedure a judge must use to decide if prior
crime evidence is admissible. First, you must decide if
the evidence is relevant to an issue in the case, such as

proving motive. *Then* you must decide if the relevance of the evidence is outweighed by the prejudice to the defendant that inevitably occurs if proof of another crime committed by the defendant is introduced at trial.

'In deciding the relevance versus prejudice issue, a judge must consider four factors, one of which is the certainty that the defendant committed the other crime. The burden of convincing the court on that point rests on the state and I haven't heard a single piece of evidence that connects Mrs. Griffen to the Rizzatti murder.'

'Does Mr. Geddes have to convince me beyond a reasonable doubt that Mrs. Griffen killed Miss Rizzatti before I can let in the evidence of the Rizzatti murder?'

'No, Your Honor. If I remember correctly, the cases hold that you must be "certain" Mrs. Griffen killed Miss Rizzatti, but that is still a high burden. There is a case, *Tucker* v. *State*, from Nevada that I would like to call to your attention.

'In the spring of 1957, Horace Tucker called the police to his home in Las Vegas. Tucker was unshaven, he looked tired and he had been drinking. A detective found a dead man on the floor of Tucker's dining room. The man had been shot several times, but Tucker said he found the body when he woke up and had no idea what happened. A grand jury conducted an extensive investigation, but did not indict Tucker because it deemed the evidence of Tucker's guilt to be inconclusive.

'Roughly six years later, in late 1963, Tucker phoned the police again. This time they found a dead man on the couch in Tucker's living room. The man had been shot to death. Tucker looked like he had been drinking. He said he awakened to find the dead man and had no idea how he got into his house or how he was killed.

'This time, Tucker was charged with murder. At his trial, the prosecutor introduced evidence of the first murder over a defense objection. Tucker was found guilty of murder, but the Nevada Supreme Court reversed because it found nothing in the record that proved that Tucker killed the first man. The court held that evidence of a prior crime is inadmissible unless there is proof that the defendant committed the uncharged crime.'

'That case is absurd,' Geddes said. 'I don't care what they do in Nevada. A Nevada case isn't precedent here. I don't think Oregon law requires me to jump through all these hurdles to get this evidence before a jury.'

'Calm down, Mr. Geddes. I'm not that impressed by that Nevada case myself. But it's clear that this issue is too complex for me to decide today. I'm going to dismiss the jury until we clear this up. I want briefs on the prior-crime issue from both of you by Friday.'

Judge Baldwin looked worried. 'One matter greatly concerns me, gentlemen. If I allow your motion, Mr. Geddes, I may also have to grant a defense motion for mistrial or a continuance because of the prejudice to the defense of reopening at this stage. I'm deeply troubled that the defense may not have the ability to investigate these new allegations against Mrs. Griffen during trial. I want this prejudice issue thoroughly briefed. This is a death penalty case and I am going to make absolutely certain that both sides have a fair trial.'

2

'Why didn't you tell me that a witness heard you threaten to kill Justice Griffen when we discussed the Overlook?' Matthew asked Abbie as she paced back and forth across her living room.

'I don't remember seeing her. I was upset. I just stormed out of the motel room. I was so mad, I don't even remember what I said to Robert.'

Matthew walked over to the French windows and stared out at the back lawn.

'I don't know if we can avoid asking for a mistrial if the judge lets Geddes reopen the case,' he said grimly.

'We've got to go on,' Abbie said, turning toward Matthew with a look of desperation. 'I couldn't go through another trial. I'd be trapped in this house again.'

'You've got to consider the possibility. If the jury starts thinking that you may have murdered Laura Rizzatti, they'll forget everything else they've heard. And the judge is right. How can we possibly investigate the Rizzatti murder while we're in trial?'

'But we're winning. If the case went to the jury now, I'd be acquitted.'

'Geddes knows that. It's one of the reasons he wants Judge Baldwin to rule that he can introduce the evidence.

It would force us to move for a mistrial and save him from losing the case.'

'That bastard. I hate him.'

Abbie stopped in front of Matthew. Her shoulders sagged and she began to sob. The pressure she had been under since her arrest was suddenly more than she could bear. Matthew took her in his arms. Tears streaked her face. She was so forlorn Matthew would have done anything to make her smile. Without saying a word, he stroked her hair and held her.

Finally, Abbie stopped crying. She rested her head against Matthew's shoulder for a moment. She felt as light as a feather, as if her tears had carried away all her emotions and left her hollow. Then she slowly tilted her head back and kissed him. The kiss ended. Abbie rested her cheek against his and he thought he heard her say, 'I love you.'

It was the voice of someone who had given up everything but one basic truth.

Matthew felt dizzy. He pulled back and felt pressure on his hand. Abbie kept hold of it, turned her back to him and led him toward the stairs. He followed behind her and walked into Abbie's bedroom in a trance, his heart beating so fast he was having trouble breathing. Abbie turned toward him. She unbuttoned her blouse and stepped out of her skirt. She was wearing a white lace bra and silk bikini panties. Matthew marveled at her smooth, olive skin, the hard muscle, the curves and flat places. The mysteries of a woman's body. Compared to Abbie, he was pathetic.

Abbie moved into Matthew's arms. He could feel the warmth and texture of her satin-smooth skin. She unbuttoned his shirt, then knelt as she slipped off his pants. Matthew kissed the top of her head and smelled her hair. There was a fragrance of flowers.

Abbie stood up and unhooked her bra. Her breasts were full and high. Her nipples were erect.

'Take off my panties,' Abbie whispered. Her desire paralyzed Matthew. How could a woman like Abbie want him? She read the confusion on his face and touched the tips of her fingers to his lips. Matthew began to shake. He had never felt such desire, had barely allowed himself to dream of it. Abbie's hand strayed to his penis and the fingers that had traced along his lips performed a different kind of magic. Then Abbie pushed him gently and he fell back onto the bed and into his dreams.

Matthew reached across the bed until he found Abbie's hand. As soon as his fingers touched hers, they entwined. They lay side by side without speaking. Matthew had never felt such peace. If this was all he could ever have out of this life, it would be enough, but he believed now that it was possible for him to have more than this single night with Abbie.

'If we win, will you go back to the district attorney's office?' Matthew asked.

While Abbie thought about his question, Matthew stared at the ceiling. With the lights off, the moonlight cast shadow patterns of the limbs of a giant elm on the white surface. The silhouette swayed gently in perfect rhythm with the calm pulse of Matthew's heart.

'It would be hard to go back, Matt. Jack and Dennis stood by me, but I don't know how I'd feel working there after being a defendant.'

'Have you ever thought about defending cases?'

Abbie turned her head and studied Matthew.

'Why are you asking?'

Matthew kept his eyes on the ceiling. There was a tremor in his voice when he spoke.

'I love you, Abbie, and I respect you, more than you can imagine. You're an excellent lawyer. Together, we would be the best.'

Abbie realized what he was asking her. Matthew Reynolds had never had a partner and his law practice was his life. She squeezed his hand.

'You're already the best, Matthew.'

'Will you consider what I've said?'

Abbie rolled over and stroked his cheek.

'Yes,' she whispered. Then she kissed him softly, then harder, then harder still.

3

Tracy went directly from the courtroom to the Multnomah County law library and started researching the law governing the admissibility of prior-crime evidence. The words on the page were starting to blur when Tracy began reading *State* v. *Zamora*, an Oregon Supreme Court decision that discussed the prior-crime issue. For some reason the case sounded familiar, but she did not know why. It had been decided two years before she started clerking, so it wasn't a case she'd worked on, and she did not recall reading it before. Then the names of the cases on Laura's yellow legal pad flashed in her head and she recognized *Zamora* as one of them.

Tracy skimmed the case. The defendant had murdered a clerk and a customer in a convenience store in Portland. A 5-2 majority reversed the conviction because the trial judge admitted evidence of a prior, unconnected robbery in violation of the rule excluding evidence of prior crimes. Justice Lefcourt had written for the court with Justices Pope, Griffen, Kelly and Arriaga joining him. The public defender had handled Zamora's appeal.

Out of curiosity, Tracy pulled the volumes holding the other cases that Laura had listed on the sheet from the yellow legal pad that Tracy had found in Volume XI of the *Deems* transcript. *State* v. *Cardona* had originated in Medford, a small city in southern Oregon five hours' drive down I-5 from Portland. Tracy did not recognize the name of the attorney who argued the case. Justices Kelly, Griffen and Pope had joined in Justice Arriaga's majority opinion reversing Cardona's conviction for distributing cocaine. Justices Lefcourt, Sherzer and Forbes had dissented.

The majority interpreted the search and seizure provisions of the Oregon constitution as forbidding the procedures the police had used when searching Cardona's apartment, even though the same procedures would not have violated the search and seizure provisions of the United States Constitution. There was nothing unusual about this. The United States Supreme Court had become increasingly conservative. Some state courts could not stomach its ideologically motivated opinions and had begun fashioning a jurisprudence based on interpretations of state constitutions that were frequently at odds with federal law.

In *State* v. *Galarraga*, Roseburg police stopped the defendant for speeding. After writing a ticket, they asked for permission to search Galarraga's car. According to the police, Galarraga consented to a search that revealed automatic weapons, money and cocaine. Justice Kelly reversed the conviction on the grounds that the search violated the provisions of the Oregon constitution. Justices Arriaga, Pope and Griffen had joined in Justice Kelly's opinion. Bob Packard represented Galarraga.

Tracy skimmed the cases again, but could not see a connection between them, other than the fact that all three cases had been reversed. One was a murder case and two were drug cases. They were from three different parts of the state. Two involved state constitutional law issues, but *Zamora* was reversed because of a violation of Oregon's evidence code. Different lawyers had represented the defendants.

The librarian told Tracy she was closing up. Tracy reshelved her books and drove to the office, where she dictated a memo on prior-crime evidence for Reynolds.

362

She placed the cassette on his secretary's desk with a note asking her to type it first thing in the morning. Barry was cooking her dinner at his apartment. Tracy called to let him know she was on her way and turned out the lights.

Barry served her spaghetti with meat sauce, garlic bread and a salad, but all Tracy could do was peck at her food. Barry saw how exhausted she was and insisted that Tracy sleep at his place. Tracy didn't argue. She staggered out of her clothes, collapsed on the bed and fell into a deep sleep as soon as her head hit the pillow. Soon she was lost in a dark forest. The trees were so high and the foliage so thick that only stray rays of sunlight were able to fight their way through the black-green canopy. In the distance, Tracy heard a muffled sound, strong and constant, like whispered conversation in another room. The dark woods terrified her. She felt trapped and her breathing was labored. Tracy struggled toward the sound until she broke into a clearing and found herself on the shore of a river that raged and swirled downstream toward an unknown destination.

As often occurs in dreams, the landscape shifted. The trees were gone and the land around the river was flat and barren. Someone called to her from the opposite shore. It was a man. She could not hear what he was saying because of the roar of the river. She strained to see him clearly, but his features were blurred by the reflected sunlight. To reach him, she would have to swim the river, and suddenly she was fighting a current that swept her downstream.

Tracy panicked. She sank below the surface, then bobbed up again. She was drowning, dying, when she splashed into a calm section of the river. She gasped for air, still unable to swim to shore, but no longer in immediate danger. The current spun her toward the far shore, where the man miraculously appeared. He shouted to her, but the water roared in her ears, baffling the sound. Then she saw that he was holding something. She watched his arms fly upward. The object sailed toward her. Tracy reached up to catch it and saw a ball rotating slowly through the air. The minute the ball touched her hands, Tracy bolted upright in bed, jerked out of sleep by a truth that frightened her more than any nightmare she'd ever had.

The offices were dark except for the reception area, where the lights were kept on all night. Tracy let them in with her key and Barry punched in the alarm code.

'It's in here,' Tracy said, leading Barry to the small room next to Matthew's office where they were keeping the defense evidence.

'I hope you're wrong about this,' Barry said.

'I hope I am, too.'

The evidence was arranged on a table. Tracy looked through it until she found the photographs and negatives in the FotoFast envelope. She set the negatives aside and shuffled through the photographs. There were shots of Abigail Griffen, pictures of the beach and the ocean, exteriors and interiors of the cabin and the photo of the shed

Matthew had used on cross-examination to destroy Charlie Deems. Tracy checked the dates stamped on the negatives. Some of the early pictures on the roll had been taken in June, but the bulk of the negatives, including the photo of the shed, were dated August 12, the day Deems testified that he had met Abbie at the cabin and the day Abbie claimed she had been attacked.

Tracy studied the photograph of the shed. Barry looked over her shoulder. The photograph showed the interior of the shed. Tracy could see the volleyball net, the tools and the space where a box of dynamite could have sat. In the middle of the space was the volleyball.

'I'm right,' she said dispiritedly.

'Are you certain?'

'Yes. While you were looking around, I walked over to the edge of the bluff and sat on the stairs. On my way, I looked in the shed. The volleyball was resting on the volleyball net. You had the ball when you found me sitting on the stairs, and we played with it on the beach. On the way back to the car, you tossed the ball into the shed. I have a very clear mental picture of the ball coming to rest in the empty space.

'We were at the cabin in September, Barry. The ball was on the net when I opened the shed door. If the ball was in the empty space on August 12, how did it get onto the net? And how can the ball be in the exact position we left it in September in a photograph taken in August? The only answer is that this photograph was taken after we were at the cabin and it's been phonied up to look like it was taken in August. Only I don't know anything about photography, so I have no idea how it was done.'

'Well, I know a lot about cameras. I have to on this job. Let me see the negatives and I'll try to figure this out.'

The negatives were in cellophane slipcases. Each strip contained the negatives for four pictures. Tracy handed the stack of negative strips to Barry. He held up the strip with the picture of the shed to the light. All four negatives were dated August 12.

Barry sat down at the table and picked up the Pentax camera. He turned it over and studied it. Then he looked at the strip of negatives again. Barry frowned. His brow furrowed. He examined the negative strips for all of the photographs. Then he laid down the strip with the negative of the shed and placed another strip directly above it. He studied the two strips, then he removed the strip without the picture of the shed and put another strip in its place. He repeated this with all of the negative strips. When he was done, Barry's shoulders sagged and he closed his eyes.

'What is it?' Tracy asked.

'You're right. The picture of the shed was not taken when the rest of these pictures were.'

'How is that possible if the negative is dated August 12?'

'That's the easy part,' Barry said, picking up the camera and pointing to a digital readout on the back. 'The Pentax 105-R camera has a mechanism for setting the date that is similar to the mechanism you use to set the date on a VCR or a digital watch. The person who took the picture simply reset the date to August 12, took the pictures he wanted, then reset the camera to the correct date.'

'But there are pictures of Mrs. Griffen on the roll of film. The roll had to have been taken before she was confined to her house.'

'It was. When FotoFast developed the film, it was in one strip. FotoFast cut the strip of negatives into several strips, each with four shots on them. The strip with the shot of the shed was the only strip that was not taken on the date stamped on the negative.'

'How do you know that?'

'When film is placed in a camera it's blank. It doesn't have any frames demarking where each photograph will be. The frames are formed when you take a picture. But each roll of film does have numbers imprinted on it that don't appear on the photograph but do show up on the negatives below the frames when a picture is taken. These numbers start at I and go 1, 1A, 2, 2A, and so on. You can see them here,' Barry said, pointing out the numbers.

'These numbers are spaced along the bottom of the roll of film at a set distance from each other. The distance doesn't change, because the numbers are imprinted on the film when the film is produced.

'Whoever did this went to the coast after we were there. He had the negatives of the film Mrs. Griffen gave you. He took out one strip that would be in the natural sequence on the roll for the shot of the shed to appear. In this case it was the strip with the numbers 15 to 16A. Then he took photographs with the Pentax using the same brand of film Mrs. Griffen used. When he came to the shot that would be numbered 15, he copied the shot Mrs. Griffen had taken at that point on the strip. 15A is the fake shot of the shed. He took the shot showing the shed without any dynamite. Then he duplicated shots 16 and 16A, finished the roll, had it printed by the same FotoFast store that printed the roll Mrs. Griffen took and switched the single strip.

'Look at the strips,' Barry said, holding up two he picked at random. 'Each row of film from the same company is manufactured like every other roll. If you take two rolls of film from the same company and lay them side by side, the numbers will line up. If you take a ruler and measure from the tip of one roll to IA and from the tip of a second roll to lA, the distance will be identical. But there's a little piece of film at the end of each roll of film called the leader that you place in the camera when you roll the film into it to get the film into a position where a shot can be taken. Every person does this differently. That means that the numbers will be in a different place in relation to the frames that are formed when each picture is taken on one roll than they will be on another person's roll.'

Barry put down one of the strips he was holding and picked up the strip with the shot of the shed. Then he held one strip directly over the other.

'On every negative strip but the one with the shot of the shed, the number is on the edge of the frame. On the strip with 15 to 16A, the numbers are slightly closer to the center of the frame. Can you see that?'

Tracy nodded.

'That's impossible,' he continued, 'if that strip was on the roll with the rest of the shots.'

Barry put down the strips. 'What I don't understand,' he said, 'is how Griffen was able to get away from her house, take the picture and make the switch without setting off the electronic monitoring system.'

'You don't understand because you don't want to, Barry,' Tracy said sadly.

Barry stared at Tracy. 'You can't think . . .'

'It's the only answer.'

'Bullshit,' Barry shouted angrily.

'I don't want to believe it either. But the simple fact is that Abigail Griffen could not have left the house. And even if she was able to defeat the electronic monitoring system, there's no way she could have known where on the roll to fix the faked strip. We had the negatives here along with the camera.'

'Ah, no,' Barry said in a voice so filled with grief that Tracy felt herself melt with pity for him.

'It was Matt,' she said softly. 'It has to be. He had access to the negatives and the camera and he's a great photographer. You would have to know an awful lot about cameras to come up with this scheme.'

'But why, Tracy?'

'You know the answer to that, too. You've seen how she's played him. He's so in love with her that she only had to whisper the suggestion and he'd do it.'

'Not Matt,' Barry said desperately.

'He's a brilliant attorney, Barry, but he's not a god. He's just a human being.'

Barry stood up and paced the room. Tracy let him work it out. When Barry turned toward her he appeared to have made a decision.

'What are you going to do?' he asked, his voice flat and cold.

'You know I don't have a choice. I have to go to Judge Baldwin. This is a criminal offense. If I don't tell the court, I'm guilty as an aider and abettor.'

'You can't do it, Tracy,' Barry begged her. 'If you tell Baldwin, Matt will be destroyed. He'd be disbarred. Geddes will go berserk. He'll make sure Matt goes to prison, for God's sake.'

Tracy placed a hand on Barry's shoulder.

'Don't you think I know that? But what else can I do? He broke the law. And you're forgetting something else. Griffen wouldn't need a fake photograph unless the dynamite was in the shed. Deems knew about the dynamite, because Abbie showed it to him, which means she asked Deems to kill her husband. If she convinced Matt to fake the picture, it's because she's guilty. If I don't tell the court, Abigail Griffen will go free. She's a murderer, Barry. She killed Robert Griffen.'

Tracy paused and her features became devoid of pity. When she spoke, her voice was hard as granite.

'She may have done something else, Barry. She may have killed Laura Rizzatti, my friend. And I'm not going to let her get way with that.'

Barry had not heard her. He was too overwhelmed by the facts he was forced to face. He looked at the floor and, in a voice on the edge of tears, he said, 'I don't believe it, Tracy. He's the most honorable man I've ever met. He would never fake evidence in a court case.'

'I understand how you feel, but I can't keep quiet about this.'

Barry's face fell. Tracy had never seen another human being so distraught.

'If you do this, you'll do it without me. I won't hurt Matt. And if you do . . .'

Barry couldn't go on. He simply stood in front of Tracy and shook his head.

'Barry, please. Don't do this to us.'

'Don't do this to Matt.'

'What about Griffen? Do you want her to walk away from a murder charge?'

'I don't care about Abigail Griffen. One hundred of her are not worth one man like Matthew Reynolds. Think of all the good he's done. All of the sacrifices he's made. Let her walk, for Christ's sake. Don't crucify Matt. Don't destroy him.'

'He broke the law. I'm an officer of the court. You're asking me to betray everything I believe in and to let a cold-blooded murderer go free.'

'I'm asking you to be human. We're talking about a man's life. And not just any man. Think about what you're doing.'

Tracy shook her head. She could not believe what Barry was asking of her.

'I can't let this go, Barry, but I'll talk to Matt before I go to see Judge Baldwin and I'll give him a chance to show me I'm wrong.'

Barry looked directly into Tracy's eyes. His own were dead.

'Do what you have to do, Tracy. But if you destroy Matthew Reynolds, I can never see you again.'

Chapter Twenty-six

1

For the sake of appearances, Matthew did not spend the night with Abbie. At four-thirty in the morning, he let himself into his house through a back door and climbed a staircase that went straight to his living quarters. Forgotten for the moment was the turn the trial had taken. Tonight, all of his dreams had come true. Not only had he and Abbie made love, but he had learned that she really loved him.

Before he went to bed, Matthew took out the manila envelope with the articles about Abbie and the photographs of her. This time when he looked at the photographs he did not feel longing or despair. In fact, they evoked no emotions. For the first time, he understood that the photographs were not Abbie. She was a warm, vibrant person. These two-dimensional images were as insubstantial as ghosts. He could not bring himself to destroy them, but he felt uncomfortable looking at them, as if by viewing the pictures he was betraying the woman he loved.

For the first time in a long time, Matthew awakened to sunlight. He showered and made himself his usual breakfast of toast and black coffee. One of his correspondence chess games had taken a peculiar turn. In a position where Matthew thought he held a slight advantage, his opponent, an architect in Nebraska, had made an odd and unexpected knight move that had him worried. Matthew carried his mug into the den and sipped cooling coffee until he was satisfied that he knew the architect's strategy. He addressed a postcard, wrote his move on the back of the card and descended to his office. Matthew's secretary was surprised to hear him humming.

A memo on the law of prior-crime evidence was waiting on his desk. Reynolds read the memo, then buzzed Tracy's office. There was no answer. He buzzed the receptionist.

'Do you know where Tracy is?'

'I haven't seen her this morning.'

It was nine-thirty. Tracy was normally in by eight at the latest.

'Please tell her to see me as soon as she comes in,' Reynolds said. Then he picked up the memo and walked down to the office library to read the cases Tracy had cited.

2

Tracy offered to drive Barry to his apartment, but he chose to walk the twenty blocks of night-time streets back to the loft. Barry cared for Tracy, he might even love her, but he could not bear to be with her and he desperately needed time to think. Tracy was relieved to be alone. The pain she and Barry had caused each other was too intense. She needed time away from him as much as he needed to be apart from her.

Tracy arrived at her waterfront apartment at two-thirty. She tried to sleep, but gave up after tossing and turning for half an hour. Whenever she closed her eyes, she saw the face of Laura Rizzatti or Matthew Reynolds.

Around three-fifteen, Tracy got out of bed and wandered into her kitchen. She poured herself a glass of milk and walked over to the sliding-glass door that opened onto her terrace. The terrace overlooked the Willamette. She pressed her forehead to the glass and stared at the lights on the Hawthorne and Morrison bridges. The ghostly glow of headlights swept over them like a legion of spirits aswirl in the night. After a while, Tracy was too exhausted to stand up. She curled in a ball on her sofa. Her eyes refused to stay open, but she could not sleep. The sadness of it all suddenly overwhelmed her. Laura and the judge dead, Matthew Reynolds's career on the verge of destruction and her relationship with Barry in ruins. She began to sob and made no attempt to hold back her tears. Her body shook quietly as she let herself go. When the dawn came, her tears had dried.

'There you are,' Matthew said with a friendly smile when Tracy walked into his office at eleven-thirty. Tracy could not help noticing how relaxed he looked. She, on the other hand, was exhausted and drained of energy. It had taken all of her courage to come to Reynolds's office to confront him.

Tracy shut the door and sagged into a chair.

'There's something we have to talk about,' she said.

'Can it wait?' he asked pleasantly. 'We've got to whip this memo into shape and I have some ideas I want to run by you.'

'I don't think the memo matters anymore, Mr. Reynolds,' she said sadly.

Reynolds frowned. 'What do you mean?'

'I know Mrs. Griffen is guilty,' Tracy said.

For a moment, Reynolds did not react. Then he looked at her as if he was not certain he'd heard Tracy correctly.

'What are you talking about?'

Tracy took the FotoFast envelope out of her purse and laid the photo of the shed on Reynolds's blotter.

'I spent last night looking at the negatives with Barry,' she said. 'He explained how it was done.'

Reynolds looked confused. He glanced at the photograph, then back at Tracy.

'I'm afraid you've lost me.'

'This photograph of the shed is a fake. It was taken in September. We'll have to tell Chuck Geddes and Judge

Baldwin. We'll have to resign from the case.'

Reynolds studied the photograph, but made no move to touch it. When he looked at Tracy there was no indication of guilt or fear on his features. If Tracy had not seen the way Reynolds controlled his emotions in court, she would have concluded that he was innocent.

'What makes you think the photograph was faked?' Reynolds asked calmly.

Tracy told Matthew about her trip to the cabin with Barry and explained about the position of the volleyball.

'It must be a coincidence,' Matthew said. 'The ball was in the position in the photograph on August 12. Then Sheriff Dillard or one of his deputies moved it onto the net when he checked the shed for the dynamite.'

'I hoped that was the solution, but it's not.'

'Then how could the negative have August 12 stamped on it?'

Tracy explained the way the fake was created, hoping that Matthew would drop his pretense and admit what he had done. As she spoke, Reynolds grew agitated and began to shift in his chair.

'But how could Mrs. Griffen have created the substitute strip?' Matthew snapped when Tracy was through with her explanation. 'It's ridiculous. She's been confined to her house since the last week in August.'

'She didn't make the fake. Mrs. Griffen had an accomplice. Someone who had access to the Pentax and the negatives. Someone who knows enough about photography to think up this scheme.

'How could you do it, Matthew? She's a murderer. She killed a good, decent man for money and she killed a good friend of mine.'

Reynolds tried to maintain his composure, but he failed. Moments before, he had been the happiest person in the world. Now everything was slipping away from him. His shoulders hunched and he slumped in his seat. He took a deep breath. When he spoke, his voice was barely above a whisper.

'I'm sorry,' he managed. 'I know how this looks, but, believe me, it's not what it seems.'

Matthew's chest heaved. It took him a moment to regain his composure.

'Abbie had nothing to do with the photograph and she didn't kill her husband or Laura Rizzatti.'

'I don't believe that.'

Matthew paused again. Tracy could see he was trembling. He closed his eyes and let his head fall back. When he opened his eyes, they were moist with tears.

'When you interviewed with me, I told you about several fine attorneys who have visited a prison after dark and left with their client dead. Then I told you that neither I nor any attorney who worked for me had ever visited a prison after dark. That wasn't true.

'When I was eight years old, I visited a prison after dark. When I left the prison before dawn, the man I had spoken with was dead. He was my father. I loved him very much. He was executed for the murder of a young woman with whom he worked. The prosecutor convinced a jury that my father had been having an affair with this woman and had killed her because she threatened to tell my mother about their affair. My father swore that he loved my mother and was only the girl's friend. The jury didn't believe him and he was executed in the electric chair.

'Two years after he died, the real murderer confessed. He worked with the woman and they were having an affair. My father had simply been the woman's friend. He was executed for a crime he never committed. If it wasn't for the death penalty, he would have been freed from prison and I would have had my father back.'

Matthew leaned back in his chair and closed his eyes.

'I know I must disgust you, Tracy. Preaching about morality and honor and dishonoring myself and my profession. But I had to . . . I was compelled to . . . I saw no other way.'

Matthew stopped again. He looked across the desk at Tracy. His eyes pled for understanding.

'She's innocent, Tracy. I'm absolutely certain. And I couldn't bear the thought that she might die. She doesn't know a thing about the photograph of the shed.'

'But how could you invent evidence?' Tracy asked, the words catching in her chest.

'I can't do it anymore,' Matthew said. 'Fighting for every inch, every minute I'm in trial. Having to be perfect, every time, because my client dies if I'm not perfect. It's worn me down. I've lost my confidence. I know I'm going to lose someday. That a client of mine will die.'

Reynolds paused again. Tracy could see him struggle to come up with the words he spoke next.

'You have no idea what my life has been like. I'm so alone. At first, my loneliness was a badge of honor. I had my crusade against death and I didn't need anything else. Then the crusade became an ordeal. So much was expected of me. I wanted someone to share my pain and there was no one. Then I met Abbie.'

Reynolds's face showed surprisingly little emotion, but tears rolled down his cheeks.

'I love her, Tracy. I couldn't live with myself if she was the one I couldn't save. I simply could not let her die. I just couldn't.'

'It's easy to fool yourself about a person you love,' Tracy said gently. 'What if Abbie did murder Justice Griffen and Laura?'

'It's not possible. I . . . I know Abbie too well. She's being framed. The metal strip proves that. And what about the money? Where did Charlie Deems get a hundred thousand dollars?'

'She could have paid Deems to kill Justice Griffen. She's a very wealthy woman.'

'Then why would Deems go to the district attorney and implicate Abbie? No. Someone else killed Justice Griffen and framed Abbie.'

Tracy was so certain of Abbie's guilt when she entered Reynolds's office. Now she did not know.

'What are you going to do?' Matthew asked her.

Tracy remembered Barry asking that very question.

380

'What choice do I have? I'll have to report you to Judge Baldwin this afternoon. Do you think this is an easy choice? You're one of the finest human beings I've ever known. If I go to Judge Baldwin you'll be disbarred and go to prison. But if I keep silent, I'll be abetting what you've done, I'll be opening myself up for the same punishment and I'll be betraying my oath as an officer of the court.'

'I'm not thinking of myself, Tracy. If you reveal what you know to the judge, he'll have to tell Chuck Geddes. Geddes will use the evidence in Abbie's trial and she'll surely be convicted.'

'But she didn't know. You said so.'

'Geddes doesn't have to believe that. If he finds out about the photograph, he'll argue that Abbie did know it was a fake and there will only be my word that she didn't. Geddes will use the fact that I used a doctored photograph to rehabilitate Charlie Deems. The jurors will believe he saw the dynamite in the shed. They'll believe that a prosecutor who kills, then tries to subvert justice by fabricating evidence, should die.

'If you tell Judge Baldwin what I've done, you'll be signing the death warrant of an innocent woman.'

3

The climb up the three-hundred-foot rock wall had been slow and relatively uneventful until Tracy reached a narrow ledge that stretched horizontally across the cliff face for sixty feet. The ledge was three quarters of an inch at its widest point, fading into nonexistence in spots.

Tracy had missed the sloping overhang that jutted out ten feet above the ledge and forty feet below the summit, because, from the base of the cliff, looking up, the overhang appeared to be the summit. Tracy stood delicately on tiptoes with her body braced against the rock and carefully studied the overhang. It covered the ledge like a canopy and the rock on either side of the overhang was too smooth for Tracy to work around it. It would be maddening to come this far and be this close to the top without being able to finish the climb.

Tracy had been studying the underside of the overhang inch by inch for several minutes when her foot dislodged a small rock. She paid no attention as it plummeted down, smashing into fragments at the end of its flight, because her concentration was riveted on a crack that ran through the middle of the overhang. The crack appeared to be wide enough to let her insert her hand, if her hand was open and rigid. Tracy thought about the crack and what it might let her do. Her plan would depend on split-second timing and the chance that the crack would widen as it worked its way into the rock. But Tracy's situation left her no choice. Her only alternative was to admit defeat and descend the cliff.

Tracy was dressed in a loose-fitting, long-sleeved white top and baggy black spider pants that zipped over her form-fitting rock shoes. The day was dry and cold. If it had rained, she would not have attempted the ascent. The solo climb was dangerous enough in good weather.

The maneuver she was contemplating was risky, but Tracy could not let herself think about the danger. Nervous tension is a climber's worst enemy, because it can make a climber's hands sweat and jeopardize the security of a good handhold. While she thought through her plan, Tracy dipped both hands into the chalk in a fat purple bag fastened behind her at her waist. The chalk would keep her hands dry.

Tracy stared at the crack and relaxed her breathing. Behind her, the wilderness spread out like a green carpet, but Tracy saw only the gray uneven surface of the rock wall. She scanned the area above her for handholds. When she was rested, Tracy worked her way up the rockface until she was just under the overhang.

Tracy turned and balanced on her foothold, then she extended her right arm slowly until her hand was in the crack. Please, please, please, she whispered to herself as her fingers inched upward. She breathed out slowly as she felt the narrow crack widen to form a pocket in the rock.

Up this high the air was as blue as the sky in a fairy tale and the clouds were pillows of white. To succeed, Tracy would have to float on the air. She watched the clouds until her body grew as light as one of them. She was gossamer, butterfly wings, puffballs blown from a dandelion.

Tracy made a fist with her right hand, increasing its width until it was wedged into the crack. She breathed in, then expelled violently, pushing out from the cliff with an explosive thrust. Her right hand was a ball of iron. For a moment it was her only contact with the world. Then she pivoted on it, swinging upward past the outer rim of the overhang. Her free hand reached high. It would only have a moment of contact in which to grip tight enough to support her body.

Tracy twisted and the fingers of her left hand found a hold just as the force of the swing wrenched her fist from the crack. For a second, she dangled in space, halfway between safety and oblivion. Then her fingers tightened and she drew her body upward in a one-armed pull-up. The right hand arced over the lip of the overhang and gripped. A moment later, Tracy was over the top, stretched out on her stomach, adrenaline coursing through her as she trembled with elation.

The summit was now an easy climb, not worth more than a casual thought. When she reached the top, Tracy turned slowly, looking across the evergreen forest at the peaks of rugged, snowdusted mountains all covered by a sky of the clearest blue. This was the world the way an eagle saw it. Tracy inhaled the sweet mountain air. Then she sat on the edge of the cliff, unhooked her water bottle and took a drink.

The climb had forced Tracy to forget about everything except the rock. Now that the climb was over, there was no way to avoid thinking about the conflict that dominated her every waking moment the way the Cascade Mountains dominated the skyline. Matthew Reynolds's life was an inspiration to every attorney who undertook a death penalty case. If Tracy did what the law and the Canon of Ethics required, she would bring him down. All of Matthew's good deeds would be forgotten, because of a single act committed for love.

Tracy had decided that she would never reveal the truth behind the photograph if she knew for certain that Abigail Griffen was innocent, because a jury that learned about the photograph would convict Abbie and probably sentence her to death. It was the possibility that Griffen was guilty that made Tracy's predicament so difficult.

Matthew was convinced that someone was framing Abbie. There was certainly enough evidence to support that conclusion. Griffen was brilliant. She would never use the same type of bomb Deems had used in the Hollins murder, knowing it would make her a suspect. If she did use a bomb, she wouldn't be stupid enough to leave a piece of it in her garage. The strip of metal Torino had found in the garage was not even from the bomb, making it likely that it had been planted to frame Griffen. Then there was Deems. If the $100,000 was a payoff for perjury, Abbie was innocent.

Which brought Tracy to the next question. If Abbie was innocent, who was guilty? Deems was the easy answer. But someone paid Deems $100,000 for something. Whether it was to kill Justice Griffen, frame Abbie, or both, there still had to be someone else involved. But who? And what motive did they have?

Suddenly a thought occurred to her. She had been assuming that either Abbie murdered the judge and Laura because they were lovers or the two murders were unconnected. What if Laura's murder and the murder of Justice Griffen were connected, but someone else killed them? That would put a whole new slant on the case.

Justice Kelly was a possible suspect. Had she lied when she said that her sexual relationship with Justice Griffen meant little to her? What if she was insanely jealous and killed the judge and Laura because Griffen had taken Laura as his lover?

Then Tracy remembered the transcripts and the cases on the sheet of legal paper. Laura had been upset about something for weeks before her death. It would have been natural for Laura to tell Justice Griffen what was bothering her, especially if, in addition to being his law clerk, she was also his lover. What if the transcript and the cases were evidence of something illegal? Were they what the murderer was looking for when he ransacked Laura's office and cottage?

The transcript was a public record that anyone could get, but Tracy had read the transcript and had no idea why it was important. It was the same with the cases. Nothing she had read in them had alerted her. Having the transcript and the list was meaningless unless you knew what to look for. If Laura's killer learned that Justice Griffen had the transcript and the list of cases, and suspected that the judge knew why they were important, he would have a motive to kill Justice Griffen. But how could she possibly figure out why the cases and the transcript were important or if they even had any significance?

Tracy wished that she could forget about the case and stay forever on this perch where she could be above it all, but she had to descend to earth. She felt defeated by the case but she had to keep going. She had no choice. If she could not solve the murders, she would have to tell Judge Baldwin about the fake photograph. Tracy sighed and took a mixture of nuts and dried fruit from a plastic bag in her side pocket. She chewed slowly and took another drink of water. Then she carefully checked her climbing gear and started her descent.

Chapter Twenty-seven

1

As soon as she woke up Friday morning, Tracy slipped into a heavy sweater and jeans and carried a bran muffin and a mug of black coffee onto her terrace. As she ate, Tracy watched the drawbridges rise to accommodate a rusted tanker with a Spanish name and a Liberian flag. She wished Barry was sitting beside her. Tracy missed him. He was a kind and considerate lover. More important, he was a kind and considerate man. She understood why Barry wasn't with her. She admired him for his loyalty. But she wished he was helping her and she knew that she would lose him for good, if she hadn't already, unless she could prove Abigail Griffen was innocent.

After breakfast, Tracy called in sick. It was not a complete lie. She was sick at heart and could not imagine being in a place where she would see both Matthew and

Barry. The receptionist told Tracy that Judge Baldwin was taking the prosecution's motion to introduce evidence of Laura's murder under advisement and had dismissed the jury for the weekend. Tracy hung up and called Bob Packard's office.

'I wanted to thank you for lending us the transcripts,' Tracy said. 'They've been very useful.'

'Glad I could help,' Packard answered.

'I was wondering if you could help me again.'

'What do you need?'

'Could you tell me a little about a case you handled in the Supreme Court? *State* v. *Galarraga*.'

'Is Ernesto going to be a witness in the *Griffen* case?'

'No. Why do you ask?'

'He knows a lot about Charlie Deems.'

'He does?'

'You didn't know?'

'No, I didn't.'

'Do you know who Raoul Otero is?'

'He's mixed up with narcotics, isn't he?'

Packard laughed. 'That's like asking if Babe Ruth is mixed up with baseball. Otero is a major Mexican drug dealer with a distribution network that covers large parts of the western United States. Charlie Deems was the Portland distributor for the Otero organization. Ernesto Galarraga worked for Charlie.'

Tracy thought about that for a moment. Then she asked, 'Do the names Jorge Zamora or Pedro Cardona mean anything to you?'

Tracy listened intently to what Packard had to say. As soon as she hung up, she made a call to Medford and talked to the district attorney who had prosecuted Pedro Cardona. When the call was over, Tracy was certain she had discovered the importance of the cases on Laura's list. She felt sick to her stomach. Coming so soon after her discovery of Matthew Reynolds's crime, it was almost too much to take in. If she was right, and could prove it, she could give the state Justice Griffen's killer and save Matthew Reynolds from disgrace. Tracy looked at her watch. It was only nine o'clock. She had time to do the necessary research at the law library and be at the Supreme Court by one.

2

Alice Sherzer gave Tracy a hug, then ushered her into her chambers.

'Are you surviving Matthew Reynolds's sweatshop?'

'Barely,' Tracy answered tersely.

'Is the job as much fun as you thought it would be?'

'Matthew is a brilliant man and a great trial lawyer,' Tracy said, avoiding a lie.

'How do you like trying a major murder case?'

'That's what I wanted to talk to you about. Mrs. Griffen's case.'

Justice Sherzer looked surprised. 'I don't think I can do that, Tracy. If she's convicted, there's a good chance the court will have to hear her appeal.'

'I know that. But I've discovered something that involves the court. Something you have to know. It bears not only on Justice Griffen's murder but also on the murder of Laura Rizzatti.'

'I don't understand.'

Tracy paused. Her stomach heaved and she felt light-headed. The full import of what she was going to say had not fully dawned on her until now.

'Judge, I think Justice Griffen and Laura Rizzatti were murdered because they learned that a member of this court is influencing the outcome of cases involving the Otero narcotics organization.'

Alice Sherzer stared at Tracy for a moment. Then she shook her head. 'I don't believe that for a moment,' she said angrily.

'Hear me out. I know how you feel. I've been sick with the thought of it, but I can't see any other explanation for what I've found.'

Justice Sherzer frowned. Then she pressed the button on her intercom and told her secretary that she did not want to be interrupted by anyone.

Tracy told Justice Sherzer about Laura's reaction when she had caught her reading the *Deems* transcript and the way Laura hid the names of the cases on the legal pad. Then Tracy explained how she found the transcript and the yellow sheet in the evidence taken from Justice Griffen's den.

'I'm sure Laura figured out a connection between the cases and told Justice Griffen what she discovered. I think they were both murdered to prevent them from disclosing what they knew.'

'And what is that?'

'I still have no idea why the transcript is important. But I'm certain I know the significance of the cases.'

Tracy gave Justice Sherzer a summary of the cases. Then she said, 'Ernesto Galarraga worked with Charlie Deems and they both worked for Raoul Otero. Jorge Zamora was an enforcer for Otero. He murdered one of their rivals in a convenience store. He also killed the clerk to make the hit look like a robbery. Pedro Cardona was a front man for Otero in southern Oregon. He was trying to establish a distribution network in Medford when he was busted.

'Deems, Cardona, Zamora and Galarraga all worked for Otero. They were all convicted, but their convictions were reversed by a divided court. Justice Lefcourt was in the majority in *Zamora*, but he dissented in the other cases. Justices Griffen, Kelly, Arriaga and Pope were in the majority in every one of the cases.

'In every case but *Zamora*, which was reversed on an evidence issue, the court reversed on a novel legal theory. In *Deems*, the majority adopted a rule involving confessions that is the law in only three other states. In *Cardona* and *Galarraga*, the court interpreted the Oregon constitution in a way that ran contrary to the interpretation of the Fourth Amendment to the federal constitution. I talked with the DA who prosecuted Cardona. He was shocked by the reversal. There was a U.S. Supreme Court case right on point. He said the trial judge upheld the search without batting an eye and the Court of Appeals affirmed with no dissenters.

'I spent two hours this morning reading the criminal cases the court has decided in the past five years to see if I could find any other cases that fit this pattern. I think that's what Laura did. Justice Sherzer, those cases are unique. There are no other criminal cases with this exact voting bloc in the past five years.'

'How did Laura stumble onto the pattern?' Justice Sherzer asked.

'I have no idea. The cases are spread through a five-year period. The reversal of any one of them should have gone unnoticed. I think something in the *Deems* transcript tipped her off, but I have no idea what it is. What I strongly suspect is that either Justice Kelly, Pope or Arriaga is working for Raoul Otero to influence the other judges to reverse cases in which important members of the Otero organization are the defendants. Somehow, this justice learned that Laura knew what was going on and had told Justice Griffen. I think that's why they were killed.'

'How could one person guarantee three other votes?'

'There were no guarantees. But some of the judges, like Frank Arriaga and Justice Griffen, were very sensitive to defendant's rights and you know how an undecided vote can be influenced by a passionate advocate.'

'Tracy, listen to what you're saying. Can you honestly imagine a member of this court murdering Laura and Robert?'

393

'No, but I can imagine him paying Charlie Deems to do it. I think the hundred thousand dollars that Matthew found in Deems's bank account was the payoff for a double killing.'

'Tracy, this doesn't make sense. I know these people.'

'Did either Justice Pope, Arriaga or Kelly take the lead in trying to reverse these cases during conferences?'

'You know I can't reveal what goes on in conference.'

'You've got to. We're talking about a double homicide and the possibility of an innocent person being convicted for one of them.'

Justice Sherzer sighed. 'You're right, of course. But I can't remember the discussions of those cases. Some of them took place four years ago.'

'What about *Deems*. It's fairly recent. Who pushed for the reversal?'

'I believe Frank Arriaga was very concerned about the use of the informant. He and Stuart argued vehemently about the case.'

'Why did Justice Griffen write the opinion?'

'Frank was going to do it. Then he got hung up on a complex land-use decision and he asked Robert to write it. They were in agreement on the issues and Robert didn't have any outstanding decisions, so he volunteered to help out.'

'Can you think of any reason why Justice Arriaga would work for Raoul Otero?'

'Certainly not! And I cannot imagine Frank killing anyone. That's preposterous.'

'What about money? Is he in debt? Does he have a drug habit? Anything like that?'

'Frank Arriaga is a dear man with a rock-solid marriage and two children who adore him. I don't even think he drinks, for God's sake. You're way off base if you think Frank is your killer.'

'Then what about Mary Kelly?'

Justice Sherzer frowned. 'Money wouldn't be the motive. She was a very successful corporate attorney and has done quite well in the stock market and real estate.'

'Did you know that she and Justice Griffen were having an affair?'

'No, but I'm not surprised. Mary's marriage is not particularly happy.'

'If they were seeing each other when Laura was killed, Justice Griffen might have confided what Laura told him without realizing that he was alerting her. If Justice Kelly is the murderer, that would explain how she learned that she was in danger.'

'I'm afraid I can't help you, Tracy. I can't think of anything that would lead me to conclude that Mary is dishonest.'

'Which brings us to the most likely suspect. Arnold Pope is a conservative ex-DA. What was he doing voting to reverse the convictions of two murderers and two drug dealers?'

'Arnold is a peculiar man. He's the most obnoxious and contrary justice with whom I have ever served, but a lot of what he does is a pose. The man is very insecure and he desperately wants our approval. He knows he's seen as a buffoon and he knows everyone resents the way he ran his campaign and the fact that he replaced a brilliant justice who was well liked and widely respected. So to prove he is a legal scholar, too, Arnold occasionally takes positions that run counter to his image.'

'Do you know about Pope's run-in with Laura?'

'No.'

Tracy told Justice Sherzer about the confrontation in the library.

'I told Justice Griffen, the day I left the court. He said he was going to tell everyone about it.'

'He was very upset when Laura was killed. Maybe he forgot. What are you planning to do, Tracy?'

'I don't know. I was hoping you could help me. I thought that you might recall something that would shed some light on this if I told you what I'd discovered.'

'I'm sorry to disappoint you. But I'm still far from convinced that one of my colleagues is a killer who is working for a major drug dealer. It's too fantastic.'

'As fantastic as a justice and his clerk both being murdered in less than a month? It could be coincidence, but I don't think so. I've been thinking back to the night Laura was murdered. I was in the library working on a memo for you in the Scott probate matter. When I came downstairs, there was a light on in Laura's office, but there were no other lights on in the clerks' office area. I looked in Laura's office. I could see someone had ransacked it, so I reached for the phone to call Laura. That's when I heard the door to the clerks' area close.

'I wasn't thinking straight or I'd never have done it, but I rushed into the hall. There was no one there. I rushed to the back door and didn't see anyone in the parking lot. I was upset and I didn't want to stay alone in the building, so I calmed down and headed for my office to leave my notes with the idea of finishing the memo in the morning. That's when I discovered Laura's body. Do you see what I missed?'

'No, I don't.'

'Where did the killer go? I was in the hall seconds after the door to the clerks' area closed. If the killer left by the front door to the building, I would have heard it close. It's the same with the back door. And there was no one in the parking lot. A stranger to the building would have high-tailed it out, but someone who worked in it would have just as likely run upstairs.

'The person who killed Laura had to be familiar with the layout of the clerks' area to hide so quickly and to be able to get out in the dark without me hearing. I think the killer rushed upstairs, waited for me to go back into the clerks' area, then snuck down the stairs and left. This all points to the killer being a person who was very familiar with the court.'

Justice Sherzer mulled over what Tracy had told her. When she made her decision, she looked grim.

'I still don't buy your theory, but I'm going to discuss it with Stuart.'

'Thank you. And try to think back to the conferences. If

I'm right, the justice who's behind this had to have been working very hard to swing the necessary votes. If you can remember who the common denominator was in all four cases, you'll know the murderer.'

3

Tracy started back to Portland on the interstate as soon as she left Justice Sherzer. She was certain she knew why Laura and Justice Griffen had been killed. What she did not know was the clue that had tipped off Laura to the identity of the judge who was working for Raoul Otero. No one was going to believe a Supreme Court justice was on the take without proof and she had to believe that the transcript held the proof.

As far as Tracy knew, Laura had never heard of Charlie Deems, or his case, until Deems's appeal was filed in the Supreme Court. If that was true, then the information in the transcript had to concern the crooked justice, but Tracy had read the transcript and none of the justices were mentioned in Volume XI.

Tracy arrived home at 4:30 and went for a run along the river. She wore only shorts and a tee shirt even though it was cold. She was still sore from her climb, but the exertion soon warmed her. When she was into a comfortable pace, Tracy began reviewing what she knew about the Griffen and Rizzatti murders. She exhausted the subject with no new insights.

Tracy turned for home. A light drizzle dulled her enthusiasm for the run. She wished Barry was there to keep her company. She always felt so comfortable when they were together. Would Barry really leave her if she told the court what Matthew had done? The possibility was real and the thought of losing Barry frightened her. But would their relationship change if she sold out her principles to keep them together? Wouldn't the sacrifice kill the feeling between them anyway?

Tracy felt a tightening in her chest that had nothing to do with exertion. What she and Barry had was so good. Why couldn't it last? Tracy knew Barry was special the first time they kissed. She would always remember that morning at the beach below the Griffen cabin and the wonderful picnic afterward.

Tracy stopped in mid-stride. The Overlook. She bent over and rested with her hands on her knees. They had gone to the Overlook after their picnic and she had looked at the register. It had been right there all along. Tracy stood up, oblivious to the rain and cold. She followed her train of thought to its inevitable conclusion and knew she was right.

Tracy raced back to her apartment. She showered quickly and changed into clean clothes. She was impatient to look at her notes from the visit to the Overlook, but she wanted to wait until the staff was gone and, hopefully, Barry with them.

The rain stopped by 6:30. Tracy was relieved to see that the lights in Matthew Reynolds's living quarters were out

when she arrived at the office. She let herself in through
the back door and found her notes from the visit to the
Overlook in her case file. Tracy reread pages 1289 and
1290 of Volume XI to confirm her suspicions. Then she
went back to her car and drove to Salem.

4

At exactly 7:20 on Friday evening, moments before Tracy
turned off I-5 at the second Salem exit, Bobby Cruz parked
his car on a narrow gravel side road and walked across a
field that bordered the farmhouse where Chuck Geddes
was hiding Charlie Deems. The field was damp from the
rain that had stopped around seven o'clock, and there was
an ozone smell in the air. When he reached the house,
Cruz circled it cautiously, peering into windows so he
could figure out the number of targets.

The two cops assigned to guard Deems were watching
a Blazers game on the TV in the living room.
Unfortunately, Deems was not with them. If he had been,
Cruz could have held all three at gunpoint, shot Deems
and escaped without having to kill the cops. Now he had
to take them out. He couldn't risk Deems escaping while
he dicked around in the living room tying people up.
Cruz didn't mind killing cops, but Raoul was paranoid
about doing anything that would bring down heat on the
business. He knew he'd have to listen to Raoul scream at
him, but Raoul's ass wasn't on the line.

Cruz slipped through an unlocked side door into a short hallway that led to the kitchen. To the right was a stairway to the second floor. Cruz guessed that Deems was probably sacking out in an upstairs bedroom.

When Cruz stepped around the corner into the living room the cops looked shocked. One of them was drinking a glass of soda and balancing a plate with a sandwich on his lap. He jumped up. Pieces of bread, a slice of tomato and slabs of turkey went flying. Cruz shot the officer in the forehead while he was going for his gun. He was dead before his plate shattered on the hardwood floor.

The second officer had fast reflexes. While Cruz was shooting his partner, he was rolling and ducking. He almost had his gun out when Cruz shot him in the ear. Cruz took a second to check the bodies to make certain they were dead.

There was a silencer on Cruz's gun and both kills had been accomplished with a minimum of noise. Cruz moved to the living-room entrance and scanned the hall. He strained to hear any sound that would indicate that Deems was on the move. When he heard nothing he went down the hall to check the kitchen, before going upstairs to finish his work.

Cruz crouched low and swung through the kitchen door into more pain than he could imagine. The pain covered every inch of his face. It blinded and paralyzed him and it deafened him to the cry of animal rage that came from Charlie Deems's throat as he stepped out of the kitchen and turned the cast-iron skillet sideways. This

401

time, instead of smashing the flat of the pan into Cruz's face, Deems swung the edge against his right shin. Bone snapped and Cruz collapsed on the floor.

When he swung the skillet, Charlie's face looked crazed, but a horrific smile transformed his features into a demonic mask as he watched Bobby Cruz twitch on the hall floor. The pan had smashed every part of Cruz's face, and it was hard to make out his features because they were covered with blood.

Deems caught his breath. Cruz's gun was on the floor where he had dropped it as he staggered back after the first blow. Charlie picked it up and put it on a hall table. Then he methodically crushed the fingers on both of Cruz's hands. When he was certain Cruz was incapacitated, Charlie looked in the living room. The cops were so obviously dead, Deems didn't bother to look at them closely.

Cruz moaned. 'Time to go to work,' Deems sighed. He went into the kitchen and traded the skillet for several sharp knives and a pitcher of ice water. When he came back into the hall, Cruz was looking at him with glazed eyes.

'Hey, Bobby. How you doin'?' Charlie asked with his trademark grin. Cruz sucked air.

'Sorry about the teeth.' Deems chuckled. 'It's gonna be tough getting dates for a while, amigo.'

Cruz tried to say 'fuck you,' but his mouth didn't work right. Deems laughed and tousled Cruz's hair.

'Sorry, Bobby, you're not my type. I'd rather fuck Abigail Griffen. But thanks for the offer.'

Cruz mumbled something and Deems smiled.

'I bet you just cursed me out again. Am I right? But that's not necessary. A smart guy like you doesn't have to resort to this macho bullshit. In a situation like this, you should be using your brains. Of course, you weren't using your brains when you came in the side door. Didn't you wonder why it was the only door that wasn't locked?'

Deems paused to watch Cruz's reaction, but Cruz wouldn't give him the satisfaction. That was okay. Charlie loved a challenge. He squatted next to Cruz and continued speaking as if they were friends seated in a bistro sipping a good dark beer.

'I knew Raoul was gonna send you after me sooner or later, so I've been watching for you. When I saw you creeping through the tall grass like a wetback crossing the border, I slipped downstairs and fixed it so you could get in.

'Now, I should be angry, because you just tried to kill me, but I'm not. You don't know it, but you've given me the chance to do some really naughty things without getting caught. See, I'm going out for a while. Then I'll come back and call Geddes. I'll tell him how you killed the cops and tried to kill me. You're gonna be my alibi. Is that some great plan or what?'

Cruz still stared defiantly. Deems looked amused.

'Don't be that way, Bobby. I don't know why you're mad at me. I'm not mad at you. In fact, if you tell me where you stashed your car, I promise I'll kill you quickly. What do you say?'

403

'Kiss my ass,' Cruz managed. Deems laughed.

'These offers of sexual delight are hard to pass up, but I'd rather play *Jeopardy!* The guards used to let us watch it on the row. It's my favorite game show and I'm damn good. Bobby, do you know how to play *Jeopardy!*?'

Cruz refused to answer. Deems drove a knife into his thigh. The scream pierced the air and Cruz's right leg shot forward, causing more pain in the fractured shin.

'Sound check,' Charlie told Cruz. 'I had to make certain that you can talk, because you can't play *Jeopardy!* unless you can answer the questions.'

Deems pulled out the knife and Bobby groaned. Deems splashed some ice water on Cruz's face and slapped his cheeks. Cruz opened his eyes. Deems slapped him again, hard, and said, 'Pay attention. Here's how the game works. I'm gonna give you the answer and you have to say the question. Like if I asked, "He was the first President of the United States," you'd say, "Who was George Washington?" Get it?

'Now, if you get all the answers, you get the grand prize. It's an all-expenses-paid trip to Hawaii for you and the wife and kids, plus a Buick convertible. Sounds good, right? But if you miss the question, uh-oh, there's a penalty. I'll keep you guessing about that.'

Charlie winked at Cruz and noted, with satisfaction, that the macho glint was leaving Cruz's eyes. Fear was their new resident. Cruz was tough, but Charlie was crazy and he was sounding crazier by the moment. If there was one thing tough guys like Cruz could not deal with, it was the unknown, and crazy people were the ultimate unknown.

'Our first category is American history. Here's the answer. "He was President Millard Filmore's Secretary of State." What's the question?'

'What?' Cruz asked.

'Wrong answer, Bobby. Watt was a Scottish engineer who made improvements on the steam engine.'

Deems grabbed Cruz's right hand and stabbed him through the palm, pinning the hand to the floor. Cruz fainted. Deems threw ice water in his face and waited patiently until Cruz revived. Then he leaned over and whispered in Cruz's ear, '*Jeopardy!* is a pretty violent game. It can hurt to get the wrong answer.'

'Okay, okay, I'll tell you what you want,' Cruz whimpered, his eyes wide with pain and fear.

'That's not how it works, Bobby. You have to wait for the question. However, it is time to play *Double Jeopardy!* There are two grand prizes. The first prize is a trip to Disneyland, where you get to meet Miss America. The second prize is you get to fuck her. Pretty good, huh?'

Deems smiled and picked up another knife. 'Unfortunately, there's also a double penalty for a wrong answer. It's both your eyes, amigo. Ready? Here's the answer. "He won the Pulitzer Prize for Poetry in 1974." What's the question, Bobby?'

'Please, Charlie, please,' Cruz sobbed.

'Buzz!' Charlie shouted in Cruz's ear. 'Time's up.'

Deems grabbed Cruz's chin and put the blade under

Cruz's right eye. Cruz began to tremble violently. He tried to shake his head from side to side, but Deems held it steady. Tears ran from Cruz's eyes.

'The car's by the field,' Cruz screamed. 'On the gravel road.' Deems smiled coldly. He shook his head from side to side in disgust.

'I'm disappointed in you, Bobby. I was sure you'd hold out a little longer. I guess you're not so tough after all.'

Deems picked up the gun and shot Cruz between the eyes. Then he took Cruz's car keys from his pocket, went upstairs and changed his clothes. When Charlie left the house, he was feeling good. Bobby Cruz had been a great preliminary and he was ready for the main event.

5

Arnold Pope's front door was opened by a short woman with leathery skin and a sour expression.

'Mrs. Pope, I'm Tracy Cavanaugh. I used to clerk for Justice Sherzer. We met at the clerk's picnic.'

'Oh yes.'

'Is Justice Pope in? I have something very important I need to discuss with him.'

'It's almost eight o'clock, Miss Cavanaugh. Couldn't this wait until tomorrow?. Arnold's had a very hard day.'

'I wish it could, but it's urgent. I promise I won't be long.'

'Very well,' Mrs. Pope said, not bothering to mask her disapproval. 'Step in and I'll ask Arnold if he'll see you.'

The Popes lived in a modern ranch-style home in the hills south of Salem. The entryway where Tracy waited had a stone floor and white walls. There was a small marble table against one wall. A slender blue-gray pottery vase filled with daffodils stood at one end of the table under a mirror with a gilt frame.

'Tracy! Good to see you,' Justice Pope said affably, smiling at her as if she was an old friend.

'I'm sorry to come by so late.'

'No problem. Myra says you have something important to discuss. Why don't we go back to my den.'

Justice Pope led Tracy to the back of the house and down a set of stairs to the basement. To the left was a wood-paneled room where two BarcaLoungers were set up in front of a big-screen TV. In one corner was a small desk. A bookshelf with Reader's Digest condensed books, some best-sellers and a scattering of law books took up one wall.

The smile left Pope's face as soon as they were alone.

'You have some nerve coming to my house after telling those damn lies to the police.'

'I was very upset when Laura died. She was my friend. I wanted to help the police and it did look like you were making a pass at Laura.'

'Well, I wasn't. And I don't appreciate people talking about me behind my back.'

'That's the way it appeared to me. If I'm wrong, I apologize, but Justice Griffen told me you'd done something like that before.'

'What! I never . . .' Pope stopped. He looked furious. 'I'll tell you something, Miss Cavanaugh. I know all the clerks mooned around about Robert Griffen, the great protector of constitutional rights, but Griffen was no angel. He's the one who made passes at the clerks. I'm surprised he didn't put the make on you. Now, what's so important that you had to interrupt my evening?'

'I've come across some information that suggests that Justice Griffen's murder and the murder of Laura Rizzatti may be connected. Can you tell me why Laura was upset when you talked to her in the library?'

'I shouldn't give you the time of day after you started that damn rumor and I don't see how our conversation in the library can possibly bear on Laura's murder.'

'Please. I promise you it's very important.'

Pope frowned, then said, 'Oh, all right. I'll tell you what happened. Then I want you to leave.'

'Thank you.'

'That meeting was Laura's idea. When I got there, she asked me why I voted to reverse the *Deems* case. I told her that was none of her business. I must have sounded angry, because she got upset. I put my hand on her shoulder and told her to calm down. That's when you appeared. As soon as she saw you, Laura backed away from me. She looked frightened. I had the impression that she was concerned that you'd overhear us. In any event, I left and that was all there was to it.'

'Why did you vote to reverse *Deems*?' Tracy asked.

'That's confidential.'

'Justice Pope, I have reason to believe that one of the justices on the court was paid to influence cases involving the Otero narcotics organization. Over the past five years, four cases involving members of this group have been reversed. You, Justice Griffen, Justice Kelly and Justice Arriaga voted to reverse in each case. I think Laura Rizzatti figured out who was taking money from Otero. If one of the other justices put pressure on you to vote for reversal, that justice may be the person who killed Laura Rizzatti.'

Pope looked at Tracy as if she was insane. 'That's absolutely preposterous. Are you out of your mind?'

'No, sir. I have evidence to support my suspicions.'

'I don't believe it. And I can tell you that none of the justices put any pressure on me . . .'

Pope paused in mid-sentence, suddenly remembering something. He looked uncomfortable. When he spoke, he no longer sounded sure of himself.

'There is some horse trading that goes on among the justices. I felt very strongly about a fishing rights case, but I couldn't get a majority. One of the justices told me I'd get my majority in the fishing case if I changed my vote in *Deems*. Well, I was on the fence in *Deems*. It bothered me that the police used an informant the way they did. Deems deserved the death penalty, but I thought the law had been violated. I wouldn't have done things that way when I was DA.'

'So you switched your vote.'

'Right. And the other justice gave me my majority in the other case.'

'You also voted to reverse in the *Galarraga*, *Zamora* and *Cardona* cases. Think back. Did the same justice do anything to win over those votes?'

'My God,' Pope said, and suddenly grew pale.

'Which justice was it?' Tracy asked, certain she knew the name Pope would tell her.

6

Abbie had prepared chicken with apricots and avocado in a light cream sauce. The dish had been complemented by a fine Vouvray. It was one of several dinners Abbie had cooked for Matthew, who was beginning to appreciate cuisine more extravagant than the steaks he normally ate.

While Abbie was putting the finishing touches on their dinner, Matthew built a roaring fire in the living room. After dinner, they carried their coffee cups to the couch and sat side by side in front of the fireplace. Matthew had been distracted in court that morning during the hearing on Geddes's motion and he had been quiet all evening. Abbie was not surprised by his courtroom demeanor. They were both concerned about the possibility that Judge Baldwin would permit the state to reopen its case. But Abbie expected Matthew to loosen up when he was alone with her.

'What's wrong?' Abbie asked, putting her hand on top of Matthew's.

'Nothing,' Matthew answered, wishing he could enjoy

the evening but finding it impossible to be happy knowing that Abbie's freedom and his career depended on whether Tracy Cavanaugh decided to tell Judge Baldwin about the fake photograph.

'You've been so quiet. Are you sure nothing is bothering you?'

'It's the case,' he lied. 'I'm worried that I won't be able to convince Judge Baldwin to keep out the Rizzatti evidence.'

Abbie put down her coffee and turned toward Matthew. She put her hand on his cheek and kissed him. 'Don't think about law tonight,' she said.

Matthew put his cup down. Abbie snuggled against his chest.

'Very touching,' Charlie Deems said from the living-room doorway.

Abbie jerked around and Matthew sprang to his feet. Deems gave them his goofy grin and ran his finger around his left ear to clean out some wax. He wore a pressed shirt and ironed slacks. His hair was slicked back. He looked like a farm boy at a 4-H meeting, except for the gun with the silencer that dangled from his right hand.

'Looks like you two are having a real good time,' Deems said.

'What are you doing here?' Abbie asked, standing beside Matthew.

'I came to visit,' Deems said, walking casually across the room until he was two arm lengths from them. 'I'll bet I'm the last person you expected to see. Am I right?'

411

'I'd like you to leave.'

'I bet you would. Then you and Mr. Smart Guy here could do the nasty thing. Course, if I was in your shoes, I'd want me out of this house, too. And I don't blame you. Me being a previously convicted murderer and all. What did you call me during my trial? An animal, devoid of feeling.'

'What do you want, Mr. Deems?' Matthew asked.

'I might want revenge on the person responsible for putting me in that teensy-weensy cell on death row. I remember every minute on the row, Miss Prosecutor.' Deems smiled wistfully, like a man recalling a sweet summer morning. 'Did you know that the toilet in the cell above us leaked. Did you know we was double-bunked for a while. Man, was that cell crowded. I had to eat my dinner sitting on the crapper. That's quite an indignity. Some people put in that situation, finding themselves with the person responsible for it, might be filled with rage and an uncontrollable impulse to do the responsible person some type of outrageous harm.'

Deems paused for a heartbeat. Then he broke into a grin. Abbie's mouth was dry and her senses were more alert than at any other time in her life.

'Rape. Am I right? Bet it's what you thought of first. You're probably picturing it right now. Can you see yourself naked, tied up on the bed, screaming, with no one to help you? At my mercy? That's not a pretty picture.'

Deems let the thought linger. Then he took a step toward Abbie. She moved into Matthew.

Deems smiled again. 'I was hoping to get you alone

for a long weekend, Counselor. Unfortunately, I'm a little pressed for time, so I'm gonna have to do you now.'

Matthew stepped in front of Abbie. 'You will not hurt her.'

Deems laughed. 'What are you gonna do? Cross-examine me to death?' The smile disappeared. 'I didn't appreciate the way you set me up so I'd look like a fool. In fact, I don't appreciate either of you. So, first, I'm gonna have my way with the little lady, while you watch. Maybe you'll even learn a thing or two. Then I'm going to make sure you both die very slowly. And I'll watch.'

Matthew lunged while Deems was speaking. The move surprised Deems. Reynolds drove him into the wall, but this was the first fight he had been in since grade school and he had no idea what to do next. Deems brought a knee up between Matthew's legs. Matthew gasped and sagged. His grip on Deems loosened. Deems saw Abbie race out of the room and quickly head-butted Reynolds. Matthew staggered backward. Deems heard Abbie pounding up the stairs and shot Reynolds in the side. Matthew looked dazed and crumpled to the floor.

'We're gonna get to the good part soon,' Deems said, 'so you stay right here. Any objection?'

Matthew gasped from pain. Deems kicked him hard in the ribs and Matthew fainted.

'Objection overruled.'

Deems turned toward the stairs. He listened for a moment, then climbed them. At the top he shouted, 'Come out, come out, wherever you are.'

There was no response.

'The longer it takes me to find you, the longer it will take you and your boyfriend to die.'

Deems paused for an answer, but there was only silence. He looked down the hall. There were two doors on one side and three on the other. He eased open the first door. It was an empty guest bathroom.

The next door opened into Abbie's bedroom. Deems liked it. The bed had a headboard and a footboard to which he could tie Abbie's hands and feet. He smiled in anticipation. Then he dropped beside the bed and looked under it. Abbie wasn't there. But, he thought, she might be in the closet. He stepped to the side and whipped open the door. A wall of dresses screened off the back wall. Deems ripped the curtain apart and made certain Abbie was not hidden in the shadows. Then he stepped into the hall.

'You're pissing me off, bitch,' he screamed. 'Get out here now or I'll start cutting off your boyfriend's fingers.'

Deems waited, hoping the loud threats would flush Abbie from hiding the way beaters flush lions for big-game hunters, but the hall stayed empty.

Deems smashed open the door to the guest room. He heard a whimper from the closet and smiled coldly. He heard another muffled sob and relaxed. Deems put the gun on the guest bed. He did not want to risk shooting Abbie and spoiling his fun. Then he tiptoed to the closet door, counted to three silently and whipped the door open, screaming, 'Surprise!'

But the surprise was all his. Abbie was sitting on the

closet floor with her back braced against the wall. The handgun she carried in her purse was aimed at Deems. Her face was set and there were no tears on her cheeks. It dawned on Charlie that Abbie had lured him to the closet with phony sobs and whimpers. He felt a momentary flash of fear, until he remembered his dark angel.

Charlie straightened slowly and raised his arms straight out from his sides as if they were angel wings. Suddenly he knew his angel was in the room, a shimmering presence, ready to protect him from all harm. He did not fear the gun, because nothing could hurt him while his angel stood sentry.

'What are you going to do, shoot me?' Deems asked with a smirk.

Abbie did not answer. She pulled the trigger instead. Deems's eyes widened in disbelief when the first bullet hit him and he died with a look of utter confusion on his face.

Chapter Twenty-eight

1

Judge Baldwin took Abbie off the electronic surveillance program at Jack Stamm's request the day after she killed Charlie Deems. She was at Matthew's side on the Thursday morning after the shooting, the day the doctors at St. Vincent's Hospital permitted him to have visitors for the first time.

Tracy waited until the end of visiting hours and convinced Abbie and the others to leave on the pretext that she had a confidential legal matter she had to discuss with her boss.

'How are you feeling?' Tracy asked when they were alone.

'Okay,' Matthew managed.

'I brought these for you,' she said, holding out a vase filled with roses. 'Where should I put them?'

Matthew slowly lifted his right arm and pointed toward several other vases that decorated the window. The nurse had cranked his bed into a sitting position. There was an IV in his left arm and a breathing tube in his nose. He looked tired, but alert. Tracy pulled a chair next to Matthew's bed.

'You don't have to worry anymore. I'm not going to tell anyone about the photograph. It would have been the hardest thing I've ever done, Mr. Reynolds. You have no idea how much I admire you.'

Their eyes met and Reynolds nodded a silent thank-you. Even now, it was hard for Tracy to think about how close she had come to destroying this fine, decent man.

'Why?' Matthew managed.

'I know Mrs. Griffen didn't kill her husband.'

'Who killed him?' Matthew asked with effort. His voice was hoarse.

'Just rest. I'll tell you everything.'

Tracy summarized her investigation and explained how the link between the cases Laura had written on her legal pad led her to the discovery that a Supreme Court justice was fixing decisions for Raoul Otero.

'What I couldn't figure out was how Laura had discovered the cases. They were spread out over several years, she wasn't on the court when most of them were decided and there didn't appear to be any reason for her to run across all four at once. The more I thought about it, the more certain I was that the answer was in the transcript, but I came up blank every time I read it.

417

'After Charlie Deems was arrested for the Hollins murders, the police searched his apartment. On page 1289 to 1290 of the transcript, a detective explains the significance of several messages that were left on Deems's answering machine. One of the calls is from an Arthur Knowland. Knowland needed some shirts and wanted Deems to call as soon as possible. Detective Simon testified that people who deal in drugs rarely call the drugs by name. Instead, they talk about shirts or tires. That meant that Arthur Knowland was calling to buy cocaine from Charlie Deems.

'Remember when you sent Barry and me to the Overlook to see if we could discover the identity of the woman Justice Griffen was meeting there?'

Reynolds nodded weakly.

'Well, I checked the register at the motel for the day that Mrs. Griffen confronted her husband after receiving the anonymous call. Justice Griffen hadn't registered in his own name. I wrote down a list of the names in the register. An Arthur Knowland was registered at the Overlook on the day Justice Griffen had sex with Justice Kelly.'

Reynolds's eyes widened as he saw immediately the significance of this information.

'As a result of Neil Christenson's investigation, we learned that the judge was also meeting Laura Rizzatti at the Overlook. I checked the register again and I found an Arthur Knowland registered on several occasions.

'I believe Laura found out that the judge was sleeping with Justice Kelly. I know she was infatuated with the judge from the way she acted when she talked about him to me. Finding out that the judge had another lover must have driven Laura to make the anonymous call to Mrs. Griffen. She must have been racked with jealousy and furious with him, but she still loved him.

'Then Laura ran across Arthur Knowland's name in the transcript and remembered that the judge had used that name when he registered at the Overlook. When Laura found out that the judge was buying drugs from Deems, she must have become suspicious of his reason for voting to reverse the *Deems* case. I think she checked to see if there had been other suspicious reversals since Justice Griffen came on the court. She found the other cases and realized that Griffen was on the take.

'Griffen needed money. He was using cocaine, and we know he was living beyond his means. I don't think he would have been able to resist a bribe in the amount Otero could offer. Who knows, Otero may have had evidence that Griffen was using drugs and blackmailed him with it.'

'My God,' Reynolds said. His voice sounded hoarse. There was a plastic pitcher next to the bed. Tracy filled a paper cup with water and helped Matthew drink it. Then she eased his head back onto the pillow.

'Laura called me the evening she was killed and left a message on my answering machine. She said she was in trouble and needed my help. While she was talking, there was a knock on her door. That must have been Justice Griffen. Laura was so in love with him, I think she

419

convinced herself that she was wrong to suspect him and told him everything she'd discovered. Then Justice Griffen killed her.'

Reynolds looked stunned. He closed his eyes and rested for a moment. When he spoke, it was with great effort.

'Who killed Griffen?'

'Charlie Deems. Remember the attack on Mrs. Griffen at the coast? She thought the intruder was Deems. This is all speculation, of course, but I'm betting it was and that Justice Griffen paid Deems the hundred thousand dollars in the account Barry discovered at Washington Mutual for a hit. It would have been worth the price. If Mrs. Griffen died before the divorce became final, Justice Griffen would have inherited all of her money. When Deems failed, Griffen would have wanted the money back. Maybe he made the mistake of threatening Deems.

'Deems was insane. He was also highly intelligent. Killing the judge and framing the woman who put him on death row for the murder is a truly twisted idea. And it's just the type of plan a maniac like Deems would devise.'

'I think you're right. You must go to Jack Stamm.'

'I will. But I didn't want to go without your approval. You're still the boss.'

Matthew tried to smile. Then, he started to cough. Tracy helped him drink some more water. Then she said, 'I'm going to go now. You need to rest.'

Matthew's eyelids fluttered. He was exhausted and medicated and staying awake was not easy. Just before

Tracy turned for the door, she heard him whisper, 'Thank you.'

Barry Frame stood up when Tracy left Matthew's hospital room.

'How did he take it?' Barry asked.

Tracy took both of Barry's hands. 'I think he's really relieved.'

'The poor bastard. He's been through hell. First worrying about what you'd do. Then getting shot.'

'You understand that I had no choice until I figured out that Abbie didn't kill her husband.'

Barry looked ashamed. 'I owe you an apology. You were always in the right. I just . . .'

Tracy squeezed his hands. 'No apologies, okay? Sometimes right and wrong aren't black and white.'

'What would you have done if you learned that Abbie was guilty?'

'I don't know and I'm glad I never had to make that decision.'

Tracy picked up her attaché case.

'Let's go to Jack Stamm's office and give him the evidence.'

2

That evening Abbie was sitting next to Matthew's bed, holding his hand, when Jack Stamm entered the hospital room.

'How is he doing?' Stamm asked Abbie.

'He's out of danger, but he'll have to stay here for a while. Is this a social call?'

'It is not. I wanted to tell Matt myself. I'm glad you're here. It saves me a trip out to your house.'

Matthew and Abbie stared at Stamm expectantly. Stamm broke into a grin.

'Chuck Geddes and I just spent an hour with Tracy Cavanaugh and Barry Frame. I'm dismissing the indictment tomorrow.'

'Does Geddes agree?' Matthew asked.

Stamm stopped smiling. 'He has no choice. His key witness is not only dead but thoroughly discredited, and his key evidence isn't evidence anymore. Chuck won't admit Abbie was framed, even after hearing what Ms. Cavanaugh uncovered, but I always believed in Abbie's innocence and I am now one hundred percent convinced of it. The Attorney General agrees. As of half an hour ago, Chuck Geddes is no longer a Multnomah County special deputy district attorney.'

Stamm looked at Abbie. 'I hope you know that I had no choice when I stepped aside and turned over the prosecution to the AG.'

'I never blamed you, Jack.'

'I'm glad. This prosecution has been very hard on me.'

'Matthew told me about your part in having me released from the jail. I'll always appreciate that. I don't know how I would have held up if I had to stay locked up there.'

'You would have done just fine. You're a tough guy.'

'Not as tough as I used to think.'

Stamm was embarrassed. He looked away for a second. Then he said, 'I want you to take a vacation with pay for a few weeks. Then, as soon as you're rested, I want you back at work.'

Now it was Abbie's turn to look away. 'I'm not coming back, Jack.'

'Look, I know how you feel. I've talked to everyone about this. There's not a soul in the office who doesn't want you with us. Hell, you're one of the best lawyers in the state. We need you.'

'I appreciate that and I want you to thank everyone. Hearing what you just said is important to me. But I've had an offer I can't turn down.'

Stamm looked back and forth between Abbie and Matthew.

'I'll be damned,' he said. Then he broke into a grin. 'I guess some good came out of this after all.'

'Will you be our best man?' Abbie asked.

'Hell, no. In fact, I'm going to jump up when the minister asks if there's anyone who objects to the wedding. If you think I'm going to let you two gang up on my office without doing anything to stop you, you're crazy.'

PART SEVEN
AFTER DARK

Chapter Twenty-nine

The way Tracy Cavanaugh was feeling, you'd think there was bright sun and a profusion of flowers outside her window, instead of a pounding downpour and predictions of solid rain for the rest of the week before Christmas. Tracy was humming while she worked and smiling when she wasn't humming, and there was more than one reason for her high spirits. The case against Abigail Griffen had been dismissed because of her detective work, Matthew was almost fully recuperated and would be released from the hospital in two days and her relationship with Barry was terrific.

A knock on her office door made Tracy turn away from her computer. On the monitor was a draft of points for the oral argument in the Texas case. Matthew wanted her to come with him when he argued before the Texas Court of Criminal Appeals.

'Tracy,' Emily Webster, Matthew's secretary, said excitedly, 'Dennis Haggard just called. They're dismissing the case against Jeffrey Coulter. Mrs. Franklin flunked the polygraph examination.'

'Fantastic. I'll tell Matt when I go to the hospital this afternoon.'

'The wedding invitations arrived,' Emily said, handing one to Tracy. 'Why don't you bring him a sample.'

'Sure.' Tracy grinned. 'He'll get a kick out of it.'

'Could you give him this, too. It's Dr. Shirov's bill. I want Mr. Reynolds to approve it before I write the check.'

Emily handed Tracy a sheaf of papers and left the room. Tracy set down the invitation and Dr. Shirov's bill and went back to work. Fifteen minutes later, she stopped typing and walked down to the library to check a case. She found the volume of the United States Supreme Court reporter she wanted and brought it back to her office, laying it on top of Dr. Shirov's bill so she could copy the passage she needed. When she was done, she closed the book, revealing the part of the bill that set out an account of the hours Dr. Shirov had spent on the case, the dates on which he had worked and the reason for spending the time.

Tracy frowned. Something was wrong with the bill. She picked it up and shook her head. It was obviously a typo. Tracy decided to straighten out the problem so Matthew wouldn't have to deal with it from his hospital bed. She was certain he would want Dr. Shirov paid promptly.

'Dr. Shirov,' Tracy said when she was put through to

the scientist, 'this is Tracy Cavanaugh at Matthew Reynolds's office. I'm sorry to bother you. I have your bill here. I'm going to bring it to Mr. Reynolds when I see him at the hospital this afternoon.'

'How is he feeling?'

'They're releasing him in two days. There's no permanent damage.'

'That's a great relief. Give him my regards.'

'I will. About the bill. There's a mistake on it. I'm certain it's a typo. I wanted to get the correct date, so we can pay you.'

'Good. I'm going on vacation and Matt's check will be welcome.'

Tracy laughed. 'I'll make sure we send it out pronto. Do you have your copy in front of you?'

'Let me get it.'

'Where is the problem?' Dr. Shirov asked a moment later.

'The first entry on your time records. It says Mr. Reynolds called you about the case in early October.'

'Yes.'

'We didn't know we would need you until the trial was halfway through. That would have been in mid-November.'

The line was silent for a second. Then Dr. Shirov said, 'The date is correct. I remember the call because Matt rang me at home.'

'Can you give me a summary, so I can refresh Mr. Reynolds's memory in case he has any questions?'

'Oh, it wasn't much. He said he was going to be in trial soon and might have a rush job for me. He was checking to make certain I would be in town. That was pretty much the whole thing, except for some small talk.'

'Did he tell you what he wanted you to do?'

'Not specifically, but he asked about the availability of the reactor.'

'Thanks, Dr. Shirov.'

'Remember to give Matt my regards, please.'

'I will.'

Tracy hung up and stared at the monitor. The words blurred. Her heart was beating so fast, it felt like it might blast out of her chest. Tracy walked out to Emily Webster's desk.

'Where does Mr. Reynolds keep his account ledgers?'

'I've got them.'

'I have to see if he wrote a check to Dr. Shirov in connection with the Griffen case,' Tracy lied.

'I'll look it up for you.'

'Don't bother. I'll do it. It could take some time.'

Tracy took the trust account ledger and check register to her office. She went back several months, but could not find what she was looking for. When she brought the ledger and register to Emily, the secretary was getting ready to leave for lunch with the receptionist.

'Who's minding the store?' Tracy asked.

'Maggie is sick. We're having the answering service handle the calls during lunch. You're the only one in. If you want, I'll tell the service to put your calls through.'

'No. That's okay.'

Tracy forced herself to wait five minutes after everyone left. Then she locked the front door and walked quickly up the stairs to Matthew's living quarters. She had never seen them before. At one end of the hall was a small kitchen. She went through the drawers quickly, finding only kitchen utensils. The next room was Matthew's bedroom. She hesitated before violating his privacy. The idea of searching his bedroom repulsed her, but Tracy steeled herself and entered.

The contents of the room gave no clue that it was the twentieth century. The oak bed was large, its head and footboards polished and ornamented with hand-carved floral designs. There was a standing mirror next to a chest of drawers that may have been part of a set some pioneer shipped around the Horn.

On the chest of drawers were several photographs. They were old. The first showed a man and woman standing together. The man was tall and solid. He had an easy smile and short steel-gray hair. The woman was slender. Neither person was handsome, but both were strong-featured with faces that radiated intelligence, humor and compassion.

The second photograph was of the man. He was dressed in a suit, walking down the steps of a courthouse, his back erect, his hands manacled in front of him. The photo was part of a newspaper story. The headline read: OSCAR REYNOLDS SENTENCED TO DEATH.

The third photograph was of Matthew and his father.

They were standing by a stream in the forest. Matthew must have been six or seven. His father held a fishing rod in one hand and his arm was draped around Matthew's shoulder. Matthew beamed out at Tracy so proud to be the one his father was honoring with his touch.

Tracy felt like she might cry. She took a deep breath. When she was back in control, she started going hurriedly through the drawers. Matthew's clothes were whites and blacks. There were no golf shirts, no tennis shorts, nothing that hinted at leisure. Nothing that hinted at anything but single-minded devotion to his cause.

Across from the bedroom was Matthew's study. Tracy glanced at the position on the marble chessboard. She had been bringing the postcards from the correspondence games to the hospital and recognized it.

Tracy looked up from the board. Around the walls stood collections of famous closing arguments, biographies of Benjamin Cardozo, Oliver Wendell Holmes, Felix Frankfurter and other great Supreme Court justices, a set of notebooks with every death penalty case decided by the United States Supreme Court and volumes on philosophy, psychology, forensic medicine and other topics related to Matthew's work. Tracy fingered some of the volumes, running her hands down their spines. This was Matthew's private sanctum, where he developed the ideas he used to save human lives. This was where he thought his most private thoughts. If there was a place in this house where Tracy would find the truth, it was here.

Tracy worked quickly, worried that the lunch hour

would end before she was done. She was halfway through Matthew's rolltop desk when she came to the bottom right drawer and found the manila envelope. She reached in and touched the bankbook. She had prayed that she would never find what she was looking for. Now that she had it, she was afraid to open it.

Tracy leaned back and the antique wooden chair creaked. There was $300,000 in the account after Matthew deposited the $250,000 he received for defending Joel Livingstone. There was only $150,000 the week after Justice Griffen's murder.

Tracy's hand shook as she emptied the contents of the envelope onto the blotter. She felt dizzy. She knew what she was seeing, but she wished with all her heart that it was not there. First were the articles about Abigail Griffen. She moved them aside and saw the photographs.

'Oh, God,' she whispered as she shuffled through them.

There were pictures of Abbie outside an office building in a business suit, talking earnestly to another attorney, and Abbie in the park across from the courthouse, resting on a bench, her head back, face to the sun, oblivious of the fact that her picture was being taken with a telephoto lens. Then there were pictures of Abbie at the house where Justice Griffen was murdered and the rental house where the metal strip had been found. One shot showed Abbie gardening in her yard in jeans and a tee shirt. There were several shots of Abbie inside both houses that had obviously been taken through a window at night.

Tracy picked up a set of 8½ x 11 photographs, taken with a telescopic lens from the woods on the edge of Abbie's property, which showed Abbie by her pool in a bikini. The first shot showed Abbie stepping through the French windows onto the patio and the shots followed her to the side of the pool. Several more photos showed Abbie in seductive poses: languorously stretching like a cat; lying on her side with her knees drawn up looking like a child; and resting on her forearms with her face to the sun. A final set, taken in extreme close-up, concentrated on every part of her body.

Tracy thought back to the wilderness photographs she had seen on her first visit to Matthew's office. Especially the shot of the doe and her fawn in the clearing. She realized, with horror, that Matthew had stalked Abbie with his camera the way he had stalked the deer.

But it was the final batch of photographs from the manila envelope that brought everything into focus. The shots Matthew had taken at the cabin on the coast. Abbie circling the cabin with her Pentax camera on the day she was attacked, Abbie walking on the beach, pictures of Abbie taken at night through the window. In several, she was naked, wandering through the living room unselfconsciously, searching for something. In the next group of pictures, she was terrified and racing through the woods.

Tracy could not feel the pictures in her hand as she slowly shuffled through them. In the next shot, a man in black was staring away from the camera. In the next, he was facing it. The man was wearing a ski mask but he had the physique of Charlie Deems.

The last group of photographs solved the mystery of the intruder's identity. Matthew had captured Charlie Deems, the ski mask removed, standing in the recesses of a deserted parking lot under a streetlamp talking to Robert Griffen.

Chapter Thirty

Tracy Cavanaugh sat beside Matthew Reynolds in his hospital room and imagined instead that they were in a narrow cell in the penitentiary after dark. The image would not hold. The concept was unbearable. The idea would not leave her.

'The outline for oral argument is excellent,' Matthew said as he reread the last paragraph of the document Tracy had prepared for the Texas case. Though Reynolds looked tired, and his pale skin seemed thin as parchment, a glow suffused him.

'Thank you,' Tracy answered stiffly.

Reynolds took no notice of her mood. He put down the outline and examined the wedding invitation again. He held it up and beamed with happiness.

'I think they did a good job, don't you?' he asked.

Tracy did not answer. Until now, she had been unable to tell him the real reason for her visit.

'Tracy?' Reynolds said, putting down the invitation. She was staring at the window. It was streaked with rain. Tracy shivered.

'Do you remember telling me about your father?' Tracy asked. 'The way you felt growing up. Losing him and loving him so much.'

Tracy paused. A hard and painful lump had formed in her throat.

'What's wrong?' Reynolds asked, his face clouding with confusion and concern.

'I tried to imagine what that must have been like for you,' Tracy went on. 'Knowing he was going to die and not being able to save him. Now I know how you felt.'

Reynolds cocked his head to one side, but he said nothing.

'It wasn't just the photograph, was it? You created *every* piece of evidence. You manufactured the bomb and the duplicate metal strips, then you lured Abbie to the rose garden so you could plant one of the strips and the Clorox bottle in her garage. You paid Charlie Deems fifty thousand dollars to testify against Abbie. You told him what to say and you created the account with the hundred thousand dollars, so you could destroy him on cross.'

Matthew's eyes were fully alive and focused on her. She had his full attention.

'What are you talking about?' Matthew asked evenly.

'When was the first time you knew the state thought

437

the metal strip was significant?' Tracy asked, ignoring his question.

'After Torino's testimony. You know that.'

'I also know that you called Dr. Shirov before the trial started to make sure he would be in town, and that the reactor would be available. What possible reason would you have to do that, unless you knew you would need his testimony to discredit the testimony of Paul Torino?'

'If I understand you correctly, you're saying that I murdered Justice Griffen and framed his wife for his murder.'

'That's exactly what I'm saying.'

'Have you forgotten that Abbie and I are going to be married?'

'No.'

'Do you understand that I love Abigail Griffen more than I love life?'

'Yes. And that's why you did this monstrous thing. For love. Bluffing won't do any good. I know everything. I've seen the pictures.'

Matthew's eyes widened. 'What pictures?'

'I was in your study.'

Matthew's face was suffused with rage. He rose halfway out of his chair.

'You were in my rooms? You dared to go through my private papers?'

Tracy was so drained that she could not feel fear or anger or even sorrow any longer.

'Was that worse than what you did, skulking in the dark, violating every rule of decency, because of your obsession? Peeping in Abbie's windows, raping her with your camera?'

Tracy stopped. Matthew sank back into his chair as if he had been slapped.

'Why?' Tracy asked, fighting back tears. 'Why, Matt?'

Matthew looked out at the rain. For a moment, Tracy was afraid he would dismiss her. Then, in a voice that sounded as if it came from a distance, Matthew said, 'She would never . . . It was my only chance. My only chance. And . . . And he would have murdered her if I hadn't stopped him. It was the only way to protect her.'

Matthew leaned back and closed his eyes.

'Have you any idea what it was like for me, growing up with a mother who killed herself, the stigma of being a murderer's son, and this face? I had no friends and the idea of a woman loving me was so alien I never ever let myself consider it, because I couldn't stand the pain it would bring me. My only escape was into my imagination and my only salvation was my mission.

'Then I saw Abbie. She was prosecuting Charlie Deems. I had dropped in to watch the trial because Deems wanted to hire me and I was curious to see how his case was being tried. She was so radiant I was struck dumb. I followed her that very first day. I couldn't keep my eyes off her. That night all of my defenses crashed and I saw myself for what I was. A pathetic little man so frightened of the world that I used my father's death as an excuse to keep from living. I was less than human. I was an animal burrowing deep into the ground, afraid of the light. And that light was life itself. And I realized that life was meaningless without love.'

Matthew leaned forward, desperate for understanding.

'Do you know what it's like knowing that everything you do must be perfect or someone will die? I never sleep peacefully. The fear that I'll make a mistake makes it impossible. Until I saw Abbie, I coped by fooling myself. I truly believed in my mission. I was like a religious zealot who can walk barefoot across coals because his faith shields him from the pain. When I saw Abbie, it was like losing my faith in God and suddenly seeing that there is only a void.

'I knew Abbie was my salvation. She was color in a world of grays. Only the thought that she was walking the earth kept me going.

'The week before we went to Atlanta, she told me she was going to the cabin. When Joel Livingstone accepted the plea, I flew home and went to the coast. I camped out in the woods and spent two days with Abbie.'

Matthew colored. He looked away. 'I know what you think. That I'm twisted, a monster. I am all that, but I couldn't help myself. It was something I'd been doing ever since I saw her. I never even bothered to rationalize my actions. She was like air to me. Without her I would die.

'Then Deems tried to kill Abbie. I saw him go in the cabin. I was paralyzed. I had to save her, but I had no idea what to do. When Abbie ran into the woods I followed.

'My father taught me how to move through the forest

without making noise. I waited and watched. I saw Deems searching for Abbie. He was so close that he would have seen her if he turned around. I did the only thing I could think of. I used the flash on my camera to distract him. He chased me, but it was easy for me to elude him in the dark. He must have panicked, because he only searched for a short time, then he went to his car.

'Up to this point, I had no idea that it was Deems who had tried to kill Abbie, because he wore a ski mask. I followed him to find out his identity. Deems drove to a bar and made a call. Then he drove to Portland to the far end of a motel parking lot. The lot was deserted, but there were streetlights. I took a photograph of Deems meeting Robert Griffen.'

'I know,' Tracy said. 'I saw the photograph.'

'Then you understand what that meant, Tracy. *Griffen had hired Deems to kill Abbie.*

'My first thought was to go to the police with my photographs. They would arrest Deems and he would tell them about Griffen. But I couldn't do it. I'd have had to explain why I was in the woods outside Abbie's cabin in the middle of the night. The police would have told Abbie that I was . . . was stalking her. She would have despised me and I would have lost her forever.

'That's when I first considered killing Justice Griffen. But Deems would still be alive and I wasn't certain about his motivation. Was he helping Griffen just for money or was it also revenge that motivated Deems? The problem seemed insoluble until . . .'

'You realized that you could get rid of Griffen and co-opt Deems,' Tracy said.

'Yes.'

'And you also realized that you could be with Abbie all the time if you were her attorney and she was in jail or under house arrest.'

Reynolds nodded. 'I would be the only one she could confide in. We could meet and talk every day. I hoped that over time she would forget what I look like, and I hoped that when I saved her, she would be grateful enough to . . . to love me.'

'How could you be certain she'd hire you?'

'I couldn't. But I would have volunteered if she hadn't come to me.'

'What if she turned you down?'

Reynolds blushed. 'She would never reject my offer of assistance. I am the best at what I do. Everyone knows that. Abbie always knew that.'

Tracy shook her head. 'What if you misjudged? What if Abbie had been convicted?'

'I would have confessed. But I knew I could control the trial. Especially with Chuck Geddes prosecuting.'

'You couldn't know that Geddes would assign himself to the case.'

'That was my only sure thing,' Reynolds answered with the tiniest of smiles. 'Chuck Geddes would never turn down a high-profile case like this and a chance to have his revenge on me for his previous humiliations. No, that part of the equation was the simplest.'

'How did you know so much about the bomb?'

'The bomb was of simple construction and I heard Torino testify about it at Deems's trial.'

'And the strip?'

'Deems wanted me to represent him when he was charged with the murder of Hollins and his little girl. Before I decided against taking the case, I looked at the evidence. I saw the strip with the notch. I saw it again when Paul Torino explained its significance at Deems's trial.

'To fool the police the evidence had to be so convincing that they wouldn't think they needed to conduct more sophisticated tests. I took two pieces of steel from different manufacturers. I checked with the companies to make sure that the composition of the two pieces of steel was different. Then I put the pieces side by side in two vises and I cut them at the same time. I took the front part of the first strip and used it with the bomb. I took the end of the second piece and left it in Abbie's garage after luring her to the rose garden. I knew the strip I used on the bomb would be mangled in the explosion and that the piece in the garage would look enough like a match so that the police wouldn't bother with any other tests.'

'What if Jack Stamm hadn't called Torino to search the house and garage for explosive devices?'

'Deems was supposed to tell the police that Abbie wanted him to make the bomb in her garage. They would have searched it.'

Tracy shook her head. She could not help admiring

Reynolds's brilliance even though he had put it to such a twisted purpose. Reynolds was a chessmaster who had thought out every move and anticipated every possible problem.

'You knew how to get in touch with Deems by using the phone numbers in the old file.'

'Yes.'

'How did you convince someone like Deems to co-operate with the police?'

'I left copies of the pictures from the coast and from his meeting with Justice Griffen in a bus-station locker. We spoke on the phone, so he never met me. I told him that the police would arrest him for the attack on Abbie and the murder of Justice Griffen if I sent them the photographs. Evidence of prior similar criminal conduct is admissible, even if a person has been acquitted of the crime, as you well know from your research in Abbie's case, if the prosecution has evidence of a signature crime. The notches in the bombs were unique. I explained to Deems that no jury would acquit him once they heard the evidence about the Hollins murders.

'To sweeten the pot, I told him I would pay him fifty thousand dollars if he testified against Abbie and told the exact story I made up for him. I let him think I was someone Abbie had convicted. A criminal with a grudge. I convinced Deems that the best revenge would not be to kill Abbie, but to make her suffer on death row for a crime she did not commit.'

'Did you tell Deems to say that Abbie had shown him

the dynamite in the shed and suggested he use it in the bomb?'

'Yes.'

'Why did you do that when Abbie didn't tell you about the photos until after she was arrested?'

'I saw her take the pictures. I knew she'd shot some footage behind the house. If she hadn't remembered about the undeveloped film, I would have led her to remember it.'

'Just as you tricked her into loving you?' Tracy said, not meaning to be cruel, but unable to help herself.

Reynolds reddened. 'This was my only chance to let her see past this face. To let her know that I love her. To give her a chance to love me for what I am.'

'It was a trick, Matt. You brainwashed her. You arranged to have her placed under house arrest. You isolated her and made her dependent on you. You . . . you trained her, the way you train a dog. That's not love she's feeling. It's something you created. It's artificial.'

'No. She does love me,' Matthew answered, shaking his head vigorously.

'Love is something that comes from your heart. Would she still love you if she knew what you did?'

Reynolds looked stricken. 'You can't tell her,' he said desperately.

Tracy gaped at Reynolds. 'Not tell Abbie? My God, Matthew. This is murder. You killed a man. I'm going to have to tell the police. I came here to give you a chance to do that. If you confess, Jack Stamm may not ask for the death penalty. You can hire an attorney to negotiate for you.'

'No.'

'What choice do you have?'

'You can keep it a secret, the way you did with the photograph. I'll quit my practice.'

Tracy leaned forward until her face was inches from his. Was it possible that Reynolds did not understand the magnitude of what he had done?

'Are you insane?' she asked. 'Do you think this is some minor ethical violation like commingling funds? This is murder. You used a bomb to kill a Supreme Court justice.'

Matthew started to argue with Tracy, to use the powers of persuasion that had saved so many lives in the past, but he stopped and turned away, realizing suddenly that the moment he had feared had arrived. He was part of the case he could not win and the life that would be lost was his own.

'I'm going to give you two days to turn yourself in,' Tracy said. 'Then I'm going to the police.'

Reynolds turned back. He looked desperate.

'I'll destroy the evidence. I'll say you're lying. I'll deny we ever had this conversation. Last week you claimed Deems killed Griffen. This week it's me. Stamm won't accept your word against mine.'

Tracy wished she could just walk away and do what Matthew wanted, but that was impossible. She shook her head sadly.

'I have the pictures, your bankbook and the faked photo of the shed. If I give them to Jack Stamm, you run the risk that he will believe Abbie was in this with you. If you confess, you can save her from having to go through a second trial.'

'Griffen was a murderer,' Matthew implored Tracy. 'He killed your friend Laura Rizzatti, and he paid Deems to kill Abbie. Can't you let this be?'

Matthew's eyes pleaded with Tracy, but she stood up and turned away. As she did, she remembered the question Matthew had asked her the first time they met: 'Tell me, Miss Cavanaugh, have you ever been to Stark, Florida, to the prison, after dark?'

That image of visiting the prison after dark and leaving before dawn with her client dead had haunted Tracy. When she was with Matthew in Atlanta, when she was sitting beside him during Abbie's trial, when she worked on the brief in the Texas case, she had been driven by her fear that someday the image would become reality if she did not give her all every moment of every day.

Silent tears rolled down Tracy's cheeks as she closed the door to the hospital room behind her. In the moments she had spent just now with Matthew Reynolds, she had finally learned how all those brave attorneys felt in the prison, at the very end, after dark.

Epilogue

Abbie parked in the visitors' lot of the Oregon State Penitentiary, then walked down a tree-lined lane to the front door of the prison. On either side of the street were friendly white houses that were once residences but now served as offices for the staff. Looming over the charming houses and their neatly trimmed lawns was the squat, square bulk of the prison with its thick egg-yolk-yellow walls, barbed-wire fences and gun towers.

After checking in at the visitors' desk, Abbie walked through a metal detector, down a ramp, through two sets of sliding steel bars and down a short hall, where she waited while her escort unlocked the thick metal door that opened into the visiting area.

Abbie identified herself to a guard who sat on a raised platform at one end of a large, open room crowded with prison-made couches and wooden coffee tables. The guard called Matthew's cellblock and asked for him to be sent down. While the guard spoke on the phone, Abbie looked around the room. Along the far wall, a prisoner was waiting in front of a vending machine for a paper cup to fill with coffee. The prisoners were easy to identify in their blue jeans and work shirts. They played with children they saw once a month, leaned across the coffee tables toward their parents or stood in the corners of the room pressing against a wife or girlfriend, trying to steal a few moments of intimacy that would help them forget the dreariness that pervaded their prison lives.

'He'll be down in a few minutes,' the guard told Abbie. 'You can use one of the attorney rooms.'

On the left, outside the large visiting room, was an open area. Along two walls were windows. Behind several of the windows were prisoners deemed too dangerous to be allowed into the visiting room. Their visitors sat on folding chairs and spoke to them on phones.

Also in this area were two glass-walled rooms where prisoners could meet their lawyers. Jack Stamm had called the superintendent and obtained permission for Abbie to use one of these rooms. She closed the door and waited for Matthew, dreading the meeting, but knowing that she had to see him, no matter how painful the visit might be for both of them.

Abbie did not recognize Matthew at first. The starchy prison food had caused him to gain weight. His face had filled out and his hips and waist were fuller. She even detected the beginnings of a paunch. When he entered the room, Abbie stood up and searched his face for a clue to his feelings, but Matthew was keeping his emotions hidden. When he paused in the doorway, she thought he might change his mind and leave. Instead, he offered his hand. She took it and held it for a moment. Then they sat down.

'Thank you for coming to see me,' Matthew said. 'Aside from Barry and Tracy, I haven't had many visitors.'

'How are you getting along?' Abbie asked, not ready yet to talk about her real reason for visiting.

Matthew smiled. 'Quite well, actually. There's a real demand for my skills here. I was most frightened of physical assault when I came to the prison, but I'm under the protection of the prisoners. It seems I have many friends here. People I've helped. And there are many more who can use my assistance.'

Abbie laughed. 'I guess putting a criminal lawyer with a mission in prison is a little like letting a kid run loose in a candy store.'

They both smiled. Then Abbie sobered.

'You know why I didn't come sooner, don't you?' she asked.

'Tracy told me what you said to her.'

'I hated you at first, Matt. It was the pictures. When I learned about them . . . About the spying . . . It was such a shock.'

Matthew looked down. 'I wish I'd never taken them, but I couldn't help myself. I was so in love with you and there was no way I could tell you. To me, you were unobtainable. I just couldn't believe that anyone so beautiful would even look at me, let alone fall in love. I'm surprised you don't hate me still.'

'Tracy told me what you did when Deems chased me in the woods and that you killed Robert to save my life. She explained why you framed me for Robert's murder. She wanted me to talk to the judge at your sentencing, but I couldn't. It's taken me a while to accept that you did everything for me so I would love you.'

Abbie looked up at Matthew. He leaned forward expectantly.

'Jack let you plead guilty to manslaughter because of everything that came out about Robert and, mainly, because you killed him to save my life. You're eligible for parole anytime, since there isn't a mandatory minimum sentence for manslaughter. I've written to the parole board. I told them I want to be present to speak on your behalf when they meet to decide your case. I know that you never wanted to hurt me and I want you to know that I forgive you.'

Matthew slumped forward as if he had been struck in the chest. 'Thank you,' was all he could manage.

'Are you okay?' Abbie asked.

'Oh yes,' he answered.

Abbie noticed the guard announcing the end of visiting hours. She had intentionally come toward the end so the visit would be short, in case it went badly. Abbie stood up.

Matthew took a deep breath and composed himself.

'Will you visit me again?' he asked.

'I don't think so.'

'I understand. What are you going to do?'

'I'm not sure. I've quit the district attorney's office. I'm thinking about traveling for a while. I still need to put some space between myself and what happened.'

A guard knocked on the door.

'I've got to go now. I'm not going to wish you good luck. I don't think you need it, because I know you're going to come through this.'

'I'll always love you, Abbie. Everything I did was for you.'

Abbie reached out and touched his shoulder. 'I know that, Matthew.'

She took one last look at Matthew, then she opened the door and joined the line of people leaving the visiting area. Matthew knew that he would never stop loving Abbie and that he had lost her forever. He understood that there was no way she could love him now. Even so, he did not feel sad. He had saved Abbie's life and that made everything he had gone through and was going to endure worthwhile. And even if it was only for a little while, she had loved him and that was more than he ever hoped for.

And now he had been forgiven.

THE LAST
INNOCENT MAN

Phillip M. Margolin

An explosive novel of suspense, as a trial lawyer faces his
worst fear – freeing a dangerous psychopath – and risks
paying the price . . . in blood.

The papers call him the Ice Man. David Nash, defence
attorney – cool, unruffled, practically unbeatable in the
courtroom. Most of his clients are guilty. A few may be
monsters. Suddenly the Ice Man is assailed by doubts and
unanswerable questions. What is the cost of each victory,
each rapist or murderer set free – to society and to
Nash's soul?

Then comes a case that may be Nash's redemption. A
client whose innocence he can believe in, a rising lawyer
and family man accused of the brutal murder of an
undercover vice cop. But as the case moves towards trial,
new doubts grip him: what is truth and what is carefully
fabricated falsehood? Is Nash, a master at handling juries,
being manipulated himself? And by whom? By the time
Nash's perfect case is finished, the questions become a
matter of life and death.

THRILLER
0 7515 1464 0

A *Warner* Book
Available from May 1997

HEARTSTONE

Phillip M. Margolin

A heart-stopping novel that begins with two vicious
murders – and ends in a web of corruption, lies, and
twisted passions.

Richie Walters, all-American boy. Elaine Murray,
cheerleader. They made the perfect couple. And that
evening out at Lookout Point – Richie fumbling at the
buttons of her blouse, Elaine thrilled and terrified – they
were about to take the final step. But the step would never
be taken. Richie Walters would die that night – die in a hot
and savage ecstasy of violence. Elaine Murray too would
die. But not that night. Or the next. She would live long
enough to know just how lucky Richie had been . . .

'I was somewhat reminded of *In Cold Blood*, but in some
ways this is a better book . . . it's fascinating reading – the
classic "page-turner" – and I admit to being stunned and
shocked at the unexpected ending.'
Dorothy Uhnak, author of *The Investigation*

THRILLER
0 7515 1463 2

A *Warner* Book
Available from December 1996

TRUE CRIME

Andrew Klavan

A blazing hot day at the height of a Missouri summer. Two men meet for the first time through the bars of a cell on Death Row. Steve Everett's life is unravelling; Frank Beachum's life is about to end. They're both running dangerously low on luck. Beachum was convicted of murder six years ago and sentenced to die by lethal injection. Everett is the reporter. Despised by his colleagues, unfaithful to his wife, he's looking for a big story to get his life and career back on track. And in the dwindling hours before midnight, the only hope they have is each other.

There are eighteen hours to go. In those hours, Frank Beachum is going to be pushed to the very limits of his faith and look over the edge into a nightmare. And Steve Everett, in spite of himself, is going to risk everything, even his own life, in a breathless attempt to save him.

'impressive . . . coolly detached, immensely detailed and totally convincing'
Sunday Telegraph

'the minutiae of the execution process is both repellent and gripping; and the tension is superbly placed'
Sunday Times

'a blunt instrument of a crime story which bludgeons tension all the way'
Daily Mail

THRILLER
0 7515 16821

Warner Books now offers an exciting range of quality titles
by both established and new authors. All of the books in this
series are available from:

Little, Brown and Company (UK),
P.O. Box 11,
Falmouth,
Cornwall TR10 9EN.

Alternatively you may fax your order to the above address.
Fax No: 01326 317444
Telephone No: 01326 317200
E-mail: books@barni.avel.co.uk

Payments can be made as follows: cheque, postal order
(payable to Little, Brown and Company) or by credit cards,
Visa/Access. Do not send cash or currency. UK customers and
B.F.P.O. please allow £1.00 for postage and packing for the
first book, plus 50p for the second book, plus 30p for each
additional book up to a maximum charge of £3.00 (7 books
plus).

Overseas customers including Ireland, please allow £2.00 for
the first book plus £1.00 for the second book, plus 50p for each
additional book.

NAME (Block Letters) ....

....

ADDRESS ....

....

....

☐ I enclose my remittance for ....
☐ I wish to pay by Access/Visa Card

Number ☐☐☐☐☐☐☐☐☐☐☐☐☐☐☐☐☐

Card Expiry Date ☐☐☐☐